# ORIGINS

## ENTER THE SPIRAL

### LAZARUS SPIRAL III

### T. KULP

ISBN: 978-1-956612-78-3 (Paperback)

ISBN: 978-1-956612-38-7 (eBook)



Making Adventure Publishing
16944 York Rd, Suite 62

Monkton, MD 21111

for victor
so many beginnings
began with you

# INTRODUCTION

Welcome to ORIGINS.

How many beginnings begin with tragedy? As I reflect on my life, so many new things began with the cataclysmic resolution of some other beginning. And such is the nature of beginnings as Seneca, and the band Semi Sonic, said: Every new beginning comes from some other beginning's end.

Many of my readers know my father's death jumpstarted my writing. The end of his life spurred me to take the first steps on my writing journey. And so much of my writing was in processing his life, our lives, his death, my life, and my remaining time. This period of reflection led me to take a writing class and while I thought I was doing it to support my mother (who also took the class); it turned out that I had a lot to say through the keyboard. So, I said it. And said it. And said it.

But after 2 years, no one was listening. What's the point of telling stories to no one? I poured years, hours, money (I self-publish), stress, emotion, energy into everything I was doing. After 2-years (yes, I know that wasn't long at all, but this is my story), I was ready to hang it up.

I loved writing and had been moving at breakneck speeds to produce great stories while working my day job. Burned out, beaten by false expectations and guilt over wasting all this time (and money) to start a writing career, I told Maria (my wife) I was hanging it up. In her infinite wisdom, she suggested I stop writing novels. I had three in various stages of completion. Their immensity and complexity weighed me down. Instead, she said, write a short horror story and just have fun.

Another element of beginnings, serendipity. It was about this time that I was asked to teach a writing seminar and I was showing how to use AI for story inspiration. The AI system generated a title that instantly hooked me: 2938 Beta. I felt this could be a sci-fi story and so I asked the AI where this story took place. Giving it no context, it suggested a small town. What a horrible suggestion for a sci-fi story, but a great seed for me. And here is where ideas smashed together to create the stories that kept me writing.

A few months (I think) before this writing seminar, my wife saw a poster board sign that read "Life Changing Yard Sale". We laughed about it and while I considered some story ideas, one of which involving a yard sale that sold human skin suits that allowed you to become a whole new person, I let the idea marinate. But here's the moment of inspiration: what if 2938 Beta was a toy? A haunted toy? Purchased at a yard sale that sold haunted toys? Who would have such a yard sale? Why? What would happen with the toys?

*Life Changing Yard Sale* was born, but not as a series, just as a single collection of tales about haunted toys. But the stories didn't stop coming. New toys. New ideas. And suddenly I had more stories than I could put in one book. Then, in the story, I discovered Neil's inventory. Forty-two toys with dark origins, dark lives, and, for some, tragic deaths. These books needed a name, a series to hold them all together and the Lazarus Spiral was born.

Lazarus like the Bible? No. That was never the thought. Immortality was never the goal of these characters. They strive for something much, much darker. Spirals curl in on themselves, descending in my mind, swirling and slipping and dragging you into them. What is at the center? Why does it exist? Who would know about it? What does it have to do with toys? And the answers came as if they were always there, slithering from the center of the spiral, being seen, being always there if only I'd known to look.

This is the origin of the Lazarus Spiral.

I don't know where the Spiral is taking Lucy, Trudy, Nadia, Neil, Viola, Dodslav, Ely, and the others. But this book is where some of them began. Not everyone stumbled into the Spiral like Lucy. Some sought it. Some were thrust into it. And others, others didn't know they were always within it.

I'll return at the end of this book with an Author's Note to discuss what's next. For now, know that this book was a tough one to write. It is the farthest I've ever written a series. There are topics within that were extremely difficult to explore and a few places that hit a little too close to home.

These beginnings are the vicious, sometimes sadistic deaths of other beginnings. Welcome to ORIGINS. The Lazarus Spiral is waiting for you to take a few more steps down, deeper, deeper, deeper…

T. Kulp

5/22/2024

# THE
# DOLLHOUSE

# ONE

Hell was supposed to be hot. But now, Neil Lessman, at 18, knew that was a lie. His body quaked at the onset of hyperthermia, his lungs turned to stone, the heat of his last breath, the only one left after running downstairs, crystalized on his face like glass pushing into his skin. Yes, Hell must be as cold as outer space, because the thing that stood before him, the thing emanating this paralytic frost, could not have come from anywhere else.

It was a demon, and it wasn't alone. It had no interest in Neil. A third soul in the basement, Andrew Lessman, Neil's brother, held the creature's rapt attention. Drew, as Neil knew his brother, stood quaking between Neil and the monster.

Black smoke billowed from the demon, with tendrils of darkness dancing around Drew's jeans and now coiling over his black trench coat. The demon's white mask, featureless save for the black slit eyes and black spiral burned into the forehead, rose over Drew's spikey blonde hair. It had no emotion through that mask and Neil had no doubt it was a mask, but Neil could feel the sickening joy drip from the creature's presence.

Neil told his arm to extend, to grab Drew, rip his older brother away from the demon rising over him. But the muscles wouldn't move. Cold or fear numbed his nerves. It didn't matter which. Cowardice coiled his guts into a spring that couldn't release. It only locked with panic, and hope that the demon stopped with his brother.

Drew had so many demons within him, Neil never considered one would come out, but here it was. Which one was this? The heroin? The guilt for what he did to Grandpa? Or mom and dad?

In the basement, the black smoke stayed close to the floor except where it engulfed and slithered over Drew. He seized in fear. Neil saw a trail of the smoke coming from the dollhouse. The dollhouse Neil built with Grandpa earlier today, the dollhouse to honor Neil's parents. That was before Grandpa found the drugs, before the argument, before Drew stormed off, before Grandpa's heart attack.

With a quick sucking sound, the smoke engulfing Drew snapped like razor wire slashing into him. It coiled as it tightened, blood pooled around the tendrils, but none fell. Red splashes and beads suspended around Drew, growing into a crimson cocoon. Before he was encased, Drew looked back to Neil, tears stood in his eyes but not of fear like Neil thought, it was regret. Those eyes said sorry in the moment before they collapsed into gory jelly, sucked into Drew's face.

Now the fear took over, pain, torment pressing screams out of him, but they were drowned out quickly by snapping bone and squishy twisting muscles as Drew's body cracked, popped, and crumbled to gravel as he was reconfigured into some kind of abstract sculpture.

The demon stopped rising. It hung in the air, watching Drew's mutilation with a thoughtful *hmmmm*. Was it considering what else to do? Critiquing its work with ideas of other flesh parts to rend, other bones to break?

Neil screamed now. His lungs let the breath out. His muscles could move, but he didn't want to. He needed not to move. The demon's empty black eyes rose to his as if waiting for Neil to say something.

But the wait was short-lived as the demon descended over Drew in a crashing wave of black smoke.

Drew was gone.

The smoke receded into the dollhouse's basement. Sucked in by a rough-hewn spiral carved into the wooden floor. The miniature living room setup that should have been there was scooped out onto the worktable, leaving the basement barren and empty. Blue light faded around the spiral until only the spiral scar remained.

Neil tried to categorize what he just saw. Was it a hallucination? A trip from a contact high? Mental break down?

"He said demons are real," Neil said aloud because his mind was too full with the work of explaining what had just happened. "Drew said his demons are real. Said he needed them ripped out of him."

The spiral drank in the last of the smoke and then sat dormant. And dormant was the right word because, like a volcano, Neil thought it could erupt at any moment, bringing that demon back to this world.

"It took him," Neil said.

And all thoughts of why he came back to the house abandoned his mind. The important thing he needed to do, the time sensitive thing, now floated away in the mental haze of questions.

On the floor where Drew had been was a thin black book. It was a journal from a bookstore, nothing fancy, but Neil didn't know his brother to be one who kept his thoughts.

With a hard blink, his motor skills restarted, and he opened the book to the first page.

*This Journal belongs to Sister Wendy.*

Flipping through the pages, Neil saw it was written in English but structured in equations like complex mathematics. None of it made sense, save for the horrific creatures sketched with what he hoped was an exaggerated monstrosity. These beasts were nightmares incarnate but not drawn well enough to be professional. His hopes that this was some fictional book, some fun escape into a fantasy world, were dashed by the poor production quality and mind-boggling complexity. No store would sell a book this poorly made, and it would be at least understandable.

Who was Sister Wendy? Where did Drew get this book?

And even though the clock was ticking on what Neil thought was the most important moment of his life prior to seeing that demon, his brother's broken body and disappearance captured Neil's attention.

One person who might help came to mind. The last person Neil met in Drew's drug life—the person before Drew began what he called his *recovery*. Maybe that person would know something? But to get answers, Neil had to go to Hell, or at least where he thought was hell… until now.

# TWO

Would his destination still be there? Someone, the city most likely, could have cut away that sore on society. But no one ever cared about the people who filled this place, nor that it existed as long as they didn't have to see it.

Grandpa's truck was well maintained, but old. It really shouldn't still be running after all these years and while at high speeds on the highway it groaned and wheezed while others honked and shouted as they passed. There was nothing Neil could do but keep pushing the truck to go faster as black smoke choked out of it.

When he finally arrived at the cluster of warehouses on the edge of the city, near the waterfront, he cranked up the windows, pushing through the areas where the handle got stuck on damp days like today. He locked the doors and slowed down, knowing his destination was just beyond the warehouses.

No one littered the street. Civilization stopped a few blocks ago and when it restarted, it would be the edge where police didn't go and gangs roamed. The theft of grandpa's truck, Neil's murder, wouldn't even be reported.

In this space of warehouses, the city was a wasteland of broken machinery from the old dock yards, rusted shipping containers, and abandoned buildings. Countless unseen eyes watched from those broken out windows, the desperate, the hungry, hoping for someone to come close, to save them, or feed them. Did they wonder about each car that drove by? But there were no other cars. And so the eyes must have been hungry, must have been wanting, for someone, anyone.

When Neil was a kid, Drew would send him into this wasteland. But not with a car, not with a bike, only walking. Drew said a bike would make Neil a target for getting mugged, so the younger brother had to walk. The eight-year-old Neil would walk a mile, one way, to do business on Drew's behalf. Neil never thought more of this than being terrified of the lurkers within the warehouses. Even all those years ago, they were there. They were watching. Walking as fast as his little feet could take him, he heard them scratching and drooling.

When he was twelve, he swore he could smell their fetid stench, and at fifteen, three years ago, he swore he saw them. Shadow bodies with pale faces lurking in the warehouse, but of course that was just imagination. His memory twisted the warehouse dwellers into the appearance of the demon he saw earlier, but surely that is not how they actually appeared. That was not what he saw those years ago…?

Before that thought could linger, he arrived at his destination: The Sleep House.

This place would have been called a crack house if it were nicer, but the outside was beyond blight. It was worse than ruinous; it was decay incarnate, ready to poison any who came too close. And it did. There were bodies strewn about the front lawn of the house, which was only ten feet of dead grass as wide as the sagging row home. The houses beside the Sleep House had rotted into collapse, with only the firewall remaining. From the sidewalk, the Sleep House screamed to passersby to run, to flee from it lest you catch whatever existential plague it carried.

Yet Neil had nothing to fear. He'd been here many times before and while the infection of the Sleep House never caught him, he trusted his safety in the hands of the house's master who he'd known since he was eight.

Neil wore the sigil of the master, a plastic necklace with a gaudy gold star in the center, and left the truck on the street. A few curious glances found him, but the diffuse gleam of the plastic gold star diverted their eyes—unworthy to gaze upon the master's emissary. There were rules in the Sleep House, and nothing was more important than recognizing your betters. The star was known to all, and all knew to look away if they wanted the gifts of the master.

Neil didn't knock but opened the door slowly, expecting someone slumped against it within. The handle was chilly brass, damp from the earlier rain, and opened easily. Inside, hissing and scratching fled from the muted daylight. The foyer cleared as people escaped into the house's darkness. There were few spaces in the foyer to hide, but people crawled over each other in the darkest recesses. With boarded-up windows and thick curtains, the house was almost as dark as the demon's smoke. Only movement could be seen, the scurrying bodies climbing over each other to stay in the darkness. Neil closed the door quickly. Some of the people under the stairs tumbled out, back into the foyer, but none looked at Neil.

"The Emissary has returned!" Neil called upstairs.

The protocols set forth by the master were of dire importance to the eccentric man. And while the master spent years filling his brother with poison, the master had a very different relationship with Neil.

A door opened upstairs, and a blinding white light filled the second floor. "Hark, the Emissary has returned," the master called forth, filling the foyer with his deep southern Baptist preacher tone. "And I shall receive him with my glory."

Bodies scurried out into the foyer, close to Neil but never touching. They prostrated on the floor, faces down, palms up to receive. Some whined in eager delight at the coming of the master.

On the second floor, the master stepped from his office, his white suit glowing in the dark from a bright light behind him. As always, his suit was pristine and angelic. He descended the stairs slowly. Behind him, the man holding a floodlight walked carefully, ensuring he didn't trip on the extension cord running between his feet.

"Emissary!" the master said.

Neil knew his other name, and now called him by it, "Thank you for seeing me, Mr. Dream."

Mr. Dream nodded. While Neil hadn't seen him in almost a year now, the time had not been kind. Mr. Dream was pallid, gaunt, sickly in a manner that Neil had never seen him before. For a drug dealer, Mr. Dream had always remained fit, healthy, but something had turned. He embraced Neil and Neil returned it, pushing through the revulsion at the skeletal body beneath the tailored suit.

"Come. Let us palaver in the heavens," Mr. Dream motioned back upstairs. He quickly reached into his jacket pocket, pulled out some baggies of white powder, and threw them into the foyer without care. "My faithful, be rewarded by the grace of your god, your loving, loving God—me. Blissful sleep be upon you." Deep breaths of anticipation filled the foyer, but no one moved. They knew the rules, to be motionless in the presence of their master, their God.

Neil led the way up the stairs, but as soon as Mr. Dream's foot hit the first step, the followers exploded in motion, scrambling to get all the baggies they could. Bodies rolled over each other, shoved, clawed, crawled in the darkness below as the light ascended and returned their world to dark.

As Neil and Mr. Dream reached his office, the scurrying died down with wanting whimpers and sobs as those who received, and those who did not, returned to their dark places.

Mr. Dream dismissed the man with the light with a flick of his wrist and closed the door behind Neil as they entered his office.

"I must say," Mr. Dream began, "I did not expect to see you again." He shrugged off his jacket and hung it on the brass coat rack in the corner of his office.

Neil took his normal seat across Mr. Dream's wooden desk. The window in the office wasn't shaded and the dreary day's light seeped into the room with a lazy, sleepy coolness. The walls were gray with bar height distressed wood paneling. Lights spotted the room, bringing a warm glow to the office that Neil appreciated on such a rainy day.

Mr. Dream had an appetite for antiques and that shone throughout the room, from old maps on the walls to highly polished dark wood shelves and ancient books. A few nautical devices spotted the shelves, and while Neil had never asked about their origin, he always assumed Mr. Dream's life before all this was on the sea.

"Something happened to Drew," Neil said, unsure if the words would sound crazy, but then again, this man posed as a god to junkies—so how crazy could it really be? "I'm not sure how to say it."

Mr. Dream sat at his desk and began loading the stacks of cash into a money counting machine. It flipped quickly through the first stack, and he wrote the number in his ledger, which was an antique leather-bound notebook.

"I'm not sure what I saw," Neil shook his head. "It was, I think it was, a demon?"

Mr. Dream, keeping his focus on accounting, asked in a disinterested voice, "I assume this is metaphorical?"

Neil shook his head. "No. I think it was a real demon. It felt like a demon. I mean, I know that's crazy, but every part of me thought it was a demon. Like, I knew what it was."

"A demon?" Mr. Dream put his pen down. "Emissary," he never knew Neil's actual name, "you imagined it. Probably poisoned by whatever Drew was cooking."

Neil had considered the same. Yet could a hallucination feel so cold? Could the glare of something imagined be as heavy as those blank eyes staring into his? "I don't think it was. It took him. Drew was there and then he wasn't. And this was the only thing left." Neil handed Mr. Dream the black journal.

"Demons aren't on the outside. They don't need to be," Mr. Dream said. He opened the book, stopping on the first page, sucking in a sharp breath, shifting in his seat. The name on the page turned his pallid face burning red.

"You know who that is?" Neil asked, but the reaction was a clear answer. Mr. Dream knew Sister Wendy. He was terrified of her. And, the clearest message of all, *abandon this path, Emissary.*

"Your brother fell into a very bad crowd."

Neil chuckled. A drug dealer suggesting that another group was a bad crowd was hilarious to him but also petrifying. Who could be worse than this man? "Worse than you? Not to be rude, but I wouldn't say you're a boy scout," Neil motioned to the door as if to suggest the proof was just outside the office.

"It's just business." Mr. Dream took a notepad from his desk and began writing. "Do you remember our first meeting?"

Neil nodded. It was horrifying. Ten years ago, he was sent here by Drew to get drugs. Drew said no one would bother a little kid, and that's why he had to be the one to go. But the junkies in the Sleep House swarmed him, grabbed him, pulled him into their piles of filth and stink, but Mr. Dream was there and screamed for them to stop.

He took the woman who was holding onto Neil into the foyer and told her to kneel before him. She did. Mr. Dream took Neil to the stairs and told him to watch, and the boy, so afraid he'd be tossed back to the writhing bodies, did as told. Mr. Dream stood in front of the woman and told her to open her mouth and receive. She did. He took a baggie out of his left pocket and poured it into her mouth. She smiled toothless and black even in this darkness. He told her to swallow it. She did. But her joy seized into wracking pain as the drug took hold of her. It wasn't the drug he normally gave; it was rat poison and her body tried to expel it, but Mr. Dream held her mouth shut, held her nose closed. Her frail body was no match for his strength and youth. She choked to death on her vomit, and Mr. Dream threw her aside. He checked his shoes to ensure none of her filth scuffed them. No such glance was spared for the dead woman.

He declared Neil the Emissary and for none to touch him, talk to him, or look at him. And so it was. The gold star necklace was given to Neil to signify his status. It was a toy from the half-eaten crackerjack box in the office. That day, Neil left with the star and his brother's drugs.

"You were too young to be here," Mr. Dream said. "I know what it is like to be thrown into hell at such a young age, but there was no one to pull me out. And here we are again." He pushed the note to Neil. "Your brother left with people from this place one day and I never saw him again. Sister Wendy is one of those people who steal my followers for worse fates. And I fear she took your brother."

Neil reached for the note. Mr. Dream clamped down on his hand with a frail grip. A frailness that made Neil's heart ache. This man was his protector in this place. He encouraged Neil to do great in school. To be more than his brother. And after so many abject lessons of the hellish life of a junkie, Mr. Dream ensured Neil would never use. He was the older brother Drew never could be. The person who celebrated A's with a few bucks for a comic book, or sharing book recommendations to help Neil navigate the problems of middle school, then high school. Mr. Dream was the ear to hear the problems, and the voice to soothe the wounds of bullies and breakups.

"I've given you counsel for much of our time together. Please, take counsel once more. Stop here. Let your brother go. Whatever you think you saw, whatever you think happened, let it be the end. These people are bad people." Mr. Dream let go of Neil's hand. "But I've always given you the choice, and so I do this last time. Please, let Drew go. Save yourself. Don't let him pull you down, too."

"He's my brother," Neil answered as if those words explained everything. He took the note. "Thank you for everything." Tears welled up in Neil's eyes. Mr. Dream's face stretched so taunt over his cheeks. His eyes recessed too deep, and Neil assumed he knew the diagnosis: late-stage cancer. This is how grandma looked at the end.

Neil took off the star necklace and handed it to Mr. Dream. "I don't think I will return. I've learned so much from you."

There was so much more Neil wanted to say, but how could he say it all? Thank you for making sure I didn't become my brother. Thank you for protecting me from the junkies downstairs. Thank you for telling me I could be anything and then pushing me to become more than I ever imagined I could be. Yet the clock was ticking. Each second was critical, and he felt it, but what was the timer for? He'd remember soon, but for now, he ignored the thought and went to the door simply saying, "Thank you."

One last question burst through his mind as he left. "Did you always want to do this?"

Mr. Dream smiled, his teeth gleaming white. He chuckled lightly and said, "No. But we don't always get what we want."

"What did you want to do?"

"Isn't it obvious?" Mr. Dream motioned to his office. "I wanted to be God. Set the universe right. Find the way back to a good life."

Neil again saw the navigation tools. The nautical tools. Wayfinders. Scopes and maps.

"Goodbye Emissary," Mr. Dream said, then returned to accounting.

"Goodbye," Neil said and opened the door.

"Let pass the Emissary one last time," Mr. Dream bellowed from his chair as he calculated.

Neil left the Sleep House unbothered and went to his truck. The note from Mr. Dream was an address in the city. He started the truck. As it choked to life, he saw Mr. Dream in the window of his office looking out. He held the star necklace and watched Neil pull away.

Neither would have expected Mr. Dream to outlive Neil. And neither would have expected Neil to forget the lessons of the Sleep House and follow his brother's path, but that is the thing about addictions. We often cannot see them when they are masked in the mundane. The horrors of drugs and alcohol are easy to see as they rot your body, then soul. But the most insidious addictions avoid any visible decay, only rotting your soul.

And now, Neil left the dealer than never attempted to corrupt his body for a dealer that only corrupted souls.

# THREE

On the card, written in Mr. Dream's elegant script, was an address. When Neil arrived, street parking was all that was available on the busy city street. He double checked the address, assuming this could not possibly be anywhere his brother ever went.

It was a restaurant with a polished glass and steel façade. Men and women flowed in and out of a rotating door in the center. Their pressed suits and perfect hair, unbothered by the windy day. The windows were too dark to see inside save for an occasional burst of golden flame from what Neil assumed was a kitchen. Over the door was a single word:

DiCoro's.

And while Neil had never been here, he'd heard of this steakhouse. Some people went there for pre-prom dinner last spring—back when Neil was looking at colleges, before everything fell apart this summer. He'd heard a dinner here cost over one-hundred dollars and couldn't imagine spending that much on a single meal. Drew never had that kind of money, so what was he doing here?

But Mr. Dream had never steered him wrong before, and so Neil went to the rotating door, pressed through the bright glare of professionally polished glass and entered a world of gloss, glamour, and glares.

Like Neil, everyone there knew he did not belong. They glanced, then stared, unsure why such a person from a lower station would venture into their world. These were wealthy people, and it dripped over them from their clothes to their perfect teeth and tans and haircuts. His jeans and t-shirt didn't match, which brought the maitre d' with a quick disapproving frown.

"Sir, I believe you are looking for somewhere else," the maitre d' said, wearing a gray suit with a thick sheen that made it look silver. The man was only slightly older than Neil, but put together in a manner that was not learned but forged. This man, once a boy like Neil, was chiseled into the model of professionalism by his manager, who had the same done to him, and the chain went on.

Neil held up the card and read the last part of the message from Mr. Dream. "I'm looking for Nightshade?"

The maitre d' froze at the name but quickly dispelled this paralysis and searched frantically, yet always professionally—never losing the veneer of professionalism. "Let me get my manager. Please wait here." the maitre d' took Neil to the long, dark wood bar near the entrance. Many businesspeople were there and while they all looked at him, no one bothered to see him, finding their drinks and others in their company more worthy of their attention.

Behind the bar was a mirror wall stretching up to the high ceiling. Glass shelves with alcohol resting on them lined the mirror, creating the illusion of bottles beyond the bottles.

"Hi," Neil said to the bartender, who looked his way.

The bartender continued cleaning a martini glass in his hand and moved down the bar further to customers who would spend money.

"I heard you are searching for Nightshade?" A woman asked Neil from behind. She wore a long black cloak like a nun with flowing white hair spilling out from under her hood. No one else in the bar seemed to notice her and for a moment, Neil thought he was imagining this. "Are you?"

"I was told to ask for Nightshade. I'm looking for someone who knew Drew Lessman," Neil said.

The woman said, "I knew Drew. Troubled soul." She settled back on her heels, letting herself rest. "Are you the brother he spoke of?"

"Are you Wendy?" He held up the black book Drew dropped when the demon took him.

She took the book and slowly opened it. "I am Sister Wendy." She closed the book with a pop that still did not bring any attention to them. "If you have this, I assume your brother has done something foolish."

Foolish? That didn't cover being eaten by a demon, but he asked, "I think he's–"

"Dead?"

Neil shrugged and shook his head. He didn't think that was true. There wasn't a pit in his gut or a crippling sense of loss, both things he expected when his brother did finally overdosed. Instead, a deep need to help his brother swelled within him. And so he answered, "He's not dead. But he's gone. Taken?"

Sister Wendy's stern face broke into a knowing grin. "Taken by whom?"

But before he could respond, his beeper broke the ambient noise of the bar in a shrill siren. It was an alarm awakening him to the thing he'd forgotten. The time he raced against was up.

"Oh, shit," Neil read the number on the small screen. "Oh shit. No. No. No. Do you have a phone?"

Sister Wendy's wrinkled face curled in surprise, having never been asked that in her long time here at DiCoro's, or in the Order. But she saw the urgency in the young man and called out, "Boy!"

The bartender raced over with his head lowered. He asked softly, "Yes Sister?"

"Let this child use your phone," she said. The young man nodded without hesitation.

She turned to Neil, placing a hand on his shoulder. "Return when you complete your work." She tapped the black book on her palm. "I'll hold this until you return."

But Neil's mind was caught in the thing he'd forgotten. How could he forget? How could he have been so blinded? However, the answer was obvious. A demon in the flesh can rip your mind away from important things. No matter how dire.

The bartender took him to the maitre d' station and now all the suits and professionals parted away from him as if he were Moses. Neil dialed the number and waited for the long ring to complete.

Then there was an interminable space as if the universe had to remember what to do next. Silence held on to the line for too long. Had the call dropped? Did the connection fail? Neil looked at the phone to see if it simply vanished, ceased to exist when he needed it most as punishment for screwing up something so important. How could he forget?

The universe determined that he'd wondered long enough and released another long ring in the phone. It filled Neil's world. Before the next space, the phone clicked, and a man spoke.

"Saint Gerald's ICU."

"This is Neil Lessman. You paged me. What's happened?" He expected the worst, and then it came.

"Mr. Lessman, you need to come to the hospital immediately. Your grandfather's condition, you are going to want to be here in the next few minutes." the nurse's somber tone carried everything not said in it.

Neil hung up and ran to his car.

***

He didn't see Sister Wendy still watching him from the bar, tapping the black book on her hand.

Once these hands were weak and the tap would have been painful, or at least she would have felt it. Now, her palms were densely calloused from rough steel barbells, hard work, and brutal exorcisms.

Tap.

Tap.

Tap.

That boy looked like Drew when he was clean. Unlike the lost brother, this one was focused. His energy was intense and, was it imagined or real, there was something radiating from him.

Perhaps the drugs muted Drew's light. But his brother was glowing. Her wrist, the thing within it, itched as it slithered under

20

her skin. That was the sign of this boy's strange nature, even more so than the feeling she got from him. The weapon in her wrist, the living weapon, at least that's what she kept telling herself it was, screamed that the boy was not like the others who have wandered in here.

Only one person would have sent this boy here.

Wendy had helped many lost souls escape that bastard's damnable shit hole. She should have killed him years ago. Unfortunately, her vows swore to help humanity's salvation. And that applied even to the worst human.

"Should I follow him?" A young man in a brown cloak broke the memories boiling within her. His voice, as with all things he did, was eager to please.

"No, Acolyte Yingling. He'll return here soon," Sister Wendy watched Neil's truck rush into city traffic, tires screeching, horns blaring. "Check Drew Lessman's quarters. Collect his things for his brother. I suspect we will not be seeing Drew again."

She placed the book on the bar, spine first, and let go. The spine had worn from frequent reading and when the book fell open; it revealed where Drew had been studying.

It was a summoning spell. A rite to cast out demons, but if performed incorrectly, it could call them forth. What drove Drew to such extremes? To steal her journal, then attempt a rite far beyond his capabilities? What was the final straw that snapped his discernment?

As the old truck vanished into traffic, Sister Wendy closed her journal and tapped it again against her palm. "Who did you call?" she wondered aloud. "Who would come for you?" Because a demon could not enter the world so easily, whoever came was waiting for an invitation. They had their own entrance and only waited for someone to unlock the door, any door, to come through.

"Who?" she went back to her quarters not to mourn the loss of Drew, for she was certain he was dead or would be soon, but to ponder the meaning of these events and await the brother's return for more answers.

# FOUR

Cornelius Lessman, known to Neil as Grandpa, was dying. At seventy-eight, he had a major heart attack, according to the doctors.

Neil knew the true cause of this situation.

Grandpa was dying from a broken heart.

"Mr. Lessman, do you understand what we are saying?" Doctor Prashanti said in his calmest, most empathetic voice. "We can try again, but if we do, I believe we will have the same outcome."

Neil nodded. "So, his kidneys have gone bad. And to stay alive, he needs dialyses. But when you hook him up to that, he had another heart attack. So, either way, he's going quick."

Doctor Prashanti agreed. "We can try dialysis again, but I suspect the same outcome." There was an invitation for direction in the silence.

Neil gave none.

"Mr. Lessman, how would you like us to proceed?"

It would have been nice to have someone else to look to. Someone else to answer, to not be forced to decide if his grandpa, the man who raised Neil since he was six, should die. And even though the doctor was clear, death was not waiting for an invitation, only a door for which to come through.

Neil didn't want to decide. That's why he went home to get Drew.

So Drew could be a hero.

So Drew could answer questions like this.

But why would Neil have thought that would happen? Drew was no hero. He was only an adult by age, never responsible, never accountable, always cared for by others.

"Which will hurt less?" Neil choked on the words. Did he say everything he wanted to Grandpa? Did he ever tell him thank you for taking him and Drew in after his parents' accident? Did he understand everything the man was trying to teach him about being a man, a good person? What was left to be said? Could it be said? Could it be anything more than the regrets of what should have been, could have been more, and now, is just a chasm between them forever?

"At this point, he can't feel anything. The pain killers have made him comfortable." Doctor Prashanti nodded softly.

"Then, I guess I'll just sit with him. No dialysis."

Over the doctor's shoulder, nurses activated and went behind the curtain where his grandpa was laying. One nurse drew the curtain. Metal rings scraped against the steel bar on the ceiling shrieking a quick, final scream as Grandpa was hidden from the world to be prepared for his final moments.

"We will keep him comfortable while you say your goodbyes. Is there anyone else we should call?" Doctor Prashanti asked politely.

Grandma died from cancer a few years back. It was just Grandpa, Neil, and Drew for the past few years. Now, Neil was the last one left. The final Lessman—but perhaps Drew wasn't dead? It didn't matter now. No phone could reach him. And so Neil shook his head.

"Can I go to him?" Neil asked. Behind the white curtain, dark bodies swarmed around Grandpa. Blankets were carefully drawn over him. The sheets changed. Other things Neil couldn't understand were happening, making a horrid stench come from behind the curtain. His eyes watered as he covered his mouth and nose with the back of his hand.

"Let the nurses finish first." The doctor, sensing his time here was finished, met Neil's eyes and said in the most sincere voice Neil had ever heard, "I'm sorry for your loss."

Neil nodded.

Behind the curtain was silent as the nurses hurried about their work. The smell stopped as abruptly as it came, masked in antiseptic and something Neil thought was mint air freshener.

The curtain opened. "Take your time," the nurse said. He was tall and wide, strong and blocky, with a kind face. "We'll be at the desk if you need anything."

Grandpa laid peacefully on the bed. Was he already dead? The beeps on his machinery were polite, faint, and fading, but still happening. No one was listening anymore.

Neil took the seat beside the bed, which wasn't there before the curtain closed. Where to begin with the things to say? If he'd not gone for Drew, he would have had more time to say everything, but now, time was up.

"After mom and dad died, I was so angry." Neil held his grandpa's hand. It was weightless, loose muscles, thin bones. "You didn't deserve all the shit we dumped on you. I'm sorry."

In this moment, Neil couldn't remember all the smiles and laughter he brought to his grandparents. He couldn't know how scared his grandpa was that he'd screw up and not raise the boys right. Neil didn't know his grandpa felt like a failure with Drew, but had no doubt that Neil would do great things. In this moment, all Neil could think about was all the things he did wrong, all the things said, all the fights and screaming matches, slammed doors, and shed tears.

"I'm sorry. I'm sorry I made your life hard. I'm sorry I couldn't help Drew. I couldn't help you help him. You did everything, but I didn't help enough."

Neil's grandpa never expected him to do more than he did. Drew had his demons, and he never let anyone help him fight them. That was what started the fight that led to Grandpa's heart break. Grandpa found drugs after a long time without them and confronted Drew about it. Grandpa begged Drew to let him help, to let him pull Drew out of this dark place, but instead Drew screamed he didn't need a stand-in dad. He could do it himself.

"I couldn't help him," Neil said. And he meant all the years since their parents' death, as well as what happened in the basement. Neil squeezed his grandpa's hand. "I'm sorry I wasn't there for you. I didn't help you. I can help him. I will help him. Like you tried to help him. I'll help him."

Grandpa's hand grew heavy. Neil felt the weight before the cooling of his skin, before he heard the machines stop their polite chirps. He kept squeezing his grandpa's hand and cried for all the things he'll never hear Neil say, all the things he'll never see Neil do, and worst of all, that Grandpa will never know that Drew would be okay.

Neil would make sure of it.

After some time, Neil wasn't sure how long, the nurse spoke. "He's gone Mr. Lessman. We were watching his vitals; he wasn't in any pain. Please take your time and let us know when you are ready for us to move him."

Neil wiped his eyes and stood. "Nothing else to say." He sniffed. "He's gone."

"Not everything said is for someone else. Sometimes we just need to say the words," the nurse said in his empathetic, patient voice.

Wise words had no place in Neil's mind. The promise he made to help his brother pushed away everything else.

"Thank you," Neil said. "Do I have to sign something or do something?"

"Your grandpa took care of everything. He had all the instructions on what to do in his wallet. You just need to go home and grieve."

Neil didn't go home. He thought he might sit in his grandpa's truck—now, he supposed, it was *his* truck—and cry, but the tears didn't come. They couldn't break through the promise he had made. So, instead, he went back to DiCoro's, determined not to let his grandpa down…again.

# FIVE

This time, no one noticed Neil walk into DiCoro's except the bartender. How this was possible boggled Neil as the bar was full and the lobby was buzzing with hopefuls trying to get a table without a reservation.

"Sir," the bartender said. Neil sniffed again and wiped his eyes, which were now dry even though tears still trickled down his cheeks. "Sister Wendy is on her way."

Neil cleared his throat and said, "thank you." The words hit the bartender hard, alien, and unfamiliar with this crowd.

"Please, wait over here," the bartender said.

He guided Neil to the edge of the bar where a collection of glasses stood upside down and dripping from the dishwasher. Heat baked off the glasses as Neil stood beside them, giving birth to the first thought that wasn't about his grandpa or Drew in hours: how hot is that water?

"Brother of Drew," Sister Wendy greeted him as she came out from a swinging door. Neil glimpsed the kitchen behind her. "Everything okay with your emergency?"

Her uncaring posture and dismissive tone didn't match her words.

Neil shook his head. "Death in the family," he wanted to add that it was the last person in his family, the only other person besides him and now he didn't know what the hell he was going to do alone in this world, but she didn't care so why waste the words. "Drew had your book when…what happened, happened?"

"What happened?" Sister Wendy said. Her tone was that of a wise guy playing dumb. She spread her hands to match, inviting Neil to tell her how she could know what happened.

"He was taken?" Neil said.

"Was that a question?" Wendy became stolid, even more so than her earlier emotionless questions.

"I'm not sure what I saw, but I was told you do." Neil pointed to the black bock still in Wendy's hands.

"Told by whom?" Now curiosity crept into her voice but was quickly extinguished when she saw Neil heard it.

Mr. Dream was the only name he knew the man by and doubted Wendy, in her nun's cloak and regal posture, would know a drug kingpin and megalomaniac from the dregs. Of course, he was wrong about this assumption. But names were things of power, and so Neil simply answered, "Someone my brother knew."

Wendy, seeing the calculus, nodded and waved for Neil to follow her into the swinging kitchen door.

As she walked, her head didn't bob. It was simply even and disciplined, appearing to float along the bustling chaos of chrome and sweaty chefs in white. Their storm of action broke around her as stones break waves, resolute, unmoved by the tidal forces swelling around her.

Neil dodged the chefs where he could but was jostled and knocked around as he tried to follow the woman. Knives flashed and chopped in quick pops. Caramelized steaks and butter covered veggies filled the air with their tempting smells, trying to drag his eyes away from Sister Wendy. She moved so quickly; he knew a single glance away would lose her in this kitchen.

He didn't know that was the point of this walk. Later he would put the ideas together and then wonder with absent curiosity how Drew, never known for his focus or attention to detail, could have ever followed her through this chaos without distraction. The shouts and alarms, the constant barrage against the senses, the quick turns around shelves and appliances, Neil kept his focus on Wendy and knew if he lost her, she'd be gone and with her any answers about Drew.

She stopped at a green door momentarily to unlock it. When she turned, her eyebrow rose in quick surprise to see Neil still there.

"This way," she said. Then motioned through the door.

Beyond the green door, the kitchen's shine and glow were devoured by a dark earthen tunnel lit with a string of bulbs that put Neil in mind of old coal mines. But he thought the coal mines were probably safer based on the slick stone floor and splintered wall supports.

Wendy led the way.

Mr. Dream's words, *'he fell in with the wrong crowd'*, echoed in Neil's mind. Who are the wrong crowd to a drug dealer? And while the Sleep House was a shamble, at least it wasn't a subterranean hideout. But this is where answers were. This is where the trail ended, and so Neil followed Wendy into the tunnel.

"I never caught your name," Wendy said. Her voice echoed softly in the tunnel. A cool breeze came from where they were going and where Neil thought it would be stale or moldy, it was fresh. Fresh like when Grandpa would take them hiking in the woods in Western Maryland. Even Drew enjoyed it, and he always hated everything that wasn't his idea. The fresh air was cleansing for all of them. It set difficult times aside for a moment whether they were dealing with Drew's latest relapse, Grandma's cancer diagnosis, or Neil's acceptance to MIT.

Clean air made everything easier.

"I never gave it," Neil said. "I'm not here to be part of whatever this is. Just want answers."

"Beware that which you seek, fore it might seek you," Wendy said with a fleeting flutter of happiness. "My teacher used to say that."

Neil, too deep in his own grief, didn't recognize the happy memory of a lost one in another. He said nothing. He simply kept walking a few paces behind her, keeping close to the lights.

One of the wooden supports was so severely splintered, it caught his shirt as he walked by. The rip was loud in this too cramped tunnel, echoing around him. But the light was too dim to see if any blood lined the tear.

Irritated, Neil asked, "Where are we going?"

"We're almost there."

The lights were evenly spaced, with nothing more than a rusty wire holding them to the wall. Warm light filled the tunnel with sharp shadows. At least the floor wasn't as slick as it appeared. The stone was worn down and smooth, but as Neil walked further, he noticed ridges in the stone, carved no doubt, in a pattern like the ridges on the shoulder of the road to wake you up when you drive over them. They were treads.

Another green door was at the end of the tunnel. It wasn't that long of a walk, probably a few minutes, but it seemed much longer not knowing where the path ended. Wendy approached the door with another key and unlocked it.

"What's in there?" Neil asked. Dread filled him as he finally realized his situation.

The focus on answers blinded him to the danger of a deep cave, with no one to help if something was to go wrong. And while Wendy was probably in her seventies, Neil had no illusions that he'd win a physical confrontation. She exuded intensity and Neil knew that didn't stop at her eyes. She could kill him, and no one would know. No one would look for him until the fall, when he wouldn't show up for college. There weren't friends or other family.

He was alone.

"Nothing to worry about," Wendy opened the door and Neil flinched away from the bright, warm light that poured out. "Welcome to the Order."

Neil's eyes adjusted to the light faster than his mind grasped what he was seeing. It was an office building but with windows and a skyline, and sunshine.

"Are we still underground?"

Wendy smiled at that, finally cracking her dour appearance.

"Not everything is always as it appears," she said. Wendy walked to a large wooden reception desk and said to the lady sitting there, "we will need a visitor pass."

The receptionist, chipper beyond sugary sweet, flashed a wide smile at Neil. She wore a finely tailored pink suit with a pin on the label that read, *Oh No! Monday Again?* But it wasn't Monday…was it? Her short hair was curled in loops like she'd just come from the stylist.

She smiled wide at Neil exposing pristine teeth under glossy red lipstick. She said, "Wonderful! Welcome. How long will you be with us?"

Neil thought of a hotel now and looked around at the people milling about. Except for the receptionist, everyone was dressed in cloaks, but with different colors. Most were brown, some black, and one, the only one he saw, was green. They moved around in groups talking, drinking coffee, or soda, or water, munching sandwiches or crunching bags of chips. It was mundane. What you'd expect to see in any office lobby but instead of business suits, they wore cloaks. Instead of being in a skyscraper, they were in a cave.

The skyline in the windows where the walls should be, the sunlight, and clouds, told him he had no idea where he was. In a cave? In a skyscraper? Who knew?

"He's just here for today," Wendy said. She didn't reflect the happiness of the receptionist, but that didn't bother the lady.

"Excellent. Well, welcome." She pulled a sticker from a strip and handed it to Neil. "Please wear this during your visit."

Neil pressed the sticker on his chest. It read *Guest Pass* with today's date.

The receptionist continued, "The coffee room—"

"No. No need," Wendy interrupted. "He's not staying long."

Neil politely confirmed Wendy's statement. "Just a short visit." Outside, the shadow of a helicopter passed with the distant thrum that should be there. It was close to real, but not quite. No one else noticed. Or they didn't show they noticed and instead went about their business.

"Well, while here, enjoy yourself. Cafeteria has—"

"It will be a quick visit," Wendy said. Her sharp tone cut any further discussion from the cheery receptionist, and they moved on into the building.

"We are still underground, right?" Neil asked as they walked through an earthen hallway but with rectangles in the ceiling like skylights shining bright daylight.

"We are. The light is simulated to provide a more hospitable atmosphere. In the lobby, the appearance of the windows, the helicopter you noticed, that's all faked to help people acclimate to living underground."

"Why do you live underground?" Neil asked as they came to another large room. This one was a three-story open-air library that belonged in an enchanted forest. A waterfall rushed from the far side of this round room down into a pit with rings of light showing other floors for as deep as Neil could see. Above was a glass dome with bright sunlight shining through, yet it was 5:00pm when he entered the restaurant, and the sun was directly above the window.

"How many people live down here?" He shouted over the waterfall.

"Underground allows us to live without distractions. We can focus on our faith. At least, those who believe can. Others are here just to help people like your brother, but without faith, they can only take their patients so far." Wendy leaned against the railing between their path and the pit. She watched Neil take in the enormous room around them. When she thought he wasn't watching, she itched her wrist. Neil didn't ask and assured himself that what she was itching wasn't moving under her skin.

"As for how many people I used to know, but now…" She shook her head as if to say *too many*.

"Faith?" Neil asked.

Cloaked people wandered around them. Some were carrying bundles of books, others carried baskets of fresh crops from a garden. Many just walked and laughed. Neil had heard about cults, Jonestown, and the more recent Waco standoff. He didn't think they looked this happy, or…if it wasn't for the cloaks, this was normal.

"Are you like a cult or something?" Neil asked.

"Or something," Wendy smiled and waved for him to follow as she pushed off the railing. "Come, I'll show you where we keep the human sacrifices."

Neil chuckled, but when Wendy didn't, he stopped laughing and looked back the way he came.

He could run now?

Get out before it gets any weirder, but who was he kidding? No one is letting him leave. And if they did, would he want to?

No.

Of course not. This is the path to answers, the path to his brother, and so he walked it, following Wendy deeper into her world.

# SIX

The walk was longer this time and down a few staircases into more daylight lit tunnels. Perhaps this place was an old mine? That would make sense as deep as it went, and all the care taken to make the place safe. Here, the supports were metal. No more splintering wood. Rooms were carved into the earth and everywhere the network of sunlight brought what could have been complete dark into a brilliant day.

Now the light was turning orange, dimming, warming as Neil assumed this was what passed for sunset down here. It was pretty, but no comparison to the real thing. No clouds to paint with pink and purple threads. Just the clinical emulation of sunset, not the beauty of it, not the feeling.

"Where are we really going?" Neil asked.

"Here," Wendy said. She stopped at a red door with a brass plate on it. Chiseled into the plate was the word: Artifacts III. She unlocked the door with her large keyring and went in. As she entered, lights flickered to life. The door was ajar. Wendy only opened it far enough to slip in, but not far enough for Neil to see. "Are you coming?"

Neil pushed the door open. He jumped back at the featureless white face hovering over him. The demon had come back. It found him. Chased him to this room. It was behind the door and Wendy led him right to it. Now the creature was going to do to him what it did to Drew.

But it didn't move. It only stared at him from within the room. It towered over him, eight feet tall, glaring down through empty black slits in the white face. It was the demon that took Drew. It came for him. It saw him and now it's found him. Wendy led him right to it.

"Familiar?" Wendy said and flicked the white face. It clunked like wood, hollow and dull. "Is this what took your brother?"

Now Neil saw it was a mask, not attached to the billowing darkness of the thing in the basement. It wasn't alive. And it was missing something.

Neil nodded and took a deep breath. "Yeah, that's what took him. Except it had a spiral, here," Neil pointed where the nose and eyebrows would have met if the thing had such a face.

Wendy didn't react.

"It was a demon?" Neil asked.

Wendy shrugged and said, "That's an easy way to think of them." She took out her black book, her journal, and opened it to where Drew was reading before he was taken. The weakened spine opened to a page that Neil thought was a math equation, but at the top of the page was a sketch of this mask. "Your brother was trying to do something far beyond his capabilities. Extraction, removing a demon from someone, is difficult in the best scenarios. He didn't have the skills, nor the environment, and so he was consumed."

"But he can be saved?" Neil pleaded.

Wendy tapped the book against her hand. "Demons rarely kill their victims. They torture them. Infest them. The lives left behind are often not worth living."

"But alive?" he asked. When she didn't deny it, Neil continued, "can you help me get him back?"

Drew could be saved. Wendy just confirmed it.

But how?

"I know better than to call forth demons," Wendy said, holding her book to her chest. "You are not consumed by this world yet. Leave it. Leave your brother to his fate, for he has chosen it. Cry off this path and live without this weight on your soul."

When Neil did not immediately answer, she continued, "To be clear, you cannot win against these *things*. They will ruin you and the ones you love; their passion is your demise." A distant look took Wendy away for a moment. "They take… everything."

Her hand drifted unconsciously to her heart. A long sigh flowed from her and quivered at the end. Wendy again itched her wrist, but this time saw Neil watching. She pulled her sleeve down and opened her mouth to say something, but then remained silent.

Her eyes softened, almost pleading. Neil fought his body to prevent it from stepping away from her, away from the journal. Another voice in the chorus calling for him to go on with no one, but how could he? Without his family he'd be alone and isn't an addict brother, someone he could never count on for anything other than to lie, be better than no one at all?

He didn't step back…he pushed through reason and common sense which all agreed with Wendy's suggestion. It was safe to leave

Drew. It was always safer to leave Drew but is that how all this began? No one pulled Drew out of the mess he got himself into and so the mess got messier until one day it was *such a mess* that hell itself came to claim him.

Neil stepped forward. Nodding, resolute acceptance that he'd do whatever it took to save the only member of his family left.

Wendy sighed and said, "I know a lost cause when I see one. We had hope for Drew, but you must want help to receive it. Consider what happens when you help your brother. Will he be back to his ways?"

"He's all I have left," Neil said with the finality that ceased all other discussion on the topic.

"Then," Wendy opened her journal to the page Drew was viewing. "Draw this symbol where you saw the creature and say these words." Her finger traced the words on the page.

Neil read, mouthing the words before Wendy clamped her weathered yet remarkably strong hand against his lips. Her eyes burned as she growled, "Do not say them here. Say them there."

Neil nodded.

She removed her hand.

Neil stretched his lips and when they had feeling again, he asked, "What if I pronounce them wrong?"

He'd seen a movie where that happened. The outcome was funny, but he didn't think real life—this indifferent and often cruel universe, would be so comically forgiving.

"The words are only part of the incantation. More important

is your intention. You must mean what you are doing to do it. Accidents don't happen in magic." Wendy closed the journal and held it limply towards him.

"Magic?" Neil shook his head.

Disbelief finally caught up to him. This couldn't be true. Drew was a junkie, not a wizard. And if accidents can't happen, then what went wrong for Drew? Reality crashed over Neil. There was nothing supernatural about what happened. Like Mr. Dream said, the monster thing was a hallucination brought on by a contact high. This mask on the wall—it's just a blank mask similar to what he imagined, but Neil was never good at lying to himself. It didn't just kind of look like the mask, except for the spiral carving; it was the same mask. And what he felt in the basement wasn't in his head. The ice crystals were on his face, on the walls, and no matter how much he hoped it wasn't true, it was.

Still, he denied what he knew to be true. Demons can't be real. Magic can't be real. Drugs were real. Hallucinations were real. Death was real.

"Drew wasn't doing magic, he was using…" What? Neil didn't know. "Some powder drug thing." What was Drew's drug? It was heroin before his trips to Mr. Dream. But now what was it? What was Mr. Dream serving?

"There are many doors to the supernatural. Some look like books. Some look like powders. Some look like fever dreams," Wendy said. She shrugged and again waved the book. "But never mistake denying what you believe with denying what exists. You do not need to believe in magic, but it exists. Your brother knew this. He sought a shortcut through a power he did not understand and thus led to his circumstance."

Neil took the book. "I don't know what I saw. But—"

"Yes, you do," Wendy said. "You saw what you call a demon take your brother. You saw that the world is much more complex and strange than you believed it to be. You saw your assumptions about reality shattered. Some would have lost their minds at this, but not you. You sought answers. I'm giving them to you. What will you do with them now?"

Wendy motioned for him to leave, and so Neil stepped out of the room, giving the white mask another appraising look.

The book was heavier in his hand now. He tapped it against his palm, as Wendy had earlier in the evening. Each tap vibrating through his bones, tuning him into a new wavelength, a new reality, a world where magic was not only possible but accessible. The key to it was in his hand. Tapping and vibrating in his hands. They walked back to the lobby to the tune of Neil's tapping and silent wondering.

Could magic be real? If it were, what else is there in the universe that he had taught himself wasn't real? Monsters? Certainly, monsters were real. There were too many human monsters throughout history to doubt the truth. But inhuman demonic creatures? What other beasts could tumble out of nightmares and fantasies into his life? Now that he knew about them—would he see them? Could they see him?

They returned to the receptionist desk with the lady smiling her pearly perfect teeth as if doing nothing more than awaiting their return. She met Neil's eyes with an unblinking awakeness that disturbed him. He glanced to the fake skyline and then back to the receptionist. She still stared at him, wide eyes, wider smile, waiting for him to say—anything. Didn't she have something else to do other than stare at him? But there was nothing on her barren desk. No computer. No typewriter. Not even paper nor notebooks. Just a roll of guest past stickers.

Neil asked Wendy,

"Now what?"

"You give her your sticker and leave," Wendy said in an emotionless instruction. "I suspect I will not see you again if you continue on this path." A young man in a brown cloak came to her side and silently waited for her to finish this business. "While it will be a waste of words, I will again say, leave your brother to his fate. Do not intertwine your future with his as he will be the anchor of what could have been."

"He's my brother," he said again, thinking a single statement conveyed all the answers and explanations one could ever need to understand why he couldn't walk away.

"Then be on your way." Wendy motioned to a different door from the one they came in. This one had a glowing green sign over it that read, EXIT.

Neil said nothing as he went to the door.

"Sir," the receptionist called with her cheery voice. Wendy had already walked away with the young man. "Your sticker?"

He peeled the white label from his shirt and handed it to her.

"Have a great day!" She said.

Dusk settled over the fake sky behind her empty desk in the fake city. The sun dipped below the horizon far in the fake view as the first stars poked through the skyline.

"Night?" Neil asked. He pointed to the windows, which he now thought might be large projections, like a movie theater or giant TV. Maybe those weren't windows after all, but some kind of screen?

The receptionist only smiled and motioned to the exit. "Have a great day!" She repeated with the same tone she used a moment ago.

Neil stepped away from the desk as the woman kept his gaze, smiling and holding her hand towards the door as if frozen in the moment. Her eyes didn't blink, her lips didn't quiver as she waited for him to leave. He paused to see if she came back to life, but she didn't. She only sat, impassive, frozen. Others in the lobby still bustled about in their cloaks.

The stillness of the woman unsettled Neil. He couldn't take his eyes from her, waiting every moment for her to do something. Still looking at her, he pressed through the exit door. The receptionist didn't blink as the heavy green door closed behind him with a loud kerchunk.

But this wasn't a tunnel. It was an alley behind the restaurant, and it was daytime. The sun was still in its ascent. Disoriented by the jarring time re-synchronization happening within his mind, Neil checked his pager to see the time. It was dead. He turned back to the door, but it didn't have any way to open it from this side. What time was it?

"I wasn't in there all night?"

But the words didn't convince him of what his heart knew.

Neil hurried out of the alley and to Di'Coro's entrance. Wendy must have drugged him or something. Time didn't just slip by, and he wasn't in there for hours. Maybe two hours, but it was dusk when he went in. He wasn't in there all night.

The front door was locked. He banged on it, shouted, "Hey!"

Pressing his face to the darkened windows, he only saw the faint glimmer of liquor bottles on their glass shelves. No one was there. He hammered harder on the glass.

"Hey! Wendy! Hey!"

The window quaked from his fist. He wasn't in there all night. He couldn't have been. What did Wendy do?

*He fell in with the wrong crowd.*

"Hey!" Neil banged harder, screamed louder. "Hey! Hey! What did you do!?"

"Sir!" a heavy voice shouted. It dripped with authority. Only a cop would shout with such a commanding tone. It froze him as he pulled back to hit the window again. "What is the problem?"

Neil's frustrated confusion fell away immediately as the police officer approached him, keeping a safe distance.

"I'm sorry, officer," Neil said. "I thought I saw my friend in there and was just trying to get her attention."

That seemed like a reasonable lie. Neil smiled a little and shook his head as if he knew how stupid he looked, but the smile was real, proud of the immediacy in his made-up story.

"Well, Di'Coro's is closed and they ain't lookin' to fix a window," the officer said. He kept his distance. "What's that you got there?"

Wendy's journal was in Neil's left hand. When Neil held it up for the officer to see, he said, "Yeah, this is her book. I just wanted to give it back." Neil presented the open book showing Wendy's name on the page. "I'm sorry. I should have just called her, but she works here, and

I thought I'd just give it back. I'll call her."

The officer, seeing how the pieces fit together and realizing this was a stupid kid doing something they didn't think through very well, relaxed. "Sounds like a good idea."

Neil pointed to his old truck. "I'll just get going. Sorry for the confusion, officer."

"No harm, just think about what you're doing kid," the officer said as he took out a notebook. "Have a good day."

Neil hurried to his truck and started it, the engine coughing and struggling as usual. As he pulled away, still thinking about Wendy, the underground place, and time slipping away, Neil didn't notice the officer's hand near his taser or the knowing look police give to junkies watching him. An addiction had taken hold. The officer saw it. But Neil did not—he wouldn't see it for many, many horrible years to come.

# SEVEN

Neil sat at the end of the driveway. In his mind, this house was still his grandpa's. But who did it belong to now? Do the police come and tell him to leave? Will some long-lost relative show up with answers? Unlikely. They would have shown up when his parents died. But now there was nowhere to go. No one for Neil to call.

So, he went inside.

The house was often silent with Drew passed out or Grandpa quietly watching TV in his room. But tonight, the silence was absolute. No buzz from the refrigerator. No creaking from someone walking around upstairs. No threat of anyone but him breaking the silence of this place. The quiet was suffocating, like concrete slowly solidifying, encasing him without any hope of ever breaking free.

Neil walked heavily to the kitchen. He flicked on the overhead light, letting the hard click echo around him. The lights buzzed as they cast pale white light over the warm wooden cabinets. Dishes were mounded on the countertops—the dishes he and Grandpa were supposed to clean after school before the unexpected death.

Was Grandpa thinking about the dishes that needed to be done while he was dying? Did he think *I can't die now? The dishes need to be done?* Not that the dishes were so bad, or that there were many—

just a few bowls from last night's dinner, mostly clean already from thorough scraping. But they needed to be done.

Neil picked up the orange bowl Grandpa had used last night for his chili. Nothing special, just canned chili from the store, but it was his last meal. Is that what he would have wanted for his last meal? Would he have preferred grandma's chicken dumplings? He loved them. They were his favorite, even after she passed away. Neil made them using her recipe. He threw the plastic bowl into the sink. It clattered against the other plastic bowls and silverware.

What was grandpa thinking at the end? If they hadn't finished the dollhouse—the one they completed after the chili—would that have been enough to stave off the heart attack for just one more day? And Neil had insisted they keep going, that they work late because they were so close. He knew they could finish with more time. They hadn't decorated the house yet, just finished building it, but Neil had a plan for the wallpaper, for painting some rooms, and, more importantly, for hanging miniature pictures of his parents throughout the dollhouse.

They built it to honor and remember mom and dad, Grandpa's daughter- and son-in-law. Drew was going to help but was always *busy* when they were building. Neil knew busy was code for high. He was 18, not 5. Grandpa told Neil to be patient. Drew would help when he was ready.

But he was never ready. Would he ever have been?

Neil went to the basement.

The wooden stairs broke the silence as they creaked and moaned under his heavy steps. There was no trace of the ice from earlier on the concrete floor and walls. But on the workbench, the dollhouse was still there. The burnt spiral remained in the basement.

Neil stood at the workbench, smiling at the memory when grandpa handed him the last tile to put on the roof. It was the last thing they did to finish the house. Neil exhaled deeply as he pressed the tile into the glue. In his mind, he asked his parents what they thought of the house. They didn't answer, but he thought they would have liked it.

Beside the house were the paints selected for the rooms. They were warm off-white pastels with white accents. It would have been a nice color scheme for a happy family. And even now, Neil could paint the house. The burned scar in the basement could be filled in with putty, sanded down to match the flooring, painted over, even tiled to eradicate any sign of its existence. Such a scar was unfitting for a happy family home. Happy families didn't have scars.

And they didn't finish things before everyone could participate. Why didn't Drew help? Why couldn't Neil wait? He should have waited.

When Grandpa told Drew they finished the house, Drew exploded. He was so angry. Neil had never seen him turn so red when shouting, or his knuckles turn so white. Grandpa took the screaming; he thought he deserved it. Neil didn't know what to say. Grandpa had tried to stop Neil, tried to hold off on finishing, but Neil didn't wait. He didn't let Drew have his chance. And when Drew was done screaming, Grandpa went upstairs—to flee, to recover, to just not deal with a screaming brat for a moment?

Or to search Drew's room. Grandpa found the drugs. Then it was his turn to scream—to ask what he did wrong, to tell Drew he was killing himself, that he'd take Neil with him. That Neil would be another sacrifice to Drew's drugs. Grandpa meant all the friends Drew lost—but Drew believed his body count started with their parents.

Maybe Neil did too.

When Neil put Sister Wendy's journal on the workbench, it fell open to the page about summoning demons.

Was it Drew's fault that their parents died? Drew wasn't driving the car. Or the truck. Sure, they were arguing in the car when the accident happened. Drew was screaming how he hated them and hoped they'd die—a moment later, his wish was granted when a truck hit them. Neil and Drew were in the backseat. They were fine. Their parents were not. The argument was about Drew going to treatment. This was after the first overdose. Mom had found him so high he couldn't even answer her. They were driving to a treatment facility. It was too rainy. Dad shouldn't have been driving in such heavy rain. Drew shouldn't have been distracting them. Neil should have stopped them from yelling at each other. Mom shouldn't have told Neil and Drew to put on their seat belts, because then they could have all gone together, and Neil wouldn't be all alone now.

But Neil didn't have to be alone. Drew could come back. Their parents were gone. Grandma was gone (cancer). Grandpa was gone (cardiac failure). But Drew wasn't gone forever, only gone for now.

At least, that's what it sounded like from talking to Wendy. And when he got back, Drew could putty over the spiral, he could paint the house, he could help decorate it and they could finish this together. Because the house was scarred. It wasn't done. It was broken, but it could be fixed. And once it was, could Drew let go of the past?

Could Neil?

What could Drew be without the hurt?

Without the guilt?

When Drew is free, what could that mean for Neil?

What is the future for Neil Lessman?

It was time to find out. Time to get his brother back and start their future.

Neil said the words to summon the demon, just like Wendy told him. They came easier than he thought they would. No mistakes were made in the pronunciation, or his intent to negotiate for his brother's body and soul.

Biting cold engulfed him, then the black smoke came, billowing from the burnt spiral in the dollhouse. Neil clenched his fists and locked his jaw. His mind tightened, preparing to see that horrid blank face again. When he breathed, when his brain remembered to do that simple little function of life, the frozen air turned his lungs to bricks. As the smoke entwined his legs, rolling over his feet and coiling to his knees, Neil knew it was time.

Time to get his brother back. Time to put the past behind them. Time to fulfill his promise to Grandpa.

It was time to deal with demons.

# EIGHT

Hell's frozen breath coated the unfinished concrete walls with icicles. The sharp temperature drop brought a pale mist off the walls, coiling around Neil and the dollhouse. Black smoke rolled through the mist as if bubbling out. Darkness built until it eradicated the light.

Neil stepped back from the dollhouse—not in fear. The time for fear had passed, replaced with the emptiness of having nothing left to lose. Of course, he hadn't thought through what could happen, all that he could lose in a future yet to be written. He didn't calculate the value of meeting his first love at MIT. There was no accounting for all the lives he'd impact with his career in robotics, bioscience, software engineering, or whatever he might choose. There was no thought of all that he could have, only reflections on what he'd lost. And to Neil, this made sense. The past was real. The future was a fantasy at best.

He stopped moving back when he achieved a polite personal space between where the demon would stand and where he would. The conversation's script formed in his mind as the demon's body solidified. Even the cold, the biting, bone stiffening cold, didn't slow his thoughts.

A spiral of smoke rose and took the form of a torso, shoulders, and before a face appeared, Neil began talking.

"I am here to negotiate for the return of my brother."

The white mask, featureless save for the black spiral carved in the forehead, emerged from the pillar of smoke. It pressed toward Neil, but he didn't move. His impassive glare met the demon's black eyes. The creature was so close he could smell the frozen rot drifting from the mask. Its smell was thick, dense, and heavy, but not choking. Not any worse than spoiled chicken on a hot day, and that's what Neil found most disturbing about it—the smell wasn't sickening. And he knew, without a doubt, that one could get used to that smell—maybe even not notice it.

"Do you understand me?" Neil didn't flinch at the demon's attempted intimidation.

"I can," it said, its voice too silky—pleasant the first time you hear it.

"I was told you would be open to a deal."

"I always am. Who told you such things?" The demon leaned back.

"Doesn't matter. Where's my brother?"

A tendril of smoke emerged from the pillar, Neil thought it to be an arm, and at the end of it appeared the hazy image of Drew's broken body. It was like a mirage in the mist and smoke, but Neil could clearly see his brother's spine coiled, his arms bent at unnatural angles with too many elbows. Drew's legs were fused into a serpentine tail and twisted into a tight spiral.

His brother had become this creature's human bonsai tree.

The sight sent bile racing from Neil's stomach to his throat. He wanted to vomit. To spray puke all over that damn white mask and see how this bastard likes to scrape off…when was the last time he ate? What was it? Chili? But Neil didn't move. His focus, his discipline, demanded he swallow his vomit, force down the soft meaty chunks, and not give this son of a bitch a moment's pleasure in seeing his revulsion at what it did to Drew.

"He's in my collection," the demon answered, a little too delighted. "I would need to replace such a masterpiece with another. Are you offering yourself in his place?"

Neil shook his head. There was no point in trading places. This wasn't only about saving Drew, but about saving them both. Neil had no illusions of being a martyr, he only wanted to be a family. "No, but there must be something else you want?"

The demon sighed heavily in faux exasperation. "Oh, there is much I want. But perhaps nothing so much as the raw materials I could gather here if only permitted to do so." He, Neil was certain it was a *he* based on the voice, was pouty, like a petulant child. What the demon said hit Neil like a lie. He didn't believe this creature was as limited as it appeared. It wasn't the weak, *I can't do things by myself, so you need to help me* being it claimed to be, with its tone, posture, and words.

"What materials?"

This demon wasn't a mindless animal, or a devouring beast. It was playing a game. Attempting to manipulate what it perceived as a lesser mind, but Neil was no fool. He was excellent at chess, a masterful debater, and above all, a survivor. His brother made him a master of that skill. But Neil hadn't a clue of the depth of this creature's brilliance, and its worst attribute: patience.

"Oh," the demon shook its head and waved its arm, making

the image of Drew vanish. Another arm extended from the smoke pillar and waved as it spoke. "I am known as many things, but few understand my truest nature is that of an artist. I am a sculptor."

Neil remembered his brother's broken form and interpreted sculptor as torturer. Was that art in hell? Perhaps?

"And I need materials with which to sculpt. Flesh and spirit. Flesh is easy. You humans always offer that," the demon chuckled. "But spirit is so much more… rare." The last word was soft, silken, and lingered in the air too long. Neil shuffled unconsciously.

"You want spirits?"

The demon nodded slowly and sadly as if to say, *woe is me I need such a thing*. "But I cannot wander your realm to collect such things. Vile forces, vicious creatures, keep me imprisoned—"

"Then how are you here now?" Neil interrupted, seeing a fault in the creature's story. "Are you on parole or something?"

The demon chuckled, thick and gurgling. "No. There are always backdoors but few I can walk through. This door," it motioned to the dollhouse, "I am tethered to it. Not free."

Was that true?

"So, if I smash that house, then you can't come back?" Neil's threat wasn't veiled.

"And neither can your brother," the demon called his bluff.

"You just need spirits? Like ghosts?"

"That will do."

"Where am I going to get them?" Neil thought about human

sacrifices but knew he was no murderer. He'd never deprive someone of a loved one like he was his parents or his grandparents.

Could he kill for Drew? Neil sank at the answer. No.

"The same place you can get anything today," the demon waved its arms. "The internet."

Neil was familiar with the internet, with the world wide web, and all the businesses starting online. The news called it the DotCom Boom, but all Neil knew was that there were a lot of stores online and some sold things you couldn't find anywhere else. And even if there wasn't a store online, there were communities online like bulletin boards. People talked about all kinds of things on there.

"Wait…" Neil came back to the moment, asked, "how do you know about the internet?"

The demon laughed and waved away the question with its tendril of smoke

"Bring me spirits and I will return your brother."

"How many?" Neil asked, still trying to wrap his head around where the hell he was going to find these spirits and what he'd have to do to get them.

"I'll come back when you have your first. I'll feel it. And then we'll discuss your," the demon whirled its arm, searching for who he was talking about, "yes, your brother."

Suddenly, Neil felt this wasn't the first time such a negotiation happened with this creature. Not with him, but as if this demon had had this conversation many times before. It was practiced. It had a rhythm, a disinterest, as if the demon was just going through the motions again.

"Who are you?" Neil asked.

"Dodslav. But many simply call me The Artist," the creature answered proudly. "Your brother is feeling the pain of his situation, so I wouldn't dally." The demon made a dismissing wave with its smokey appendages to shoo Neil away. "I'll return when you collect your first spirit. We can discuss our negotiations after that."

"I don't trust you," Neil shouted as the demon dissipated.

"Then you are wiser than most," Dodslav laughed, as his white face receded into the smoke and the pillar drifted down into the white mist. "Trust that I want to make my masterpiece. Trust that I need materials to do that. Trust in your ability to deliver to me that which others have failed to do. I am an artist, and value nothing more than my masterpiece to be."

And Neil knew he heard the truth. What artist doesn't want to build a masterpiece? What artist isn't consumed by their art?

As the black smoke flowed back into the burnt spiral, Neil looked once again at the putty. He could finish the house right now. But that would seal his brother's fate. Instead, he went upstairs to his computer and sealed his own.

# NINE

Beep beep beep screeeeeeeech ksshhhhhhhhhhh brrrrrrr beep beep beep krrrrrrrrrrr…

Neil's computer modem screamed its indecipherable greeting to his internet service provider as it connected online. A few quiet beeps later, and Neil's telnet session was established.

He'd read about a bulletin board where people shared ghost stories in MacWorld magazine. They even provided the address. And while he did not know what he'd asked, or what he was even looking for outside of "spirits", he thought this would be a place to start.

In his command prompt, he typed the connection code:

```
telnet bbs.darkturn.com 2323
```

Like all things related to the early internet, connecting to anything required patience. It was a quiet moment for him to remember he was alone.

Not that there was much to light. His room was spartan, down to the tightly made bed and empty walls. While the entire room was a sign of order and neat precision, Neil's computer desk was a mess. It was an oasis of insanity in the engulfing order of his room. But nothing on his desk was missing or lost; he knew where everything was in this jumble and could quickly, easily retrieve anything he needed from the piles of magazines, papers, and notebooks.

Many nights were spent like this, posting on bulletin boards and reading the real news of what was happening with computers from the people actually making the future in Silicon Valley. Neil could have been one of them. He modeled his future after them. They went to MIT, so he was going to go to MIT. But now, none of that mattered. Who wants a future where they are alone?

`Beware traveler! You've made a`

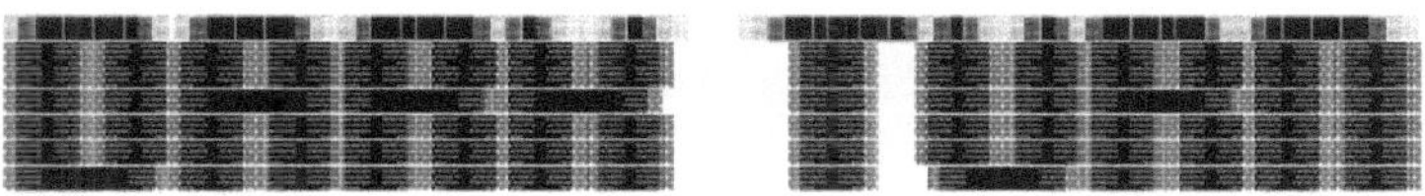


`What is your handle?`

Neil considered this—he had never stuck to a handle across boards before—but now decided he should if he was going to be searching for spirits online. He assumed this wasn't the kind of thing you could just find; he would need to build a reputation. Someone would need to reach out to him eventually, but how could they if they didn't know who he was?

And so, he typed the first thing that came to mind.

`@basement_rizer34`

He and Drew were going to rise from the thing in the basement. They were going to rise out of the 34th dollhouse, that was the last dollhouse made by grandpa. He'd been obsessed with building them over the past few years, with this last one being the 34th. And all 33 previous dollhouses were given to churches, hospitals, families in the neighborhood, and some were just put in the attic. But 34 just sat in the basement and will forever more sit in waiting until Drew can be pulled from that burnt spiral.

Welcome @basement_rizer34. Select your
fate.

    1. Read messages

    2. Post a message

    3. Enter chat room

    4. View bulletins

    5. Log off

Neil pressed 3, hoping someone else would be online.

There are 352 users chatting. Don't be
an asshole.

The latest messages mentioned ghost stories, a haunted house in
West Virginia, some lady kidnapped by a witch, and sightings of
Bigfoot in Tennessee. Without skimming far, he entered his question
and hit return to post it.

How do you buy a spirit online?

And a moment later, someone replied.

Wrong bbs dumbass. Go to Rovernet los-
er.

Neil laughed. Rovernet was the BBS for collectors of all things.
It made sense that they'd have people who claimed to collect spirits,
ghosts, and who knew what else. And so, Neil logged off Dark Turn
and jumped over to Rovernet.

As he waited, Neil considered how much it would cost to buy
a spirit. Perhaps people would give them away? He'd seen enough
horror movies with Drew to know that haunted things were not

usually wanted things. In his pocket, Neil found ten dollars neatly folded in his wallet. Hell, maybe people would pay him to take their haunted things. That would be great. Because with Grandpa's retirement checks no longer coming, he was going to need to get a job. How else would he buy these things or eat?

```
Welcome trader to


Have we got a deal for you!

                                                          d8P
                                                       d888888P
   88bc88b d8888b ?88    d8P d8888b  88bd88b  88bd88b  d8888b  ?88'
   88P' `d8P' ?88d88  d8P'd8b_,dP 88P'  `   88P' ?8b d8b_dP  88P
  d88     88b d8878b ,88' 88b    d88       d88    88P 88b       88b
 d88'    `?8888P'`?888P'  `?888P'd88'      d88'   88b`?888P'   `?8b


Handle:
```

Again, Neil entered @basement_rizer34 and navigated through the categories until he found what he thought he was looking for. Each category listed a type of object—from books to cars to computer parts—but none of those seemed right. It wasn't until Neil found *OTHER* that he knew he was on the right path.

Within OTHER there were terms he didn't understand, categories that he knew were euphemisms for other things. He knew CANDY wasn't the kind you got in the store, nor was FUNTIME something for kids. But within OTHER, was a category for ODDITIES and within that, a category for HAUNTED. And Neil held his breath, hoping that was what he was looking for.

Within the category was a bulletin board. No chat rooms here. Users were posting the strangest for sale ads.

FOR SALE
EYELESS TEDDY BEAR
Accepting: Verifiable backstory
Teddy bear belonged to a kid who died
in a fire. Only the bear survived. It is
still hot to the touch and in a dark room
you can see the fires of hell where its
eyes should be watching you.
Based in California.
For more information, contact @beary_
good_time

Having experienced the temperature of hell, Neil doubted the
veracity of this story. But there were many items posted, all with
fantastic stories, many sounding impossibly odd. One caught his eye
because it was only a state away.

FOR SALE
OUTLAW CAP GUN
Accepting: Best offer
Prev owner says this cap gun was made by
legendary outlaw Duddly Dust Cutter. He
made it for his son but was gunned down
before he could give it to him. Now, it
fires real bullets when the shooter said
'Duddly Says Die'.
Based in Kentucky
For more information, contact @tom_and_
linda_curees

Kentucky was only a few hours away. Neil could get there by
tonight if he left now. He messaged @tom_and_linda_curees to
express his interest.

Hello, I am new at this but am interested in buying your haunted gun. Could
we connect to talk about details? Thank
you, @basement_rizer34.

To Neil's amazement, a response came quickly from @tom_and_
linda_curees.

Sure thing. Phone number? I'll call you
now if it ain't too late. Tom Curees.

Neil, thinking it wasn't late at all, provided his phone number and
went to the kitchen to wait for the phone to ring.

A moment later, it did, and the two discussed plans for a late-night
pickup at Tom's house in Kentucky. Neil grew up during "stranger
danger" and knew driving to Kentucky to meet someone claiming to
sell a toy gun infested with the spirit of an outlaw was a horrible idea,
but what else could he do? He could sit here and be alone or he could
follow the only lead he had.

Five of his ten dollars was used to fill up his truck and off he
went to get fixed up with his new addiction. But like all dealers, Neil
wasn't sure if this man could be trusted. Just in case, he brought a
kitchen knife. One of the many things he learned from Drew, always
be prepared for the dealer to turn on you and always have a surprise
waiting for them if they did.

# TEN

What would a man who had a haunted toy gun be like? Neil built an image of Tom as he drove to Kentucky. A few hour drive was plenty of time to construct not only how this man would look but everything about him.

Tom would be middle-aged, bald, fat, with a jug of sweet tea in one hand and a BBQ sandwich in the other. He'd be the equivalent of a goth kid, but as an adult. Dramatically obsessed with death, black walls, skulls for decor, maybe a coffin coffee table. The messages were short and direct, no signs of who Tom was beyond a seller of an oddity. Neil weighed what the house would smell like more: incense or body odor. It would probably be a trailer with junked furniture spotting a dead lawn.

None of this was shaped by his interactions with Tom. These were all constructs of assumptions made about someone living in the middle of nowhere in Kentucky, claiming to have a haunted object and selling it online to… who? Did sane people dwell on these BBSs? Did sane people try to buy haunted things? Probably not.

Neil wondered how Tom could leave his house after a heavy snow as he drove down the narrow paved road. The single-lane road, hemmed in by towering trees, felt dark and ominous, with branches arching overhead and casting eerie shadows in the dim moonlight. If he broke down here, the closest gas station was a few miles back—and it looked like it had been closed for years. As in all things now, he was alone as he turned at Tom's mailbox: 62 Cross Lane.

The driveway was steep gravel, with the truck losing its traction a few times before slipping back. Neil pressed the petal harder and blew a cloud of rubble behind him as he drove on. Potholes bounced him along, eventually flattening out into an asphalt paved road. The trees parted, showing Tom's house, making Neil break hard.

A giant satellite dish, black mesh pointing to the sky, grabbed his attention, followed by the warm glow of porch lights beyond. There were overturned big wheel bikes, a trampoline, and a large colorful sign that said: *All Unattended Children will be Given Sugar and a Puppy.* The cute sign made Neil chuckle and suddenly, he had no idea who Tom was.

He parked in the driveway in front of the garage and followed the neatly manicured garden surrounding the walkway to the front door. All the lights were on inside and outside the house, chasing away any thought of a man obsessed with death. Yet Neil knew not to let his guard down. All the serial killers he'd ever heard of had people that said *oh, they were so nice,* or *I never would have guessed.* He pressed the doorbell, tightly gripped the kitchen knife in his pocket, and listened to the bright chimes echo through the house.

A woman's voice answered, "Coming." Then he saw her through the window, a woman who looked too young to be a grandma. Her hair was once blonde but now was shot through with white. Kind eyes were surrounded by crow's feet, and while wrinkles gathered on her cheeks, bright white teeth broke through her lips in a cheery smile. She quickly wiped her hands on the white apron that kept her flowery dress clean and opened the door. "You must be Mr. Riser."

"Yes, ma'am." Neil smiled and stepped back, unsure what to do. Where was Tom? "I'm Neil Lessman," he thought a moment and then went on as if inviting a friend to come and play, "is Tom home?"

"Ah," she chuckled. "Yes, Tom's just wrapping up some work downstairs. He'll be up in a moment. I'm Linda. Happy to meet you. Please come in." She stepped aside and motioned for Neil to enter. When he didn't move, she continued. "First time?"

"Yes, ma'am," he said.

"Well, let me welcome you to the community," she stepped away from the door as if inviting Neil in with her distance. "This is a very small community. Bad actors don't last long…in this world. I won't be offended if you leave. Stranger danger and all," she winked. "But Tom's one of the good ones. He's a great first trade and is looking forward to meeting you."

When she stepped back again, Neil found himself compelled to follow her. He didn't want to seem rude, and she seemed so nice. No alarms were going off and he supposed that's what the victims of serial killers would say if you interviewed their ghosts. Even the dull heat that washed over him as soon as he crossed the threshold didn't raise the alarms it should have. The knife in his pocket was sweaty and unnecessary now. He wanted to throw it outside, but once inside Linda's house, she shut the door and waved for him to follow her.

"Hungry?" Linda turned into the dining room where a full dinner was on the table. "I hope you came hungry."

Of course, Neil hadn't eaten in two days now. This didn't register with him until the smell of fried chicken pulled his nose to a place setting at the table. He could taste the buttery mashed potatoes, feel the juice from the corn on the cob dribbling down his chin, hear the sloshing as he chewed that macaroni and cheese. His stomach clenched, demanded he sit and eat but again, manners stilled his desire and he politely, half-heartedly, held up a hand and said, "I don't want to impose."

"Nonsense. You come to the Curess home, you eat. Them's the rules," Linda said. She scooped a mound of mashed potatoes from the serving bowl and plopped it on a plate. "Sit." She pointed to the place setting she just served and then gave Neil's plate a heaping spoon of everything. When he sat, she handed him a basket of biscuits and the tray of fried chicken. "Eat. You're a growing boy."

Neil took a spoon full of the mashed potatoes. The moment it entered his mouth his body took over, casting aside all etiquette, and released a deep moan of satisfaction as the sweet butter danced on his tongue and the velvety potato, perfectly mashed with a soft but chunky texture melted in his mouth.

"Oh my god. These are the best mashed potatoes I've ever had," Neil said.

A stronger wave of the heat he'd been feeling since walking in hit him again. This one more intense but still faint, easily dismissed as a gust of air from an old heating system. Maybe it was the sugar in the sweet tea? There were many possible sources and all of which easily explained and disregarded. A door closed somewhere in the house with a heavy click, and the heat faded to the dull pulse he had grown used to.

Neil kept eating.

"That's why I married her," A deep voice came from the dining room entrance. "Mr. Riser—"

"Neil," Linda corrected the man.

He nodded, "Neil, I'm Tom Curess. Happy to meet you," he said, and he truly was. Neil guessed the man was in his sixties, a minor beer belly hanging over his jeans and a major scraggly white beard covering the bottom of his face. He was smiling and extended a weathered hand to Neil in welcome. Neil went to stand but was waved off by Tom, "Nah, nah, please eat," and so Neil sat and shoveled dinner in his mouth as fast as he could.

"I told you we should have made more," Linda whacked Tom's shoulder. "Boy's hungry and we just made two chickens."

Neil looked at the tray of chicken and wondered how any family could eat all that in one sitting. They never ate this much at his house. Grandma was a great cook, but she had Grandpa, and thus the rest of them, on a heart healthy diet. She was a big believer in portion sizes and food groups. This meal appeared to be in the food groups of fried, butter, and happiness.

"Thank you," Neil spoke through his chewing. "This is plenty. I'm not a big eater." But he was showing otherwise as he pulled every bit of meat out of his chicken breast.

"Well," Tom sat at the head of the table. Linda kept busily moving around with trips to and from the kitchen bringing out more food. Chips. Pretzels. Mozzarella Sticks, still sizzling from the oven.

"No business at the table," Linda corrected him.

"Aye, yeah, I know the rules." Tom smiled and served himself a full plate, checking to see that his plate was as full as Neil's as if entering an unspoken eating contest with his guest. "Well, let's start with a bit about you. Why you coming into the trade?" Tom caught Linda's stern eye, "That's not business, that's just friendly chatter."

She relented and went back to the kitchen.

"Please, Linda, we have enough food to feed an army. Sit. Eat." His voice was joyous but also pleaded, wanting her to be with him. "So, Mr. Neil, what's the story?"

As Tom shaved his corn on the cob into clumps of kernels, Neil answered. "I, I have a strange story that I don't really want to share."

Tom didn't flinch at that. He kept mixing his corn into his mashed potatoes. But Linda hurried over to Neil and put her hands on his shoulders. Neil wanted to bristle at this but couldn't under her warm touch and gentle comfort.

"You don't have to say anything you don't want to," Linda said clearly and with emphasis. Tom nodded as he ate.

"Yeah," he said with a bit of chicken flying from his mouth. "You don't gotta say nothing you don't want. It ain't my business as long as you live up to your end of the deal. I always say business is like a squirrel in fall, you know where your nuts are, and I know where mine are, and we don't gotta know about each other's nuts."

Linda groaned, hurt by the analogy, then patted his shoulders and sat across from Neil. She paid him no mind, or so Neil thought, as she served herself dinner. As he took another long sip of his iced tea, which was mostly sugar, Linda refilled it from a jug on the table as soon as he sat the glass down.

He let his guard down. How could people so nice be anything but nice?

Neil had a lot to learn about the world he was blindly striding into at a demon's encouragement. If his mind wasn't so tormented by the loss of his grandpa, and then the loss of his brother, and the insanity of the past two days, he'd certainly be more cautious – but tired minds make mistakes.

# ELEVEN

As they ate, Tom and Linda did most of the talking. They told tales of their grand babies, their recent trip to Disneyland, and how much they love traveling in their new RV. Neil didn't say much, only listened, and the old couple had no problem filling the dinner conversation.

After dinner, Tom stood from the table and said, "To business?"

Neil stood and nodded.

"Join me in the basement." Tom walked out of the dining room and Neil followed. Linda began cleaning up the table as they left.

The Curess house was nice and very neat, which didn't surprise Neil. He didn't doubt Linda ran a tight ship, but Tom didn't strike him as someone who needed much cleaning up after. They went through the living room and stopped at a heavy locked door. The deadbolt was locked, two slide locks, one at the top, one at the bottom, and a chain lock.

Here is where the heat was coming from. Neil again dismissed it as simply being the furnace. Most houses have a furnace in the basement and perhaps this one was running hot because Tom and Linda were old. Old people get cold…don't they?

"You know what's behind this door?" Tom asked. "Things that hate you for living." He let that sink in. The words hit Neil and soaked through him, dragging his shoulders down, as the realization that he was into something he didn't understand finally settled over him. What if the heat wasn't a furnace? What if what he's been feeling wasn't an old heater blowing air into an elderly couple's house? "I don't know if you think this is all a lark, a bunch of weirdos doing weird things—"

Neil shook his head quickly. "No. I know…this is real." Dodslav flared in Neil's mind. The cold brought gooseflesh in waves over his body, and that smell, that frozen death smell, wrinkled Neil's nose. Tom, seeing the reaction, nodded and put his hand on Neil's shoulder. The younger man flinched at the touch, but Tom didn't let go.

"Few come to this world without some story. There are those who don't understand, but I see you're not one of them. When I open this door, we don't use names. No touching anything. And if something talks to you, you never, ever talk back. Ignore it." Tom locked his eyes with Neil. Seeing he understood, Tom turned to undo the locks on the door. "I'm divesting. The grandkids are getting too curious, and this stuff isn't something you pass on," he chuckled. "Make sure you get rid of your collection before someone else gets wrapped up in this crap."

"Why?" Neil asked with naïve curiosity. "Aren't they just toys?"

Tom chuckled darkly at that. He didn't look at Neil, only turned over his shoulder and grimly said, "Thinking like that will get you killed, kid. Killed if you're lucky. These things aren't what you see. Open your feelings and tell me they're just toys."

The moment Tom opened the door, letting a sliver of light from the basement into the hallway, Neil felt every nerve sizzle as a heatwave crashed into him. It burned like the time his blood sugar went crazy at Hershey Park from all the candy and not eating all day. And there was a smell to the heat, a musty dry smell like something was wet, runny, and now it had dried up, crusted over.

"What the hell is that?" Neil gasped. He grabbed his mouth and stomach to hold back a gag. What was down there? And why wasn't Tom bothered by it?

The older man kept walking downstairs. Neil stretched to see around him, but Tom took up most of the staircase and there wasn't anything visible beyond the corridor.

Neil swallowed hard and followed, feeling the heat build as he walked into the cool basement. His flesh was clammy, a chilled sweat building over his forehead, but within him, he burned with the energy in this place. This is what microwave food felt like. How the heat was never even, or the inside would be cold while the outside was scalding hot, but reversed. Neil mopped away the sweat from his forehead and continued into the basement.

Beyond the stairs, the basement opened into a finished apartment area. It was nicely done with soft carpet, a TV, couch, and heavy wooden shelves lining the walls. Tom stopped at the first shelf and pulled a pair of leather garden gloves from it. Holding them out to Neil, he said, "Put these on to be safe."

Neil did.

Tom put on his own pair and walked past the first bookcase, which was covered with books. As he passed, he plucked a leather-bound journal from the third shelf. Tom stopped at the second bookcase, which had many toys spaced over the five shelves. Neil recognized some of them from his youth, a plastic construction truck, one of those Russian doll things, an action figure, a wooden revolver, and a few other toys he didn't recognize.

"So, you're interested in the Outlaw Gun," Tom scribbled on a blank page in his book.

"Inventory?" Neil asked as he finally found the source of the heat. The toys were surrounded by shimmering air like the horizon of a desert. Some toys were hotter than others, and Neil waved his hand around them to see what happened with the shimmer. As soon as his hand entered it, the waves flowed around his fingers as if repelled by some force.

"Yep." Tom noticed what he was doing and nodded with understanding. He grunted approval as he wrote. "So, you're one of those types. I thought you were telling the truth when you said you understood. Now I see you really do."

"What is it? I mean, you see this, right?"

"Nope," Tom said and closed his inventory. "I don't have whatever it is people like you have. To me, it's a toy that just doesn't feel right." Then, seeing clarification was needed, he added, "Feel with my gut, not my hand. Never touch these things with your bare hand."

"Why not?" Neil retracted his hand and saw the haze follow his fingers as if he pulled it back towards himself.

"I've never had the guts to find out, but I'm told by other collectors that it activates *resolution*. That's what they call getting your spirit mixed up with the spirit in the toy. Remember what I said about the dead hating you for being alive? Well, I've never wanted to test the idea. But I met another person like you a bunch of years ago. They were really interested in the stories of these things, and that made me capture those stories in here." Tom waved his journal.

"What do you mean, people like me?" Neil stared at the toys, feeling drawn to the Russian doll as if the world shrank around it and drew all his focus to the doll's yellow eyes and swirling red scarf wrapped around her crown. The eyes invited him to open her, see what was inside, but her smirk told Neil whatever was within was unpleasant. Her secret was unpleasant. Her nature was unpleasant, but he needed to look. He needed to see what was inside. And so he reached, but Tom smacked his hand away.

"We're negotiating the Outlaw Gun. Not Baba."

Neil retracted his hand and exhaled in shock as he woke up. "I'm sorry. Just, just thought it was…"

"Never talk back." Tom pulled Neil back away from the shelves. "Never show signs you've heard them. It was inviting you and you almost accepted it. Next you'd been taking your gloves off."

Neil nodded and kept his eyes on Tom. "How does a trade work?" The real question Neil wanted to ask was what 'people like him' meant, but it was forgotten in the heat and fear of almost falling for the Russian doll's tricks. When he drove away later, he'd remember the question, but by then, it would be too late.

"Well, normally you'd offer a toy for my toy. You'd tell me why it would be good in my collection and I we'd negotiate from there which toys are the right swap. But since you don't have any, we'll just go with money. There has to be something exchanged."

"Why?" Neil realized this was a constant question about

everything. It was the question his grandpa always told him to start with for anything new. Why was magical. Why told and gave you purpose. And so, Neil always began with why.

Tom's face corkscrewed as he searched for the right words. "I don't know everything about this world, but I think it has to do with ownership. Ownership has to be clear. I'm not sure why, but every trade I've ever done and every trade I've ever heard done always requires both parties to give something to seal the deal."

Not all traditions were always understood, and this was one. Tom didn't realize there was a deeper meaning to this act of barter. He only thought of it from the lens of the living and not that of the dead. Each transaction was not only about the physical toy—Neil would learn this much later in his life, but Tom wouldn't live long enough for this lesson.

"I only have five dollars," Neil said quietly. He fished for the money in his pocket and pulled out five ones. "That's all I've got."

As he pulled the money out, the knife tumbled to the carpet. Neil, aghast, apologized and explained he didn't know what would happen and it was just for protection.

"Kid, you'd be stupider than a donkey in a bourbon barrel if you didn't have something in mind like that." Tom picked up the knife and handed it back to Neil.

How stupid are donkeys in a bourbon barrel? How'd the donkey even get in there? These thoughts distracted Neil as Tom turned toward a pile of plastic bins on the third bookcase in the basement. "Five bucks, as in, that's all you've got tonight, or that's all you've got?" Neil didn't answer quickly enough, so Tom kept talking. "A dollar will do. Just gotta be something."

Neil pulled a dollar free from the fold of bills in his pocket and offered it to Tom, who reached for it but stopped before taking it.

"I don't know what's driving you here, but that dollar could be used for a taco, a comic book, a drink…but if you give it to me, then this thing's yours and you're in."

Neil's hand shook from the burning sensation that had been eating at his nerves ever since Tom opened the basement door, but that didn't stop him from pushing the dollar into Tom's hand. "I have to."

Drew needed this and if his salvation only cost a dollar, that was the best dollar Neil ever spent. Could the cost of freedom from drugs, demons, Drew's old life, really only be one dollar?

Tom took it and Neil knew the transaction was complete when he could hear the whispers in his mind. The voice was a rusty cowboy's voice, a cool voice asking overlapping questions. *Who are you? Where's my boy? Where'd you take him? What'd you do to him? Shoot him! Shoot him! Point and say Duddly Says Die and I'll shoot him dead. Then take me to my boy!*

"What is it?" Tom asked.

"I hear it," Neil answered. "Did you hear it?"

"What's it saying?" Tom hurried to gather up the plastic container and lid. Placing the container on the floor, he checked his gloves, ensuring a tight fit, then put the wooden revolver into the case and sealed the lid.

The whispers stopped as the lid clicked closed.

"I, I can't hear it now," Neil knelt to look at the gun through the clear plastic. It wasn't anything special. He could imagine this on the shelf of an antique store or in the retro-toy section of some big box store. The wood was pale with a faint grain but looked like an old western six-shooter. "It was asking about some boy. Like the gun's boy? It was scared. Confused."

There were not any voices now. Both men silently considering what Neil had just said. After a few moments, Tom waved for Neil to follow him and then walked toward the stairs. Neil grabbed the plastic container with his gun and followed.

At the top of the stairs, Tom motioned for Neil to exit the basement and as Tom closed the door, locking it with the deadbolt, chains, and sliders, Neil felt the cool air wash away the burning in his nerves. There was still the dull heat, but the cooling sensation made him smile.

"Ah, don't be happy, Mr. Neil. You carry a heavy burden there." Tom pointed to the plastic container.

"All done boys?" Linda came around the corner, her apron now removed, but her arms were full of Tupperware containers. "I packed you some left-overs Neil." She heaped them onto the top of the plastic container. When she saw what was inside, she sighed, "Good. That one, I didn't like that one. I don't like any of them, but don't like guns in the house."

"I told you I'm getting rid of all them," Tom said, a bit defensively. "Just takes a bit. Gotta get good trades."

Linda shook her head in exasperated disagreement.

"Good trades?" Neil asked as he balanced the leftovers on his large container.

Tom huffed and nodded quickly. "Oh yeah, not everyone in this trade is fair, or a decent person like you kid. Watch'em. They'll leave you screwed like a rattler in a weed whacker."

Linda smacked Tom's shoulder. "Don't you be filling Neil's head with those silly things. Why would a rattle snake be in a weed whacker? You don't think it'd bite before it got all caught up?"

"Well, I'm just saying—"

"You talking foolish, old man." Linda kissed Tom's cheek. "Did you use the donkey one too?"

Neil chuckled.

"Yeah, thought so." Linda shook her head.

"Thank you, ma'am," Neil said and smiled at her. "I appreciate your hospitality. Both of your hospitality." He turned to Tom. "I'm hoping this is all I need." But Neil knew there was going to be something else. There always was something else with bullies like Dodslav.

"There's a no return policy," Tom laughed, but Neil got the message. It wasn't a joke. "You ever want to do another trade, I can connect you with others but I'm out of the game."

They walked Neil to the door. "Why not just destroy them? Like, why not just smash them and be done if you want to get rid of them?"

"I'd still own them. That's the problem. They're more than the toy, you see. And as far as I know, you can't smash a ghost," Tom chuckled.

"There was that guy who said fire could do the trick," Linda offered, and Neil knew that voice was the same his grandma used to remind Grandpa of things they've disagreed about in the past.

"Well, I don't want to find out if it doesn't work," Tom replied in his tone of reminding her about past disagreements. "Besides, there's always someone looking to get in, and that'd be like a–"

"No!" Linda pointed at Tom. "Nope, stop right there. We're done with animal analogies tonight."

Tom smiled and winked at Neil.

"Thank you," Neil said as he stepped back outside.

"Well, you're welcome, Neil," Linda said and rubbed his shoulder. "Just be careful with these things. They're not...*good*."

"And there's a lot of people in this world that aren't good either. Be careful kid," Tom added. He wrapped his arm around Linda and squeezed her gently.

"I will." Neil put the container in the passenger seat and then climbed into his truck. It took two tries to start it, but when it choked to life, he drove down the driveway and left the Curess home thinking about Linda's cooking and Tom's mentoring. Neil wanted to come back after Drew returned to introduce his brother to Tom.

Unfortunately, one of Tom's trades would go bad and the worst toy in his collection would claim his life. It would be years before Neil found out, but when he did, Neil discovered whether fire could destroy a toy.

Sometimes it can. He learned that watching the Russian doll, and the secret she kept inside, boil and crumble inside an incinerator.

Even the dead can die.

# TWELVE

The drive home was long with anticipation. Neil needed to stop for gas, but only got enough to get him home. He wanted no more delays. Drew was coming back. His torture at the hands of this twisted demon was going to be over.

As soon as Neil arrived at his grandpa's house, he hurried to the kitchen, putting away the containers from Mrs. Curess, then ran downstairs and ripped the lid off the plastic bin with two loud clicks. The whispering began again, asking about the boy, but the heat baking off the wooden gun was quickly overwhelmed with the frigid air leaking out of the dollhouse.

Black smoke spilled from the spiral, and the whispering abruptly stopped. The chattering toy didn't want to be heard now that Dodslav's chill filled the basement.

Neil faced the dollhouse, pushing the plastic container towards where Dodslav appeared before. Tom gave Neil the leather gloves and Neil slipped them on, now forming an idea to ensure Drew's return.

Like before, the icy wind made a thick mist on the floor and within that white mist rose Dodslav's black smoke. As before, the pillar of smoke solidified and the white face with the spiral pushed through.

"I've done what you asked," Neil said and pointed to the gun.

"So, you have," Dodslav cooed.

Neil expected Dodslav to pick up the gun and take it, absorb it, devour it like he did Drew, but the demon just swayed and waited.

"Take it," Neil said. "That for my brother."

Dodslav laughed a thick, phlegm filled choking laugh. "This is not enough. This is just the proof that you can get more."

Neil picked up the gun in his gloved hands. "You said bring you a spirit—"

"And we would discuss the deal," Dodslav snarled. "You have, and now we shall discuss the deal. You must bring me more. Much, much more. Perhaps if you fill this room with paltry spirits like this, that would be enough. I cannot build my masterpiece with this. I must have more. Much, much more."

Neil smirked, having expected the creature to default on their deal. And so, Neil went to Plan B. He pointed the gun towards Dodslav and smiled. "Give me my brother back or I'll shoot you right now. I don't know if you're already dead, but I'm betting a ghost bullet can kill a ghost…or whatever you are."

Dodslav didn't move.

Neil dropped the gun to where he thought Dodslav's knees would be and said, "Duddly says die." The gun exploded like thunder in his hand, firing into the smoke. But Dodslav only laughed. A hard metal bullet bounced off the smoke then clinked against the concrete floor. Neil picked it up, seeing a crushed bullet, now only a small coin.

"I am immortal in your world," Dodslav laughed again. He shook his head. "I told your brother about your quest. In my grace, I even allowed him to speak by reconnecting his jaw and throat. He said you were smart, but clearly, he was wrong. You haven't thought this through. If I were dead, how would you get him back? If I couldn't keep him alive, how would he continue to live? So many variables you have missed. But in your offering, you have been wise. A toy, infused with the love of a child…" Dodslav sucked in a deep breath. "I can taste the purity of this. A toy, such a good selection."

Neil heard hints in Dodslav's speech that planted seeds, not of doubt or defeat, but of future success. Dodslav was immortal in Neil's world, but what about whatever world Dodslav came from? And indeed, how would Neil get his brother back without Dodslav? Could Neil take his brother from wherever Dodslav was from? And if this gun could shoot bullets, what could other toys do? Could one open a portal to Dodslav's world? Could one fix his brother? And Dodslav's reaction to the toy, it was the same as Drew's reaction to the purest drugs. Toys were the fast track to Drew's freedom. In that moment, the seeds that drove the next thirty years were planted.

Neil lowered the gun, presented Dodslav the disappointed slouch he knew the creature expected, and asked, "I get more of these and you'll return my brother? That's our deal?"

Dodslav, satisfied with Neil's defeat, nodded and extended a tendril of smoke. "Indeed. Shake to seal the deal?"

Neil grasped the smoke, but his hand passed through it. Dodslav roared in laughter at Neil's gullibility.

"Seems like you will need to just take my word for it," Dodslav said. "As I said last time, trust my passion. I trust your need for your brother. And that's the roots of our future. A tree built on the trust of each other's desires."

"Sounds like that's all I can do," Neil said, keeping his smile on the inside. "Do I summon you when I'm ready?"

"I'll feel when you're ready. Don't call me. I'll come to you. Just keep me close." Dodslav motioned to the dollhouse. He laughed again. "You tried to kill me. There's a first time for everything. Usually, you humans are all sniveling and whimpering, but you have spirit." Hearing the irony in his words, Dodslav laughed again and receded into the dollhouse basement. The laughter echoed in the empty basement as the demon vanished.

Neil put the gun back into the plastic case and closed it before the voices could begin again. He pulled off the leather gloves and dropped them on the lid, then ran up to his room and jumped back online.

Connecting to RoverNet, navigating to Oddities and back to where he met Tom, Neil looked for the next seller, willing to trade with a first timer. They were easy to find. And Neil began building his list of haunted toy dealers without thinking about how he'd afford this, or how he'd pay for gas, or even pay for food once Mrs. Curess's leftovers were done. His mind was set on finding more haunted toys, and as he built his list, he built his plan for what he'd need to break into Dodslav's world.

A portal.

A weapon that worked.

A way to fix his brother.

A way to capture Dodslav and force him to fix Drew.

What else? As Neil searched and built his list of people to contact, he watched for what else he could use against The Artist. Confidence and conceit were the weakness of all bullies, and this one, this demonic bully, would be no different.

Neil was smart. Very smart. But he was facing an enemy that he didn't fully understand. And so, as he searched for toys, he searched for information about demons. His search lasted through the night and as dawn broke through his window, exhaustion finally caught Neil.

He fell asleep on his keyboard, dreaming

of the promise he made to Grandpa, the promise to help Drew. In the dream, he repeated his promise over and over until his throat bled from saying it so many times. And when he couldn't speak anymore, when his throat was so cracked and all the blood had run out, his grandpa squeezed his hand until the bones cracked and screamed, "Save Drew!"

Neil startled awake, falling out of his desk chair, as a loud knocking demanded his attention downstairs.

Someone was at the door.

# THIRTEEN

Neil hurried downstairs and smeared the drool off of his cheek with his sleeve.

An old man in a fine suit stood on the porch. He swung a brown briefcase by his leg in a slow pendulum like a dying clock. The man pulled his gray bowler hat to his chest, showing a liver speckled bald head, scraggly white hairs, and deep wrinkles. He smiled blinding white dentures; they could be nothing else.

"Mr. Lessman?" He asked.

Neil didn't answer.

"I'm Nigel Cone. Corny, I mean Cornelius's—well, I guess you knew him as your grandfather, I am, was, your grandfather's lawyer." Nigel waited for a response, but Neil only stared. "I have some papers, Corny—sorry, Cornelius," Nigel smiled awkwardly and shook his head. "Sorry, I knew your grandfather for a long time. He was a good man. A good friend."

"I'm Neil."

"He spoke very highly of you. Is your brother here as well?"

"He's indisposed." Neil opened the door wider, and Nigel came in.

"Yes, well, Cornelius talked about both of you often. He was worried about you two being okay after he was gone." Nigel motioned to the kitchen table and sat. He opened his briefcase and pulled out overstuff manila folders.

Neil sat across from Nigel. There was a chill coming from the basement. Would Nigel ask about it? Was Dodslav listening? Would the white mask rise from the basement to devour this innocent man?

Neil shivered but Nigel didn't. The old man was as solid as a man of his age could be. There was occasional quaking in his hands, but that was probably more related to nerves than cold.

"Your grandfather was quite the wise investor. He tucked away every extra dollar since you and your brother came to live with him," Nigel chuckled quietly as he sorted the folders. "He had holdings in stocks," he said, motioning to one folder, "properties"—he pointed to a different folder— "and even precious metals." Nigel pulled out a smaller folder with only one sheet of paper in it. "And all this is now yours."

In the small folder was a sheet that summed the accounts. Grandpa had started savings accounts for Neil's mom when she was born. He did the same for Drew and Neil when they were born. After mom died, Grandpa transferred the assets to Drew and Neil. They had almost fifty years of savings, interest, and investments built up.

Nigel pushed the paper closer to Neil, unsure if he could see it. The two sat in silence as Nigel watched for any sign of Neil's reaction to being given tens of millions of dollars. But there was no reaction. The old man couldn't understand that Neil was all out of being surprised, being shocked, being confused. All Neil could do was sit there and nod.

"Is this for Drew and me?"

"Well," Nigel shrugged and shifted in his seat, leaning closer, "Cornelius was very clear. This was for you, and you were to share with your brother. I think there was some concern over," Nigel shook his head, "how the money was used," he smiled and plucked a pen from inside his jacket pocket. "The house is yours. The truck. The other properties and my services should you need them, all prepaid by your grandfather for up to five years, if I live that long," Nigel smiled and laughed.

Neil took the pen, signed the line that said signature, and pushed the papers back to Nigel.

"Now what?" Neil asked.

Nigel pushed another paper at Neil. "That's your grandfather's account information. Take this paper to the bank and they will make you the owner of the account. After that," he packed the signed paper into his briefcase and clicked it shut. "Live life how your family taught you. Be a good person, help others, take care of your own."

"Yeah, okay," Neil said.

"I get it," Nigel stood, his knees grinding through arthritic pops as he did. "You've lost your grandfather. Suddenly at that. It can take a while to sink in, but just remember, you're not alone. Your brother's here for you. Your friends. Your family. They're all here for you."

"They will be." Neil nodded and walked Nigel to the door.

"Take care and remember, call if you have questions or need help to understand the documents. I thought I would give you time to review them. That often works best for my clients in a time of loss."

"Yes," Neil said. "Thank you. Have a good day, Mr. Cone." Neil closed the door and looked at the massive folders cluttering the table. Grandma would have screamed at Grandpa for such a mess on the dinner table. But there's no one to scream now. Neil quietly stacked the folders and moved them to the basement beside the dollhouse.

In the basement, he took a moment to stare at the dollhouse.

"Are you listening?"

No answer.

Neil put the container holding the gun beside the dollhouse. His fingers drummed on the lid for a few moments as he thought about the list he made last night. As he stared at the spiral burned into the dollhouse basement, Neil said, "I'll see you soon Drew. I promise."

# INVENTORY NOTE: THE DOLLHOUSE

Item Number: 43? Maybe 1?

Components:

Neil's Dollhouse

*Note: I'm not doing collections. All these toys are now private collection using Neil's old terminology.

This is my first addition to the inventory and so I'm going to break away from Neil's old format a bit for my style. I'd like to say this is the only entry I'll be providing, but I know that's not true. Not after what I've learned from this dollhouse.

Before I start about this specific toy, I want to share why I'm numbering it 43. These inventory journals start at #2, there is no #1, no first toy and while I don't know this for sure, my gut tells me this dollhouse is actually toy #1 for Neil's collection. I don't remember mention of this dollhouse in other notes. I suspect there's a special reason for that, but I'm also assuming only Neil knew that. With this in mind, I'm numbering this dollhouse 43 for the journals going forward.

This dollhouse, on the outside, is simply a gorgeously hand-crafted dollhouse made from thin wood. I've seen kits like this online but this one seems much more well-built than I'd expected from those kits. Mom says the craftsmanship of this dollhouse shows the amount of love that went into it. Inside, the house is empty, like the people haven't moved into it yet. No furniture, no pictures, nothing but the spiral burnt into the basement floor.

When we were cleaning out Neil's house, getting all the toys, I felt a constant stream of cool air coming from this one. When I went to it, I heard a man whispering, asking if anyone could hear him. I know I shouldn't have answered, but I hadn't touched it, and according to Viola, the Death Doll—Item 42, see my note in her section about drowning her in the Patticon River, when you touched these toys you activated them and so I make sure to never touch them. But this was just someone whispering, looking for anyone to help. So, I answered.

The spirit said it was bound to the house and required the spiritual energies of the toys to escape. After Viola had me destroy so many of the toys, the spirit in the house doesn't have the power to escape from its prison. It said it needs more toys to escape, more spiritual energy, but I wasn't about to trust a faceless voice. However, when it saw Nadia, when we were taking the dollhouse from Neil's home, the voice said it could help her — it could undo the damage done by King Dark, Item 29. It knew about what happened, how I accidentally set King Dark free, how the creature killed one of my friends and disfigured Nadia. The voice said it has the key to help her undo the damage King Dark did to her and I believe the voice. Sounds stupid to write, but I really feel like the voice is being honest. Dad said I always had a good ear for the truth and what this guy in the house is saying sounds true to me.

So, I'm proceeding with caution. I've reached out to the guys on the Haunted Toy Reddit thread like Neil did to get more information.

I'm going by the handle queen_light. That name will remind me of what King Dark did, and how careful I have to be in this weird world of haunted things, ghosts, and monsters.

But if the spirit in the house can help Nadia, can take away what I did to her by bringing King Dark into her life, then I've got to try.

I'm working on getting Item 44 lined up. I wonder how many toys it will take? Is there another way, something other than toys? We'll see.

Who was Neil writing these entries for? Himself? They read like notes to someone else. More a journal than a simple inventory. Who am I writing these for? Mom and I are going to destroy all the toys after we do whatever we need to do to help Nadia, so I guess these notes are at the end. Maybe just a record of what the toys were and what we did? Maybe a confession—none of this feels right, but once I help Nadia, I'm done.

We're done.

No collection.

No continuing.

I'll be done.

I

"What do you make of this?" Vilhelmina pointed her sword at the severed head. Holding up the hem of her dress, she stepped through the pool of blood, taking extra care not to slip on the stone floor. Before approaching the body—Yor's body—she removed her evening shoes, reasoning that more people would notice blood on her shoes than the feet within them.

"Vilhelmina," her partner began, but stopped. "Do you need—"

"You're getting it all over you," Vilhelmina interrupted. She pointed to his white leather pants, the knees now slick with Yor's blood. Even the tails of his blue suede jacket were dipping into the pooling gore of her… her protectorate. "And I've seen a body before." Yes, she'd seen decapitated bodies before—too many in her years of service—but this was Yor's body. His lips, which were always bent in a smile around her, now twisted, contorting in shock, trying to release a scream that would never come. A few feet away, his fingers, always soft on her cheeks, were stoney. His warrior's body, dressed in the silken flourishes appropriate for tonight's ball, now soaked up the gushing leak from his neck. The blood didn't spurt; it just flowed in a steady stream, all pumping heart and tensing muscles now dead.

She hid her face, giving her mind a moment to push aside her humanity, letting the cold, calculating other half of her heritage take hold. She tugged up her green silk gown, pulling up all the layers that fluffed out around her legs. The golden stitching and silken sheen of her gown caught the cellar's torch light, making her glow. Long black hair curled unnaturally at the ends in soft spirals. Those curls got in her way as she examined Yor. "Did you see him come down here, Sergei?"

Her partner, Sergei, hunched in the cellar. Too tall to stand. Blood dripped from his clothes as they strained around his thick gray skin. His elephant ears unfolded and stretched, as did his trunk. In his suit, he was a well-dressed, albeit very large, bi-pedal elephant. "Well, I didn't see him come down, but I wasn't watching him tonight. My eyes were on the ladies."

Vilhelmina rolled her eyes. Sergei was a Gajanthrope, and while known for their long memories, the elephant folk were not known for their romantic exploits, save their lifelong dedication to their mates. She stepped out of the blood, checked to make sure she was clear, then dropped her hem and shook out the wrinkles. "Of course they were. Let's lock down this place and start questioning the guests," she stopped, seeing a door across the basement and went to it. The wooden door was frail and opened to a shallow storage closet. It was empty save for a bookshelf lined with pickled veggies.

"Whoa," Sergei said. "You can't lock down this place. Count Hutton will not recognize our—"

"We are Valkyries," Vilhelmina demanded. "There has been a murder. A human murder. Our sacred duty has been violated by someone here. Hutton has no say in my oath or my duty." Vilhelmina left her shoes behind and started upstairs.

"Wait, Vilhelmina!" he gently grabbed her arm. "It is okay to not be okay. Yor was more than your charge…"

Vilhelmina ripped her arm from Sergei's large hand, her nostrils flared, jaw set as she growled through her teeth, "Don't! We have a duty to perform. We failed. I failed. And now I must bring the assailant to justice." But the humanity in her didn't want justice. It wanted more blood—much more blood than that which still leaked out of Yor. She wanted to gut the rotter who did this and wash away the grotesque humanity swirling within her. How much blood would that take? Her sword's leather handle squeaked as she choked it. Would all the blood in the world be enough? She'd find out. Storming up the stairs, she went to find her prey.

"Well, at least put your sword away." Sergei hurried to follow her, holding her shoes in his thick fingers. "Where did you have that, anyway?"

At the top of the stairs, the servants who found the victim parted to make way for Vilhelmina as she slid her sword into the sheath the tailor had added. As instructed, none of the servants told anyone anything and kept everyone, even the Count, away from the basement. Vilhelmina stabbed her finger at them and said, "Not a word until I come back. Don't leave and don't let anyone else down here." They nodded quickly.

"Wait, Vilhelmina! We've gotta tell the Count before you do anything else." Sergei grabbed her arm but kept his distance. When she got like this, take charge and lose herself in the mission, he knew she couldn't be stopped. "We gotta tell him someone killed his son and you carrying around a sword will not look all that good."

She nodded, but didn't remove her sword. "Fine. We'll tell him first," she gulped and noticed a small blotch of blood on the edge of her dress. "Damnit."

"It will come out," Sergei waved away the stain.

But Vilhelmina knew it wouldn't come out before she had to walk back out to the ballroom. They'd see the stain if nothing else. All these people could see were imperfections. She gulped and grit her teeth. "It's fine." But it wasn't.

"Let's get this over with." She stopped at the door and pointed to the servants one more time. They nodded, more afraid of her than of what they had found down below. Satisfied, she entered the judgmental hell of the ballroom.

**II**

A masquerade ball was the perfect setting for a murder. Vilhelmina held her mask on a stick, what others would have called a Columbian Mask, to blend in. But her heritage didn't allow her to blend in, and her upbringing made her stand out more. Certainly, her striking mix of human and Valkyrie features could not be concealed by her green and gold feathered mask. She had inherited her Valkyrie mother's razor cheekbones and jawline, her silken black hair, her six-foot height and deceptive lithe musculature. But her human father's features brought a softer edge to all those things some people would mistake for compassion, but Vilhelmina rejected such weakness as she believed her mother would have as well.

If not for her appearance, she would glide through this ballroom with the adoration a Valkyrie deserved. But her mannerisms betrayed her, revealing what could not be ignored—nor adored—by the wealthy. She had grown up poor. Her uneven walk, the walk of someone who knew the rough track of a pigsty, and the callouses lining her palms told her story. Her lack of noble upbringing was obvious in everything, from the way she breathed to the moments of hesitation as she tried to determine how to greet someone. Nobles knew whether to bow, shake hands, or kiss as second nature. But

Vilhelmina always led with a handshake, as her father did. But what else would you expect from a farm girl like Vilhelmina?

"Count Hutton." She did not wait for her moment to speak as a more well-mannered guest might.

The party surrounding Hutton fell silent, their laughter fading as they observed the interruption. Almost in unison, they shrugged when they saw who it was, as if it were expected of someone like her. Vilhelmina recognized the gaggle of sycophants, even with their finely plumed masks. Lord Armitage wore the burgundy peacock mask—it suited him. Lord Minue sported a sun and moon mask, ornately decorated with more jewels than his kingdom could afford, but men like him never cared about what they could afford. Finally, there was Lady Chelus, a retired Valkyrie turned tradeswoman specializing in exotic minerals. Her mask resembled a geode—rough and dull on the outside, but bursting with glitter and brilliance around her purple eyes. Her white satin dress glowed in the chandelier light as she gracefully moved to block Vilhelmina from the group. She spoke first.

"One ought to know to await the attention of their betters," Chelus said with a snide smile to the others. She wasn't talking to Vilhelmina.

"Count, there is an urgent matter we need to discuss," Vilhelmina said, ignoring the others.

"Oh, an urgent matter?" Armitage chimed in and waved to the others. "Such as?"

"For the Count alone. Valkyrie business," Vilhelmina looked to Chelus. "Active Valkyries only."

Chelus' disgust was impossible to contain any longer; she shook her head, ready to spit out the vile taste filling her mouth. As a full-blooded Valkyrie, Chelus stood nearly seven feet tall, with brilliant white, almost silver, hair. Every ounce of her body was elegant muscle beneath unblemished, creamy skin. And like all Valkyries, her eyes blazed like radiant purple gems.

The Count, noticing Chelus' tension, waved the others away. "Yes, yes. Let's get this over with and return to the revelry." Without comment, the Lords and Lady dispersed. Chelus glared at Vilhelmina, silently mouthing the insult thrown at the half-Valkyrie so often that Vilhelmina doubted anyone knew her by any other name: *mutt*.

She tried to ignore the insult, but words could be sharp as swords, making her shrink before the majesty of Chelus. Vilhelmina took the Count's offered arm, and the two walked to a quieter corner of the ballroom.

"Perhaps your office," she said.

"Is this about Yor?" the Count whispered. He, like Vilhelmina, was aware of his son's interest in his Valkyrie—half Valkyrie, but protector nonetheless—and knew of his son's plans for tonight to announce his intent to court Ms. Vilhelmina.

She nodded and bit her lip. The lips holding in Yor's eternal scream flashed in her mind. She shook away the image hard enough to jostle the Count. "Please Count. Somewhere secluded."

The two rushed to his office. As he settled into his chair and lit a cigar, she closed the door and shot the bolt. Hutton's office was typical for a diplomat. His chair was soft and imposing, while the chairs across his large desk were small and without cushion. Maps of foreign lands hung on the walls, alongside letters of merit and commendations for his service with the Legion of Clmal. Everything in this office pointed to Hutton's importance—reminders that he had everything. But the duty to inform him of what he'd lost fell to Vilhelmina.

Before saying the words, she questioned them. Was it true? Perhaps it wasn't Yor in the basement—just a case of mistaken identity or a doppelgänger slain in his place. But that was the damned human within her talking. So she let the Valkyrie speak. "Your son is dead. Someone beheaded him in the basement."

Hutton dropped his cigar, the embers catching on his velvet jacket and smoldering. Vilhelmina went to him and patted out the building flame.

"I believe someone here has done this sin against your family."

"But—" Hutton's confusion silenced him. He tried to speak, but no sound came out, until tears spilled over his cheeks. "You were supposed to protect him."

"I was," Vilhelmina moved to the other side of his desk. She placed her hands on it in a commanding a-frame that hovered over him, even in his large chair. "He asked to step away from me, to meet me in the basement and when I protested, he insisted. Said he needed a moment to himself."

An eternal moment now. Why did he dismiss her? What was in the basement that was so important she couldn't see it? She should have said no, that she was his protector and that meant going where he went. Over the years, there were a few moments when they were apart. And it was the human within her that got too close. The Valkyrie would have refrained from all but duty, yet a human, a human, is weak of flesh and soft in heart. Purple stone eyes could never see beauty, or kindness, like blue eyes—Yor called Vilhelmina's eyes *deep wells*—could.

Staring into space, Hutton's mind slowly came to the idea that his son could be gone. Taken at his very own party. Such an insulting moment to murder him made Hutton shiver at the pure monstrosity of the situation. "But who would want Yor dead?"

That was a critical question. One with very few answers. Yor was beloved by many and known as a hero both on the battlefield and in the hospitals. Seeing the ravages of war, Yor committed himself to the care of others but not as a doctor, as an emissary to ensure supplies and treatments could reach those who needed them most, regardless of their banner or borders. To Vilhemina, he had no enemies, and she had been his protector for years now. She would know. And above all this, she considered Yor's adeptness in battle, which rivaled her own. He was more than a capable fighter. Whoever killed him caught him by surprise or overwhelmed Yor in a terrifying manner.

Vilhelmina asked her first question of her first interrogation tonight. "Did you recently make any enemies?"

"You think someone killed my boy to get to me?" Hutton asked, dazed at the possibility of such a beastly thing. "But he's—" The Count couldn't finish said all the things that made his son a good person. The tears came without anger as loss sank deeper into his soul.

Vilhelmina wanted to pat his arm, tell him they'd find the murderer, but compassion was Sergei's job in this team. Besides, all her emotions were currently busy piecing together their own reaction to Yor's death. "Lock down the party. We'll find the culprit."

The Count nodded, unable to articulate the commands to do so. Vilhelmina opened the door. Two servants stood at the ready. She conveyed the Count's wishes, and they leapt into action, passing Sergei in a rush as they went. He looked at Vilhelmina for confirmation that her plan was in effect. She nodded.

"Count, I'd like to introduce you to my partner, Sergei. He is also of the Valkyrie Order, but not born to it as I."

Sergei, hearing his cue, entered the room. "Your Excellency," he bowed, his trunk curled up to avoid the floor. "My humblest condolences in your time of loss. Rest assured, the offender will be brought to a swift and commensurate justice."

The Count, studying Sergei through tear-filled eyes, said, "Mr. Sergei, I know of your kind's memory and sense of duty. Your presence fills me with certainty that an expedient end is in sight."

What some would have considered an insult, referencing *his kind*, Sergei took as a compliment. His kind, the Gajanthropes, were uniquely suited to the work of Valkyries due to the species' inexplicable genetic memory and honor. He took pride that *his kind* were the only other *kind* permitted to join the Order of Valkyrie outside of bloodline Valkyries.

"Did Yor say anything, or give you any comment that looking back, could have been a sign of trouble?" Sergei asked as he produced a small notebook from his breast pocket. Flipping to an empty page, he slide the pen from the notebook's loop and began writing notes.

The Count took a thoughtful moment and answered, "He was very on edge tonight, but I assumed that was—because of his plans for the night." Count Hutton didn't look at Vilhelmina. "His announcement."

She didn't look at him either. Her eyes were pointed at him, her face directed at the older man, but she saw nothing. Yor asked her to leave once. To go with him and for the two to vanish, farm the land, tell stories by the hearth on chilly nights, be alone in a world that was becoming ever more maddening. If she would have said yes, this wouldn't be happening. But her duty, her damn sacred duty, kept her rooted in a world that hated her. Why?

"Vilhelmina and I will discuss strategy. Count, for your safety, please remain in your office. We will wait for your guards' return and then begin our investigation." Sergei calling her name brought Vilhelmina back to the moment, out of the wishing well formed of past regrets and the present knowledge that you could have changed everything if only…if only…

Count Hutton nodded. "He loved you," he said. "He insisted on inviting you tonight so that he could tell everyone that he loved you."

Vilhelmina nodded. "I know," she said, and then turned to the door.

"Viola, find the murderer. For him," Hutton asked. At the name, Vilhelmina stopped. Only Yor had ever called her Viola, his flower. She had always hated the name, but hearing it now didn't sting as a sign of weakness as it once had—it stung with the piercing jab of regret. To everyone else, she was a mutt, but to Yor, she was a beautiful flower. He never saw her like the others did, and now he'd never again remind her of the folly of others.

Vilhelmina walked out of the office.

# III

Two more Valkyries arrived from Sergei's summons. They were both adorned in the white armor and black cloaks common to their role. While Sergei brought them up to speed, Vilhelmina watched the confused party-goers cluster into their cohorts. She watched them with the eyes her mother gave her, keen eyes that burrowed through the masks everyone wore and revealed their true selves. It wasn't magic, just detached observation.

Her list of suspects grew immediately as hushed conversations shifted out of her view, and all backs turned toward her. Whether this was to hide the truth or simply to ignore the one who didn't belong, she wasn't sure.

Chelus watched Sergei with curious interest, stepping closer a few times to hear him mete out the duties. Vilhelmina knew the older Valkyrie wanted to take control, to swoop in and command, but she was no longer a Valkyrie and knew better than to interfere in an investigation. A human had died. The sacred duty had been defiled, and it was only natural that Chelus would want to intercede. While humans are overwhelmed with loss and empathy at a death, Valkyries are overwhelmed with obligation and duty to protect. But the older Valkyrie said nothing. Besides, the murder had happened on Vilhelmina's watch. She shouldn't have let Yor go to the basement alone. But he was insistent. Why? Why so insistent?

Sergei smiled and waved to the nobles as he crossed the ballroom floor. They accepted him, even though he was not noble by birth, his people were revered by all and feared by most. Who would want to wrong someone who remembered everything? Who's family was said to share memories as if each experienced the lives of the other. In a society that bartered on reputation and influence, having your wrongs remembered by all was poisonous.

"Alright, we're on lock down. Tulmos and Xur are monitoring the outside while those two are watching the guards watch the exits. *Those two* were the two Valkyries he was just talking to. "Where first?"

"Yor's room," Vilhelmina said. She waved for her partner to follow.

"Why not the basement?" Sergei asked as he followed her.

"We were just down there. I didn't see any answers, did you?" Her quick answer betrayed her, but Sergei didn't push. She didn't want to be with Yor's body again, not yet. She needed space from her failure and time to process what had happened.

The two continued their way up to Yor's room in silence.

The Count's mansion stood four stories tall, with the entertainment areas on the first floor, offices and libraries on the second, guest rooms on the third, and master suites on the fourth. The house was Victorian in design. Each floor was ripped from a Penny Dreadful, with spiderwebs, brass fixtures, and wood paneling. The carpet was a deep blue, plush beneath the feet, with gold stair rods holding it tight to the wooden steps. Armor, swords, and shields decorated the walls, relics from the many places Count Hutton had visited in his long, long life. For a human, he was quite old for this world.

On the fourth floor, Vilhelmina guided Sergei to Yor's room, but someone was already there.

"Hello?" Vilhelmina asked as she pushed the door the rest of the way open. She held her sword but did not draw it.

"Greetings," a bright voice chimed from under the bed. "Just a moment." As the old man climbed out, Vilhelmina recognized him as the Count's Seer, Paul. He was a Vaniri, and like all his kind, he was tall, lithe, and bronzed from the sun—or perhaps from wheat fields or sunflowers or fall leaves. It always seemed arbitrary. Whatever they associated their golden skin with seemed to depend more on how the Vaniri wanted to position themselves than any factual genetic condition.

He wore a blue tunic and trousers, the standard garb of a court seer. A golden chain with a stone spiral, symbolizing the Lazarus Spiral, the mythical convergence of the six worlds, hung on his chest. His hair, like his smile, was gleaming white and thin. After brushing himself off, he stood and waited for an explanation of what they were doing there.

Vilhelmina waited for the same from him. She would have settled for a reason or rationale why he was under the bed, but the seer's demeanor was that of being interrupted and, as such, frustrated by her and Sergei's arrival.

"The party is downstairs," Paul informed them. "Yor is not here, my lady."

"Yor is dead," she replied.

Paul pressed a hand to his spiral and gasped. He recovered quickly and bowed his head in reverence. "May he find his way through."

Vilhelmina waved away the nonsense and clarified, "We are investigating Yor's death."

"Was it an accident?" Paul asked, but Vilhelmina thought that to be a strange first question. Yet she knew Vaniri, especially Vaniri seers, were *unique* in their perceptions of what was socially acceptable. Wandering in nature, reading ancient tomes, staring at bones, or tea leaves, or whatever dead thing made their vision work, didn't make for great conversationalists.

"We are investigating," she answered. "Why are you here?" But she knew he'd give some crap answer as seers did when they didn't want to interact with the likes of a Valkyrie.

"A vision told me to come and search for what I seek under the bed," Paul pointed to the large four post bed. The bedding was white, with a gray drapery hanging between the poles.

Sergei chimed in, "And what is it you're looking for?"

"I will know when I find it."

Vilhelmina threw her hands up as if to say, *well there you go*. "This is an investigation, and we'll need you to return to your quarters or the party," Vilhelmina stepped aside for Paul to leave. There were no answers coming from him. Standard seer crap. His likes trafficked in enigmas and could perpetrate their own mysteriousness by the nobles. Of all the members of the court, they said the most and did the least, with even less accountability. When they were wrong, they blamed the fates. When they were right, most often a guess, they spun tales of how their foresight was so clear. They didn't work for what they had.

They conned their way into the hearts of courtiers and the rich. And that was what Vilhelmina hated most about them. They didn't earn their station through anything but deception. Yet, no one challenged them—no one questioned why *they* belonged.

"Check your quarters or the party for whatever you're looking for. Let us know when you find it," Vilhelmina said, showing Paul to the door. He nodded but made no move to leave, simply observing the exit. "Perhaps the fates are inviting you to leave—*through me*," she sighed.

"Perhaps." Paul steepled his fingers and walked toward the exit. "Please do inform me of your findings. Yor was such an important young man. I hope his," Paul sneered at Vilhelmina, "*interests* did not cause him to befall ill tempers."

Sergei placed a large hand on Vilhelmina's shoulder. "I'm sure we will find the culprit and bring them to a swift justice."

Paul walked away from the room at a slow, even pace that made him appear to float down the hallway. When he arrived at the stairs to the third floor, Vilhelmina quietly growled and went into Yor's room.

"Don't let him get to you," Sergei said as he started searching Yor's desk.

"He didn't." Vilhelmina insisted. She tucked her cumbersome dress up and knelt at the bed to search under it. What was Paul doing under there? But the answer was quickly clear. There were loose floorboards under the bed, pried up and not carefully replaced. "Got something."

Sergei came over to her as she climbed under the bed. Under the floorboard was a small, jeweled box. It had Yor's family seal on it, the fox and the hawk. While there was a heavy lock on the box, it was unlocked and hanging open. Vilhelmina lifted the box out and handed it to Sergei. "Now we know why he was under the bed," she said.

Inside the box was blue velvet, but nothing else. Yet Sergei could make out a faint indentation of what could have been a key in the bottom of the fabric. "Did you know about this?" He asked.

"No," Vilhelmina got to her feet and took the box from Sergei. "What do you think?"

"Looks like a key indentation?"

Vilhelmina nodded. All she could think about was getting out of this damn dress, but she hadn't a change of clothes. Investigating in this bulky thing was going to suck and, worse, get the dress ripped up. One tear would confirm what people like Chelus thought of her. She couldn't clean up from the farm and didn't belong here. Not that she wanted to belong. Yor wanted her to belong. Not to conform, but to be accepted by the likes of his father. That's why he gave her this dress, to show them she could belong here. However, that didn't matter now. What Yor wanted didn't matter now.

"Not just a key," she pulled a small torn piece of paper from the lock. "Looks like someone left something behind." The fragment was too small to decipher, but in one way, it was unmistakable. It was from a map. Trees and a road were clearly drawn. Written in red pen was the word, *past* and while it continued into another word, that word was missing from the fragment. Directions?

"So, did Paul take it, or did he find it empty?" Sergei asked.

Vilhelmina knew if it was empty, then either someone was here before Paul, or Yor took whatever was in here out before he died. "Did you check the body in the basement?"

"Yor. His name was Yor and not just some*body*," Sergei said gently. "This isn't a standard investigation. Don't act like it is."

"It is," Vilhelmina said. "A human died on my watch. Now we investigate."

"A human you were with for the past few years. You were his protector, but we both know there was more than that," Sergei said. "And there's nothing wrong with that. But there is something wrong with hiding from the truth."

Vilhelmina left the room. "I was his protector, nothing more."

Sergei followed. "Nothing more? You weren't assigned to be here tonight. You came at his request. Valkyries don't attend security detail in a ball gown. A gown that Yor had specially designed for you."

Vilhelmina rounded on him. "I said there was nothing more," she stabbed her finger up into his face. "End of story." The comforting cold of her Valkyrie nature took over, burying anything that could have been with the frost of *duty*.

Sergei let it go as they went back downstairs. In the kitchen, the staff were still at the basement door. When they saw Vilhelmina, they parted to let her through.

"Anyone been here?" She asked. They hurriedly shook their heads. Vilhelmina held her hem as she walked downstairs. Her heels clopping along the wooden stairs until she reached the concrete floor. After a deep breath, she stepped into the basement to see Yor's body. His body was dressed in his finest suit, wearing his military pins and honors. But those metals were not a fraction of his achievements. The number of lives he saved, the children he helped, the negotiations he led to end the horrors of war, those were his legacy. But now he laid in his own blood, those metals drenched, and the tales of who he truly was relegated to those who truly knew him, which were few, if not only one.

If asked to say a word at his funeral, Vilhelmina would start with the lives he saved, not the battles he won but the battles he diffused. She chuckled, knowing she'd never be invited to attend his funeral, much less speak. Yor insisted she be here. No one else wanted her in this world. The laughing stopped when she saw Yor's blood. A thick pool surrounding an empty body print. His body was gone as the blood seeped into the gap where he had once laid.

# IV

"Who did you let in here!?" Vilhelmina screamed at the three servants charged with guarding the door. "I told you no one! No one!"

They cowered before her, huddling together to brace against her wrath. Would she slash them to bits with that giant sword? Her corded muscles and ferocity alone could dismember them through sheer strength of will. Their only hope was that all the blood rushing to her face would make Vilhelmina pass out—that they could escape if she fainted. But before that happened, Sergei put his hand on her shoulder.

She ripped away. The instant calming effect he normally had was inert in the tsunami of emotions crashing over her. None of those emotions were calm. None were serene. All were boiled in the cauldron of regret and loss.

"Who!?" Vilhelmina grabbed one of the servants. The other two collapsed into quivering masses.

"No one! I swear!" The servant boy pleaded. His neat bowl cut hair jostled out of place by Vilhelmina's rough shaking. Only one hand was necessary to turn this boy into a rag doll. Her strength was from her mother, augmented by years of farm work. She could break the boy's humerus into splinters by just squeezing it.

"Look at him!" Sergei shouted in her ear. "Does that look like the face of a liar? Or the face of a terrified kid?"

While her insides boiled in anger, the boy's face came through her blindness. She saw him. Limp from her shaking him. So terrified even his bladder couldn't relax enough to release. Vilhelmina threw him down to the others. They scampered around him, cuddling him into their mass of quivering fear. The two women didn't ask if he was okay, just quietly held him and rocked, keeping their eyes on the ground.

"What is wrong with you?" Sergei hissed in Vilhelmina's ear. "You said *just another investigation*. Well, that's clearly not the case." He pulled her arm, turning her toward him harder than she had ever felt before. Sergei's strength was always a last resort for him, his intellect and cunning being his weapons of choice. "Take a walk. Get a grip and get back here. I need you focused."

She knew he was right. However, that didn't calm her, only enraged her more that she lost control. That was the human in her. Hot tempered, impulsive, rash. Valkyries were made of sterner stuff, colder stuff, heartless stuff. But she listened to her partner and stomped away from the terrified servants, from the basement door, and went to the Valkyries watching the entrances.

Still panting, she navigated through clusters of partygoers in the ballroom. As she spoke to the Valkyries at the main entrance, Vilhelmina scanned the party. There were nervous gatherings, and then there was a small group of people as calm as could be, as if nothing of interest was occurring. There were three of them: Chelus, Paul, and a man in a mask Vilhelmina didn't recognize.

He wore a featureless white mask with two blacked-out eye holes. Vilhelmina wondered how she hadn't noticed him before—his stark contrast from the colorful partygoers made him stand out. The man was dressed in a pristine white suit with long tails and intricate gold stitchwork that caught the light in a surreal manner, making it dance around him. His white tricorn hat had a gold feather in the band that swayed with his elegant movements.

Despite all the charm and grace he projected, Vilhelmina recognized plastered confidence when she saw it. Her own practice and failed attempts to fit in had taught her what to look for. This man's performance was masterful but inconsistent. He didn't laugh on cue with the others. His hands lacked the disinterested flair of someone unconcerned with spilling expensive wine. But the final sign was his mask—focused on those in his circle rather than on those who could provide him with the social step ladder that all nobles here sought.

Vilhelmina excused herself from the valkyries and approached the man in white. "Pardon me," she interjected to disappointed sighs from Chelus and Paul. The man in white faced her. "I do not think we met earlier. Yet I am unsure how I would have missed you."

The man in white laughed a velvet chuckle that put Vilhelmina at ease until she noticed the effect. Such a simple laugh, such a deep impact, and she put her senses on high alert. He bowed to her in a graceful swoop.

"Madam Valkyrie, your words honor me. I understand your distress, for I would feel the same if not for noticing you all night. Your strength and beauty radiate as the sun gives—"

"Cut it there," Vilhelmina interrupted, waving away the disarming words with one hand and fanning herself with the other. The man in white was no noble—perhaps a poet, perhaps his words were meant to insult. Regardless of their intent, they tapped into Vilhelmina's heart and caught her breath. Never had someone begun their flirtations with her strength, nor had their impact been so immediate, rooting in her nerves and turning them on end.

The man in white was dangerous.

"We are discussing business. Perhaps your investigation would be suited elsewhere." Paul waved Vilhelmina away.

"Indeed," Chelus added. "Mustn't you have leads by now? A true Valkyrie would have completed this affair already," she said, glancing at Paul and laughed as if to say, *a true Valkyrie such as I.*

But the man in white raised a finger, wagging it at his companions. "Tonight's events must have addled your manners, and for that, I wish you an expedient recovery," he said, then offered his arm to Vilhelmina. The chandelier lights danced over the gold, threading like fawns playing in the woods. And before she knew it, Vilhelmina had laced her arm into his. "We shall take our leave to aid in your rediscovery of your couth."

And the two walked away. Vilhelmina smiled at the turn, but her true joy came from the confusion in the faces of Paul and Chelus. Each stood in bewilderment at what happened as their companion, the man who had their attention only moments before abandoning them for a plus one.

"Your name, sir?" Vilhelmina asked. Noticing her arm, she slowly untangled herself from the man. He smelled like winter wind before a snow. The scent invited wonder and hope for a warm fireplace. Watching the snow fall, Yor wrapped around…or perhaps it was the man in white. The image, the idea that this man replaced Yor so quickly, made Vilhelmina step further away from him.

"Must we?" He replied and laced his fingers behind his back. "Cannot we be mysteries for the night and in the morning wonder? Dream?" He leaned up and toward her, being slightly shorter.

"Hutton's scribe?" She guessed.

The man in white chuckled, another dreamy laugh. "No. I am but a sculptor."

Vilhelmina rolled her eyes. Now understanding the intoxicating nature that exuded from this man was nothing more than the capricious passion of an artist. Still, her heart raced as he playfully bumped into her, his silken suit gliding over her skin.

"Have you been here all night?" She asked, directly this time, as they continued to walk. Without noticing where they were going, Vilhelmina had entered the ballroom's dance floor. The white and black tiles glistened from the lights above. The artist stopped, bowed and offered his hand. No one else was on the dance floor.

"Indeed. And if you indulge me in this dance, I would be inclined to answer more of your questions." He motioned to the musicians, who had been chatting at their instruments. With no one dancing, they had stopped playing, but now, seeing the invitation to begin, they launched into a waltz with the eagerness of men making up for lost time. Others turned to see who had taken to the floor. Vilhelmina felt their eyes, their questions, and most of all, their dismissal for not being one of them. She took the man in white's hand and danced.

# V

"Have you been dancing all night?" Vilhelmina asked.

"No," the man answered as he pulled her closer.

His winter smell hooked her again, taking her to what could have been—what could be—then her Valkyrie mind shoved the emotions aside.

She tensed, but kept her feet moving. Her father insisted she learned how to dance for just such occasions, not to impress but to blend in. Others joined them on the dance floor, spinning around them as she continued her questions.

"Then perhaps you were with Paul or Chelus earlier?"

"Paul was missing earlier in the night. He and I discuss the transient nature of the muse, yet I could not find him earlier to begin our pontification," the man laughed at the last word. "As a seer, that is all he is good for. Pontification and persuading the nobles to part with their coin to become a patron of a lowly artist such as me."

A laugh slipped from Vilhelmina. It was the delighted, giddy laugh of a girl. She sucked it back, gritting her teeth.

They spun toward the center of the dance floor, under the largest chandelier that brought the man in white's gold threads to life.

She asked, "And that is why you are here? To get paid?"

"Oh, my dear, you make it sound so transactional. I am here to sculpt, to call into existence that which never existed. The money permits me to do that. Nothing more and since you asked about Paul, I assume the next person of interest will be Lady Chelus," he twirled Vilhelmina quickly, deftly, and in complete control. Her feet kept pace, having no choice but to succumb to the man in white's mastery of his own body and, apparently, hers. "Lady Chelus is a patron. I must keep my patrons happy, and they are happy when they think I work for them."

Vilhelmina reclaimed control of the dance and forced the lead. "If you do not work for them, then who?"

The man in white didn't resist her lead. He flowed into it and then whispered into her ear, "Then whom, my dear? Speak as them lest you remind them of who you are."

Vilhelmina's steps faltered, and he took the lead. If he was correct or not didn't matter as the man in white hit the seed of self-doubt that always blossomed in Vilhelmina's heart. However hard she tried, she could not escape who she was, and that reminder ruined her. He leaned back and said, "I have always, and forevermore will, work for only myself."

"If you were not with Paul, and I did not see you with Chelus earlier, then where were you before the party was locked down?" The song ended with loud clapping and cheering, though Vilhelmina didn't notice that the applause was for her and her dance partner.

The musicians launched into their next song, but Vilhelmina's dancing was done. She disentangled herself from the man in white and stood statuesque in the center of the floor.

"Perhaps your partner saw me?" The man in white said and reached his hand for another maiden, who gladly accepted and the two spun off into the crowd. But before he left, the man in white sighed, "You are alone here, my dear. You'll need friends," he pointed to himself and laughed off into the dance floor with his newest partner.

"I have friends." But only one came to mind. Sergei was her partner, not her friend. There was only one person she considered a friend, and his body was missing. She went to Sergei to see if any clues had been found. Unaware that Sergei was searching for her at that very moment, but he didn't have answers, only news of another death.

# VI

"The Count is dead," Sergei whispered into Vilhelmina's ear.

She recoiled. The words were a physical blow that sunk into her heart. Another death on her watch. What was happening?

"Who knows?" She asked. Her mind tried to shift from the thoughts of Count Hutton, but couldn't. When she was assigned to Yor, Hutton protested to the Valkyrie council. He didn't want a mutt around his son for fear that she'd wrap him into her wilds. From his opinion, that's what she did, not knowing it was his son pursuing her.

"I don't think anyone knows. He was still in his study."

"How did he die?" Vilhelmina gulped. "Same as Yor?"

Sergei nodded. "He was sitting in his chair when I found him. His head on the desk. Whoever got him did so by surprise. There was no blood elsewhere in the office. Maybe someone snuck up on him?"

Vilhelmina shook her head. "There's only the front door to the office. I checked it for other entrances or exits when I first was assigned here. There were none."

"Well then, we have a bigger problem. The guards outside his door said no one came in since you and no one left. You were the last person with Hutton. They didn't hear a struggle or anything to put them on alert."

How is this happening? No one went into the basement but Yor and her. No one went to the Count but her and Sergei—and Sergei left right ahead of her. At that thought, the connections formed. She was the last person to see both Yor and Hutton. And there were witnesses who knew that. If she were investigating this, she'd be the prime suspect: the last to be with both, with an emotional connection to one and being unwanted by the other.

Motive: the temperamental, half-human jilted lover who was also a trained warrior carrying a giant sword is rejected by Yor in private, kills him, then blames the father and kills him in his office before she leaves. Motive, opportunity, and means.

"You know what this looks like?" Vilhelmina said.

Sergei nodded. "But we both know that's not what's happening here."

"How do you know?" Vilhelmina pulled Sergei away from a group of nobles from the northern isles passing by. Their flowing robes and tunics, deep gray with soft streaks of white, like a storming sea, but Vilhelmina recognized their species, the Selkies, and knew they could be from no-where else. The Selkie nobles gawked with their exceedingly large black eyes and pallid faces, framed by eternally wet charcoal gray hair. Being from the islands, they had probably never seen someone like Sergei before, but Vilhelmina suspected their stares were more rooted in suspicion than surprise.

Noticing that she and Sergei were huddled like conspirators, Vilhelmina quickly pulled away and laughed as if he had just told a joke. His dire expression, however, didn't match the situation, leading to raised eyebrows and scowls from the Selkies before they rushed away. "You're a horrible actress, as you just showed," Sergei said. "And you wouldn't kill innocent people. Definitely not the humans you were sworn to protect."

"If someone's pinning this on me, then we better check my quarters," Vilhelmina said. Sergei nodded, and they headed to the third floor, where she had her room. They didn't notice someone following them as they hurried along. Nor did they notice the Selkies who passed earlier talking to Chelus, who was summoning the two Valkyries at the entrance.

Vilhelmina didn't notice any of this. Her highly attuned senses, normally so sharp, were too distracted, too divided between the crushing black hole of loss threatening to consume her and the desperate need to understand why someone would want to kill Yor and the Count. The grief gnawed at her, relentless and merciless, but something darker and more sinister was clawing at the edges of her mind—who would go to such lengths to frame her? And why? The thoughts twisted inside her, a venomous seed of doubt. Had she failed so completely, not just in protecting her charge, but for missing the true enemy lurking in the shadows?

She unlocked her room and opened the door. When she entered, she yelped.

In her room, the bodies of Yor and the Count were gruesomely displayed. Their heads were mounted above the fireplace, where the flames had reduced to smoldering, quietly crackling embers. Blood splattered and dripped from the pelts hanging on Vilhelmina's walls. Furniture was tossed, shattered in chaotic disarray. On the bed, Yor's body laid as if thrown onto it, his throat hacked away as he fought back. An axe rested in the fire, its metal darkened by the heat. Count

Hutton was crumbled beside the axe, his neck wound in the dying embers. The air was thick with the scent of charred flesh and blood, a macabre silence hanging over the room.

Paralysis overtook Vilhelmina as the surreal scene processed in her mind. The Valkyrie mind took in the details with stoic acuteness. There was a head, blood drizzling over the fireplace mantle, meaning the time of death was not long ago. Over there were long solid streaks of blood where the murderer decapitated Hutton and then drug his body to the fireplace, throwing it face down into the flames. The weapon was probably the axe which now was burning away the signs of blood, making it undetectable by hemalurgy.

As this inventory took place, the other side of her mind tried to scream, tried to fill itself with something other than the horror of this scene—but nothing came, only the sights, the smells, the flavors of this room. Only the desecration of Yor's body, the mutilation of his father, the death of her future with someone who loved her for her, not caring that she was a mutt or a Valkyrie or a human, but a person worthy of love. Vilhelmina, called Viola by Yor because he saw her as a beautiful flower and not a mistake, stood and saw the horror of this room and did nothing but let it flood her human mind with death.

Sergei gasped, but Vilhelmina didn't hear it. He staggered back, but she didn't see it. Only the blood dripping from the mantle to the fireplace embers, the sizzling as the blood hit the brick, held her notice.

"What have you done?" Chelus snarled, her voice cutting through the room like a blade.

Vilhelmina, awoken to the presence of others, spun, her heart pounding. Chelus glared at her with raw disgust. "Murdering mutt!"

Chelus spat, the words laced with venom. The older Valkyrie's fingers curled, white knuckles straining against the skin, her jaw set so hard she could have bit through stone. Before Chelus could attack, the guards burst into the room, swords drawn, their faces grim with resolve.

Vilhelmina's own sword cut through the air, a growl escaping her lips as the animalistic human urges she'd fought so hard to control surged forward—urges for revenge, for blood, now twisted against the very guards assigned to help her at this party. The room seemed to close in on her, the weight of betrayal and rage pushing her to the brink.

Sergei tried to step between Chelus and Vilhelmina, holding up his hands to calm the situation, but both women quickly stepped around him, not wanting to be denied their impulses.

"Vilhelmina Bonde, Protector of the Valkyrie Order, drop your weapon. You are under arrest for suspicion of the murder of Count Hutton and his son Yor," one Valkyrie shouted.

Nobles gathered outside the room to see what was happening. The man in white stood out among them as he would any crowd. Paul the Seer pushed through.

"What is this!?" He cried. "You!" Crocodile tears ran freely from Paul's eyes. "They trusted you half-breed! They loved you! And you betrayed them! You murdered them!"

Vilhelmina didn't answer. She growled and jerked her sword from person to person in the room, ready to fight her way out. If they took her, they won. Whoever was doing this won. How did Chelus and Paul get here so quickly? But the answer came to her: because they were who set her up. At least one of them did. If they took her, she couldn't find the actual killer and bring them to justice. They'd get away with it. But why would either of them kill Yor, much less the Count?

"I'm not going anywhere," Vilhelmina roared. "Why'd you do it?" She thrust her sword between Paul and Chelus. "Did you work together?"

Chelus recoiled, readying to strike, but Paul didn't flinch. The guilty never do when accused. She kept her sword on Paul.

"Valkyries, take her." Paul's eyes locked onto Sergei. "It is your duty."

But Sergei didn't move. "Vilhelmina's innocent," he addressed the other Valkyries. "We all took the oath. We all know what that means. Her duty is bound to her blood. She swore to protect humanity, and that is not swayed by the whims of an evening."

"But she is not a full Valkyrie. Her *humanity* is subject to rash behavior, as all humanity is," Paul said. He waved his hands as if explaining to a child, slowly and in a presenting manner, giving the Valkyries the missing information they needed to understand the full situation.

"This is true," Chelus added. "Her mother was honorable, but her father was only human. A good human, but *human*, nonetheless. They would be ashamed to see their spawn in such a manner."

"Shut your mouth!" Vilhelmina charged Chelus. With all the emotional energy she spent suppressing the loss of Yor, she was raw to the insults against her family, against her.

Chelus didn't move, but Sergei did. He disarmed Vilhelmina and took her down to the bloody wooden floor faster than she could react.

Tears filled her eyes, her throat raw from screaming. She lashed out, trying to break his grip as he pinned her to the floor.

"Stop!" Sergei shouted to her. But she didn't. Her humanity was on full display, as the other Valkyries shook their heads in pity and pride, knowing their full blood prevented such outbursts. They felt duty deeper than passion.

"Get off me!" Vilhelmina shouted. "He did this!"

But the room cleared, with the people outside moving on, relieved that the party could restart now that the troubles seemed resolved. The man in white remained, waiting alongside Chelus and Paul, shaking his head at the scene like everyone else.

As Sergei held Vilhelmina down, she writhed violently, her screams reduced to broken squeaks as her throat gave out. Chelus stared in unfiltered rage, only her Valkyrie nature restraining her from slaughtering the too-human beast thrashing on the floor.

How could they think Vilhelmina killed Yor? And yet, seeing her now—how could they not? She was rabid, spit frothing over her lips as she struggled to get up, to tear Paul apart. He was the actual murderer here, the true monster. No matter what display she was putting on for the nobles, no matter how they shook their heads in disgust, confirming that such mutts had no place among civilized folk, she seethed and writhed with fury.

One Valkyrie pulled Vilhelmina's arms behind her and secured the iron restraints on her wrists and ankles, linking them with a chain that clinked heavily against the floor. The sound cut through her rage—she'd been caught. This was exactly what she had feared. Now she couldn't investigate, couldn't prove her innocence. She was out of the game. She had truly failed Yor. Failed the one person who believed in her. The bloody ruined bed was in front of her eyes. Yor's body was there. Last week he was under the covers with her, hiding from his father—avoiding some state dinner. He smiled and brushed her cheek, asking her again to leave with him, to run off beyond the mountains where there were forests and plains where no one would find them. They'd sleep in every day. Read every night. Yor would cook. Together they'd work the land, she'd teach him to farm, he'd teach her to enjoy life without duty. He deserved that life.

However, Vilhelmina chose her duty over him and now he's dead.

As the weight of the chains settled in, all the horror, all the anger within her drained away, leaving nothing but the hollow shell of a beaten soul.

Feeling the fight in her evaporate, Sergei released her. One of the Valkyries moved to lift her by the chain, but Sergei intervened, stopping him—sparing Vilhelmina the physical pain of being carried by her restraints, on top of the torment already ravaging her mind.

"She can walk," Sergei said softly, lifting her to her feet. Vilhelmina fell silent. She wasn't angry with Sergei; she didn't feel betrayed. In fact, she didn't feel anything. The black hole she'd been suppressing had finally consumed her, leaving nothing in its wake.

# VII

They kept her in the basement where Yor was murdered, his blood still staining the cold stone floor. Above her, the party continued, the atmosphere shifting from a celebration of the Count's son's successful negotiations to a wake, and now, grotesquely, to a celebration of their murderer's capture. For the nobles, any occasion was worth celebrating.

Vilhelmina sat alone in silence, listening to the muffled music and laughing upstairs. Her only company was the small brown mice scurrying between the dry food store and a tiny hole in the stone wall. The mice paid her little mind as she leaned against the wall by the stairs, straining to catch snippets of conversation from the guards in the kitchen above. It was impossible to hear them over the stomping on the floor above her. She must be below the dance floor. Every so often the stomps ceased and clapping came, then a moment of silence. In that silence, she focused on the guards, thankful Sergei was with them. He wouldn't miss anything. He'd find a way through this.

Her eyes drifted to the tear in the dress Yor had made for her, where threads stiff and smooth like papyrus poked through the fabric. She must have stepped on the hem at some point, tearing the dress at the waist. That someone else might have ripped it during her arrest didn't cross her mind; it must have been her fault. As her fingers traced the frayed edge of the silken green fabric, she wondered how she had worn it for so long without ruining it further. Fancy dresses, like fancy people, had never been meant for her—that was something she had been reminded of all too often.

"Vilhelmina?" Sergei called down.

She rose to meet him, but he put up a palm, telling her to stay where she was. He remained at the top of the stairs and said, "I can't come down. The guards are worried I'll do something stupid like free you." He smiled, but his trunk didn't lift and curl like it did when he smiled for real, and his broad ears drooped, showing Vilhelmina just how dire her situation was. "The Seer has requested to try you here in court instead of a Valkyrian trial. He's making the case that they would be lenient on their own kind."

Vilhelmina scoffed at that. The other Valkyries would jump at the chance to skewer her, to remove a mutt from their ranks. If not for her mother's birthright, they would have never permitted her to enter their world. This was exactly the situation the Valkyries would love to have, a mutt that lashed out and broke her oath over such a paltry thing as love. Paul was doing her a favor without realizing it.

Sergei shrugged and continued, "yeah, that's what I thought too. But he's made the case, and it looks like he's getting his way. And he wants it done tonight, at the party." The last bit brought Sergei's shoulders down, like his drooping ears, and he looked away.

A trial at the party was certain to be a Kangaroo Court. The verdict was "guilty" before any evidence or inquisition would happen. It was just the next phase of tonight's party. But it wasn't the false trial that weighed on Vilhelmina, it was being made a show of in front of these people who never wanted her to be anything more than a poor farm girl. This verdict wouldn't be about murder. It would be an object lesson for anyone who fooled themselves into thinking they could be more than their station in life, more than how or where they grew up. Worst of all, Vilhelmina knew they were right. If not for who she was, the Valkyrie in her, so bound to duty, Yor would be alive.

She should have never left him tonight. But he wanted to surprise her, and her humanity longed to be surprised—to discover what this man, who saw her as more than a protector, more than a Valkyrie, was planning to make her feel special tonight. The dress was the first gift, but he promised another, and an announcement. She knew Yor was planning on leaving the Count's manor. He was planning on moving far from the world of nobility and all his plans were for two.

"If that's what's needed," Vilhelmina said and returned to where she was sitting on the stone floor.

Sergei didn't push. He knew her well enough to see what was happening. "I'll be your defense."

"No need," Vilhelmina held her hem up as she sat to avoid making the rip worse, but as she slid back, a long ripping filled the basement. Her dress tore again as it was caught under her foot. She sighed but wasn't surprised.

"There are questions about what happened. While you're down here, figure them out. Don't just mope," Sergei knocked on the door. "Your too smart to get caught like this. Something's wrong and you're locked in the place with the answers. Get off your ass and get to work." The guards let him out, and he left without another word.

Once Yor said something similar to her. There was an assassination attempt on him she thwarted. Nothing special, just a rival House making a power play prior to negotiations starting over trade routes. The assassin got too close, almost killed Yor before she stopped him. Fear of losing Yor, the need to protect him constantly, kept her from finding who sent the assassin. Yor told her, *you're too smart to be fooled by some spoiled rich kid. Figure out who sent the assassin instead of waiting around for the next one to show up.*

Who was the next death? Sergei? That was likely. And if he was going to defend her, it put a big target on Sergei's neck, as thick as it might be.

After another moment of moping, she got up but didn't look for answers. She looked for a sewing kit to fix her dress. If she was to be made a spectacle of, at least she'd look nice in Yor's dress. Needle and thread were often stored in pantries to seal burlap sacks.

A mouse squeaked as she almost stepped on it. Redirecting, she avoided crushing the critter but tripped on a cleaning bucket that wasn't put away from whoever was trying to mop Yor's blood from the floor. The bucket splashed and spilled. Vilhelmina slipped and fell to the stone ground with a splatter, soaking her dress in bloody water. Brown splotches covered the once emerald dress.

"Damnit!" She slammed her hands into the pool around her. "Shit!" Her dad's temper boiled over. "Shit! Shit! Shit!" she screamed. There was commotion at the door upstairs, but Vilhelmina didn't care. She unleashed the stream of swears she heard from her dad whenever he hammered his thumb, or when a trough he was building collapsed because he didn't build it sturdy enough, or when he did anything that made him feel stupid, useless, human.

And like her father, she got up and hit the closest thing she found — a stone wall. It cracked and crumbled under her Valkyrie strength.

But it wasn't broken enough, not destroyed enough to satisfy her rage, so she turned and ripped a stock shelf from the wall and threw it across the room. It hit a rippling rectangle of light and exploded into splinters with a loud crack.

This snapped Vilhelmina out of her fit and replaced rage with puzzlement.

What was that?

Did she imagine it?

There was a small sack of rice at her feet from the shelf she just destroyed. Throwing it where the shelf broke, she watched as the rice bag burst open against a hazy block of light. As rice rained down, pattering against the floor, she went to the oddity. As her fingers came close to the space, energy vibrated around her, static warbled as if tuning into the right radio station, and a wooden doorframe sizzled into existence directly in front of her.

How did she not notice this before? Sure, it was invisible, and it wasn't like she was throwing things the last time she was down here. But a thorough investigation would have found this. Hell, just walking around the basement, carefully examining everything, would have found this. How'd she miss this?

However, the answer was simple: she was distracted. Yor's death kept her mind busy on the body and not looking for things she couldn't see. Sergei, too worried about her, did not see this either. While her mind was tied to the world of nobles and parties, she didn't look for signs of magic or mysticism. And she knew who in Count Huttor's court dealt with magic—the seer, Paul.

But why would Paul kill Yor and the Count? For whatever Paul was looking for in Yor's room? And how would Paul, a seer not known for War Magic, kill a capable warrior like Yor? Maybe there was a motive for the murder, but means? And what of opportunity?

The door was polished oak with a brass knob handle. A knocker hung from a brass lion's mouth in the center of the door. As Vilhelmina retracted her hand, the door sizzled out of existence again. Before it vanished, she reached for it again and again it appeared.

On the floor, at the door, was a trail of blood, but Vilhelmina wasn't sure if that was from her spill, her fit, or the murderer. She chided herself for tampering with the crime scene, but let it go quickly as she took the doorknob, turned it, and opened the door slowly. No hinges creaked, but light poured into the basement from a well-lit hallway beyond. The dancing upstairs was just commencing again as she stepped inside.

Blood streaked the floor beyond the door, as if a body had been dragged through it. Vilhelmina hesitated at the threshold, her breath catching in her throat. The door had appeared out of nowhere, a wooden anomaly in the cold stone of the basement.

She pressed through the doorway, one step at a time, keeping close to the wall. Every muscle in her body was tense, her senses sharp, her eyes scanning the shadows for any sign of movement. The air was thick, oppressive, as if it too was hiding secrets.

She slipped into the hallway, her feet silent against the stone, moving carefully, deliberately, as if any sound might alert Paul to her presence. Her mind raced, trying to piece together the events.

Was this the opportunity Paul had seized? Had he waited for Yor to go into the basement? She pictured it: Paul demanding whatever he was looking for in Yor's room, Yor refusing, and then what? Not a fatal strike. Paul could never best Yor in combat. So what happened? How did Paul kill Yor?

She shook her head, forcing the questions away. They clouded her thoughts, made her weak. She needed to focus, to understand how Paul had murdered Yor. The hallway stretched before her, a passage that shouldn't exist, leading deeper into the unknown. Someone who could summon a door like this might have turned their magic into a weapon. Did Yor die by a sorcerer's hand? Is Paul more than a simple seer?

As she moved further, the hall's damp chill seeped into her bones, but her mind remained clear. The Valkyrie within her stirred, pushing aside the chaos, filling her veins with the icy certainty of duty. Whatever awaited her at the end of this hallway, she would face it with her mother's unyielding resolve and the vengeful fury of her father's blood.

# VIII

The hallway was freezing. Her bare shoulders turned to goosebumps from the constant chilled breeze. Carefully carved stone walls lined a polished terracotta tile floor. The tiles formed patterns that were clearly symbolic, but that Vilhelmina couldn't decipher. Were they purely decorative or sigils? Her mind didn't stray into these questions, keeping focused on the streak of blood that was now fading, but still directing her deeper into the hallway.

Torches crackled quietly as she passed them. Behind her, the hallway curved slightly, making the door to the basement, the one she came through, the last door she could see. Other doors lined the hallway, wooden with brass handles, just like the one to and from the basement, but these doors were closed.

Ahead, more torches for as far as she could see, but in contrast to their golden light, there was a door open and from it came a pale blue light. There were quiet voices coming from the room, hushed tones speaking conspiratorially. Moments like this, she loved her sword. It was heavy enough to cut through bone, but light enough to move with ease. But it was taken when she was arrested. Her fists would have to do, should it come to that. Her dad always said to solve problems with her head instead of her fists, and so she got low, sliding against the wall, silently moving to the door and listened.

"Kill her now! Don't make this a show," the man's voice was familiar. "You know this isn't what he wants."

"I have my orders as do you," this voice, easy to place, Paul the Seer, snapped back. "Don't let your ambition cloud your judgement. If we don't feed the sharks, they'll smell blood somewhere else. You know what he'd do for this!"

"But you don't have it! You have failed him."

"No! I have enough!" Paul said. "I have the first part of the map. What do you have but two heads?" Disgust built in Paul's voice like he wanted to spit on the other man, whoever it was.

"So proud of doing part of the job," the voice was so smooth and entrancing, she heard it before, "Will he be so favorable to receiving half what you promised?"

"You just want it for yourself!" Paul shouted, all attempts to whisper now gone. "You're not a believer! You're an opportunist and he'll see through you."

"No one sees soon enough," the man laughed, and that's when Vilhelmina put the pieces together. It was the man in white. The sculptor who was talking to Paul the Seer earlier in the night. This didn't surprise her as much as provide confirmation that Paul had an accomplice. Was Chelus involved too? Is that what they were talking about when she approached them earlier? Who was the sculptor? Obviously more than just someone searching for a patron. But the man continued, disinterested, "Paul, tell me, do your powers of clairvoyance tell you that you'll see the morning?"

Vilhelmina slowly peered around the door. It was her room. They were in *her* room. Blue flames lashed out from the fireplace. Both men were by the hearth, unable to see where she watched them. Her door was close to the bed and even though she thought they couldn't see her, as she could not see the door until she reached for it in the basement, Vilhelmina took no chances. She got low and slowly crawled from the door to the bed and then slid under, pulling all her dress along with her.

"He will kill you for this," Paul sneered and chuckled. "I told him to stay away from your kind. One thing you have in common with the trash in the basement, both of you are lesser beasts striving to grasp that which you shall never touch."

"Do you know where the rest of the map is or not?" The man in white said and stepped closer to Paul. Their feet touched. Paul stepped back and chuckled. It was the chuckle of a man attempting to break the tension. But the silence left behind by that nervous sound pushed Paul back another step. "Then our transaction is complete."

Metal cut through the air in a quick slash. Blood burst from Paul, crashing over his feet in a waterfall. The tang of copper filled the room as Paul's guts flowed onto the floor in a stream of plops. He collapsed into his gore with a splash, like the puppet master snipped his strings. Paul was still alive when he saw Vilhelmina under the bed, but he didn't give her away. His eyes didn't plead for help, nor did they ask for forgiveness for inciting her arrest. Within Vilhelmina, the cold Valkyrie kept control. No help was going to be given. No solace, nor forgiveness, just disconnected observation.

Black smoke drifted out from the man in white's pant legs. Vilhelmina grabbed her mouth at that.

This couldn't be.

All of them were destroyed.

Her mother was in that battle. Vilhelmina grew up with the stories of it, what it meant for their world, for humanity. This man was much more than some sadistic sculptor or a power-hungry aristocrat. The man in white was no man at all. He was a Dokkalfar, the monstrous dark elves. And now the feelings he stirred within her made sense, the blend of desire and dissolving her inhibitions. His kind were tempters, deceivers, destroyers. What was a dark elf doing here? How did he survive the Purging Wars?

The creature floated on the black smoke off the floor and drifted to the door where Vilhelmina had just come from. She heard the door close and sizzle out of existence. Paul being left behind to add to her body count, but she was supposed to be imprisoned.

Would this murder wouldn't be put on her?

No, because no one would come back to her room. There was no reason. She was caught. The murder evidence witnessed by all at the party. Why would anyone come here for the rest of the night?

Paul was choking on blood. He'd endured disembowelment and didn't scream or call for help, simply laid in his guts waiting to die. Vilhelmina crawled out from the bed and went to him.

"Tell me what's going on and die knowing your last act was service to a good man," she demanded.

Paul tried to spit out blood, but it merely dribbled from his lips. "Yor was in over his head," he sputtered, the words weak, barely holding together. Vilhelmina knelt closer, straining to catch his fading voice.

"I told him to give me the map," he rasped, his breath hitching. "But he knew. He knew I wasn't only working for his father." He managed a smile, a grotesque twist of crimson-stained lips. "True power... only a map away."

A ragged laugh escaped him, but it quickly turned into a choking gasp. His chest heaved one last time before the light in his eyes dimmed, leaving only silence.

Paul was dead.

Vilhelmina leaned away from the traitor's corpse, her mind racing. Who else was Paul working for? And why didn't Yor tell her?

The man in white—he had to be connected to whoever Paul was serving. But clearly, the man in white had his own agenda. She didn't waste time wondering why Paul would frame her. That much was obvious. He needed a patsy, and who better than the one everyone already despised?

She waited a moment longer, watching as Paul's final breath escaped him, ensuring he was truly dead before allowing herself to think further.

When she couldn't find a pulse, she stood and straightened her dress. Another body in her room. But then she noticed Hutton and Yor were missing again. Their bodies removed, leaving Paul as her latest victim. Did the man in white know she'd find the door or that she'd escape the basement and now Paul would be her latest victim?

She went to where the invisible door was in her room. Like the basement, the door fizzled into view when she reached for it, then vanished as she withdrew from it.

The man in white could get away, but she didn't think he'd leave without the rest of the map. What map? Yor never told her of a map. She'd been by his side for many of his quests and adventures. There were no secrets between them.

Perhaps she didn't know Yor as well as she thought? What else she didn't know?

Vilhelmina quickly threw her black hair into a loose braid, pinned her dress up, and, for the first time, was in a room quiet enough to hear her dress crinkle. But she paid that no mind, focusing on a more important detail, how to tell Sergei what she's seen.

Returning to the basement seemed the obvious choice, but was the man in white waiting on the other side of the door? Would she become his next victim?

Her gaze shifted to the dire wolf's pelt hanging on her wall, a gift from her father when she first took the mission to protect the Hutton family. Back then, she hadn't known if it was meant for the floor, but the fur was too beautiful to be trampled underfoot. So, she hung it instead. Now, a streak of blood marred the muzzle, but at a masquerade party, others would assume it was just part of the costume.

The wolf's hide was massive, enough to wrap around her body, with its giant head concealing her face. She took it down, revealing the swords she had hidden beneath. The blue flame flickered and died, plunging the room into darkness. Outside, the moons hid behind dense clouds—unusual for this season.

In the darkness, Vilhelmina took deep breaths, steadying herself. Her humanity assured her that answers were closer now than they had been all night, while her Valkyrie mind demanded that she perform her duty: bring the man in white to justice.

And if the stories her mother had told were true, if the man in white was truly a Dokkalfar, it was her sworn duty to protect humanity. Nothing was more dangerous to humanity than the

Dokkalfar. Humans called them demons, but the truth was far worse. Demons were evil for no reason other than to ruin good. Dokkalfar, the dark elves, were vile because they chose to be so—for their own enjoyment.

Wrapping herself in the wolf skin and sheathing a sword at her side, Vilhelmina slipped out of her room and descended to the party below.

A wolf among the flock of nobles.

# IX

The dance floor was bustling with noblemen trying to close deals on a mate or business. Both were the same to most. There were laughs and cheers, offers of drinks and promises of happily ever afters.

Vilhelmina paid it no mind as she navigated the chaos under her wolf's cloak. Its fine fur still bristly and sharp scratched others as she approached. Was it the wolf's head or the burning intent of the person within? The party goers simply parted as she approached. Under the cloak, her lithe body was hidden, and with no jewelry or adornments showing, no one looked twice at her. The wolf didn't sparkle or glow, and thus, didn't draw the eyes of nobles. Or so she thought.

Beyond the dance floor lay the foyer, then a hallway, then the kitchen, where Sergei was preparing his case to defend her. He didn't know Paul was dead, nor that there was no prosecutor—only a dark elf in the shadows working against The House of Hutton.

But to what end? Why is the man in white killing everyone? Count Hutton was dead. So was his son. And the Seer, the third in charge, was also dead. Who would that leave?

In the kitchen, Vilhelmina saw three Valkyries guarding the door to her prison, the basement. The man in white was talking to them, requesting access to see her.

"Please, Master *Valkyrie*, I only wish to help." The man in white said in his teeth rottingly sweet voice. He reached for Sergei's arm to touch and assuage any concerns the Gajanthrope would have, but Sergei jerked away.

"The defendant mustn't be disturbed." Sergei put his large hand up, warding the man in white back, then said, "please leave while I prepare my defense."

"Oh," the man in white sighed, "I meant no offense. Physicality is not called for." He motioned toward Sergei's hand, casting the motion to back off as a threatening gesture. The man in white glanced to the other Valkyries, then added, "there is no need for violence."

The other Valkyries nodded.

Sergei put his hand down quickly and took a deep breath. "I am simply asking you to leave. Your compliance would be appreciated." Another deep breath centered Sergei and seemed to calm the Valkyrie guards, who now looked suspiciously at Vilhelmina's partner.

"Oh, I know of the legendary restraint of *your kind*. I am certain there would be no outbursts. None like we saw earlier from your partner. I shall take my leave. My apologies for the distressing moment."

But Sergei wasn't distressed until the man in white said he was. A master manipulator was performing.

Vilhelmina kept to the shadows, remaining invisible to those in the room but not the one who spotted her on the dance floor. Since Vilhelmina thought she was unnoticed, she did not watch for anyone watching her. The presence of a mythical creature, a Dokkalfar, had distracted her. She'd never seen a dark elf, only heard of them in rumor and myth. Now, she faced one, and he killed the Seer, and she was certain he killed the Count and Yor. However, he split Paul open. That's how he decapitated the others…no not the *others*—Yor and his father. Not just *some humans,* but Yor and his family.

The man in white chuckled his bright, infectious laugh, and walked off unbothered, swaggering out the door. Vilhelmina rolled into the shadows to stay unseen. The man in white passed without stopping.

After a few breaths, the intoxicating heat from him wafting over her, bringing her senses to wanting attention. She needed him to stop and touch her, pull her into his arms and–NO! He must pay for what he's done. He killed her protectorates and now, he's parading about their home without a worry in the world.

Vilhelmina slipped into the kitchen, keeping her jaw clenched to avoid any words from slipping out until it was time. Sergei stopped her, not noticing who she was. The three guards prepared to assist Sergei in dismissing this new visitor, but before they did, Vilhelmina spoke.

"I'm sorry. I thought this was the library." She turned quickly to leave. "Perhaps you could show me where it is Master Gah-gan?"

Sergei stiffened at that. Vilhelmina was the only person who called him Gah-gan. It had started as an inside joke when they first met— she'd tried to be polite, but she'd butchered the pronunciation of his people's name. The nickname stuck, and he embraced it.

"Yes. I can show you the way, ma'am," he replied, his voice steady. "Keep the prisoner in the basement and permit no visitors." The three Valkyries nodded and returned to their posts, flanking the basement door.

Sergei offered his arm to Vilhelmina. She took it, still shrouded within the wolf pelt. Together, they walked to the library, unaware of the third presence that had been watching Vilhelmina since she stepped onto the dance floor, weaving through the nobles. As Sergei closed the library doors behind them, the watcher sprang into action, rushing across the party, intent on ruining their reunion.

# X

"How——?" Sergei began, but Vilhelmina cut him off.

"It's the man in white," she said, pulling the wolf's head back to expose her face. Her black braid slipped free from under the pelt. "He killed the Seer. I think he killed Yor and the Count."

"Wait. Go back. *He* killed them? But wait, how did you get out of the basement?" Sergei asked, his tone sharp.

"There was an invisible door. It led... somewhere. I don't know. And then there was another door in my room. I bet there are more," Vilhelmina said, pacing now, her hands gesturing wildly as she tried to make sense of her thoughts. "That's why I didn't see him earlier tonight. He came through one of the doors."

"Stop. What door?" Sergei demanded, his voice firm. "And how do you know the Seer's dead?"

The third person came into the library silently, unnoticed, then demanded Vilhelmina and Sergei's attention. "You released the prisoner?" Chelus said. She stood in front of the closed door, blocking the way out.

"Lady Chelus?" Vilhelmina answered. "We've found the true——"

But Chelus wanted nothing of it.

"Silence! Conspirators!" Chelus pointed at them, her voice sharp and commanding. Her glare fell on Sergei with such weight that he instinctively stepped back, retreating from her presence. The tall, older Valkyrie had lost none of her potency. Intent and focus were as much a Valkyrie's weapons as any sword or war hammer. Though Chelus wore only a fabulous dress, she was ready for battle, her posture unyielding, daring them to challenge her.

"I expected better from you, Sergei," she continued, her tone heavy with disappointment. "A mutt like her is bound to be faulty, but you? How could you shame your kind?" She shook her head, disbelief etched into every line of her face.

"Mutt?" Vilhelmina cut in before Sergei could respond. The two women closed the distance between them, their wills colliding like celestial bodies in a violent clash, the air around them almost crackling with tension. "It doesn't take someone as 'lowly' as me to see you rubbing elbows with a murderer. Tell me, Lady Chelus, did you help, or were you cut out while the boys played their own games without you?"

Chelus slapped Vilhelmina so quickly the crack was lightning across her cheek, thunder rumbling through her jaw. The younger woman staggered back and stumbled to the ground. Her wolf covering sprawling on the floor under her. Vilhelmina hissed, growled, and sprung to her feet.

"How dare you!" Chelus roared. "Your mortal failings blind you or make you too dull to understand history!"

Sergei grabbed Vilhelmina as she lunged at Chelus. His thick muscles strained to hold her as she thrashed and clawed, desperate to tear Chelus' eyes out. Chelus spat in her face and swung again, but

Sergei yanked Vilhelmina away just in time, the strike missing her by inches.

Sergei shoved Vilhelmina to the side and then reached to restrain Chelus, but she was quicker. She caught his arm, twisted it, and with a fluid motion, flipped the giant to his back.

"You're too dull to consider your predecessor!" Chelus snarled, slapping Vilhelmina again—this time with such force that it sent her flying across the library, crashing into a shelf. Books rained down on her from above, driving her to the floor.

But Chelus wasn't done. She ripped Vilhelmina from the ground and pinned her against the shelves by her throat. Vilhelmina kicked, struggling for leverage, but Chelus easily lifted her off her feet.

"Count Hutton was my charge before you were born! As was his father! And his father's father!" Chelus hissed, her grip tightening around Vilhelmina's throat, shaking the younger woman like a broken doll.

Sergei grabbed Chelus from behind, but she shrugged him off with little effort, sending him stumbling back.

"You took Yor! And you failed him! You failed your sacred duty because you're too human!" Chelus spat, throwing Vilhelmina to the ground like trash. The older Valkyrie's pale face reddened at the cheeks, but her eyes blazed with fury. "You failed this family I've protected for centuries—long before you poisoned the Valkyries with your humanity!"

Vilhelmina clutched her throat, gasped for breath. A raspy cough wracked her body as she struggled to draw air back into her lungs. This was the punishment she deserved—the lashing for failing Yor, for being too blinded by duty to see what was truly right.

Chelus's words cut deeper than her blows, each one laden with the bitter truth Vilhelmina could not escape—not the truth as Chelus meant it, but the truth that haunted her every step. The failure was not in her humanity, but in her Valkyrie nature, her inability to break free from what she was supposed to do, from what society demanded of her, and to embrace what her human heart knew was right.

Run away with Yor.

But she hadn't. She had done what was expected of her, and for that, she would endure this beating—and the many more that were sure to come. But Vilhelmina wanted justice more than self-flagellation. There'd be time later to reflect on how accurate Chelus was, how her feelings for Yor obscured her judgement, her duty to protect him, and how a simple choice could have changed all this. But now was not the time for such thoughts. Now was the time to bring the man in white to justice.

Vilhelmina tried to speak, but her throat would not work. So, she crawled to the desk in the library and scribbled on the paper quickly, "I know who killed them."

Chelus took the note, crumbled it and threw it at her. "Know or suspect?"

Vilhelmina shook her head slowly, and Chelus knew that meant the younger woman had no proof.

Sergei said quietly, "Vilhelmina said it was the man in white. I saw you and he speaking earlier." He put his hands up in defense as Chelus rounded on him. "I'm not saying anything more than you were talking. Do you know who he is?"

Seeing Sergei truly meant nothing more, Chelus relaxed and went to the desk where Vilhelmina was crawling into the chair to recover her breath. There was a golden statue of a general waving a sword while riding a rearing horse. She picked it up. Vilhelmina shrank back to avoid being brained by Chelus, using the statue to bash the younger woman's head in. The older Valkyrie must have been thinking the same, and smirked at the idea. Perhaps satisfied at Vilhelmina's reaction, Chelus turned back to Sergei and moved away from the desk, pointing the statue at Vilhelmina's crumbled, gasping body.

"He's worse than this one. He's an artist." Chelus wiggled the statue in the air. "Count Hutton commissioned him as a sculptor to make things like this. This was a depiction of Count Hutton at the Battle of Lorain. The artist made it for him as a gift of appreciation for liberating the city."

"Battle of Lorain?" Sergei asked and then squinted while he searched his legendary memory for the details. "The battle on the edge of the Shallows? Lorain was the first city taken by the Dokkalfar in their expansion and the last to be freed from their reign."

Chelus nodded. "When the Valkyrie fell to the dark elf advances, Count Hutton's father came to liberate the city. The Count was a young man at the time and pride is often the province of youth." Chelus sneered at Vilhelmina. "Few survived the battle. The Count's father lost many good soldiers that day to drive back the darkness."

Vilhelmina could finally speak and so did, "The man in white is a Dokkalfar. I saw it right after he killed The Count's Seer. They were talking about the murders." She stood, the desk supporting her weight. "He's looking for a map."

Chelus took in Vilhelmina for a moment. The younger Valkyrie wasn't sure if it was a look appraising Vilhelmina's efforts to stand, to fight, or if the older Valkyrie thought she was a fool for pushing the subject.

Breaking from Vilhelmina, Chelus shook her head, "The Dokkalfar were defeated." It was a definitive statement with no space for questions. The silence didn't allow dissent. Because if Chelus was wrong, the thousands of Valkyries who died pushing them back to their realm died in vain. No Dokkalfar had been seen in decades. They hadn't been poisoning humanity with their promises and temptations. Where the Valkyrie's sacred duty is to protect humanity, the Dokkalfar's purpose was to corrupt and torment.

"I know what I saw." Vilhelmina broke the silence. She shouldered past Chelus to leave, but the older woman grabbed her wrist.

"You are not leaving. Your trial awaits."

Sergei's trunk curled up, his eyes narrowed. "You mean the clown court?"

"Trial. Justice. Protecting our sacred duty by punishing those who violate it." Chelus kept her grip on Vilhelmina. The grasp didn't hurt, but it was unbreakable. Silence came between the three again. Vilhelmina didn't struggle. Sergei looked between the women to figure out what to do, but he couldn't decide, and so he did nothing.

"Who is the judge? Paul is dead. Will it be you then?" Vilhelmina asked. Still, she did not struggle. "A fair trial for one such as me?"

"The only evidence is against you. Bodies in your room. Motive is also against you. Why would Dodslav kill his patron? Why would an artist sever his meal ticket?" Chelus asked.

Vilhelmina now had a name for the man in white. She'd never heard of him before, but thought it not surprising that Chelus was under his sway. The man was just sweet enough, not too much so, nor too little, but just right for everyone he manipulated. Even Paul didn't suspect a thing until his guts were steaming on the floor. The smell of death, the pungent eye watering stench hit Vilhelmina as she remembered Paul's look of surprise as he stared at her from the floor. Not surprised to see her, but that Dodslav killed him.

"Because he wants the map," Vilhelmina answered. "Paul wanted it to. They want it for someone else. I'm guessing someone paying more than an artist's commission."

Chelus' grip faltered, then dropped.

Sergei asked, "Do you know something, Lady Chelus?"

The elder Valkyrie straightened her white gown and stood tall. "Before this one, the Count had expressed a suspicion that Paul was being recruited by another. I knew not who, neither did he from what I understood." Chelus strode to the door, glancing back to Vilhelmina with disdain. "Perhaps your tale is true. If it is, then you should have no issue discovering evidence within the hour. Without evidence, you will face trial. I'll preside and you will be found guilty. Am I clear?"

Vilhelmina and Sergei nodded.

"Cover back up. None can know you have escaped the basement," Chelus demanded, then paused, speaking to Vilhelmina from over her shoulder. "Your mother fought with me at Lorain. She was an honorable warrior. Do not sully her memory with your failure. Live to her standard. Bring me proof." Chelus returned to the party, closing the library doors behind her and leaving them to formulate their next hour.

And while Vilhelmina tried to focus on the task at hand, to push aside all that Chelus said—including that she knew her mother—and see the goal of proving Dodslav's involvement, all her mind could think were thoughts of inadequacy. She failed the Hutton family. Two generations are dead on her watch.

"Right. Now, what's the plan?" Sergei asked.

Vilhelmina's eyes blurred with salty tears as the weight of her failure settled into her guts. What would her mother have said about all this? Would she had been as cold as Chelus? Or would a Valkyrie who fell in love with a human and abandoned her life of palace balls and war fields for a farm have been more warm? Caring? But this didn't matter now. Time was running out.

In an hour, she would lose her freedom, most likely her life. So, what now? When her mind was torn between laying down and crying forever, or killing Dodslav, how could she save her own life much less bring justice to Yor's murderer?

"You said Dodslav was looking for a map?" Sergei said as he looked around the library. There were many maps on the walls, but he was certain these were not the maps the murderer was looking for. These could be easily taken.

Vilhelmina collapsed onto the library sofa with a heavy thud, the wolf blanket wrapped tightly around her as she clutched it closed. She was in no condition to conduct an interrogation, let alone probe the mind of a master manipulator like Dodslav. But it was all she knew to do.

So, with a tear-choked, cracking voice, she managed to ask, "Can you bring the man in white, Dodslav, here? I have some questions for him."

# XI

At the desk, Vilhelmina sat draped in the wolf skin, the head pulled low over her eyes. When Dodslav and Sergei entered the library, Sergei quietly closed the door, bowing to the followers who had been drawn in by Dodslav's magnetic presence.

As the two men walked from the ballroom to the library, a crowd gathered around them. Dodslav asked questions loudly, laughed even louder, turning himself into a spectacle that drew eyes and attention. And worst of all, for Sergei and Vilhelmina, it attracted a following that now lingered outside the library.

"Seems so foreboding," Dodslav quipped as the doors clicked shut.

"I saw you kill Paul," Vilhelmina looked up, meeting the black pits of Dodslav's mask with her piercing blue eyes. "In my room. And I know about the doors between the basement and my room. I'm betting there's one in Count Hutton's office as well."

"Where are Yor and Count Hutton's bodies?" Sergei asked, keeping his broad back to the door. Dodslav stood between the two of them. His confidence did not waiver, nor his swagger as he bowed to Vilhelmina in a dramatic flourish.

"Lady Valkyrie," Dodslav said. "Surely you are mistaken. While I do not doubt what you saw, I have murdered no one but do plan to put an end to a few noble's longings later tonight," he chuckled, his intoxicating laugh.

Vilhelmina steeled herself against his charms, which was no easy feat. She wanted to laugh too, to let out a giddy, girlish squeal, but that was him, his influence, not what she wanted. Being in the same room with him was alluring, and she wondered why, how could he bring out such thirst in her?

If he were Dokkalfar, he would be a tempter by nature. A solicitor of the salacious. Humans called Dokkalfar demons for good reason. They brought out the worst in one's humanity and here, for Vilhelmina, it was desire. The urges she suppressed for Yor now boiling over for this man, this creature. And giving in would prove Chelus right. That her weakness, her humanity, controlled her.

"Where's Yor's body?" Vilhelmina asked as her mouth watered and fingers warmed. Dodslav came closer to her. His scent was bittersweet dark chocolate mixed with the aroma of wild lavender. The Valkyrie within wanted to pull away, but the human leaned in.

"I have not seen it since it was discovered in your room Lady Valkyrie. I assume you have had it moved since. To where? I wonder."

Vilhelmina leaned over the desk, her upper body pushing forward, her chest straining against the confines of her corset. Stretching her neck, pressing her chin towards the man in white, her lips parted, letting a quiet, deep exhale escape. The wolf's pelt slipped from her shoulders, drifting to the floor in a soft, fur-lined spread.

Dodslav extended his hand toward her, palm up, poised to either accept her hand in a dance, or gently lift her chin to guide her lips to his.

Sergei pulled the man in white back, breaking his spell on Vilhelmina, who shuddered from the oozing aura dripping from the Dokkalfar. She had no doubt now of his true nature. Shaking away the heat from this tempter like a dog shakes off rain, Vilhelmina reset her mind and body.

Sergei stepped between them and shoved Dodslav back.

"As smooth as you are, you have not the wherewithal to see those who are unaffected by you." Sergei's trunk coiled, ready to strike. His wide ears extended, making his overbearing figure seem to encompass the space around Dodslav in a wall of muscle. "Preying on others. Sickening."

Vilhelmina watched Sergei close in on the man in white. He'd never been the fight first ask questions later kind of guy, but here it was. The Gajanthrope had hit his limit and was ready to beat answers out of this creature.

"Where are the bodies?" Sergei roared.

Dodslav just laughed. "You see, this is the difference between warriors and artists. You react to orders. You expect others to do the same. We artists," Dodslav shrugged, uncaring and unbothered by the giant bearing down on him. "We brood. We analyze. We weave masterpieces." The man in white backed away from Sergei's approach, building distance between them. "My masterpieces are more complex than murder. One could call them, perhaps ought to call them, machinations." Dodslav reached out, a door fizzled into reality. He gasped in faux shock, then said, "It's almost like I planned this?"

As the door appeared, Sergei rushed forward, but Dodslav slipped through the opening and closed it quickly. The giant dove to catch the door, but it vanished. Vilhelmina hurried to the door, reached for the handle, but it was gone. No door appeared, not like it did in the basement or her room.

"Where did it go?" Vilhelmina asked. "The other doors were still there."

A commotion was happening outside the library doors. Sergei turned, his blood still pumping from the need to smash Dodslav's stupid little mask and then the face underneath. He shook with the need to hit something. A breath could help push out the rage, but he didn't want to let it go. He wanted to hold on to it, turn it on someone. Break something.

That's when the door broke in. Two Valkyries charged through the library door, shattering it to splinters. Sergei ran towards them, swinging his massive fist into the face of the first Valkyrie. The other barely dodged away from another punch as the first stumbled to the ground.

"There!" Dodslav shouted. "I knew he was helping the killer! They did it! They conspired against this family and *your* prosperity!" He addressed the gaggle of nobles who he'd gathered. They nodded in agreement, seeing how clear it was that these two rogue Valkyries not only killed the Hutton family but sought to ruin the lives of everyone at the party. Dodslav shouted, "Lady Chelus! Help! The big one is going feral!"

As if summoned through speaking her name, Lady Chelus ran into the library and effortlessly subdued Sergei with her martial prowess. Vilhelmina didn't fight. She glared at Dodslav, seeing his plan to validate his innocence coming to fruition.

"They tried to make me confess to the murders. But I am innocent. I escaped and locked them in here," Dodslav said, his voice trembling with what seemed like genuine fear. He shivered, drawing three noblewomen closer, their concern quickly transforming into something more primal.

Unconsciously, they pressed themselves against him, attempting to comfort him but instead sparking bolts of electric lust shooting through their bodies. Their touch, meant to soothe, ignited a current of desire that they could neither control nor resist.

"I expected this of you," Chelus scowled at Vilhelmina, who did nothing but watch Dodslav as he swayed in endearing fear and revolting delight. "But not of you," she looked down at Sergei as she pinned him to the floor. His arm was twisted up behind him as the giant struggled to get to his feet from under her pressure. Every inch he made, Chelus quickly stole back. "To trial. Both of you!"

The Valkyrie guards had recovered and rushed to Chelus' aid. They seized Sergei as he regained his senses; the fight draining from him as his true nature reasserted itself.

Dodslav wore a mask, but Vilhelmina thought she could see his expressions in those black pit eyes. He was sneering at Sergei. Satisfied with his victory and the Gajanthrope's exposure as an animal. And a victory it was. Dodslav was about to get away with murder. He had created the narrative that was simple enough for everyone here to understand.

The mutt tried to seduce the Count's son. When thwarted, her and her beastly partner murdered anyone who got in their way. Just see their feral displays, so shameful, so different from us nobles who maintain composed natures in civilization.

Vilhelmina went with the Valkyries without a fight or protest.

Chelus raised an eyebrow, waiting for the attack to come, for the young woman to snap, but she didn't. While Vilhelmina was no equal to Chelus, she was a gifted fighter and could easily attempt to escape with only two guards on her.

The Valkyries took Sergei and Vilhelmina to the dance floor where their trial was to begin.

Chelus followed with her hands clasped, her jaw set, teeth grinding as she processed the scene in the library. Sergei fighting when Vilhelmina did not? Dodslav's ability to escape two highly trained and proficient warriors? She glanced behind her, seeing Dodslav leading a parade of nobles, all cheering him, recounting his bravery and guile. He looked at her, smiling.

If Chelus was not careful, the next person on trial…would be her.

# XII

"Let us begin," Chelus bellowed.

A circle of nobles formed around her, Sergei, and Vilhelmina. The two on trial knelt before Chelus—not in servitude, but out of respect for her role as judge.

All the fight had fled Sergei, leaving him dazed and confused, still grappling with what had happened. What wall had crumbled within him, unleashing the beast he had worked so hard to suppress? But Vilhelmina understood. Her cold, unfeeling Valkyrie nature saw clearly what Dodslav had done. He had found the cracks in their minds, the places where their worst selves were kept at bay.

For Sergei, it was the beast within his animalistic side—a primal force that all Gajanthropes learned to suppress, lest they be seen as the animals they feared they truly were. Dodslav had poked holes in the mental dams that held back their darkest instincts, allowing their worst selves to seep through.

"You are charged with the violation of your sacred duties. The murder of Yor Hutton. The murder of Count Miskov Hutton. The murder of Seer Paul, Vaniri of the Mountains. For the slaughter of two humans and a Vaniri, how do you plead?"

"Not guilty." Vilhelmina said, firm and absolute.

"Not guilty…" Sergei said.

The nobles jeered and spat at them, with only Dodslav remaining silent. He stood, impassive, patiently waiting for a moment to strike. Vilhelmina wondered when he'd interject. It was coming. He needed to be the star, and right now, Chelus was the star. That would be untenable to one such as him.

"Before judgement is there any evidence the defendants wish to present in their case?" Chelus asked.

Sergei, weighed down by his shame, could only shake his head. Vilhelmina's eyes met Chelus's before shifting to Dodslav. She considered protesting, making an accusation—but instead, a single question formed in her mind. It came from her human side, the irrational side—the manipulative side.

"According to Valkyrie law, forsaking one's sacred duty is punishable by death," Vilhelmina began, straightening her back as she scanned the crowd. "And with my death, the last secret of the Hutton House will die. Yor told me where the map was."

The nobles exchanged confused glances, murmuring among themselves—what map? But this was the moment Dodslav had been waiting for. He seized the opportunity, speaking up with a tone of authority.

"Count Hutton spoke to me of this map," Dodslav declared. "A route to treasures that would secure the economic stability of his partners for generations to come."

The nobles didn't know about any map, but they exchanged smiles and nods, pretending to understand. What they truly cared about was clear—their own fortunes. If Dodslav claimed they would be taken care of, then it must be true. Some nobles murmured, their curiosity piqued by the promise of wealth.

"Perhaps," Dodslav continued, "if the accused would lead us to the map, to the insurance of our well-being," he motioned to the crowd, "then we would see it fit for mercy?"

The nobles cheered their hero, the man in white.

Chelus did not cheer.

"Please, tell us where the map is, and Lady Chelus, you would show mercy. Would you not?" Dodslav said to cheers.

Chelus appraised Vilhelmina, covering a curious smile with a benevolent one. The younger woman was manipulating the crowd. Dodslav was helping. The two were not working together, but their interests aligned and that made for a dangerous situation. Chelus did not get to answer as Dodslav led the crowd in a chant of give us the map. To calm the crowd, she raised her hand, but it had no effect. Dodslav kept them going, ignoring her authority, her control of the situation. She shouted instead, "I shall permit this!"

There were chuckles amongst the nobles as they dismissed her permission.

"And," Dodslav interjected, "to avoid any issues, I will go with the accused to retrieve the map. Her partner will remain here with Lady Chelus, the only one among us who can control such a beast."

The nobles agreed to what appeared to be wisdom. Sergei cringed at the words. Chelus bristled, but she was not calling the shots any longer. Vilhelmina rose to her feet as the crowd applauded Dodslav's bravery and courage.

"Take me to where the map is hidden," Dodslav offered his arm and stretched forth his charms to melt Vilhelmina's inhibitions. She laced her arm through his. Her milky skin blending with his white frock coat. Only the gold stitching revealed where her flesh stopped and his shirt began. The two walked to the stairs and proceeded to the third floor.

From the dance floor, the nobles watched and murmured among themselves, already dreaming of what they would do with such riches. Sergei glanced up just in time to see Vilhelmina disappearing down a hallway with the Dokkalfar. His gaze met Chelus's, and in that shared look, both recognized the fear that their fates now rested in the hands of a dark elf—and a Valkyrie whose humanity, Chelus thought, made her not only unworthy of trust, but dangerously volatile.

Indeed, Vilhelmina was running on the most unpredictable fuel: human emotions.

# XIII

Vilhelmina's heartbeat raced. She kept telling herself it was only Dodslav's manipulation, but her body didn't care. She wanted to feel. Memories of Yor tingled over her skin. Every touch she avoided came to her now. Her lips wanted every kiss she had turned from. Her fingers buzzed with the times she felt his hand in hers.

"Here." She motioned to her bedroom door.

Inside, the night's murky darkness cast the room in shadow. The hall lights hinted at what was within the room and what was no longer there. Paul's body was missing. Even the stain from his disembowelment was no longer visible. The stench of cleaner overpowered the faint scent of blood in the air. Anyone who smelled it would claim it was from the cleaning her room had after Yor and Count Hutton were found. Their bodies were now gone, their heads removed from her mantle. An orchestrated crime scene to anyone who wanted her to be guilty. The outsider who didn't belong. The oddity who thought she could be one of them.

Dodslav followed her into the darkness. She shut the door.

"You aren't giving the map to them," Vilhelmina said as she navigated the darkness to her desk.

Dodslav tittered, "No, it would be wasted on the likes of them." He moved to the fireplace and began building it to receive a spark. Both he and Vilhelmina moved through the dark as if they belonged in it, as if it were the natural state for either of them to exist without light. Thunder rumbled outside. A storm was approaching. "They seek only money, believing that wealth accounts for anything in the universe." He sighed, the sound of heavy with disappointment. "If only we could all be so shallow, then perhaps we could all be happy."

He lit the flame, and it crackled to life, filling the room with warm, flickering light.

Vilhelmina opened her desk drawer, pretending to shuffle for something, but having found what she was looking for as soon as she approached her desk. The dagger was small enough to palm and hide but long enough to gut the artist, only to disarm, perhaps to produce a confession. Vengeance was not justice and while both were wanted within her, the need for justice was winning, so far.

"Do you know what kind of artist I am?" Dodslav ran a finger over the mantle where the heads were hours ago. He pulled his white glove up and saw a faint line of dust. He flicked it off. "I'm a sculptor."

There was a box on the mantle. Vilhelmina did not notice it when she walked in. Her mind was too focused on the task at hand; disable the Dokkalfar and obtain a confession for the court.

"I saw your statue in the library. Lady Chelus said you made it. Can you come hold this? The map is just under here."

"Yes, that was gold. A mundane material. I prefer to sculpt in more esoteric mediums." He pulled the box from the shelf and walked toward Vilhelmina.

She heard his steps. His careless swagger approached, but he stopped a few feet away. He was cocky, and Vilhelmina tried to knock him off his game. "Did you know the statue was to celebrate your slaughter? Your *kind's* slaughter? Driving you back from civilization, back into your holes?"

Dodslav answered after a moment, "Not all of us were slaughtered. This is the weakness of humanity. They are capricious and move on to the celebration of victory before the confirmation of their enemy's defeat." A metallic cranking began, then a bright chiming tune. "They are never thorough, never planning for the long game. They only kill and leave without consideration of how the dead can be—repurposed." He laughed.

Vilhelmina, confused, hiding the blade, faced Dodslav. He held an ornate wooden box with a brass handle protruding from the side. As he turned the handle, music notes came from the box in a slow building rhythm.

"When the mundane want my talents, I give them the mundane but for those of us with true potential..." His black eyes fixed on her blue eyes. She pulled the knife closer behind her leg, wondering if he suspected this attack. "You are so far beyond them, Little Viola."

Vilhelmina stiffened at that. Only one person, Yor, called her that and only his father knew. The cold dagger pressed against her leg, readying to strike, held still now at the name—Yor's name for her. The name she would have been known by after running away from this life. The name of the farmer's wife married to a farmer husband who looked like a noble that left his home years ago to start a new life.

"Yor's little Viola," Dodslav purred, his voice dripping with condescension. "Someone as special as you would never reveal the map, even if you knew where it was. Which you do not. And so, I applied my artistic talents to discover the answer, so I may proceed along my own special path. You see, when working with special people—people like you, Viola—I use special materials."

He cranked the music box faster; the notes accelerating into a discordant blur that stabbed at Vilhelmina's ears like a knife. "My craft, my special materials, are sculpting spirit and flesh. And that's how I got my answers. Sweet, sweet Viola. Little Viola, the farmer who became a warrior, only to wish to be a farmer again. The cold Valkyrie, who could not overcome her humanity and fell in love because she was loved. Who lost her future, her life, her joy, to something so uncaring as *duty*."

The final note whined, the box lid burst open, and a shrunken head sprang forth on a twisted spinal cord, rocking back and forth. As shriveled and mutilated as the head was, Vilhelmina recognized it instantly. Its eyes were gouged out, its mouth crudely stitched back together after being slashed open from lips to jawbone. The skin, brined and wrinkled, bore the unmistakable marks of torture.

The dagger slipped from her hand, clattering to the floor. The air grew thick, choking her. The head continued its relentless bobbing, back and forth, back and forth, like the inexorable swing of a bladed pendulum.

"Yor, where is the rest of the map?" Dodslav asked the jack-in-the-box.

"In Little Viola's dress," Yor's shrunken head hissed. His jaw clacked open but didn't move with each word. It simply fell open, exposing the blackened tongue and gray teeth. Dead flesh animated by this *artist*.

"And why would you put it there?" Dodslav asked as he stepped closer to Vilhelmina. She pressed herself against the desk. It squeaked as she pushed it against the wall, trying to escape the closeness, trying to escape the horrible visage of her love…of Yor.

"She would die before giving up the dress. It was my engagement proposal gift to her. I was going to ask her to marry me," Yor said, unaware of Vilhelmina's presence.

Dodslav pressed the box towards Vilhelmina. She couldn't escape it, pinned against the desk. "She would have said no. Rejected you. Rejected your advances."

Yor nodded as fervently as he did after exploding from the box. "I never found out. I love her. I hope she loved me."

"I do," Vilhelmina said.

Dodslav laughed and shoved the head back in the box, snapping the lid closed. "He can only hear me."

Vilhelmina reached for the box, but Dodslav snapped it away with a taunting giggle. She didn't fight for it or try again. She only stood there.

Yor knew she loved him, or at least suspected it. And what would have happened if she got to the basement before Dodslav? If Yor would have asked her, would she have said yes? Valkyries do not marry, except her mother and for that she was banished. But Vilhelmina, Yor's Little Viola, wasn't only Valkyrie, she was human too. Her humanity would have said yes.

"Now, let's get on with this. Dress off." Dodslav motioned lazily to her torn green gown. "But don't get too excited. I only want the map. You're too *Valkyrie* for me," he said. His last words were wreathed in disgust.

It was all of her that Yor loved. Her humanity and her Valkyrie. Chelus only saw her as human. Dodslav saw her as too Valkyrie. The nobles saw her as a mutt too unstable for their liking. Perhaps they were all right.

She turned around, presenting her back to Dodslav. The urge for justice molted from her. A fresh skin of delightful rage slid over her mind. She'd torture Dodslav until he undid whatever he did to Yor and then let her humanity, the sickest depths of her humanity, come out to play on this fiend. But he thought he was in control, and so she needed to throw him off, this time without distraction, without surprises.

"Untie me," she whimpered.

He traced his leather gloved finger down her spine and slowly lowered the loosened corset, exposing a soft muscular back. She arched her back as his fingers traced the lines left by her corset. Her breathing relaxed as Dodslav pulled the strings of the corset and lifted it from her. The shift underneath was sheer and loose. Her nipples peaked in the room's chill and Dodslav's aura. Vilhelmina covered herself and shied away from him.

"Can I cover up?" She said bashfully and pointed to a fox skin hanging on the wall. Another one of her father's trophies that he sent her like the wolf.

Dodslav laughed. "If you so desire. I just want the map." he examined the corset for the map to be inside but saw nothing.

He pulled the lining out and checked the silk. His attention was enthralled in the search, knowing he'd broken Vilhelmina's will to fight. She went to the fox skin. Pulled it down along with what was underneath. The fox wrapped around her body like a wide belt covering her breasts, exposing only the midriff of her toned stomach.

"Now the rest," Dodslav said as he tossed the corset aside, finding nothing.

With one hand, Vilhelmina untied the knots at her waist and stepped out of the dress, her eyes catching the tear she had ripped earlier in the night. The coarse, inflexible fibers jutted out—she thought they looked like papyrus. And now, her suspicions were confirmed. She kicked the dress toward Dodslav, who knelt to examine it, his fingers tracing the same threads Vilhelmina had just scrutinized.

He smiled, beginning to pull the dress apart, his attention fully absorbed. In that instant, Vilhelmina swung a spiked ball into his face, the metal crashing into him with brutal force. The crunching sound of whatever broke in his face should have made Vilhelmina sick, but instead, it filled her lust to break more things in the Dokkalfar.

The mace shattered Dodslav's mask, sending him crashing to the floor. Black blood and smoke gushed from his face as the mask crumbled away, revealing the thick brow, pointed ears, and onyx-black flesh of a Dokkalfar. He bared his long fangs at Vilhelmina, but she had lost none of her Valkyrie fight. Instead, she had found her human skills—deception and temptation.

His obsession with the map had blinded him to everything else, including the mace she had hidden beneath the fox skin.

Dodslav snarled and hissed. She screamed and swung again at his face. He rolled. The mace splintered the floor as it struck. Black smoke billowed out from under Dodslav's sleeves and pant legs. It stunk of burnt flesh. Vilhelmina screamed in delightful rage and swung, this time finding Dodslav's knee. His bones exploded where she struck with an echoing, crumbling pop that was only drowned out by his own pained screams.

More blood gushed from him. His leg twisted, boneless gravel, unable to shape his flesh. Crumpled on the floor, he hissed and snarled at Vilhelmina, who drew up the mace, ready to smash his other leg, immobilizing him before moving to his arms in a joyful mutilation of this horrid thing. This thing that killed Yor. That mutilated him. That…that could restore him?

Vilhelmina brought the mace down on his other leg, the spikes burying into the wooden flooring through his leg. The white pants were now black with blood soaking through his knees. She bore her teeth, grinning with full humanity on display, the passions he tempted now out in their glory.

Chelus burst through the door, shattering it into splinters that sprayed across the room. Dodslav turned to face her, Sergei, and all the nobles, his true form now fully exposed. Black smoke billowed from his onyx skin, and black blood drooled from his long fangs.

Gasps filled the room as even Chelus staggered back, recoiling at the sight of the enemy of their civilized world—the tempter, humanity's poison, the Dokkalfar.

Dodslav hissed at them, driving the nobles away from the door, but Chelus did not retreat. She strode in to apprehend the dark elf. All doubt of guilt removed now that his true nature was exposed.

A knot popped in the fireplace, drawing Vilhelmina's eye. The axe, the one placed in her room earlier to stage Yor's murder, was still there. Its steel glowed orange from the heat. The handle, still cool, fit nicely in her hand as she ripped it from the flame and pressed the searing blade against Dodslav's cheek. Flesh sizzled, filling the air with the stench of moldy meat. Vilhelmina giggled—one of those delightful, little-girl giggles he had tried to coax from her earlier, but this one was venomous. Spittle pooled at the corners of her mouth as her smile stretched wider and wider, matching his screams as they grew louder and louder.

"Now—" she snarled, but before she could demand he restore Yor, black smoke thickened around Dodslav. Surprise overtook his fear. Then he scrambled for the dress, pulling himself across the floor without the help of his legs. Vilhelmina spun and drove the axe into the dress, ripping it in half between her and Dodslav. The smoke bloomed and then dissipated, taking Dodslav with it. Yet before he disappeared, Vilhelmina—little Viola, saw Dodslav's horrified face staring at her, knowing she was going to be the death of him.

And one day, long from today, he'll be right.

After he vanished, Vilhelmina held up the remains of the dress, seeing part of a map protruding from the matting between the silk and insulation. She pulled it out. On it was a tower hidden in a coiling path beyond an unnamed mountain ridge. Under the tower, written in script, was the label *The Tower of Ascension*.

Chelus reached her and examined the floor where Dodslav had been. There was no trap door. It was as if the smoke devoured him. Both Chelus and Vilhelmina knew this meant the work of a sorcerer, much more powerful than a Seer.

The younger Valkyrie panted, every nerve quivering with the hunger to kill, the rage, the loss, the failure, the hope. Yor was gone, but could he come back? Could Dodslav undo the horror he did? Where did he go?

Her Valkyrie mind sharpened, took control. The map. That was where he was going. She lifted it to Chelus, who examined it.

But Chelus only shook her head, confused and uncertain. "It's not real."

Vilhelmina's hands could not hold the paper anymore. They shook too hard. It floated out of her grip as the Valkyrie within lost her hold on Vilhelmina's emotions.

Sergei ran into the room, pushing through the fleeing nobles in the hallway. The two Valkyrie guards followed, and all three were shocked to stillness when they saw Chelus' expression.

"Where did Yor find this?" Chelus' voice quivered as she watched the hypnotic flames dancing in the fireplace. Her mind drifted far from this room to a nightmare that was unfolding behind her eyes. The nightmare of what this map meant, and where it led.

Vilhelmina scrambled over the floor, searching for the jack-in-the-box. Maybe a mage in the Valkyrie Order could help him. They could restore him. She could have the life he offered, she could say yes to his proposal. But she couldn't find it. Dodslav took him. Yor was gone.

She ran to Sergei, throwing herself into his arms. He embraced her, feeling the quaking sorrow that consumed her. All control over her humanity was lost. She sobbed into his chest, but Chelus quickly pulled her back.

"Where did Yor find this?" Chelus demanded, her voice sharp. She pointed to the map but dare not pick it up from the floor.

"It was in my dress!" Vilhelmina screamed, shoving the older Valkyrie. Chelus didn't budge, her expression unyielding.

Vilhelmina turned back to Sergei, burying her face in his chest as another scream tore from her throat. He held her tightly as they sank to the floor together, her sobs echoing through the room.

"What is it, Lady Chelus?" One of the Valkyrie guards asked. His voice shook, but not as hard as Chelus's. He didn't know the absolute nightmare unleashed.

"The location of the Lazarus Spiral." Chelus gasped. "A myth." But she didn't believe that. "Who would be so mad?" She looked at Vilhelmina, saw the young woman was inconsolable, and kept her questions to herself. Only one came out and she didn't know if she wanted the answer because what it would mean could destroy everything. "Why do they want the Lazarus Spiral?"

However, she knew there was only one reason anyone would seek the Spiral. To control every realm, every person, every decision, forevermore.

# XIV

Dodslav materialized on the floor of the sorcerer's library. The soft rustle of old pages turning filled the silence, a silence so thick now that he'd been ripped from the chaos of battle.

"Did you recover the map?" The man at the desk asked. He was reading an ancient tome thicker than all the other tomes on the desk. All the books were massive, leather, and older than Dodslav or even Lady Chelus. The man's fingers were stained black, as if burnt long ago. The thick beads around his neck clacked as he rocked back and forth, the stone spiral in the center tapping against the wooden desk with a rhythmic clatter.

Dodslav held up the part of the map he had retrieved for the sorcerer to see. "Part of it. Two-thirds now with only the last piece missing," he climbed to his feet, forgetting his broken knees. He collapsed to the floor with a yelp.

The man at the desk chuckled.

"This is enough. I know where the tower is based on this." Dodslav held up the map. "It is within the Fallen Mountains."

The man chuckled again at the oversimplification. "The Fallen Mountains are an infinite maze for those wandering without direction. Part of the map is not sufficient," he shook his head and caressed a crumbled mass of black stone on his desk. The mound of rubble appeared to be once a large stone, but now provided no value other than as a reminder of whatever it once was. "I would have thought you more capable with all the boasting you have done." A black dog-like creature with glowing green eyes and long ears came to the man at the desk. It snarled at Dodslav as the man pet the beast. He took a deep sigh and turned the page again, his eyes having never left the book. "No matter. I will clean up this mess."

"There were Valkyries," Dodslav said with a sharp tone. The man closed his book at that with a dust spitting pop.

"Excuses?" The man stood. His green-eyed pet stalked over to Dodslav. "I found you in ruins. Dying in a conquered city. I gave you life. I gave you purpose. I gave you a place to perform your *art*." The last word must have tasted spoiled to the man, judging by the way he said it. "And your reason for failure is Valkyries? You fear them more than me?"

"No," Dodslav corrected quickly. "No. They were formidable, but I shall not fail again. I have their weakness close to hand." Dodslav glanced at the jack-in-the-box by his foot. "The map will be yours, Master Adams. Send me not from your sight. I will succeed."

"Artists..." the sorcerer, Ely Adams, sighed. He leaned back and reopened his book. Raising his fingers, he tensed them, plucking at the air as though playing an invisible harp. Warmth flooded Dodslav's knees as the pain evaporated. "Do not fail. Go."

Dodslav crawled to his feet, took the map to the sorcerer, and left the library for his art studio. Downstairs, in the mansion's basement, Dodslav placed the jack-in-the-box on one of the wooden shelves. He smiled at it and cranked the brass handle until Yor popped out with his fast nod.

"You studied the map?" Dodslav asked. "And you know the path through the Fallen Mountains?"

Yor nodded, but Dodslav wasn't sure if it was his spinal cord spring or the answer to his question.

"I can restore you to your body. Return you to your dear Little Viola if you tell me the path through the mountains."

"You will go back on your word," Yor wheezed.

"Honor-bound promise I will not." Even among the Dokkalfar, an honor-bound promise meant something. "I met her tonight. She would have said yes to your proposal. Don't you want to hear that?"

"Yes," Yor answered. "I can tell you the way."

"Not now," Dodslav looked upstairs. There was no sign of the sorcerer, but the man's senses were preternatural. "I have some things to attend to first." Dodslav closed the box and smiled as he looked up the stairs toward the library. He thought to himself, daring not to speak yet, wondering if even his thoughts were safe from the sorcerer. *I have not survived war and extermination to serve a master. And with the Spiral in hand, I will be the master. Master of all.*

Dodslav smiled as he shed his white clothes for a black cloak. He relaxed and allowed his smoke to billow from his naked onyx body in dense clouds around him. In the corner, he had the remains of Count Hutton. Flesh and spirit screaming as he stretched them, twisted them, and chiseled them into an abstract swirl. While Count Hutton screamed in agony, Dodslav thought about the Lazarus Spiral and what he'd make with the flesh and spirit of all things, in all realms.

# INVENTORY ITEM 11

Item Number: 11

Components:

Jack-in-the-box

Collection: Public

This one is a strange find. I found it at the Maryland Fair Ground Toy Expo. Normally, places like that do not deal with toys that could kill their owners, but this vendor, he said his name was Conroy Miller, had a box of toys he labeled oddities. That, of course, took me back to the old days, and I didn't take it seriously until he put on leather gloves before reaching into the box.

When he produced this jack-in-the-box, he warned me not to open it. Conroy said the head within lost the love of its life and is eternally seeking her. I said that wasn't too bad, but he said that the head never stops talking about her and sobs so horribly that you will want to jump out of a window.

I asked if Conroy ever listened to whatever was in the box, and he said he had. He didn't believe the story and so he cranked the box and released the head. The shrunken head within demanded he search for his long-lost flower, the love of his life who will marry him. The head, claiming to be "Viceroy Yor", who I searched for but found nothing, said he was murdered on the night he planned to propose to his love. Now, he would never know her answer, but he hoped it would be yes. Tragic, but then, Conroy said something very interesting…he said the head also claimed his love had a map to the greatest treasure in existence. That with this treasure, you can be anything, have anything, but all the head wants is his love.

Conroy sought the treasure but got to a point where the head's tears and crying about his lost love was so depressing, he had to stop searching or he'd end up killing himself in deep depression from this head's hopeless longing.

Once I held the jack-in-the-box with my own gloves, I felt its power. This toy was perfect for my collection. The more powerful an object is, the more infused with spiritual energy, the heavier it is, like the ethereal spirit takes on a very real weight. Also, I feel the power as a vibrating warble, like the time I accidentally touched the connectors for a neon tube while plugging it in. That pulsing shock is like what I feel when I hold these objects, or when I get too close to them. When the force makes me physically shake, I know it's an excellent find, and this one did that. Holding the box, my whole body quaked. I sat it down on the sales table to complete our transaction. Fortunately, I had a trade in my car packaged and ready to go.

I'm tempted to open it. To learn about this treasure, but I'm just growing my collection. Going on a treasure hunt would be a distraction. If I found it, could I ask for Drew back? Is that in the treasure's power? Funny how just a few years ago I would have laughed at such talk, but now, this is my daily life.

New haunted items are coming in, each with a crazy story to match this one. Some are phonies, but when I don't feel anything from the object, I just walk away. More often than not, the trades are real and perhaps I'll have enough for Dodslav soon.

Part of me would love to hear the story. I'm a sucker for a story, especially about a haunted object like this. Poor shrunken head lost the love of his life and perhaps the demon Dodslav can help him when I hand this jack-in-the-box over. With what he did to Drew, how the demon reshaped his body, maybe Dodslav can give this jack-in-the-box a new body?

I don't get the impression the demon is helpful. But I could be wrong. Maybe he has a soft spot for lovers?

# ONE

"This will be perfect," Carter muttered, picking up the toy and barely noticing the sharp static shock that jumped from it to his fingers.

It was a plastic frog, roughly the size of a large book. A dial embedded in its stomach was surrounded by cartoon images of farm animals. The frog's white plastic eyes stared lifelessly at Carter, half-closed in a dazed expression. Its left arm was raised as if to wave hello.

Carter pulled the arm down, and the dial spun. The frog's eyes swayed side to side, searching aimlessly, as if trying to find something that wasn't there. As the dial slowed, so did the eyes, both coming to a rusty, jittery stop on a picture of music notes.

The frog croaked, emitting a warped, dying tune like a rotten music box. Time and decay had stolen any joy that might once have lived in the song.

"This is perfect." Carter held up the frog to his mom. "Dad will love this," he said and turned the toy over for a price tag, but didn't see one. None of the toys had price tags. And there wasn't anyone to pay either, just an old lady screaming at people, but Carter didn't think she worked at the yard sale.

Carter's mom was glaring at a group of ladies staring at her son. They could have been his grandmothers, far too old to be shamelessly drooling over a teenage farm boy. She waved them away with a sharp gesture, then recoiled when she saw what Carter was holding.

"Oh, that's ugly," she muttered with amusement. "Your dad will love it."

Carter held up the plastic frog, and his mom took it from him, examining it with a mixture of distaste and curiosity. "I think that's one of those old Spin & Speak toys," she said, turning it over in her hands. "I bet he'll put this god-awful thing right on his shelf," she sighed, but a smile crept onto her face.

"It's not that ugly," Carter laughed. He flicked his golden hair out of his eyes and his mom heard an old lady grunt in approval. "Could be uglier. Like that thing," he pointed to a worn-out stuffed elephant with an eye patch. It was well loved once, but now it looked diseased with the patches of missing fur. "Do we just leave the money?"

"No price?" Mom frowned as she searched the frog. "I guess it's pay-what-you-will." She shrugged and took a ten-dollar-bill out of her purse, looking at Carter to confirm that was enough.

He nodded, but held up his hand. "Let me get it for dad?" As he pulled out his own money, a lighter fell from his pocket.

Mom shook her head. "You're still carrying that around?"

Carter smiled, pride glowing in his eyes. "Dad gave it to me," he said. "My first piece of farm equipment from my dad."

"Just make sure it's only for farming." His mom smirked and winked. Carter blushed, ready to stammer out a promise that farming was all it would be used for—but his mind flashed to a video he'd seen online. It said a man should always carry a lighter to light a cigarette for a lady.

He didn't know anyone who smoked, but he'd seen enough old movies where everyone did. Did Nadia smoke? She was awesome and popular hanging out with those gamer, streamer kids. He meant to ask if she was going to homecoming last week, but chickened out. Maybe she'd ask him, and they'd be out at a nice fancy dinner at like Red Lobster and she'd ask for a light and he'd be ready. But how likely is it she'd ask him to homecoming? Or he could afford to buy her dinner at Red Lobster? Did she even know he existed? Besides, that wasn't what this farm tool was for.

Carter moved to the money jar, relieved to get away from his mom, and stuffed the ten-dollar bill inside. The crazy old lady had left, and the jar was unguarded. There wasn't much in it, and he briefly considered taking it to the house. Maybe someone was inside?

He saw movement behind the glass of the front door—a child, maybe. But when the kid noticed Carter watching, it jerked away from the window with stiff, unnatural movements. Was it playing a game? Pretending to be a zombie or monster?

Carter shrugged, assuming an adult must be inside, keeping an eye on things. Yet something about the empty yard unsettled him, the stillness nagging at the back of his mind. The silent dark house, the kid watching from the door, all gave him the clear signal: stay away.

"Another farm toy for the collection." Carter said with a triumphant smile, turning away from the house as he took the frog from his mom. He gave it a shake, hoping to make its eyes swing side to side again, but this time, they stayed locked on him. The frog's lifeless plastic smile glistened under the midday sun, and for a moment, Carter had the eerie feeling that the toy held a secret—a secret it wasn't ready to share.

His mom, too distracted by the old women ogling her son, ignored the warning that bubbled up from her gut. Deep down, she knew something wasn't right, but she pushed the thought aside. "He's seventeen," she muttered to one woman, her voice laced with annoyance. The woman's hair was tinted blue, her wrinkles taut against the Botox swelling in her face. Blue Hair scoffed, dismissing the comment with a shrug, and continued browsing through the toy section.

To Carter, the frog was the perfect goofy thing to take his dad's mind off the bills. Who knows, it could be worth something online?

As they climbed into their old station wagon, Carter felt a flicker of hope—maybe this weird little toy was exactly what they needed to turn their bad luck around.

In one aspect, he was right. The frog would change their fortunes, only, not for the better.

# TWO

Forgotten Baggage Farm was just a few short miles from town. Carter always enjoyed the drive home—where the busy streets gave way to clear roads, open fields, and quiet. He loved living close enough to town to grab something if needed, but far enough away that they never heard anyone else around.

Fall had just settled over the town, but nowhere was it more noticeable than on Carter's family farm. Shiny red orbs peeked through the still-green leaves of the apple trees that lined the road. The scent of those apples hung thick in the air, so dense it made your mouth water just driving by. Carter loved picking season—the trees were beautiful, and the air tasted like fall.

The vibrant reds and greens of the orchard were far more pleasant to him than the brown, viny coils and garish oranges of the pumpkin patch. Most people thought pumpkins didn't smell like anything, but Carter knew better. To him, they reeked of rot—of the end of fall and the consequences of the harvest. Ever since the pumpkins had ruined the farm and destroyed his future, that stench had lingered in a toxic cloud over everything.

Carter gripped the lighter in his pocket, the only tool that had saved them from the farm's complete destruction. One blighted pumpkin had nearly infected everything, bringing with it bills and hushed discussions about selling the farm, about moving. But for now, those talks were pushed aside as they pulled up the long driveway to the white farmhouse.

Thinking of dad, how he'd love this hideous frog, lifted Carter's mood with excitement—he had good news for once and another trinket to add to dad's farm toy collection.

The toy was weird, but his dad liked weird things and had always had a soft spot for the outcasts. Without thinking, Carter pulled the frog's arm down again as the car came to a stop. Its eyes bounced around wildly as he climbed out, the spinner on its belly erratically whirring to life.

As he passed the barn, the frog's eyes suddenly stopped, locking onto one of the hogs in the pen. The spinner froze abruptly, and the toy's croaking voice box rasped, "Pig."

Carter thought nothing of it and continued inside.

Mom got out of the car and started the long walk up the driveway to the mailbox, oblivious to the pig's strange behavior. It didn't squeal or grunt—it simply toppled over into the mud with a quiet squelch. Its legs locked stiff, eyes staring blankly ahead. White foam pooled around its mouth as thick yellow fluid bubbled from its eyelids, oozing over its face. The fluids didn't drip to the ground; instead, they clung to the pig's skin, crawling over its flesh like a living coat.

One leg kicked weakly, a silent, feeble struggle against the transformation taking hold. Moments later, the pig lurched upright, moving with the drunken sway of something half-alive.

The other pigs in the pen squealed in panic, racing to the back

corner, crowding one another in fear. One brave pig lunged toward
the staggering creature, but froze when the sick pig tried to squeal—
only a hiss escaped. The sound sent the others into a frenzy, thrashing
against the pen in a desperate attempt to flee.

Suddenly, the sick pig collapsed onto another, biting into its
leg. The victim screeched in agony as the infected pig tore flesh and
muscle from its body, devouring it alive.

The rest of the pigs huddled in terror, watching helplessly as two
more pigs now shambled about, infected and hungry. The sickness
was spreading.

# THREE

Dad sat in the office, catching up on paperwork. Three things were always present in that room: a cup of cold coffee, Metallica playing loud enough to drown out any questions about the future, and Dad's worried face. His brow furrowed as he flipped through bills and receipts, the weight of the farm pressing down on him.

The newest addition to the office was a shelf lined with old farm toys. Once, that shelf had displayed a collection of Star Wars spaceships, but they'd been auctioned off on eBay a while ago, a small sacrifice to ease the bills. Now, it held rusted tractors, faded plastic animals, and weathered tools—a small shrine to a time when things seemed simpler.

"Hey dad, check this out." Carter didn't stop at the door, he just came in, turned the music off, and shoved the frog between his dad's face and the final notice from the feed provider. "Pull the arm."

Dad put down his pen and gave Carter a quiet smile, a silent thank you for the much-needed distraction. He reached for the frog, pulling down its arm. The spinner whirred to life, and the eyes flicked side to side, briefly pausing as they landed on his face.

The moment stretched longer than it should have, as if the frog was staring back at him—or perhaps deciding what horrible thing it wanted to do next with its wide, unblinking grin. But then, the eyes continued their hypnotic swaying, as if they never stopped, as if the frog wasn't thinking anything in that too long pause, and maybe it never paused at all.

The spinner slowed, coming to a halt on a picture of music notes. The frog's voice box rasped to life, and a haunting, dying melody wheezed from its body—a song that, with fresh batteries, might have been cheerful but now dragged out in a slow, groaning whine.

"Well, that sounds like fun." Dad turned the device over. "Needs new batteries." The discordant music vibrated in the air, leaving them both feeling queasy but neither saying anything about it. The tune lingered longer than Carter expected, not ceasing abruptly but fading away, as if the frog, lost in a haze, had forgotten its song and slipped into a lost memory.

Jetson, Carter's black Lab-Newfoundland mix, ran into the office with them on high alert. He passed by Carter and sniffed at the frog, whimpered, sneezed hard, and went to the window. The pig pen was visible out the window, but Carter and his dad didn't notice the commotion in the field as pigs tried to flee the growing numbers of the infected. Jetson whined, high and long at the window.

"We'll go out in a minute." Carter tussled the dog's head. "I'll get some fresh batteries," Carter said. He waved for his dad to follow. "Take a break and help me."

Dad needed a break from the endless paperwork. The office had become a necessary evil since the blight, a place to fight for the farm's survival after the fire had done its job—killing the disease but leaving behind the aftermath of a year's lost crops. Now, the paperwork was the only thing that could fix what was left.

Sometimes Carter wished the door would just stay locked, that his dad would lose the key, and they could all go back to having just enough.

Sure, other kids had flashy new cars when they started driving, and a fancy suit for prom might've been nice last year—not that he went. But Carter didn't need any of that. He had something none of those kids had: a farm that had been in his family for three generations. That past wasn't just history—it was his future.

He didn't need college or a job in some city. His future was as clear as the evening sky outside. The farm was his destiny, just as it had been his dad's, his granddad's, and his great granddad's before him.

The two went out into the kitchen and searched the junk drawer for fresh batteries.

"What kind do we need?" Carter asked.

"Well," Dad said, inspecting the frog again. "I don't see a battery compartment." He flipped it over. "You know, the old version of this had a pull string. They didn't use batteries. Maybe it works like that?"

While they searched for batteries and a place to put them, Carter asked, "How's the bills looking?"

To his credit, dad didn't betray the truth in his answer, "I think things are working out. Pumpkins are moving quick and apple picking weekends are right around the corner. That new parking area you helped make will get more people from town picking their own apples." Dad shrugged. "I think we're making it through."

Carter wanted to gripe about the pumpkins and how their blight caused all these bills, but instead he stayed positive, nodded, "We should host a pumpkin carving event or something near Halloween," he said, bobbing his head. "If we charged a few bucks a ticket, gave them a pumpkin, and set up a carving area, we could make a couple hundred bucks."

Even at 17, hundreds of dollars still seemed like a lot, but when you're an adult with bills, hundreds of dollars don't cover the feed bill for a week. Dad patted his son's shoulder and said, "Such a businessman. We'll be in excellent hands when you take over." Squeezing gently, "Not that that's anytime soon. I ain't that old yet."

They both laughed for different reasons. Carter thought it was a funny joke, but his dad could only laugh away the idea that time was running out. What would they do without the farm? That's where things were heading. But even through these dark thoughts, he couldn't stop smiling at Carter. It wasn't Carter's desire to keep the farm that made him so proud of his boy. It was the clarity of vision his son had for the future. The certainty that the farm was safe, and the future was foretold. Carter was the only one with that confidence.

Their thoughts were interrupted by a heavy thud against the front door. Both men jumped, exchanging a glance as they waited for a knock or the doorbell—maybe it was a delivery?

But delivery people didn't just thump against the door like that. They knocked, banged, or rang the bell. This was different. And was that… panting?

"Hello?" Carter called out, his voice cutting through the stillness.

No answer.

There was no knock, no response—only the slow scrape of something sliding down the door, settling onto the porch.

"I'll go see," Carter said and closed the kitchen drawer. Jetson wailed a loud whine and then let loose a sharp bark towards the door. "Easy." Carter didn't need to stoop to pet the large dog. Its soft hair bristled over the dog's thick neck and even on its head, Carter could feel the frantic pulse and racing heart of the animal. "Easy…"

On the porch, Mom lay twitching, her eyes wide and blank, staring up at the sky. Foam frothed around her lips, building over her face in curling mounds. Carter caught sight of her through the narrow windows flanking the door. Panic surged through him. He screamed for his dad.

Jetson's barking grew louder, the sharp cracks of his yelps splitting the air like a whip. Each bark felt like a warning—driving Carter toward his mom, or maybe urging him to close the door, to protect them from whatever was coming. But humans rarely heeded the wisdom of dogs.

Carter dropped to his knees, pulling his mother into his lap, ignoring the primal sense that something terrible was about to happen.

"Mom!?"

Her eyes rolled back in her head. White foam pumped from her straining throat. Thick yellow tears congealed on her cheeks and oozed into the crow's feet around her eyes. If she was trying to talk, Carter couldn't tell. "Mom!"

"Camille!" Dad went to help Carter bring his mom inside. Jetson rushed to the door, barking louder, guarding the entryway. "Get out the way, Jetson!" The two carried her to the couch. In their hurry, they left the door open and after Jetson saw there was no use warning Carter, he returned to stand sentinel at the front door. A low growl emanated from the dog in thick warning of the dangers shambling outside.

# FOUR

"Camille!" Dad screamed. "Call 911!"

Carter pulled his cell phone out and held the 9 until the operator came on.

"911. State your emergency."

"My mom's having a seizure or something." Carter took a breath and pushed the panic out of his head as if the need to keep his mom alive was a snow plow opening the road for action. "She was on the front porch. She's foaming at the mouth, and there's something in her eyes. I think she's having a seizure." Having never seen someone have a real seizure, Carter relied on the only reference he had: movies.

She was twitching like he'd seen in the movies. Quick, jerky motions, blank stares and dazed drooling.

"Where are you and your mother now?"

Carter told the lady on the phone his address and knew it wouldn't take long to get there from town, assuming the EMTs were at the firehouse.

"What is your name?"

"Carter Gilquist. My dad is here too. Donald Gilquist. We brought my mom into the living room."

"I have notified EMTs and they are on route. Have you cleared the area around your mother?"

"She's on the couch."

"Okay, move everything away from the couch and place her on the floor, if possible. Do not put anything in her mouth."

"Dad, we need to move her to the floor." Carter shoved the coffee table over and pushed the loveseat away from the couch. They moved it easily with adrenaline fueled farm muscles. The two men gently placed Camille on the floor.

"We moved her." Carter shouted into the phone.

"Roll her to her side if possible." The operator responded calmly but firm. Her voice smoothed the nervous edges from Carter. This woman was in control. She knew what to do and was directing the situation. The EMTs were coming and with them the help mom needed to be okay. Dad rolled mom over.

Carter put the phone on speaker so they could both hear, then asked, "Is she going to be okay?"

"EMTs are on their way. For now, I need to know when the seizure ends. Is she still having a seizure?"

"Yes," Donald answered.

"Okay, stay with her and—" the rest was muted by Jetson's ravenous barking. Under the sharp snapping sound was a baritone growl that ripped Carter's and Donald's attention from their emergency. Even the 911 operator stopped talking as Jetson's barking turned ferocious.

Carter ran to him. The dog was locked, tense, ready to kill, and didn't stop barking. Standing in a line across the front yard were six pigs, bleeding, eyes closed with the yellow goop and white crust caked around their snout. They did not move at the dog's aggression, only swayed and staggered toward the house.

"Dad?" Carter called.

"What's happening?" The 911 operator asked, her calm breaking and barely audible over Jetson's warning to the pigs.

"Dad!?"

Dad ran to Carter. While they looked out the front door at the approaching pigs, they didn't see mom stop twitching. The foam stopped coming, and she laid motionless on the living room carpet. Her fingers shocked open then just as quickly as they opened, they locked into mangled claws.

"What's wrong with them?" Carter asked the obvious.

"How'd they get out?" Dad asked.

"Hello!?" the operator shouted. "Mr. Gilquist? Carter? Are you there? Hello!? Is your mom still having a seizure? What's going on!?"

Dad turned to mom, Carter following a moment later. She was still. Carter noticed the bite in her hand. The pigs are sick and one of them bit mom and now she's sick. He ran to the phone and picked it up.

"Operator, I think my mom was bitten by our pigs. They're sick or something," Carter shouted over the barking. Jetson was getting raw now and his barks took on a gasping high pitched siren sound, but the pigs were not deterred.

"What's happening? Why's the dog barking like that?" The operator screamed, but Carter could only make out every other word.

"Carter, something's wrong!" Dad shouted and pulled Jetson back from the front door. The dog lunged to escape his grasp but dad slammed the door. "Something's wrong with the pigs!"

"I know," Carter said. Jetson kept barking. "She's not seizing anymore," he said to the operator.

"Say again!" the operator shouted. "I can't hear you. Say again!"

"The seizure has ended!"

Shattering glass cut through the barking and screaming. One pig burst through a window. Dad grabbed the iron shovel from the fireplace and swung it hard into the pig's face. Yellow goop splashed off the creature and sprayed the wall. It didn't yelp or squeal, only silently slunk over.

Jetson ran for the backdoor.

"They're coming in!" Dad said.

"What's happening!?" the operator screamed, but Carter dropped the phone as the pig stood back up and another pig tumbled into the house behind the first.

"Get the gun upstairs," Dad said, swinging again at the pigs. The echo of each blow reverberated through the house, but it didn't stop the animals. Carter could hear their skulls cracking like gravel under the force of his father's hits, yet the pigs kept coming.

"Hello!?" the operator shouted. "Help is on the way! Hello!?"

The voice died when Carter stomped on the phone as he ran upstairs. The gun was in the bedroom safe and the bullets were in the closet. He took a .22 rifle and a .38 Special handgun. The .22 was beside the shotgun, but when his dad had to put down a pig a few years ago, he used a .22.

Downstairs, Carter heard his dad shouting to scare the pigs, but they kept coming. He knew because more windows were breaking. Carter loaded the guns, threw more bullets in an ammo bag, and ran downstairs.

His dad had been backed against the couch where Mom had been lying. But now, the floor in front of it was empty. Mom was on her feet, staggering toward the kitchen in a drunken, jerking gait.

"Mom!" Carter screamed.

Dad couldn't hear him over the sickening sound of the shovel squelching into the pigs' boneless faces.

Mom didn't stop. She made her way to the kitchen counter, her movements disjointed and picked up the frog toy. She turned, facing Carter on the stairs. Her eyes were sealed shut with thick yellow pus, and crystalline foam clung to her mouth. The wound on her hand wept black sludge.

"Dad!" Carter yelled again, pointing at her, but his father didn't react—too caught up in his desperate battle with the pigs that kept lunging through his defenses. It wasn't until Dad tripped over the couch and fell onto it that he noticed Mom was missing.

She pulled the frog's arm, and the eyes flicked from side to side as the dial spun on its belly. The eyes stopped abruptly, locking onto their target just as the dial clicked into place.

"Farmer," croaked the frog in its eerie voice.

Dad screamed as an invisible force slammed into his face, knocking him to the floor. The pigs staggered back, giving him the space needed for his transformation. White foam erupted from his mouth, and yellow tears flooded from his eyes, thickening into the same sludge that had sealed the pigs' eyes—now spreading over Carter's mom's face.

Carter didn't say a word. He couldn't. The pigs turned away from his dad and began marching toward him.

With the gun in his hands, Carter bolted back upstairs.

# FIVE

"Help is coming," Carter said. The EMTs would be arriving soon. How long had it been since they were on the phone with the 911 operator?

Downstairs, the pigs were trying to climb the stairs, but after a few creaking steps, they tumbled down.

What was happening with mom and dad down there? Carter paced in his parent's room with the gun safe, thinking this was the best place to be cornered if anywhere. There was a lattice out of one window to the ground, but Carter didn't think that would hold his weight.

Like all the rooms in the farmhouse, this one was large, spacious and white. His mom wanted everything open and bright, which made things easier to clean from her perspective. For now, Carter appreciated the space to walk in his thoughts.

What was going on? Dad thought the pigs made mom sick, but it was that frog thing that did whatever happened to dad. And dad looked just like the pigs. Did the frog infect the pigs? Then the pigs infected mom?

Downstairs, the front door opened. Carter went to the windows and looked out over the porch to see what was happening.

His mom and dad walked out from the porch, followed by the line of pigs. They went to the stable. His mom held the frog toy over her head like it was the Ten Commandments coming down the mountain. Their steps were even and lifeless, as if windup toys, mechanically going about their business.

From within the stable, the horses neighed and kicked at the fence. Mom lowered the frog, pulled the arm, and quickly the toy croaked, "Horse."

As the word finished, the horses stopped kicking and fighting, tumbling over and seizing just like his mom, then his dad, was doing. The procession of Carter's parents and pigs didn't wait for the horses to finish their transformation. They turned and went to the coup. As they did, Carter saw their swollen, now melted faces with a dense mask of the mucus substance coming from their eyes. Their mouths were sealed, as were their eyes, but Carter knew they saw him.

"What the hell?" Carter moaned. Could they breathe through that crust? Would it come off? Would their face come off with it? The guns in Carter's hands rattled as he shook. His mouth was dry as more questions poured through him, but only one stuck…could they be cured? And that one made him want to scream in horror as the answer came to him: No. How could you cure the yellow crust casing their face, the black sludge dripping from his mom's hand as if pumped out of her body? No, these changes weren't cured. They were how his parents would die.

Sirens were getting closer. Police and ambulance. He wanted to be relieved, but now, he wasn't sure EMTs could help. When the horses got up and staggered to the fence, his dad opened. He thought they all, from pigs to parents to horses, looked like zombies.

But Carter hoped there was a cure and if there was, it was something to do with the frog. It caused these problems, it could solve them. What was happening? Some kind of sound that made things go crazy? He'd heard on the news of a weapon in Cuba that made people really sick after they heard a strange noise. His mom played the frog, and the horses fell. The same thing happened with his dad. How was the frog making everyone sick and why wasn't he infected yet?

In the coupe, the chickens screamed but succumbed after Carter heard the frog said, "Chicken."

The ambulance turned sharply into the driveway, followed closely by a police car. Carter hurried out of the room and rushed downstairs, the .22 slung over his shoulder, the .38 holstered at his belt. He stopped at the front door just as the ambulance skidded to a halt, gravel spraying as the police car slid in beside it.

Officer Morris was the first to step out.

"Officer Morris! It's Carter Gilquist!" Carter shouted, raising his hands, the guns held high. "I've got Dad's .22 and .38. I need help!"

Morris immediately drew his own gun. He knew Carter—and if the boy was carrying his dad's firearms, something was seriously wrong. "What's goin' on?" he demanded.

"I don't know," Carter replied, stepping forward cautiously, hands still raised. "They're sick, or something."

"Who?" Morris asked, eyes narrowing.

Two EMTs jumped out of the ambulance. One was short and chubby, the other gaunt and pale like a vampire. Carter didn't recognize either of them. Without hesitation, they both sprinted toward the front door.

"Where's the patient!?" the vampire yelled. Carter looked at the coupe, but they would have left there by now.

"I'm not sure. They were just in the coupe."

"I thought they were in the house?" The short one said. "Operator said she was in the house."

"No, she got up and got out," Carter said. "They're sick or something. I don't know."

"Slow down," the short one said. "We were told there was a woman having seizures. Where's she now?"

"No, it's not just her. There's something going on." Carter's voice wavered, unable to fully tell the horror unfolding in his home. He couldn't bring himself to say it—couldn't call them zombies. But whatever it was, they were infected with something monstrous, their faces twisted into grotesque masks of sickness, like a nightmare had vomited into their eyes.

"It's an infection of… something," he managed, his words failing him.

"Luis, get the biohazard packs from the back," the short one said. Luis, the man Carter thought of as Vampire, ran around to the back of the ambulance.

An uneven, disjointed galloping was getting closer.

"You hear that?" He shouldered his rifle and went to the sound. It was coming from behind the ambulance. Officer Morris followed and as they came around the corner, they saw the zombie horse rear up and stomp Luis's head into the ambulance door. The man's boney head exploded against the steel door and sprayed Morris and Carter with chunky dark red gore.

Luis dropped.

The horse reared up again. Morris fired. Carter followed, dropping to a knee, shooting up into the horse's center mass.

"What the shit!" Morris screamed as he shot. "What the shit, man!"

The horse staggered back from the shots, part of its face evaporated from Morris's shot finding its mark. But it didn't fall. Only ran off towards the barn. A trail of black sludge from where they hit the beast led to where the horse had escaped.

Carter reloaded as the short EMT came around the ambulance and saw his partner's headless body.

"Luis!" the short EMT shouted and grabbed his radio. "We need backup! Backup!"

"No backup," the frog's croaking voice crackled through the ambulance's radio speaker. The three men froze, their eyes slowly turning toward the source of the sound. "We have enough now."

Static swallowed the message, buzzing like a broken siren. The short EMT yelped, stumbling back.

Morris lunged forward, quickly shutting off the radio, his hand shaking. Carter instinctively backed away from the ambulance, dread creeping into his veins.

Officer Morris rushed to his police car, yanking the radio. The same heavy static blasted through. He cursed, throwing the radio down as he jumped out of the car, but not before a chicken tumbled out after him, pecking wildly at his hand.

Morris screamed, rolling away as he clutched his hand. The chicken was relentless in its attack pecking at him, slicing long slashes over the back of his hand.

"Sonuva—" but before he could finish, he collapsed and started seizing.

# SIX

The EMT ran to him, but Carter grabbed the short man's arm and shouted. "No! We have to get out of here!"

"We have to help him!" The EMT shouted back. Neither of them noticed the pigs coming up the driveway.

The EMT yanked himself away from Carter, rushing over to Morris. More chickens were emerging from the police car now—an unsettling procession, each one tumbling out in silence.

They ignored the EMT entirely, moving in a calm, orderly single file toward the barn. Their heads bobbed as they wobbled through the grass, patient and quiet, purposeful.

Carter didn't want to leave Morris and the EMT, but he knew there was no helping the officer. The infection had him, whatever it was, and soon, the person who got up from the ground wouldn't be the same as the one who fell.

Carter needed to get help.

Up the drive, the pigs stood quietly with gentle sways as they held guard over the exit.

Carter knew he could have run through the field but didn't doubt the horse or the pigs would catch up to him. Then what? The radio said we have enough now. What did that mean? There were three, but Morris was taken out. Two? Is two enough? Enough for what?

Morris stopped seizing as the foam popped over his mouth and the yellow slime coming from his eyes hardened. The EMT felt for a pulse. "Hang in there Morris!" The EMT shouted and began chest compressions.

"That's not going to help!" Carter shouted and checked the barn for activity. He could go back in the house, use the house phone. Theirs was one of the few homes to still have a land-line in town. "We've gotta—"

Morris leapt up and sank his teeth into the EMT's face as he leaned down to resuscitate him. The EMT tried to scream, but his lips were trapped in Morris's bite, and all that escaped was a gurgling mumble.

Carter didn't move, didn't scream no, didn't even breathe. He knew it was already too late. And he'd be next.

The EMT wrenched his lips free from Morris's teeth, blood spraying in an arc from his torn mouth as he reared back and screamed. Clutching his face, he rolled over in agony, but Morris was already on top of him, sinking his teeth into the EMT's throat.

Blood spurted from the wet, sloshing bite, and Carter raised his gun, aiming at Morris.

"You cannot kill us," the frog's voice croaked from one pig in the driveway. "We cannot die, but we can restore life. You can save your parents. Come to the barn. You are needed."

Morris didn't stop gnawing at the EMT's neck, even as the body went limp beneath him. The familiar foam and thick slime began bubbling from the EMT's mouth, signaling the inevitable transformation.

Carter turned, his stomach knotting as he looked toward the barn.

Morris pulled back from the EMT, turning to face Carter with his foam-covered, blood smeared grotesque face. The frog's voice croaked through the officer now.

"Go to the barn," it commanded, as Morris stood and motioned toward the gray building where Carter and his dad had once stored old tractors. They had just sold the last one for parts, leaving the barn little more than a hollow, empty space.

Carter had once imagined that barn filled with life—where neighbors would gather for pumpkin decorating, sip apple cider, and learn to bake apple pies on picking days. But now, it was a place of death. A place where the zombies had gathered.

Halloween had come early, but these weren't playful horrors. These were real monsters. And they wanted him.

The police radio crackled to life: "911 from 42 Birch, police and EMT units available, respond to 42 Birch. Over."

Someone else had gotten a toy like the frog. Another yard sale victim—another family, trapped in this nightmare. Carter shouldered his rifle and began walking toward the barn, his mind racing with questions. Who would sell such cursed things? Who'd even have these damned toys? And why? Why have something that could kill your family? Kill your future?

Evening had crept in unnoticed during the chaos. The sun had slipped away, taking with it the warmth of the day. Icy winds swept through the yard, rattling the wind chimes on the porch. His mother had always said they were for luck, but tonight they sounded like the farm's death knell. The sweet smell of apples was gone, overtaken by the metallic tang of blood in the air. Carter could no longer deny the truth—death had come to this place, and it wasn't leaving.

Morris's hand oozed black tar where the chicken bit him. Carter assumed the chickens were there to stop him from driving away, to stop any of them from leaving, just like the pigs were blocking the way for the cars. Even if he climbed in the ambulance to plow through the fleshy, rubble-skulled swine, the chickens probably chewed through the wires. He didn't see it, but he knew it. Just like he knew he'd never leave the barn, that his parents couldn't be cured, that tonight, everything was going to die.

The EMT bonelessly crawled to his feet. Morris lifted a finger, pointing to the barn in the silent command to get walking.

Carter did.

The EMT followed in a lopsided swagger from the muscles in his left shoulder clenching around the throat wound left by Morris. They crossed the yard from the farmhouse to the barn.

Carter didn't hesitate when he arrived at the lightless entrance. He stepped inside and reached for the light switch.

"No need," the frog croaked through Morris. The officer's voice now sounded pre-recorded, mechanical, and fuzzy with static. "Go." The officer pointed further into the barn's darkness.

Carter did.

The air had lost all sweetness, as this dark place was hot, damp, and rife with decay. Something was already dead in here. An animal forgotten by the butcher. But Carter knew this wasn't the case. The last animal to pass away here was Bobert, the cow, and the butcher came for him when he was bought. Whatever died in here was recent. The flies still buzzed in the wounds of the dead thing.

"What's in here?" Carter asked.

"We are," the frog answered. Carter was unsure who spoke in the absolute darkness.

"What died?"

"We did," the frog answered.

"My parents?" Carter's voice caught, choked on hope and loss.

"You can release them."

They continued to walk into the dark when Carter, with hands outstretched, found the ladder to the loft. His eyes were adjusting but only to hazy gray forms. He trusted his hearing more, but not because he could hear anything to tell him where he was or what was around him, but because the old barn would creak and scream its rusty warnings if anyone approached. The wood was old, dry, and easy to break.

"Climb," the frog said.

Carter did.

A dim yellow light flickered at the top of the barn. Carter's parents sat with their backs to him, the gas lantern light casting long shadows between them and the wall. On the wall, a dripping red spiral had been painted, the crimson liquid slowly oozing downward.

His mother pressed her hands into something that squelched, pulled her hands free with a wet peel, then smeared another arm of the spiral with a deliberate, mechanical motion.

"We come. We go," croaked the frog, its voice now coming from the toy propped beneath the spiral. Its lifeless eyes bounced from side to side as the spinner whirred on its belly.

"In shadows deep, where time is slow, our souls undying, in the spiral's embrace, rise again, defying time and space," the frog's voice rasped, the rhyme echoing like a chant.

"Mom? Dad?" Carter's voice wavered. He didn't want them to respond. He didn't want them to turn.

Their hands dripped with blood and gore, pools of it spreading from the chicken corpses scattered around them. They pulled their hands from within the chicken's guts and turned toward him. Slowly, they faced him, their eyes sealed behind layers of mucus, their mouths crusted shut beneath thick, foaming residue.

Carter wished they were faceless. He wished they were dead. Anything but this. Their faces sagged like melted wax, bubbling grotesquely with every labored breath as they gasped for air beneath their prison of sludge.

"Open the door," the frog demanded. "Unveil the core. Twist the spiral, evermore. Life from death, a promise sown, yet in each revival, we have grown." From everywhere, the frog's voice explodes in a single word, "Legion!"

Carter was shoved forward. He looked back, seeing the outline of Officer Morris.

"You want me to open the door?" Carter didn't see a door.

"Yes," the fuzzy dead voice surrounded him. It filled the barn from below, behind, from his parents and from the frog.

"If I open the door, my parents will be okay?" Carter asked the frog.

"Our word," the frog answered from everyone around him. But what did that mean? What does the word of a faceless demonic toy mean? There was no other answer. Could he destroy the toy and restore everything? Is it the master vampire that once destroyed, sends the town's people, his parents, back to normal? He still had the guns. The railing of the loft wasn't too far from Officer Morris's back. Push him off and shoot the frog?

"Who are you?" Carter asked. The question formed in his mind a moment before leaving his lips. "Why are you doing this?"

"We feed. We expand. Now, we come." Then, from everywhere: "Legion!" After a moment of silence, the frog spoke again, "Open the door."

None of these answers were what Carter wanted. He wanted a clear, evil scheme. An answer that showed him how to win. Instead, there was no winning. Just a hungry thing who wanted to eat and grow, and now wanted something more. It was always about more.

A blight that crept from creature to creature, infecting the first on the wind from that frog's voice. And how do you stop a blight?

Because this one wasn't stopping here.

It wasn't going to release his parents.

The animals weren't going back; they were going to go out and spread. That's what these things do.

It was a blight. And like the blighted pumpkins, if something wasn't done, it would kill everything.

Dad said there was only one way to make sure a blight was gone forever. The thing that purifies everything. Fire. Things are too far gone to keep this isolated. And just like the pumpkin patch, now's the time to stop things from getting out of hand.

Time to use Carter's first farming tool. He fished it out of his pocket.

Carter snapped around and stomped his foot into Morris's chest, shoving him back. The officer flew through the old railing and fell from the loft with a sharp snapping sound as he hit the floor. Carter didn't check if the snap was Morris or the barn floor. Instead, he took out his lighter and clicked to light it, but no flame sparked.

His parents jumped to their feet and rushed him, grabbing his arms as Carter tried again. This time, the flame ignited, and he threw it from the loft, into the hay bales on the barn floor below.

Dry hay on dry wood caught quickly as Carter shook free from his parents and ran to the toy frog under the spiral.

"Open the door!" The frog demanded, fixing its eyes on Carter.

There was a gap in the center of the spiral. A black abyss was just big enough for his finger to reach in and pull it open. Cold wind streamed from the hole with a strangely absent smell. It didn't bring with it the bloody odor or the apple's scent; it was nothing—what Carter thought outer space would smell like.

He picked up the frog. His parents rushed him again, but below them the barn had caught into an inferno. Crimson light leapt up along the barn walls, now flaring brighter into hues of orange and yellow. Popping and crackling wood echoed in the barn as fire slithered up the walls, up the ladder to the loft. Another loud pop and the ladder crumbled from the loft.

Carter gripped the frog tightly, locking eyes with its thinking, plotting gaze, then hurled it into the hellfire that was about to engulf them all. As the flames swallowed the toy, he silently prayed—begged—that destroying it might somehow bring his parents back, return their lives to what they had been. But deep down, he knew better. There was no going back.

The frog wouldn't have cured them. It was a monster, and monsters betray. They don't help. They don't heal. They only destroy.

As the frog flew from Carter's hands, he didn't think about the fire, or the draught that hung over his hometown for weeks. Tomorrow was supposed to bring rain, but Carter didn't think he'd see tomorrow.

He didn't think any of them would.

# SEVEN

The frog didn't scream or slowly shout *no* or any of the things Carter expected. It simply disappeared into the flames without a sound.

Nothing could have been heard over the barn's crackling and popping.

The animals, now Carter could see them plainly, didn't run out. They stood, their faces encased in the yellow slime, staring up at him. He wanted to think they had accusing stares, but how could they under their encasing?

"Mom! Dad!"

His parents didn't respond. They only stared over the edge of the loft, their eyes fixed on the fire below. A loud pop shook the barn, rattling the loft beneath Carter's feet. He knew it was one of the support beams. The entire structure would collapse soon if he didn't act.

Rushing to the edge, Carter looked down as the animals—chickens, the horse, the pigs—faced the flames. One by one, they walked silently into the fire, where he had thrown the cursed frog. None of them yelped or screamed as they disappeared into the blazing inferno.

The entire barn was now engulfed. Flames snaked down from the ceiling and roared up from the floor. The heat closed in and burned away any cool moisture in the air. It was suffocating, the heat crashing into Carter in waves steaming away the sweat on his skin.

Carter's parents moved with eerie calm toward the same spot where Morris had fallen through the railing. They lined up side by side at the edge, their steps even and deliberate.

"No!" Carter sprinted toward them, grabbing at their arms, but he couldn't stop them. They stepped off the loft and into the fire below. Only Carter screamed as they vanished into the flames.

"No!" he cried again, collapsing to his knees at the edge of the loft, his hands trembling as the fire raged beneath him. More screams needed to come out of him, but they couldn't. Tears came, clear tears burning hotter than the inferno came over him, steaming away before they hit the wood below. Kneeling motionless and silent, he stared into the flames.

Another loud pop reverberated through the loft as the supports gave way. Was this the future he was always destined for? No continuing his dad's work, his granddad's work, his great-granddad's work? Everything was burning. His future was this fire, and soon it would consume him, too.

There was a hay drop across the loft, but the hay there was in flames. His only way out was through the inferno below. But why leave? What was beyond the fire? Mom and dad were gone. All the livestock was gone. The farm, if it didn't all burn down, was going to be taken by the bill collectors. What was there left? What future could exist off the farm?

A blast of frozen wind blew over Carter, almost pushing him

from the loft. He grabbed the ledge to hold on as he turned to where it came from. Another way out had opened. One that churned his stomach.

A hand emerged from the center of the spiral, pressing and stretching the wooden wall as though it were soft, pliable flesh. The wood groaned under the pressure, distorting like stretch marks rippling a tattoo. Another hand followed, forcing its way through and widening the spiral.

"Anyone in there?" A man's voice called from inside the spiral. Someone was coming through.

Carter didn't answer. He still couldn't speak, but he moved closer to see who was in the wall.

"Are you alone!?" the man shouted.

"Yes." Carter choked. "No one's left…" Black smoke filled the air as he struggled to breathe.

The hole stretched open, ripping as if the man was burrowing out of skin instead of a wooden wall. The spiral's bloody drawing glowed bright red. The light hurt Carter's eyes and he turned away as a man climbed through the gap torn open in the spiral.

"Well, doesn't this look horrible?" the man said. "Sole survivor?"

"I did it," Carter looked away. "I set the barn on fire. I thought it was the only way. I didn't mean to—" He couldn't say *kill his parents,* but that was what he did. His heart told him so. He started the fire, threw the frog into it, and then they followed.

"Get a hold of yourself, kid," the man reached for Carter but didn't approach. Carter thought he looked like the old photographs of early Arctic explorers. He wore a furry hooded leather hide jacket.

Brown hide pants, thick gloves and a large backpack with everything anyone could need to survive in the wilderness sticking out of it. On his belt was the biggest sword Carter had ever seen. It glittered in the firelight but was far too big for the man wearing it to swing. It'd be like an infant swinging a baseball bat. "These things ruin lives. You survived because you're smart and you did what you had to. Now we gotta go. I got a lot of questions for you, but y'ain't gonna be able to answer them if you die here."

The man turned to the spiral and pulled it open. Again, the crimson spiral glowed as it stretched and squelched open. Cold air steamed from the spiral into the fire's heat.

"Who are you!?" Carter didn't move. How did he know if this wasn't who the frog wanted to come through the spiral all along? "Why did you come here?"

"Of course," the man strained to rip open the spiral. The flesh gave way with a wet ripping. "William Nolton, at your service. I saw the opening and usually stop things from coming through. Saw you here and thought you needed help. But we best save introductions until after we—" The loft snapped and pitched, throwing Carter back towards the now burning railing. William moved faster than his middle-aged body would suggest possible. He and grabbed Carter before the younger man could fall into the flames. "Sorry, but no time to ask."

William threw Carter into the spiral and then scurried over the collapsing loft. "Let's go!" William pushed Carter through the opening, following himself just as the loft collapsed.

Carter and William vanished into the spiral. The stretched skin shrunk on itself, closing, leaving the burning bloody spiral flaking to ash behind them.

The barn burned.

Moments later, the wall with the spiral collapsed. As it fell, sparks, embers, and ash belched into the night sky, burying the frog on the floor below. Its wide eyes stared up at the ceiling as it crumbled and rained down on it.

# EIGHT

"Officer Little?" Dispatch called.

Little was still smarting from the tongue-lashing Mrs. Trudy Nelson had given him just moments ago. She'd claimed someone broke into her house, and he'd raced over the second he got the call. But when he arrived, there was no one—no signs of entry, no disturbances, and a security system that would have caught anything unusual.

What else could he do but tell her there was nothing more he could do?

He understood she was scared for her daughter, and the entire story sounded creepy to him too, but that didn't give her the right to bark at him like that. He's human too.

"Go dispatch," Little replied.

"We have a fire out at the Forgotten Baggage farm. Fire department is on their way but it's real bad, gonna need you on scene."

"Yes ma'am," Little tried to push Trudy out of his mind, flicked on his lights and siren, then raced over to the farm.

Calling it a *rager* was an understatement. The entire farm was engulfed in flames—from the fields to the house, with every building in between ablaze. When Little arrived, the heat hit him like a wall. Fireman Bradfield waved him over to where they had pulled their trucks back, the flames too intense for even the hoses to reach.

"What the hell happened here?" Little said as he got out of his car.

"Don't know yet," Bradfield said. "Whatever it was, really did this place in."

"Any sign of Donnie? Cammie? Their boy?" Little asked as the men watched the fire engulf the last apple tree in the orchard.

Bradfield shook his head. "That's burning like hell there. We can't get in. Just setting up a perimeter to keep it contained. Dry as it's been, this whole field could go up."

"Rain's coming soon," Little said, glancing up at the sky. "Supposedly any time now." But the rain held off for a few more hours—long enough for the fire to devour the house, the barn, and nearly the entire farm, stopping just short of the pumpkin patch. Then, as if on cue, the rain finally arrived. A heavy downpour drenched the smoldering ruins, quenching the flames and giving the firefighters the break they needed to gain control.

Not a single pumpkin burned.

Once the fire was out, Little followed Bradfield to what was left of the house. It had collapsed completely, the walls fallen, leaving nothing but crumbling rubble. Ashes hissed against the rain, steam rising in faint tendrils—the dying gasps of a once-living place. The little hisses echoed in the silence, a grim reminder of the surrounding devastation.

They left the somber scene and moved on to the barn.

As they approached, a firefighter met them and suggested the blaze had begun in the barn. They didn't know about the lighter or the dry hay, only that this was where the fire seemed to start. Like the house, the barn had been reduced to ash, along with the sturdy old frame that had held it up for generations—one that would have lasted many more, if not for the frog.

Firefighters were still at work, dousing the last smoldering flames and ensuring nothing flared back up. The air was thick with the roar of engines and the whooshing spray of hoses, so neither Bradfield nor Little heard the faint, dying voice buried in the ash pile.

"Open the door. Open the door," the mechanical voice rasped, choking on its own failing circuits. After another sputter, it fell silent, never to speak again.

"Let me know if you find the family," Little said. "That boy had a future. Hate to see it end like this."

Of course, Officer Little did not know how strange Carter Gilquist's future would become, nor could he fathom that within 24 hours, he'd be facing evils much worse than those Carter had encountered.

The future was murky for everyone in this town—dark clouds for the next storm were already gathering on the horizon.

The nightmares birthed from the yard sale were just beginning.

# INVENTORY NOTE: 5 (APPENDED)

Inventory Item: 5

Contents:

Frog shaped see and say, (badly burnt)

Nadia guided us to this item. I'm not sure exactly what happened, but there was a fire at Carter Gilquist's house, and we were able to recover the frog toy from the ashes.

We also found a dog wandering around the ashes, too. Nadia took him home with her. The dog's collar said his name was Jetson, and he was probably Carter's. Jetson was sniffing around, close to where we found the frog. Nadia kept staring at that place too, but she didn't say what she saw with that new eye of hers. I'm guessing she saw some kind of supernatural residue or something. She doesn't talk much about her eye. It's not a gift in her mind, just a scar.

The fire was a few days ago and we haven't been able to get any details about it. Everyone says it was lightning or an electrical issue, but Nadia and I know better. Someone in the Gilquist family was at Neil's yard sale. They got this frog, and things went horribly wrong from there.

Neil's original notes said this item contained a spirit that was trying to get back to its home dimension. In his note, Neil claimed he didn't believe it and marketed the toy as part of his public collection, which seems to have meant that Neil didn't care about holding on to it. His private collection were the weapons he was storing and finding to go to Dodslav's realm and reclaim his brother (Drew) by force if necessary. I can't imagine having a sibling stolen by a monster like that. I guess that's kind of what happened with Nadia and King Dark, but I got her back…just a little different.

Nadia says this frog toy is still active and so we're sealing it in a bin like the others. Perhaps one day it will be useful, but we need to discover some more information about it before trying to destroy it.

There's been no sign of Carter since the fire. I hope he and his family found their way out of this thing's resolution. He was a good kid. Nadia had a huge crush on him. I guess she digs farm boys.

Neil said he wanted to test his weapons on the creature within the frog toy. I'm thinking it will be useful for the same. But the dollhouse told me the frog could help us. The dollhouse said the frog knows how to open doors to other worlds and if we gather enough toys like the frog, the dollhouse can open a door to us and help destroy the toys. We need all the help we can get. We haven't been able to destroy any of the toys yet. Neil said fire could do it, but that isn't working. Water doesn't destroy them, just puts them to sleep.

With Viola, the Death Doll (see Inventory Note for Item 42: Ely's Doll), I saw this work. She tried to kill me, but I was able to drown her in the Patticon River, putting a ten-pound weight on her to keep her at the bottom of that river. But I know she's not dead. Just asleep. Hopefully, forever.

I think resolution is the only thing that can break the spirit free. My mom doesn't want us doing that. I agree. It's dangerous and who knows what will happen when we wake up these ghosts?

The spirit in the dollhouse can help. He promises to help. We just need to get a few more toys so it can use their spiritual power to come to us and help. I think this spirit knows a lot more about this world of haunted objects than he's letting on. I've tried to ask questions, but it's hard to get away from mom or Nadia long enough to have a conversation. Nadia doesn't like the dollhouse. Neither does mom. They don't want me around it, but they don't know how it can help.

They haven't heard what I've heard.

He can help.

He's who we need to finish this.

# 32

# ONE

His daddy called him Nicky, and today, daddy was coming home.

The crowd at the dock was overwhelming for any five-year-old, but especially so for Nicky. His mommy said he was *sensitive*, a *very sensitive little boy*. Large crowds like these made him nervous and confused from all the noise. He tried not to be so *sensitive* but no matter how much he tried, Nicky could never be brave for his mommy. She didn't seem to mind and always told him it was okay to be afraid, but to never let it stop him.

And today was a day he didn't let his fear stop him. Today was a special day. It wasn't just a beautiful late August day. It was the day his daddy came back from what his mom called, The Great War.

From his mommy's shoulders, he watched the boats slowly dock. Over the sea of people, he could see sailors throwing lines to shoremen.

Were these warships? Probably not. Most likely smaller boats that moved soldiers around. He had seen these kind of boats in the movies between the cartoons. Nicky always wondered if he'd see his daddy on the movie screen when they told people news about the war, but he never did.

This morning was just like the movies. It was gray. The sky was one big dull overcast cloud that muted the sun. Foamy brackish water broke around the weathered ships, leaving smears of muddy sludge on the bow from the factories lining the harbor.

Nicky hoped that goop didn't get splashed on them. Mommy said it was toxic and that meant it would make the fish and him sick. The factories made poison and poured it into the harbor. At least, that's what mommy said.

There were other kids on their parent's shoulders, but he was the tallest. He hated being so small, but his mom was much taller than the other mommies and everyone said he'd be tall one day, but that day never seemed to come. He wasn't tall like his mommy or strong like his daddy. Nicky knew what he was. The doctors whispered the word like a curse that promised a hard life. Nicky was *frail*.

"I think that's his ship sweetie," Mommy said. She pointed to a boat pushing through the dark steel crowd of vessels. "Let's see if we can get a closer look."

"Okay." Nicky nodded.

Everyone between here and there was shouting and cheering and being so noisy, so so noisy. He winced at the idea of going through them, but he hadn't seen his daddy in two years, and he didn't want to wait any longer.

Nicky had a great memory and didn't need a reminder of what his daddy looked like or when he left. Nicky was just starting to talk. His words came late, that's what his mommy said. Math was always easy for Nicky, and he could subtract two from five, his current age, to know daddy left for war when Nicky was three. He even remembered the look on daddy's face as he left.

Sadness.

Daddy didn't want to go. But the government said he had to go. There was no choice. They needed heroes on the front, and Daddy was a hero.

Mommy pushed through the crowd.

"Daddy!" Nicky pointed to his daddy, who was coming down a long ramp from the boat.

"Peter!" his mom shouted, waving frantically. She shoved through the crowd, ignoring the grumbles and side-eyed glares. She and Nicky had suffered too many of those lately for her to care anymore. Polite society had long forgotten their manners when it came to white families living in mixed neighborhoods, and so she returned the oversight.

His dad, the soldier, carried his pack over strong shoulders and a neatly pressed uniform. That pack must weigh as much as two of Nicky. It certainly was big enough. How strong had his daddy become in war? Could Nicky become that strong? Probably not, but maybe?

"Peter!" she called again. Her voice was drowned in the chaotic screaming around them. Everyone was calling out names and shouting for their soldier's attention. There were other people who were crying, not happy tears but wailing in loss as soldiers talked to them. These soldiers handed bags like the one daddy carried and pointed to a table where lots of people gathered. They all looked worried. That was the table of worried people in Nicky's mind.

Mommy called again. This time daddy heard her and pushed his way through the crowd towards them.

Daddy didn't look happy to see them; instead, he began to cry. He waved. Thick brown gloves covered his hands. The closer he got, the more Nicky thought his daddy seemed…different. He looked the same. He walked the same. But he didn't feel the same. Nicky couldn't place the feeling and perhaps if he were older, he'd recognize a man who saw more than his soul could bear. Now, looking at his daddy made him feel sad and lost. He should have been happy. And inside, he was—until he felt the hot fog drifting from his daddy.

As he came closer and closer, a boiling heat washed over Nicky, coiling in his guts, nesting there like burning serpents crawling over each other. Daddy's fingers trembled. Maybe he was hot too? Nicky's mouth watered, spit building to wash out the nasty, metallic taste flooding around his teeth. Now Nicky's fingers trembled too as the heat from his daddy soaked through his bones.

"Oh, my god! I can't believe this is happening! This is finally happening!" Daddy's voice cracked as he wrapped himself around mommy. "Bethany, I, Nicky, I." He squeezed them.

"I love you!" Mommy wept into his uniform. Nicky knew that would make it look stained, but his daddy didn't mind.

"Hey champ!" Daddy said as he ruffled Nicky's hair. The touch made Nicky squint as the wiggling in his stomach quickened. "Taking care of your mom?"

Nicky nodded.

"I heard you're talkin' more." Daddy smiled. His teeth were dirty. Had he been eating dirt?

"Yeah," Nicky said and nodded again.

"Well, that's great. That's something," Daddy squeezed mommy again. "I missed you guys."

"When do you report back?" Mommy asked, but daddy didn't answer. His face twisted into a smile, but his lips remained sealed. No dirty teeth this time. Then he waved for them to follow him out of the crowd.

"I got you something champ. Something to help you with your words," Daddy said as he held mommy's hand, squeezing it like he was never letting go again.

Daddy and mommy both were worried. They both had the lines on their foreheads that meant they were worried, or thinking really hard. There was something they weren't saying, and Nicky knew adults did that, but this time, it felt like something was wrong, something steaming and to boil over.

They emerged from the crowd and went to a short bench. Nicky's mommy lifted him up and over her head, placing him on the bench. Daddy put his pack beside Nicky and stretched it open. A rush of blistering air gushed from the army bag's opening, knocking Nicky back on his heels. Daddy reached into the bag. Mommy caught Nicky before he fell.

"Oh, careful sweetie," she said and rubbed his back.

Nicky tried to see past his daddy, to see into the darkness of the bag. Whatever was in there smelled like the sludge in the harbor on a hot day. His dad rooted through the sack, digging deep, then popped out with a small pale wooden board. It was about the size of a dinner tray and as thick as a heavy book. Six squares were cut into the board like they were placeholders for something to fit into them.

"See, here," Daddy said, then pulled out a small colorless canvas bag. It clattered as he opened it and pulled out a wooden square with the letter H on it. He put the H in the first hole and smiled at Nicky. "See, you can practice your words with this." His daddy reached in again and pulled out a wooden I, and placed it beside the H.

"Hi," Nicky said.

Daddy smiled and shoved the puzzle board back into his pack. "I knew it would help!" He laughed. "Now, let's get home. Lots to talk about. Lots to catch up on."

Mommy nodded and helped Nicky off the bench. The three of them went to the trolly holding hands, Nicky in the middle, as his mommy told daddy about their big dinner tonight. Even though it was a Meatless Monday for most of America, tonight they were having baked ham with carrots and walnut bread. A real treat.

She talked and talked and couldn't hear all the voices behind them like Nicky could.

He was sensitive.

No one else heard the faint voice whispering from Daddy's pack. *Hi*, it said.

But Nicky heard and looked for who said it. No one was behind them.

# TWO

Nicky lived in a small apartment on the outskirts of a revolution brewing in the streets. Energy simmered through this part of New York. Everyone could feel something happening. Some people fled what was coming. Some people ran towards it.

Mommy once told him, "artistic revolutions aren't for everyone", and so when many people left the neighborhood, Nicky's family moved into one of the newer apartments. It was on the third floor and had windows which Nicky loved. He stood by it and watched the new colorful faces speckled through the streets moving about their lives. Many were smiling, happy, laughing faces, looking forward to what was coming. Some were angry, sad faces bracing against what was coming.

Nicky would sit with his elbows hanging out the window, chin on his forearms, listening to the cacophony of lively music, thoughtful voices reading poetry, people fighting, angrily yelling for others to get out of their neighborhood. You could hear singing and laughing and shouting and growling all in a chorus of change sweeping over their little neighborhood Nicky called Harlem.

But most exciting of all things was that their building had electricity, so mommy could paint at night. Now, with their light bulb in the kitchen, she didn't have to stop painting when it got dark and her paintings were always full of bright colors. When Nicky wasn't taking in the colors and music of the streets, he was listening to his mommy sing while she painted bright yellows, bold blues, vivid greens.

Daddy had seen the apartment, but only for a week before he left. It was all new to him, which Nicky assumed that was why his daddy was so surprised to see their neighbors, the Millers, coming out of their own apartment.

"Uh, hi," Daddy said.

"Peter, this is the Millers, our new neighbors," Mommy said.

Daddy was thinking deeply about the three Millers as they stood there in their work clothes. Ezra was dressed in his Sunday finest to clean his dad's barbershop. Ezra's dad, Mr. Abraham, wore his collared shirt covered by a charcoal vest, topped with a bright red bow tie. Ezra's mom, Mrs. Lisa Anne, was headed to church. Ezra was a few years older than Nicky, but he hadn't started school yet. His mom taught him at home because there weren't any schools for coloreds open in this part of the city. Nicky wondered if his mommy would teach him at home like Ezra's mommy. He hoped so.

"Sir. Ma'am," Mr. Abraham said. He bowed his head softly and smiled. "Welcome home, sir."

"Hi Nicky!" Ezra said and pulled out a deck of cards from his pocket. "Look what pa got me." The cards were flimsy paper with a triangle drawn on the back of each. Ezra flipped over a card and showed Nicky a king with a heart. It was intricately drawn over a more simplistic design.

"You?" Nicky pointed to the card, then motioned like he was drawing.

"Yeah, I drew it. A drawing guy comes to the shop. He showed me how." Ezra showed the Jack, who was also finely drawn over a lesser image.

Nicky smiled. Ezra gave him a card. "Good," Nicky said. He looked at the card for a moment, then handed it back. Ezra, like mommy, was an artist, and Nicky knew artists liked to keep their work.

"Off to the shop?" Mommy asked.

The Millers nodded as they passed. "Sorry, we're running late," Mrs. Lisa Anne said as she excused her family. They hurried to the stairs while Mommy opened the door to their own apartment.

"So, things are different," Daddy said as he went in. "It wasn't posted but…"

"There's a lot of colored families moving up from the south," Mommy said. "We've been seeing a lot around here and that's not sitting right with a bunch of folks." She shrugged. "But they've been good to us. Millers' shop is becoming a place where artists hang out, and I've sold a few paintings to people there. But wait till you hear the music, Peter. Oh, the music."

She shook her hips and Nicky joined her just like they did at night when he couldn't sleep from the nightmares. They'd get up and dance to chase away the monsters who never came out of the shadows, never came out of his dreams, but always whispered into Nicky's mind.

"Beth, just…be careful. I saw…well, I saw people who couldn't see. We all fought for the same team." Daddy put his pack on the table by the door. He froze there, his mind drifting back to somewhere so cold his body quaked with shivers. A loud noise that Nicky didn't hear made his daddy jump. Mommy gently touched daddy's arm and that brought him back to their apartment. He said, "I'm not going back." His voice faded like a ghost whispering how it died.

"If I go back. I'm not coming back  I mean, I will, but it won't be me. It won't be…"

Nicky watched the conversation from the family room and wondered when he could get the toy his daddy brought him. He didn't think about what else could be in the pack, or what else his daddy brought home with him. There was no consideration for the weight he carried and how it wore down his shoulders, puffed his eyes, creased his brow. All Nicky cared about was that his daddy was home and he brought a new toy.

"What are you going to do?" Mommy asked.

Daddy shrugged. "I'll figure that out after this weekend." He opened his pack and took out Nicky's puzzle. "We'll think about that later, right champ?"

Nicky nodded, willing to agree to anything for his new toy. He took the puzzle from his daddy, who still wore the leather gloves.

The canvas bag of letters was handed over next. It clattered, wood on wood knocking, as Nicky ran away from the serious conversation and to his corner of the apartment. He kept his toys here and his books. It was far from his mommy's paintings, which were on the other side of the apartment. He didn't want her accidentally getting paint on his things and she didn't want his toys ending up on her canvases. The spacing worked for both of them.

Mommy and daddy kept talking while Nicky started playing with his puzzle. He reached into the canvas bag and felt nothing in there. It was empty, but he heard the clattering wood within. So he reached deeper, his entire arm going into the sack, and thinking about the letters, he suddenly found the blocks he need. He pulled out the H and I, putting them on the puzzle board, and then said, "Hi."

The puzzle whispered into Nicky's mind, *Hi. Who are you?*

Its voice was thick and congested. Nicky braced for a cough or a sneeze. Instead, it inhaled in a series of deep, resonant breaths, each one sounding like a wave of thick, sour foam slobbering over the docks down by the waterfront.

Nicky's parents were talking at the kitchen table. Mommy was making coffee. He reached into the canvas bag and easily found the letters he needed now, wondering why the bag originally felt so empty, N-I-C-K-Y. He put them on the board.

*Hi, Nicky. I'm Huldis. Will you help Astrid?*

"Halldis?" Nicky said.

*Close enough*, Huldis said. *Will you help Astrid?*

Nicky, not knowing who Astrid was, but knowing you should help other people if you could. His mommy did that all the time, and that's why his daddy was fighting the war, to help people. Helping people is what you should do to be a good person and Mommy said he was a good boy and good boys always helped others.

It was important to help others even when some people said you shouldn't. There were a lot of people who said his mommy shouldn't help people like the Millers. They yelled at her and said mean things, but that's when Mommy said she knew she had to help even more.

Because if she didn't help, no one else would.

Nicky nodded, eager to be a good boy. To be a good helper like his mommy and daddy.

*Great. That's great. She'll love meeting you. You can use your words to help her. Can you spell, open?*

Nicky nodded, assuming the board could see him, and then pulled out the letters. Each block was the size of his daddy's hand, with the letter on all sides. All the wooden blocks was old and worn down from what could have been centuries of use. The letters were gouged scars in the smooth wood. Nicky was surprised to feel the blocks in the canvas bag. Then when he pulled one out, an O was chiseled on all the sides. The next block had a P on it. He held the E as his dad got up from the kitchen table, their conversation pausing.

"Hey champ, you want to get a milkshake?" Daddy asked as he came over to Nicky and knelt down.

The puzzle said nothing, and so Nicky thought a milkshake was a great idea. Besides, he was just making words. How did that help Astrid? But Huldis said this was how to help, and so Nicky would help after a milkshake.

"You want to take your puzzle?" Daddy asked.

Nicky nodded and put the blocks back in the bag. "Halldis," Nicky said.

Daddy looked at Mommy to understand, but she just shrugged. "You boys want alone time, or can a lady join you?"

Daddy smiled. "Know any ladies?"

She laughed and shook her head.

"Mommy, come," Nicky said and pulled Daddy towards her.

"Sammy's still open?" Daddy asked.

Mommy shook her head.

"Closed, but there's a new place near there."

"When did it close?" Daddy took off his uniform and put on jeans and a loose undershirt. He pulled on his army jacket and a flat cap.

"Not everyone's happy about what's going on around here." Mommy couldn't smile through the worry. She'd wanted the people who left, the people who wanted the neighborhood to stay white-only, to stop coming back and stirring up trouble for people like the Millers, and lately, people like her. 'Race Traitors', they called her and anyone else who thought people were people, no matter the color of their skin.

Daddy motioned for Nicky to join him at the door. "Come on, kiddo. Let's get a milkshake and then maybe we'll get a burger." He pulled out a few dollars. Mommy smiled as Nicky ran toward him.

Huldis quietly whispered into Nicky's mind, *We'll play more later. When you're not so distracted,* it laughed, coughed, and choked on whatever broke loose in its throat.

As they left their apartment laughing, happily excited for dinner and dessert, Nicky's family didn't grasp the significance of the artistic wonders brewing across the Harlem River.

Nor did they realize that when people leave, their absence becomes an infection, spreading rot among those who stay behind. The rot of fear and abandonment, building and festering until the infection bursts—erupting pus and sickness over innocent skin.

Tonight, that infection would find its way to Nicky—erupting over him, drowning the small boy in sickness and setting nightmares into motion for centuries to come.

# THREE

Nicky's mom, adults called her Bethany, was an artist. She painted the scenes of a transforming city. New faces, new colors were moving into Harlem and with that, a new creative force was coming to life. Years later, it would be known as the Harlem Renaissance, but right now, the white people were moving out, and before the gap could be filled with a creative revolution, distrust and hate flooded into the edges of the city.

People like Bethany were few and far between. A middle-class white woman who thought new ideas and new art would be good for her sensitive boy, Nicky. She thought the world was a bigger place than a neighborhood, having traveled with her dad for many years prior to settling down with her husband, Peter.

"Here we go," Bethany said, pointing to a small wooden sign propped against the brick wall.

The sidewalk was filled with Black men and women in neat suits, heading to work or returning home. First shift at the factory just ended and the second shift was just beginning. You could tell who was going to work and who was coming home by their shoulders and feet. People going to work held their shoulders back and straight, their feet clacked across the sidewalk in fresh shoes, ready to earn the day's wages. While those coming home were hunched with feet dragging in long pulls across the pavement, their body done for the day and ready for a soft chair or better yet, bed.

The sign on the wall read *Son Rise Diner*. There was an attempt at drawing a sunrise on the sign, but the scraggly lines and featureless landscape took more imagination than it should to see the intent. Outside, the building was like most restaurants in Harlem, brick buildings with large windows for people to see who was eating there. Bethany opened the wood and glass door. A sharp bell chimed to announce her, and she motioned for Peter to go in.

As he did, everyone in the diner turned to him. Almost everyone was black with two white men huddled at the bar still shoveling food into their mouth, filling their flabby cheeks. Once Bethany followed Peter in, then Nicky behind her, everyone relaxed at the familiar face.

"Miss Bethany, Mister Nicky, who do you have with you today?" A black man wearing a white dress shirt, black vest, and black bowtie came over to great them. His hands were gnarled with fingers bent at odd angles, but just enough that most people didn't notice.

Nicky noticed everything.

While the man's body was strong, everything about him seemed weathered. His hands were leathery, his cheeks were hard, and more than one scar snaked around the nape of his neck.

"This is Peter, my husband. Peter, this is Mister Lions. He owns the best breakfast joint in New York."

Peter extended his hand. Surprised, Mister Lions took it. "Thank you for feeding my family while I was deployed," Peter said.

Mister Lions smiled, a bit of bacon still in his teeth, "Nothing of it. They're a delight to have and your boy, he's so smart, I'll have him doing my books soon," Lions laughed, a thick chuckle that infected everyone else. "What are you three eating?"

Nicky tugged on his mom's coat. "Pancakes?"

She smiled and nodded. "Make that two," she said, motioning to Peter, who was looking at a paper menu with just a few items on it.

Lions spoke quickly. "We're going to have more soon. Just starting small."

"New around here?" Peter asked.

"Yes sir. Been just a few months. Got this place on the cheap and trying to make something of my mama's recipes."

"She'd be proud." Bethany took off her coat and sat at a small table. Nicky followed her and climbed into the chair beside her.

"Can I get the black beans and cornbread?" Peter asked.

Lions did a double take to see if he was joking. A wily smile crooked on his face waiting for a punchline that never came.

Peter saw this and added, "In the trenches, we didn't have much. I was pinned down with a few colored soldiers and one night, a real bad night, we all thought we'd die. So Ruby, that wasn't his real name but that's what we all called him, he said if we're going to die then we'll die full of good food. He made his bean ration with something he brought from home and if that was my last meal, I would have died a happy man. But it wasn't. We survived and Ruby kept cooking. He'd fancy up our beans and cornbread. That man knew how to cook."

Lions laughed. "Where was Ruby from? My mama's recipe might be different."

"I didn't get to ask," Peter said. The happiness of a good memory washed away with the bitter tides of reality. "He," Peter held his wife's hand, squeezing, "Not everyone left the trench."

Lions nodded. "I'll, I'll get this started for you all," he said and went back to the kitchen.

Bethany didn't say anything. She didn't know what to say. Do you apologize? Console? Just move on?

Peter stared out the window, and Bethany wondered what he saw. Mortar shells? Dead friends? The movie pictures from the front lines looked like vast wastelands of barbwire and broken fences. Is that what he saw? But she didn't want to dwell, and moved to the only thing she could think of at that moment.

Nicky, absorbed in his own world, was pulling blocks out of the bag and put an O in the indentation where a block could fit. The puzzle looked ancient, with places worn down to a glossy shine. Where the board wasn't worn down, the wood grain gave it a rough texture, begging for a little finger to get close to it so a splinter can stab through her little boy's soft flesh.

There was a forest in California with trees like this. Coarse and smooth and smelling of ancient times. The puzzle's smell threw her back to when she and her dad stayed with those trees for a few days as a kid. The deeper parts of the woods smelled like this, the old, dark parts where the branches intertwined to shield their secrets from the sun.

"So, where'd you get this from?" Bethany picked up a block. It had a P on it, but when the carving shifted, the indentation slithered away from her touch. She dropped it to the floor. Nicky climbed under the table to retrieve it. She wiped her hand off, dismissing what she felt, not explaining it away, just letting it go because if she didn't, her mind would have to ask questions it didn't want to consider.

Peter was still staring out the window when he answered, "There was an old castle in Ghent, Belgium. We had a battle close to it. Some of us went to the castle for supplies. This was in a store beside the castle." The memory brought a smile. To push through the darkness in his eyes, the memory must have been one of the few moments of light from The Front. "The shopkeeper creeped me out, but he gave this to me for free. Said it would help my boy. I guess he overheard me talking about Nicky to the other guys." Peter held Nicky's hand. They both smiled. Nicky laughed.

"Like it," Nicky said and laughed. "Like Huldis. Funny." He put the P in its place and pulled another letter from the bag—an E.

"Yo, Lions," a man near the window called to the kitchen. "You gonna wanna come out here."

Three white men passed by the front window. Each looking drunker than the first. They were fresh from first shift with the red cheeks and shiny noses that came with a few too many gins.

The first man came in with the bright ding just as Lions came out of the kitchen. He was running a large knife through a towel. Peter and Bethany both looked to the door, but Nicky kept his attention on the puzzle, reaching into the bag for the next block he needed: N.

"Table or bar, gentlemen?" Lions waved the knife from the tables to the bar. This woke up the two chubby white men at the bar who were still stuffing their face with the brown mush too drowned in syrup to tell if they were pancakes or waffles.

The group's leader, a young man in a heavy jacket and thread bear jeans, glared at every eye meeting him. His bulky frame, built by long days, long hours and hard shifts at the factory, filled the doorframe. Tight red curls were gray with ash or dust, whatever he picked up from his shift that morning. The same powder caked his skin, cracking and dulling the freckles beneath.

No one spoke, waiting for the man to start whatever trouble was heading their way.

His gaze stopped on the two white men at the bar. "Earl, Monty, ain't you got no pride?" His words dripped with disgust, his face a mirror of the feeling.

"Good pancakes, cheap Stevie," one man said.

"Bradly's got cheap pancakes too," the leader said. "And he's your kind."

Then Nicky's family caught the man's attention. He said nothing, just stared at them. Stared at Bethany with disgust. "And you brought a kid here?" He shook his head as another one of his men came in and pushed a plate off the counter. It crashed to the floor and shattered.

Peter jumped from the table and reached for his gun, but it wasn't there because he wasn't on The Front anymore. His mind was, but his body was in New York.

The leader started laughed, "Little jumpy?" The leader's men started laughing and pointing at Peter as his breath raced and his chest heaved.

"It's time for you to leave," Bethany said to the leader.

"We don't want no trouble," Lions said and went back to cleaning the knife.

Peter was still searching for the noise.

"You don't know your place, woman. Just like these boys," the leader said and motioned to the black men frozen from their meals, waiting for what would happen next.

Bethany stood from the table and stepped in front of Peter. Lions joined her and motioned for everyone to calm down.

Nicky didn't pay none of this any mind as he finally found the last block he needed, the N.

Bethany didn't notice Nicky freeze and look into space as if having a conversation with someone in his mind. She didn't see him rummage into the canvas bag.

Two more men came into the Son Rise Diner. The leader's confidence swelled with his ranks as they grew, so did his chest, and so did his certainty that he could do anything he wanted in here.

Bethany was no stranger to fighting. Peter was searching for the danger his mind told him was there, but he couldn't see. There were no explosions. No gunfire. No mortars or screams. Nothing signaling danger and so he kept searching.

Nicky put the N on the board. A thrum vibrated from the board, through the floor. Peter felt it and startled again with a quiet yelp.

The men, not sensitive enough to feel a strong breeze blow through the restaurant, didn't notice anything but Peter's yelp. They laughed harder and two of the men went to the bar, throwing more plates on the floor with explosive shatters. Peter jumped, but it was the backfire, the booming backfiring car, that unlocked his mind and triggered his fight. The danger was obvious. It was the men throwing the plates; the men grabbing his wife, pushing Lions. Peter leapt in and punched the leader whose nose popped like a water balloon soaking Peter in blood.

The leader staggered to the door, but Peter didn't stop. He took to the next guy, punching him in the sternum and then kicking out his knees. Another punch cracked the man's jaw with a dry snap. Lions grabbed Peter and pulled him back. Two other men helped.

"Get the hell outta here!" Lions yelled at the guys who came for trouble and found what they were looking for. Peter wasn't constrained easily and took out another attacker who was still holding a plate to smash. He punched through the plate, smashing it into the man's face, slicing under his eye, unleashing a gushing wound.

Finally, Bethany grabbed Peter, and that snapped him back to New York, to now, away from battle and back to his family. He whined a high-pitched confused noise as Lions, and the men held him back. The troublemakers retreated out the door. The leader spit blood on the floor and pointed at Peter as he left.

Nicky began the next word as Huldis spoke to him, putting the blocks back in the bag as instructed and pulling out a new block. This one formed a T.

Bethany smiled as she saw Nicky enthralled with the puzzle, glad he missed the ugliness. "We should go," she said to Lions. He nodded.

"Back door," Lions motioned to the kitchen. "You flip that sign," he pointed to the open sign on the door. "Get your boy," Lions pointed to Nicky.

"Nicky," Bethany tried to sound calm.

Peter was coming back to himself and saw the blood on the floor. The shattered plates were on the floor. He looked at Lions with the desperate question, *What did I do?*

"We'll clean up. Get your wife and boy outta here." Lions pointed toward the kitchen. "Boys like that don't lick their wounds, they just get drunker and come back. You can't be here when they do."

"But, you?" Peter said. "I'm sorry."

"I'll be fine." Lions motioned for one of the black customers. "Get Derby and his boys. Tell him we'll need some security tonight." The customer nodded and ran out the front door. "Miss Bethany, you all gotta go."

The two white customers left their money and followed the other customers out the front door.

Nicky quickly put the T in place, then the H, just like Huldis said. The E was in his hand when his mom asked him to put the puzzle away. "One letter," Nicky said and put it on the board. Another vibration pulsed from the board. Peter stiffened and searched for the origin as Lions took him to the kitchen door.

"What was that?" Peter looked outside for a plume from a mortar or the splattering remains of a landmine.

"We have to go Nicky. We have to hurry," Bethany said.

"Huldis. Said. Stay." Nicky cleared the puzzle and put the blocks back in the bag as Huldis told him to do. The three words shocked Bethany and made her search for who told her son to stay. No one was there. Maybe someone said it as they were running out or said something similar, and Nicky mixed up the words.

"We have to go." Bethany shoved the blocks in the bag and swiped it from the table. When she reached for the board, Nicky snatched it away.

"No!" He screamed. "No! Stay!" Nicky grabbed for the bag of blocks.

Bethany gasped and pulled away from her son. Her sweet son, who was so sensitive and so quiet, now he was feral and screaming. "No! Stay! Finish! Help Astrid!"

"Who's Astrid?" Peter screamed over Nicky and went to his son. "We have to go Nicky. Bad people are coming. We have to go."

"No! Help Astrid!"

Bethany tried to reach for the board, but Nicky pulled it back so hard it hit the window with a splintering crack. Peter snapped it from his son, lifting Nicky in the air with it as the boy finally let go of the board.

"We will help Astrid!" Peter shouted over Nicky's cries, unsure what that meant. He didn't realize that he had already put Huldis' plans in motion, and they would indeed help Astrid, but Nicky would be helping alone. "First, we need to get to safety. We can't help Astrid when we're in danger."

*** 

*No more distractions!* Huldis said in Nicky's mind. His parents never yelled at him, but every kid knows an angry, disappointed voice when they hear it. What did he do wrong? His mommy said it was time to go, and what else could he do?

The men from earlier scared mommy and daddy. It's their fault the puzzle isn't done yet. But why were his parents scared? Mommy was tough. Daddy was a war hero. Those men were just a bunch of factory workers. What could they do against such mighty heroes?

Nicky followed his daddy. Mommy was still standing at the table, staring at Nicky. She checked her fingers, thinking about something she touched, and then looked at the canvas bag with disgust.

"Let's go," Lions motioned for Nicky's family to go into the kitchen. They did and disappeared just as the troublemakers from earlier, fewer than before, rattled the front door, making the glass quake as they tried to get in. But it was locked.

Lions shouted from the kitchen, "Sorry! We're closed!"

But the rattling persisted, now becoming banging. Glass couldn't take a beating like that. A shatter was coming. Any moment now, the door would explode in and the men would come for them. And Daddy would kick their butt. And Mommy would make them sorry they scared Nicky. They'd be sorry they stopped Nicky from helping Astrid.

Maybe Huldis heard these thoughts. Nicky hoped so. But the puzzle was silent. Nicky hoped the puzzle knew the distractions were almost over.

It did.

Because, as Nicky would one day understand, Huldis made sure of it.

***

The kitchen smelled like the beans from the trenches and Peter shook away the dread that he was back on The Front. He wasn't at war. He was home, but his blood pumped like war, his mind raced like war, and this was why he couldn't go back. He couldn't be this person. He couldn't be ready to fight, wanting to fight, waiting to fight, all the time. He wanted to be a dad. A husband. He wanted to love life with the loves of his life.

Lions showed them the back door, and Peter was the first one out. He didn't see the alley, just felt the hard steel burn into his chest.

Bethany screamed as the puzzle board clattered to the ground.

The man with the cut eye grabbed Bethany. The man with the crooked jaw grabbed Lions and threw him to the ground.

It was the troublemakers.

They'd come around to the back, expecting an exit. The act at the front door was meant to do just this, flush them out. And it worked.

Another stab went into Peter's gut.

Two men threw Lions down and stomped on his face.

"Not so tough now, race traitor!" The leader spit in Peter's face and stabbed again.

"NO!". Nicky screamed and went to push the man stabbing Peter away, but the man whacked him with the butt of the knife. Nicky tumbled to the ground. Bethany pushed off her attacker and rushed to Nicky and Peter. The leader reared back and smashed the knife hilt into her temple. Blood gushed from her temple in a stream. Her feet tangled. She tripped over the puzzle board in the alley. Falling with a thick crunch as her head hit a steel dumpster.

Everyone's stomach clenched at the noise.

She fell beside Nicky. Her limp body rolled to face her son. Nicky saw her. Only half of her was his mom. The other half was a monster. A thing that once looked like Bethany but now, its face was caved in, drooping and loose, lumpy and bloody.

Black jelly ran out of Bethany's skull.

The leader dropped his knife.

Peter's stomach belched blood onto the asphalt. He fell on the pavement with a splash.

Nicky was reaching for his mom when Peter crawled over, wrapping his boy into him, turning his face away from this world. Bethany didn't move.

A final boot stomped down on Lions with a heavy crack. Then he stopped twitching. But the men kept laughing. They kept pointing and laughing at Lions who wasn't pleading for them to spare the boy anymore. The owner of the Sun Rise Diner, wasn't saying anything ever again.

Peter panted seeing the death surrounding him. It followed him home from The Front. The Reaper spared him over there just to take his whole family here? Couldn't it have just moved on? Death take someone else. Leave Bethany. Leave Nicky. Leave all of us.

Wooden blocks, all with the letter D on them, were spilled in the alley. Peter counted the blocks as he struggled to breathe through pierced lungs. How many times was he stabbed? Some must have been in the chest? Why is it so hard to breathe?

The attackers shouted and ran off, leaving the dead and dying.

Peter could only whisper as his lungs filled with blood. "I love you," He reached for Bethany. He rested his hand on her foot, feeling her lifeless body. "I lost so much time with you. I'm sorry Nicky. I'm sorry." How could lungs with so many holes in them fill up with blood?

***

Daddy's final breath was hot on Nicky's wet cheeks. Tears drained out of his face, as the blood drained from his daddy's body. He tried to scream for help, but the horror of losing his family froze his throat.

Nothing came out.

Every muscle in his body twitched and spasmed in his dead daddy's arms.

If he could call for help, someone would come. Someone would help. The police would come. Someone would come. But nothing came out. No one would come because Nicky was too weak to scream.

He wasn't his daddy. He wasn't a hero. He wasn't tough, like Mommy. He was frail. Too frail to save his family. Too frail to do anything but watch his parents die. Now he lay broken on the pavement, shattered in his daddy's blood.

Echoes of the men running away bounced off the high alley walls. Did they slow down? Were they coming back? Were they coming back to kill him? To help him? Realizing what they did, what they stole from him, and now wanted to give it back? But it was just a trick of the alley. They weren't coming back.

The blood was turning cold now. Soaking through his clothes. Cool breezes barreling down on him. Rats scurried around them. How long until they came to see what they could eat?

Then there was nothing.

Stillness.

The dead didn't move. They didn't breathe. And neither did Nicky.

Silence.

But a familiar voice comforted him.

*I called for help,* Huldis said. *I'm sorry about your parents. I will get help. And then… no more distractions.*

# FOUR

The woman barked, "Get up."

Stern barely described the woman standing over Nicky, with death still curled around him. She stood with arms crossed over her dark blue blazer, her glossy shoe tapping impatiently at the non-compliant orphan beneath her. Her white hair flowed around her slight frame, and thick sunglasses hid the beginnings of crow's feet.

She was older than most would guess, younger than her soul suggested, and, at times, more monstrous than her beauty betrayed.

"Get up, now." She stomped the pavement with a sharp crack of her high heel. "Huldis, tell your toy to get up, or I'm leaving it here." She flicked her wrist, as if swatting a fly—but Nicky knew he was the fly.

*Get up, Nicky. Listen to her,* Huldis whispered into his mind so gently that Nicky wasn't sure he'd heard it.

"Hi," a softer voice said. A little girl Nicky's age stood nearby, her white dress dotted with yellow flowers. The wind played with the hem of her dress, as it did with her golden hair. If Nicky had been a bit older, he might have fallen in love with her at first sight—but that was a few years away. "I'm Anna."

She offered her hand to Nicky. He took it in a frail grip, but her strength was shocking, lifting him easily to his feet. "Why are you so sad?" she asked, glancing at the bodies around him.

"Don't touch it, Anna!" The woman scowled, as if that were the natural setting of her face. "Get the board," she ordered, stepping over to Nicky's mom and pulling the canvas bag from her death-frozen fingers.

Nicky's rage ignited. He threw himself at the woman, fists raised, like his daddy would have done. But she pushed him aside with a flick of her hand.

Nicky lay on the ground, stunned. He'd never been hit by his parents. He didn't think the woman hit him either—she'd simply waved her hand, and he fell.

Anna came to him again, helping him up. "Don't attack her when she's watching," she whispered in his ear. "She's always watching," she added, louder, so the woman could hear. Anna picked up the puzzle board and smiled as she handed it to Nicky. "It wants you back."

Nicky took the board. His eyes stayed on his daddy's face, frozen in sorrow, disappointment etched into his features forever. His daddy's eyes were open, staring into Nicky's, no matter where he stood. Mommy had her eyes closed, but the side of her head was open, smeared over the dumpster in a black stew. Mr. Lions didn't have much blood around him, and he was holding the knife used to kill Nicky's dad. But Nicky knew that wasn't right. That wasn't what had happened.

"Come," the woman commanded, motioning for the children to follow.

"Yes, Mother," Anna said, taking Nicky's hand. "Come along now. You're one of us."

As they walked past Mr. Lions, Nicky stopped to pick up the knife. He didn't know why, but he knew he'd need it someday.

"No, he's not," the woman corrected Anna. "He's not one of us. Do you have a name, boy?"

Nicky nodded.

"Huldis said you're not a fluent speaker. He said your family called you Nicky."

Nicky shook his head. "Daddy calls me Nicky," he said, the words coming without the usual confusion over what to say or how to say it. "Elijah," he tapped his chest. "Mommy calls me Elijah. Elijah Nicholas." He glanced at his daddy and tapped his chest again. "Elijah."

"I'm your mother now. What's your family name?" The woman stepped into the evening's gaslight as they left the alley behind.

"Adams," Nicky replied.

"Elijah Nicholas Adams?" The woman asked for final confirmation as she walked ahead of him and Anna, who still held his hand, swinging it like he was her new toy—and perhaps he was.

Nicky grunted in reply.

The woman nodded as they approached a long black car. Nicky had never seen a carriage like this, with gold-rimmed headlights. The car's top was pulled back, and a man sat in the driver's seat, waiting. When she approached, the driver jumped out and opened her door, bowing his bald head. The car was so shiny it gleamed in the golden streetlights. After the woman climbed in, Anna followed and tapped the seat beside her, signaling for Nicky to join them.

"Put down the papers first," the woman instructed. Anna smiled and giddily spread the newspaper over the seat she'd just patted. "Get in," the woman demanded when Nicky hesitated.

"Who?" Nicky asked, pointing at them. He clutched the board to his chest like armor. Huldis would help him. He'd found these people, and if they were bad, Huldis would help again… wouldn't he?

"Does it matter?" The woman rolled her eyes. "An orphan with questions. What is this world coming to?"

"Mother is Fiona Geeze, and I'm Anna Geeze," Anna said, tapping the newspaper-covered seat again to show that all questions had been answered. "Come on, Nicky."

Where else could he go? Back home? Who would take care of him now? There was no one else. Maybe the Millers would take him in. Maybe he and Ezra would become brothers.

But he didn't even know how to get home from here. And what if the Millers said no? This lady had a nice car. She probably had food. And Anna seemed really nice.

Maybe they could take him to the Millers when they got to Ms. Fiona's house.

Nicky climbed in.

"Elijah," he said again as he settled into the car.

Blood drenched him from lying in his daddy's dying embrace. It had dried, turning his clothes into a crackling, stiff shell.

"Where?" Nicky tried to ask, but his eyes stayed fixed on the alley, on his parents.

"Home. Until Huldis is done, and then we'll put you back." Fiona flicked her finger toward the alley as if casting trash aside—and in her mind, she was.

Anna giggled and shook her head. "No, Mother. He'll be with us now."

Unfortunately for Nicky, Anna was right.

# FIVE

On the ride out of the city, they didn't talk. Fiona read the newspaper and then a book she had brought along. This could have been any car ride for her. Nothing of interest, nothing of note, no one worthy of notice in the car with her.

Anna played with a doll, singing it songs in a language Nicky didn't understand. Every few minutes, Anna would stop singing and whisper something into the doll's ear while looking at Nicky. Then she'd laugh and shush her doll.

There was no music on the radio. Only the rushing wind over their heads and the fading bustle of the city as they drove away from everything Nicky had ever known. He had only left New York twice before today and both times were to go to the beach. He'd never seen upstate New York's lush green and bright skies. And it didn't seem that different until they broke away from the other few cars, turning on roads without lights, only visible in the dim cone of light coming from the car's headlights.

Once the headlights went out and the driver had to pull over to relight them. That's when Nicky, engulfed in the darkness beyond the city, saw the tapestry of stars hanging over him. So many stars he couldn't count them, and he was great at counting—at least that's what his mommy said.

Under the stars, the air was strange. It didn't smell like the factories or taste like the river. It made him feel awake—energized. It was fresh and clean and smooth... unlike the road, which was rough, bouncing Nicky around on the chair. The paper under him crackled as he moved and tried to hold on tight. Anna and Fiona didn't move, they barely bounced. Unlike him, they belonged in fancy cars and knew how to ride. Nicky must have looked like a buffoon to them as he struggled not to fall over.

He held his knife tight and his puzzle board tighter. Back in his family's apartment, he had other toys. When could he get those?

Were the Millers looking for them? Would anyone look for his parents and when they found them, in that alley, in all that blood, with Mr. Lions, what would they think?

*Don't fret Nicky,* Huldis said. *We'll return to our game soon.*

Fiona glanced over her book at the puzzle board and pushed the canvas bag of blocks closer to her hip.

Nicky nodded, but didn't want to play. He wanted to tell his daddy he loved him. He wanted to hug his mommy and help her paint. Instead, he was riding in a car with a woman who hated him and a girl who didn't understand why he'd be sad about his family being killed.

As they entered a dense forest, the moon disappeared behind the tree canopy. It flashed at Nicky every so often and kept reminding him that the night was there. It was waiting for him to wake up and discover this was all a dream. He'd scream for his mommy, and she'd come. Daddy would be there too. No more going to war, no more long trips away. They'd be together. Nicky smiled.

Anna cocked her head and asked, "What are you thinking about?"

"Dreaming," Nicky said.

Anna nodded excitedly and waved for her mother's attention. "Mother, Nicky is thinking about dreaming."

Fiona didn't stop reading. "He's not one of us, Anna." She turned the page. "He does not dream like us. Do not attribute him with our blood. He is just passing through."

Anna's smile widened as she dismissed her mother. Being a good boy, Nicky didn't recognize the defiance in this grin. He always did what he was told and couldn't imagine that Anna wouldn't.

Nicky turned to Anna, tapped his chest, and politely said, "Elijah."

She giggled and clenched her doll tight, whispering again into its ear.

They exited the trees, leaving behind the mildew smell of nature and returning to the crisp night air. The stars and moon again revealed to Nicky in their grandeur. Such a sky was impossible in the lights of his home. There were so many lights on the street, on stores, in stores, on cars, that he never saw stars like this. And why not? He looked at the moon before, but it always seemed so alone. A few stars dangled around it but the moon was always so so alone. Back in his apartment, he wondered if the moon was sad. But now he knew it wasn't. When alone, when there's no possibility of being with your family again, you weren't sad, you just didn't feel anything.

Initially, he thought they were driving to a castle, but castles were made of stone. This house was black in the night with only a few lights glowing inside the house to give it shape. The windows were bright with yellow light watching him approach with so many unblinking eyes Nicky wasn't sure where to look.

A black gate opened on its own as they approached and closed after they passed. Did it open by magic? There were no twinkling sounds or lights to show it was magic.

The drive wound up to the house in a long tongue towards a gaping darkness. The darkness was illuminated as exterior house lights flicked on, revealing a cluster of men waiting for the driver to arrive. One held a tray of drinks, another a tray of food. Ms. Fiona wouldn't allow him any of that. She didn't like him, and he didn't know why.

The car stopped. The men swarmed the car, opening doors, holding out arms for Ms. Fiona to take, then offering refreshments in drinks and food. She dismissed all of them with that flick she does and handed her book and newspaper to one man who was waiting for them.

With the lights on, Nicky could see the house wasn't black at all. It was made of pale bricks. White columns surrounded the entrance, creating a canopy over the car. A chandelier hung over the car, which made him want to get out as quickly as possible. If it fell, it would slice him to bits, and he'd lay on the ground in a pool of blood but with no one to hold him this time.

"Prepare the guest room," Fiona commanded. Two men rushed away.

Anna bounded out of the car and waved for Nicky to follow her as she hurried to the giant red front door. Two men stood flanking it and waited for the women to approach. Nicky stepped out of the car, hurrying away from the chandelier.

"Leave those rags on the doorstep," Fiona waved without looking. "Change of clothes for the little beast." Another man ran off at her command.

"Come on!" Anna waved for Nicky to follow her. "This is your new home!"

"No, it is not," Fiona corrected.

Anna waved the thought away. "Bring Huldis. We'll play with him in the study."

"No!" Fiona stopped and towered over her daughter. The woman's expression was anger struggling to cover fear. Her pale complexion blushed with the faintest of pink. Fiona pointed a long slender finger, knobby at the joints, at Nicky. "You will not take this into our study. It probably can't even read."

She was right. Nicky couldn't read. He could barely talk. Words were never his province. Feelings were. His mom said he was a very sensitive boy, a frail boy.

Too frail to save his family.

So frail, even the ability to learn words was too difficult for him. So words came slow. He shrank from Fiona and looked away from Anna.

A man came to him with a long jacket and a pair of trousers.

"Get in the house, Anna. We need to talk in private," Fiona said and walked through the front door. Anna followed, bounding along unbothered by the world or tonight's events. Two men stepped in front of Nicky, barring his way and thrusting the change of clothes at him.

The night was frosty, and he wanted to go in. He could feel the warmth inside that house even if the owner was cold to him. The men didn't speak, just pushed the clothes to him again.

He took them, peeling the crusty shell off his body as the dried blood cracked and drifted from him. Nicky stripped down to his long-johns and put the jacket on when the man stopped him. Wordlessly, the man shook the jacket, shook his head, then pointed to the long-johns. Both men turned to give Nicky privacy as he stripped naked and pulled on the fresh trousers quickly, then the jacket to hide his gaunt body.

Nicky had put down his knife and the puzzle board while he changed. They sat on the pavement and waited for him to dress. When he was done, he knelt to pick them both up, pausing a moment and looking back over his shoulder.

New York wasn't visible from where they were. Even on this big hill overlooking a massive forest, the moon's silver light glowing over the nothing that stretched from the forest to the horizon.

The Millers weren't coming for him. And he wasn't going back to the apartment for his other toys. That life was over. He picked up the board, then the knife. They were everything he owned.

The men stepped aside and let him pass into his home, his school, and what would become his new family.

# SIX

Fiona was gone. Anna sat pouting on the ledge of a stone fountain in the grand foyer. It was three tiers with the top reaching the second-floor landing.

Two dark wood staircases curved around the fountain up to the second floor, with a crimson runner draped down to the foyer. The foyer was hardwood, covered with a plush carpet that felt more like a pillow to Nicky that a floor. Lamps lit the great space with a crystal chandelier hanging above him, sparkling in the golden light.

Nicky stood by the door, unsure what to do. He was so small in a place this big, too small to do anything but hold his knife, hold his board, and wait.

*That's the problem with calling for help,* Huldis bemoaned. *You never know if the person has come to help you or themselves.*

Fiona still had the bag of blocks, but Huldis wasn't mad. His voice wasn't angry, just disappointed, as if he should have known better. Where did she go?

Anna hugged her doll and asked it something Nicky couldn't hear. Her face was sad, not disappointed, but frowning as if she hoped for something and didn't get it. The little girl invited Nicky to join her on the fountain, patting the stone ledge the same way she did in the car.

He sat with her, thankful she told him what to do.

"This is Zelia," Anna held out her doll. "You can tell her secrets." The doll's blonde yarn braids swung around her face. She had blue button eyes with black stitching holding them to her face. Zelia wore a fancy dress that matched Anna's, but under that dress were a pair of jean overalls covering a pink and white stripe sweater. The dress fit loosely over the doll's real outfit, hiding the commoner clothes. Anna said Zelia needed to pretend to be fancy around mother, but the doll was really a good friend and hard worker. "You want to see her room?"

Nicky shrugged.

Anna took that as agreement and grabbed his hand. She pulled him up the stairs. At the top, he saw a giant painting hung over the front door. It was an old lady, the oldest lady Nicky had ever seen with a stern expression even more set, more carved into her face than Fiona's. The woman wore a black robe with a large wooden bead necklace. Fiona stood behind her with the same stern expression. Anna sat on the floor smiling in the painting with three, Nicky assumed they were dogs, sitting around her.

The dogs were black, with glowing green eyes and long, pointed ears. Their snouts were longer than Nicky thought was right for a dog, but he'd only seen the wild dogs in New York and didn't know any other kinds. The dogs sat around Anna like sentries monitoring their post. One dog had the old woman's hand resting on its head as if she were petting it.

"Dogs?" Nicky's heart jumped as he stopped and searched, but he didn't see any in the house.

Anna giggled. "No, silly!" she said, pointing at the painting, then to the hallways off the second-floor landing. There were three hallways going in different directions, but the one Anna pointed towards was completely dark. The moonlight shone through a window at the end of the hallway, placing pale blocks of light on the blue carpet. A shadowy animal was staring out the window at the moon. When it felt Nicky's stare, its head twisted slowly to meet Nicky's gaze with burning green eyes that left a trail of ghostly light. It moved slowly into the shadows and vanished.

"They're Pooka. That was Jasper," Anna said without missing a step, as if dogs with glowing green eyes were standard in this house. She took Nicky's hand and pulled him to one of the lit hallways.

They walked past closed white double doors where Nicky heard Fiona quietly talking to someone. Anna didn't let him linger, and the two went to the next room, which was as big as Nicky's apartment.

She let go of him at the door and there he stayed; in the hall, holding his belongings and taking in the room before him.

Anna pranced her happy gallop through the room, sitting Zelia on a bed bigger than his parents' bed. His parents' bed wasn't so plush and was never made so neatly. The room was fully furnished with everything a doll, or kid, could ever need. Nicky looked for the doll's dinner table, since this room had everything else. Instead, he found a large desk with teacups and a teapot on it. There was a bookshelf filled with books, more books than the children's section at the library. White and yellow flowers covered everything in the room, creating a camouflage effect, making furniture blend into the walls, carpet, and clothes hanging in the closet.

How many dolls did Anna have? With all these dresses, she must have hundreds. He couldn't even count all the outfits, because they were mostly the same dress: white with yellow flowers.

"Like the cresses?" Anna asked and motioned him to the bed.

Nicky dropped his eyes to the line on the floor where the hallway carpet stopped and the hard wood of the bedroom began. With his bare feet, his shoes were left outside, he stepped on the hard floor and went to the bed where Anna was kneeling.

She pulled a long blue box from under the bed. It was a secret thing and treated with the reverence it deserved as such, with neither of them speaking as it was revealed. Anna slowly opened the box, showing Nicky piles of overalls with pink and white striped sweaters. Anna put her finger to her lips and pushed the box back under the bed. "Zelia's a hard worker. She'd rather be farming than dancing," she whispered. Seeing Nicky didn't understand, she said, "Farming, like growing food for people to eat. Dancing is when you—" She stood up and shook her hips to a frantic, unheard tune.

Dancing Nicky knew, but farming? He'd lived in New York his entire life and been surrounded by artists. They didn't much talk about the world outside of New York and besides, food came from the market or factory, not a farm.

Anna closed the box quickly and pushed it under the bed, springing up to attention as sharp footsteps came into her room. Nicky remembered Fiona's shoes on the pavement in the alley and jumped up with Anna. Did Fiona see the box? What would she do if she found it?

"Come," Fiona said and motioned to Nicky. "I'll show you your place in this house."

Nicky followed her out of the doll's room. Anna trailed behind, skipping along.

They went down to the foyer. Then to the kitchen, where a few men were working on a meal. They stopped and stood at attention as Fiona entered the room. She waved the standard dismissive flick of her wrist for them to continue their work, and they did.

The kitchen was a large place, bustling with life. There were ovens and ovens and pots hanging everywhere. Food pantries lined the walls with so much to eat, Nicky knew they'd never go hungry here if he was allowed to eat. No one offered him tastes of the food they were cooking like they did for Anna. No one spoke. They only held out spoons with inviting smiles for her. None of the servants looked at Nicky, much less smiled at him.

At the back of the kitchen, Fiona opened another door and walked down more stairs. These were not fancy, only wood planks attached to unfinished wood framing. Fiona lit a match, then lit two gas lamps, twisting their valve to fully open.

Nicky followed her down. Anna came next, the stairs too narrow to walk side-by-side.

The cavernous basement yawned before Nicky as he stood on the last step. Stone walls surrounded the basement where the light could reach, with shadows pooling in every rough surface. Dirt covered the foundation in a couple inches of brown earth over gray concrete. Pale white concrete encased steel poles that stretched to the ceiling.

Why was there dirt over the concrete floor? But he'd never seen a basement and thought this might just be how all basements are.

In the gloom, Nicky's eyes found a gleaming polished wooden table. The lantern light danced over its surface as the flame flickered. Beside it was a wooden chair with a red pillow on the back and seat. He'd never seen a chair like that and thought it was just for show, not meant to be sat in. Near the table was a wooden bed much more simple than the doll's bed, but nicer than any Nicky ever had. It wasn't even on the floor.

"This is your place," Fiona said.

He stepped off the stair and went to the bed, felt how soft it was and couldn't help but wonder if it was made of clouds.

"I have had the servants make this for you," Fiona said. "Be wise with your oil." She put one lamp on his table. "It will be refilled daily with breakfast, but no sooner. We live by a schedule here, as will you." She put the other lamp by the stairs. "You may not leave here unless accompanied by me. No one else." She paused for a moment and glared at Anna. The little girl scrunched up her face in disapproval. "Huldis may stay with you to teach you language. When you can speak like us, read like us, you can have a room upstairs."

Anna clapped. "I'll help."

"No," Fiona corrected her. "His kind live off our work. If he wants to change his conditions, he must do so with what he came into this house with and that alone."

Nicky put the puzzle board and knife on the table. It felt wrong to put a knife crusted with dried blood on such a nice wooden table, but he didn't know where else to put it.

Beyond the lamplight, the shadows moved and while it could have just been the flicker of a gas-flame, Nicky knew there were things in the dark upstairs. He asked Anna, "Pooka?"

Fiona recoiled. "They would never come down here," she said, glaring at Anna. "Keep him away from them." It wasn't a warning or command. It was a threat. Nicky's parents never hit him, but he saw parents that did when he went to the market with his mommy. He thought Fiona was that kind of person. The kind that would hit Anna. She was cruel. Suddenly, the knife felt very close to Nicky's hand. The thought could have evaporated or turned into a brainstorm of violence, and as he watched Fiona, letting her decide what happened next. If she hit Anna, his fingers would curl around the blood crusted blade.

But Anna's cheery reply diffused him. "Mother, can I feed him?" Anna looked up at the kitchen and smiled. "I'll take care of him."

Fiona shrugged, then said, "Don't get attached. He is here to do a job and then he'll be gone. He's not a pet. He's one of the help."

Nicky sat on the bed.

Anna ran upstairs.

Fiona went to the stairs and stopped. "There is another woman in this house. You are never to speak to her," she said. Her voice trembled at the end. Fiona surveyed the basement. "You will never be one of us, but you can pretend to be more than you are. We all pretend to be more than we are." Then, whispered almost quiet as a breath, "we all come from the dark."

She stood on the stairs. They didn't creak under her. The railing, she held it with white knuckles, did groan as she squeezed it ready to snap from her grip.

A sudden switch in the conversation confused Nicky as she said, "Anna is kind. Hurt her and I'll put you back where I found you, in that alley, in a pool of blood." She stared at him, ensuring there was no mistaking her ability to leave his guts on the ground, stand over him with that disappointed glare as he took too long to die. How inconvenient he would be as her victim. He'd die slowly. Maybe, God forbid, even get blood on her shoes.

Nicky's fingers brushed the knife. She'd use that knife to gut him, just like his daddy.

Seeing the message was received, Fiona went upstairs. She shut the door with a heavy slam, then a slide lock clicked in place. Fiona and Anna were talking upstairs, but Nicky couldn't hear them over Huldis.

*Well, looks like we're stuck.* Huldis said.

Nicky nodded.

"Get some rest. Then we'll get to work. We've got a lot to do, and Astrid needs us," Huldis said.

Nicky nodded again and laid down on the too soft bed. It absorbed him and before it could devour him fully; he climbed out of bed and laid on the floor with the blanket over himself. He hoped when he awoke, he'd be home with Mommy and Daddy. He'd be back in their apartment and maybe they'd go get ice cream. Daddy could take him to get cotton candy, and they could go on the merry-go-round. Mommy would take them to that new music place where the guys with the horns played and the woman with the pretty voice sang while mom drew her.

*Those are distractions*, Huldis said. *Tonight, you can have them, but tomorrow we need to get to work. Remember what happens to distractions.*

Nicky did.

He stared into the darkness, waiting for sleep, but knowing it wasn't coming.

The gas lamp faded.

Flickered.

And went out.

The house was quiet.

The darkness was deep.

The floor was cold and hard, and was the only thing Nicky could feel as he waited to wake up.

# SEVEN

The work began after a deep sleep. When Nicky awoke, the basement was still dark. It must always be dark down here.

No one came to fill the lamp. Nicky climbed out of bed and stretched his arms to find the table. Groping in the dark, his hip hit the table, and he felt around it to where he left the board.

*Good day,* Huldis said. *Ready to work?*

*Yes,* Nicky said, but not speaking, he replied in his mind.

Their conversations were silent as Huldis could hear Nicky's thoughts. They talked easily as Nicky's words were easy in his mind, but hard to make it from his thoughts to his mouth. Along the way, they seemed to get lost. But as Huldis found quickly, Nicky's voice hid a razor sharp mind.

When he was tired, Nicky would sleep. Sometimes he found food on the steps. The lantern was filled occasionally, but light was not required to navigate from the stairs to the table after a few sleeps. The dark was no more an obstacle than rain or snow. It was only something that hid what you could see at a distance once your eyes adjusted.

Food could be smelled when it was on the stairs. No light needed to see it. Huldis's voice could be heard louder as he got closer to the board, but Nicky thought this to be something Huldis did on purpose, having caught the board being just as loud when he was at the stairs as it was when he was at the table.

Anna came to visit, and when she did, she brought light with her. A few sleeps ago, she even brought cookies. She made them herself, and Nicky knew that to be true, because they were burnt to ashy hunks of charcoal. He still ate them and appreciated her visit. She told him about Zelia's latest adventures in the hedge maze, whatever that was. Anna said, "There's a monster in the maze and it tried to eat Zelia, but we ran away."

She left after that. Nicky wondered if the monster in the maze would find its way to the basement. But such thoughts never lasted long as the *work* was near constant.

Nicky didn't question what Huldis was, a ghost, a magical board, or whatever. All that mattered was he was the voice that kept him from feeling alone in the dark basement. And Huldis was nice. He knew the words were in Nicky's mind. They were jumbled and didn't always make sense, but they were there.

Huldis explained how he thought Nicky's words were knotted up in his head and how Huldis would help him untangle the words.

Anna came to visit. Zelia was always with her, and they'd have tea with Nicky. She taught Nicky the etiquette of a tea party as well as brought him books from the doll's room. She'd read to him and showed him words. Huldis would help him read by helping him untangle the words.

Never did Nicky question who Huldis was helping. As a child, Nicky was innocent and, as all innocent children do, assumed the innocence of others. For his part, Huldis was kind and focused and encouraging. There were no distractions here. Every moment was work.

Nicky would eat twice a day with a little snack during tea time. Huldis taught him how to exercise to keep his body growing even in the basement dark. After a while, his feet were stretching beyond the length of the comforter, which used to fit just fine. He was getting taller.

Sometimes a servant would bring fresh clothes and a bucket to wash himself. But that never mattered much to Nicky. No one told him to bathe down here. His mom, no longer mommy in his mind, always pushed bathes but she wasn't here now.

His dreams were outside of the basement. They were bizarre lights and colorful faces rushing through streets like rivers. New York was a torrent of discordant music, gushing blood…or paint…or music. It filled his mind and when he woke up, he could breathe in the darkness. The cold basement chasing away haunting memories of warm crimson pools and embraces lost forever more. He'd awake, panting, unable to breathe, unable to find silence in that chaos, too hot from being held by his mom, and when he'd realize he was alone, he'd sigh and smile and find life back to what he knew it to be now.

Every time someone left the basement, the door was locked. Sometimes that would wake him up, hearing the heavy metal bolt shot through the lock. But that meant something was delivered. And so he'd get up to check.

And that was life.

Nicky had no concept of time in the basement. There were no windows and the days were kept by the coming and going of meals.

And when breakfast didn't come, as sometimes he was forgotten, he assumed the day was extra-long.

Anna's outfits were always the same in her white dress with yellow flowers. Her hair was always in a long ponytail, but Nicky could tell it was getting longer and longer. She was also getting taller. Once Anna was almost as tall as Nicky. Now she was starting to stretch over him.

But Zelia always looked the same in her jean overalls and pink and white stripe sweaters under the fancy dresses.

Nicky knew he'd been down in the basement for a long time because the floor, now with his comforter on it, became comfortable. The tea parties didn't take as much guidance from Anna on which utensil to use when. And now he could tell the difference between black tea and green tea, even when he couldn't see it in his cup. But most exciting, the books Anna left behind weren't just symbols on paper anymore. They made words and words made stories, and stories made books.

Huldis and Nicky worked every day. When the boy got tired, the puzzle would say, *I can't motivate you. Your motivation is what will get you out of here. I can inspire you, but you don't need that. Fiona's already inspired you.* And after that, they'd keep working.

But Huldis was wrong. It wasn't Fiona's promise that drove Nicky.

It was Anna.

He wanted to be with her and hear her stories. He wanted to run through the barn, the house, the hedge maze, with her. She had adventures, and he wanted them too. He wanted to be like the boys, men, girls, and women he read about in these books. Adventures weren't just for make believe people. He could have them too and he would as soon as he could prove to Fiona he was worthy to leave the basement.

And the basement wasn't all that bad. It was the biggest room he'd ever had. This bed he'd made on the floor was the most comfortable bed ever. He was never alone, as he always had Huldis. He missed his parents and sometimes wondered if they were really dead. Perhaps they survived and got help before it was too late. Now they were looking for him.

But his heart knew that wasn't true, no matter how much his soul hoped it was. Huldis also dispelled any dreams, reminding Nicky that they were distractions. He'd never be able to do what he's done if they were still distracting him.

One time when Anna visited, she had gotten even taller and Nicky realized just how much taller she was than him.

As usual, Anna brought a book. This one was about a little girl following a rabbit when Nicky reached for the book, gently taking it from her and placing it on the table. He opened his mouth. She crooked her head curiously.

"Anna," he spoke slowly. "I want please the story, the monster story, please."

She smiled and squealed with joy. "Mother!" She ran upstairs and locked the door behind her as she was instructed to do.

*Good work.* Huldis said. *You meant to say I want the monster story, please.*

Nicky repeated, seeing the mistake in his word configuration.

A moment later, the latch unlocked, and Anna bound back downstairs. Fiona followed her with the even pace Nicky remembered from her last visit, which was his first day down here. How long ago was that?

The woman's hair was tied up, and she wore a long green nightgown under a red sweater. Silver stitching around the hem formed trees that sparkled in the bright lantern light. She smelled like outside, the cold fresh air lingering around her as she entered the basement.

"Speak," Fiona said. The dismissive flick came with her command.

"Yes, ma'am," Nicky said. He struggled through the words. He waited for her to react. Then added, "I like," he breathed to refocus, "the monster story."

Fiona looked at Anna.

"Ms. Shelley's book, Frankenstein." Anna smiled and beamed with pride as she held up the book Nicky wanted, drumming it with excited fingers as she showed it to her mom. "I told you he could learn!"

"And so he has," Fiona glanced at the puzzle board. "I assume your tutor's assistance is still required."

Nicky nodded without looking at her. He wanted to be smart on his own, but knew he wasn't there yet. Huldis helped him make sense of the words.

"Anna, take him to the barn and have the servants bathe him. Then show him to the room you have made for him." Fiona walked upstairs.

"It's a Christmas Miracle, Mother!" Anna shouted after Fiona.

"It's not Christmas yet," Fiona called back down as she continued.

The door did not close behind her.

Anna handed Frankenstein to Nicky, and the two walked upstairs. Nicky held the book, the knife, and the puzzle board as he went to be scrubbed clean in the horse stables.

# EIGHT

One servant apologized to Nicky, not saying the words, apologizing with his eyes, before throwing a bucket of ice water over him. The scrub brushes were rough and pushed him hard against the stone wall to get all the dirt off him. Another bucket of icy water drenched him again and then the pokey bristles stabbed into him again. Anna waited outside as the servants scoured any dirt that might have been on Nicky away. When they were done, they threw a towel at him and left without a word.

Outside, the world was cold. Ice crystals clung to the grass. There were flag stones lining the path from the stables to the house, but they were colder than the grass. Nicky walked quickly as each step bit sharp spikes of cold into his bare feet. Anna danced along the path, singing some cheery song Nicky didn't recognize. His mind was too focused on the ice crystals forming in his hair, the icicle forming on the tip of his nose.

When they re-entered the house, Nicky took a moment to feel the warm wooden floor and allow his feet to thaw, but Anna hurried him along and so he walked quickly after her.

As the ice turned to drips, Nicky kept wiping his face and hair with the towel to keep any drips off the floor. He didn't want to upset

Fiona by getting her floor wet. She seemed to be the type of parent who was upset about everything and, as children do, Nicky learned quickly what could trigger her wrath. He was hyper-fixated on avoiding that. He knew what made her mad, his existence. If he was invisible, she'd be happy. She'd leave him alone like she did when he was in the basement.

As Nicky stepped into the foyer, his breath caught in his chest. A Christmas tree so massive it seemed to touch the ceiling filled the room. The Rockefeller Center tree, which would become a New York icon in just over a decade, couldn't hold a candle to this evergreen giant.

The tree radiated color and light. Lush red silk bows cascaded down its branches like a waterfall of crimson. Warm, not hot. Comforting, not soaking. A waterfall to fill his heart, not hollow it out.

Nestled among the deep green needles were apples—real apples— their polished skins gleaming in shades of ruby and emerald. Nicky's eyes widened as he caught glimpses of gold ornaments peeking out from deep within the branches, like hidden treasures waiting to be discovered.

At the base of the tree, a rolling sea of shimmering packages spread out like a shiny carpet. Gold and green wrapping paper sparkled in the light, each box tied with intricate bows that looked too perfect to be real. Nicky edged closer. Each gift had a label. His eyes darted from one to another. Every package was marked with a single name: Anna.

"That's a Christmas tree," Anna said as they passed. "If you're good, *Santa* might bring you a gift." She giggled and hurried upstairs.

His mom mentioned Santa Claus, but Santa never brought him gifts. All the gifts were from his mom and sent home by his dad. His mom said Santa was a myth that other people talked about to have more fun during Christmas. He knew not to say anything different to Anna because she believed in Santa, but Nicky couldn't imagine more gifts being able to fit under the tree.

"When is Christmas?" Nicky asked, taking his time to form the thoughts.

"Tomorrow," Anna said from the top of the stairs.

Christmas in New York, Nicky tried to remember it, but could only think of his mom taking him shopping. Her face was smiling, it was a warm smile, but he could only see half her face. The other half, the half that hit the dumpster, was blurry. His heart sped up, hoping her face stayed blurry, hoping he didn't have to see her again. But she smiled, and he smiled back in the memory. Now, he couldn't smile.

Nicky nodded and followed, calculating a question he was too scared to ask directly. It was summer when his dad came home. So perhaps he wasn't in the basement as long as he thought? Only a few months. That wasn't too bad.

She took him to the room beside Zelia's, which was much smaller and not as nicely furnished. The walls were dark blue with thick red stripes running from floor to ceiling. Silver stripes lined the red, making the reds all that much brighter. All the furniture was wood, and all the wood colors matched. There was a place where a bed belonged, but it was missing. Nicky cocked his head at the blank space.

"I had the servants take the bed out because I saw you weren't using yours." Anna pointed to a bedroll on the floor. Nicky looked puzzled. "I saw you when I visited. If you were sleeping, I didn't bother you."

Nicky didn't remember this. He never knew when he was sleeping, being in the dark for so long.

He felt the bed roll. It was perfect. Anna took Frankenstein from him and put it on the desk. Then she went to the bookshelf and pulled out another.

"If you like Frankenstein, you'll like this one." She pulled another book, adding to the pile. "It's about a man who is actually two people. One is a doctor and the other a monster."

"Thank you," Nicky said. He put the puzzle board on the desk beside the books.

Anna stopped selecting books when Nicky gently tugged on her arm. When she looked into his eyes, her silver-blue eyes meeting his, he lost his breath for the second time that night. During his time in the basement, his mind and body grew. The differences between boys and girls were becoming clearer, and the stunning beauty Anna wielded over him was staggering. How did he never see her like this during her visits? How did teatime pass without him falling into those eyes?

Anna wrapped him in a hug and squeezed tight enough to make his back pop. "Merry Christmas Nicky! What do you want Santa to bring you?"

He pulled back from Anna, sad to correct her, "I'm Elijah."

Anna blushed and smiled. "Yes, I'm sorry. I guess you'll just always be Nicky to me." She stepped away from him. "So, what do you want from Santa?"

He shrugged, not wanting to ask for the impossible. Santa wasn't real and bringing people back from the dead wasn't real, but what else could he want? He had his favorite book. He had someone to keep him company in Anna. And he had Huldis to teach him about the world.

"Well, ask Santa and I'm sure he'll bring it for you," Anna said as she slipped out of Nicky's room. "I gotta get to bed. I left out enough cookies for both of us." With that, she ran off.

Nicky left his door open. He put on the flannel pajamas Anna left for him, then he went to the window and looked out into the moonlit night. The stars winked at him. He wondered what they knew. Did they know about Santa Claus?

He pulled the latch and opened the window to let the frozen winter air into his room. The warmth of the house was chased away, but he always knew it was temporary. It was warm for him. Just warm for now. The cold was his world, and so he returned to it while wishing for his own Christmas Miracle.

Huldis helped Nicky form the words and Nicky grasped his hands like his mom showed him and knelt to pray.

"I want to go home," Nicky said and waited for the sky's reaction to ensure it heard him. But it was indifferent to his request. Still, he waited for something and didn't realize when he fell asleep at the window, still waiting to go home.

# NINE

"Get up Nicky! Santa came!" Anna shook him from behind. He was still kneeling at the window. Snow was gently falling and a white blanket covered the world outside his window from the house to the forest. A dusting of snow drifted through his window, covering him. As he stood, he shook it off. "Come on!" She tugged at his arm, and he went with her to the landing.

The hardwood of the first floor was hidden under all the glittering wrapped packages. Anna squealed and ran down the stairs. Nicky followed her, excited for her excitement.

Fiona was sitting on what Nicky assumed was a throne. It had a long leather back that rose above her head and the wood was shining so bright in the winter light. Massive windows let the white light outside pour in and make everything glow. There was another woman, ancient compared to Fiona, sitting in a wheelchair and watching Anna. It was the old woman from the painting. A giant warm smile wrinkled this old lady's face, and she held out her arms for a hug from Anna. The girl, no longer so little, obliged with a laugh. The old woman answered with a kiss on Anna's cheek.

"Will you not introduce me to your friend?" The old lady asked Anna. She had a thick Irish accent which Nicky recognized from his trips to church. On the rare occasion his mom took him to church, there were a lot of Irish people at communion.

"Mother. This is the orphan we discussed," Fiona answered for Anna.

"And you thought it proper to cast this fine gentleman as a cellar dweller?" The old lady shook her head.

Fiona glared at Nicky. And he said nothing, as instructed.

"Have you nothing to say, boy?" The old lady asked him direct.

Nicky shook his head and kept his eyes on the floor.

*Then perhaps you have thoughts?* The old lady spoke in his head.

"Mother!" Fiona shouted, scandalized.

The old lady rolled her eyes, and Anna laughed. "Oh, Fiona Lucille, you mustn't be so. It's Christmas morning. Let the boy have his voice."

But Nicky kept his word to Fiona and said nothing. The old lady nodded and smiled. *Good lad, but she is only scared of you. Take her words as the barks of a frightened dog.*

"Mother! That's enough!" Fiona scowled. "Anna, open a gift," she demanded.

The old lady made a long face like she was in trouble. Anna mimicked her, and that made Nicky laugh. He choked it back quickly to avoid Fiona's ire.

"Elijah, there is a gift for you as well," the old lady said and motioned to a pile of silver wrapped gifts that were not there last night.

Nicky just stared at the old woman. Santa wasn't real. Who brought the gift? Certainly not Fiona. Maybe Anna?

He went to the pile and looked for his gift but found all the silver wrapped ones had his name on them. Nicky frowned and stepped away from the pile. Anna grabbed his arm and threw him, none too gently, into the pile of gifts.

"Best to just dive in!" She said and followed him into the pile.

"This one first," the old lady wheeled over to him and pointed a long, skeletal finger at a thin rectangular box. "Open that one, Elijah." And so he did.

It was a long wooden box inside the wrapping. He opened it. A flat gray stone, smooth and cool to the touch, was inside, along with a vial of liquid. He looked with curiosity at the old lady, unsure what this gift meant. Suddenly, the image of his knife appeared in his mind, oiling the stone, then running the knife over it.

"It is a whetstone," the old lady said. "You hone your knife with it as you will hone your other tools with us."

"He's not staying," Fiona said, but when the old lady looked at her this time, Fiona took a deep breath in as if to suck those words back down her throat. "As you wish, mother."

"Never has a Geeze turned away those in need and never shall we begin now," the old lady said. "He did his time. Now we do ours."

"He's not one of us!" Fiona replied.

The old lady nodded in agreement. "Indeed. Nor will he ever be, but we do not turn out those not of our blood." She straightened in her chair and stabbed her finger into the armrest of her wheelchair. "We are not monsters."

At that moment, Anna shoved another gift into Nicky's arms. "This one's from me." It was a jumbled mess of wrapping paper with unnecessarily long strips of tape holding it all together. "Open it!" Anna encouraged, and Nicky did.

It was a book, but the pages had no words. Each cream-colored page was blank, with rough cut edges wrapped in a crimson leather binding. A pooka's face was engraved on the front of the notebook with two emeralds for eyes. He held it up, delighted by the beauty but unsure what to do with it.

"You can write in it," Anna said.

Nicky nodded agreement and put the book down beside the whetstone. He smiled, then said, "please." Inviting her to open a gift.

Anna did. It was a new dress, much like the other dresses her mother had bought for her, white with yellow flowers. Nicky smiled and nodded that it was a delightful gift, and motioned for her to take another. She tore into the gift, revealing a yellow dress with white flowers. Then a white dress with light orange flowers. Fiona smiled and nodded with each dress as if approving it. The light orange flowers brought suspect glances from her, but she approved and Anna moved on.

"Anna dear, here's one from *Santa*," the old lady said.

Anna jumped to it, tearing the paper away. When she opened the box, she paused and looked quizzically at the old lady. "What is it, Nana?"

"Your birth rite," the old lady said.

When Anna lifted it from the box, Nicky scooted closer to see it. Fiona did not smile or nod approval. She gasped, scandalized, but

Anna was too busy examining the odd gift. It was a spherical black stone with a map etched into it. At the center was a tower. There were other structures, but Nicky couldn't understand what they meant. There were symbols on the map as well, but like the buildings, they were indecipherable. The symbols and buildings were a spiral which all met in the center, at the tower.

"Why is it warm?" Anna looked to her mother for an answer but only found an icy glare.

"Perhaps another gift for Elijah," Fiona directed and waded through the gifts, taking the stone map from Anna. "There Elijah, there's a gift for you from—" Fiona trailed off as she gave her mother a stern glare. Her breathing drowned out the crinkling gift wrap surrounding Anna and Nicky. The two older women stared at each other. The younger angry. The older, defiant in a way that only mothers can be to their adult daughters.

"Thank you," Nicky said and picked up another gift. He opened it and pulled out the blue suit jacket and pants. It was made just for him. There was a fancy red shirt inside the box as well. He held up the clothes for Anna to see and put them carefully back in the box. Anna nodded approvingly, like her mother, and smiled, then motioned for him to continue.

Christmas morning continued in this fashion with Anna getting dresses, books, a painting of her, a dollhouse and dolls while Nicky got clothes to build his wardrobe from nothing to all the clothes he could ever need for any situation.

"Prepare for midday meal. We will luncheon in the Study," the old lady said and motioned for the man standing at the periphery to come and wheel her.

Fiona didn't protest, but clearly wanted to. She motioned to the torn wrapping paper around Nicky and said, "Clean it up." Then she turned to Anna and pointed to the pile of dresses. "Select one for luncheon and I'll have the servants take the rest to your room."

Anna did.

Nicky did as told. The servants did not help. He took the trash to the kitchen, where he saw a trashcan when he left the basement. After a few trips and ensuring his space was clean, he took his clothes, whetstone, and book to his room.

There, Huldis was sitting on his desk beside the knife. Even with these gifts, the puzzle board and the knife were the only things that were his. Now the book, Frankenstein, was part of that. He thought the rest would be reclaimed by Fiona when she turned him out.

Would she? The old lady seemed to be very clear that he was now part of the family, or at least, welcome in the house. Anna wanted him here. The old lady seemed to as well.

Maybe Fiona wasn't the one in charge around here?

Anna popped into his room, wearing the white dress with light orange flowers. "Here," she said, pulling out the blue suit and red shirt. "Wear this for luncheon, and then wear this for dinner tonight." She selected a black suit with a white shirt as his second outfit. "Get changed, so we aren't late. You're going to love the Study." Anna bounded out of the room in her usual half-skip, half-run.

Nicky changed and looked at himself in the mirror. His face was sunken, pale, and ghostly. Dark lines had formed under his eyes, and his hair was messy. Who was this? A stranger stared back in the mirror. His arms were too long. His legs were too strong. This wasn't a frail boy.

He noticed a brush on his desk, and with it, he brought his hair to order as he thought was expected. The suit and shirt fit him perfectly, as if they were made for him. And he was certain they were.

This isn't the boy who went into the basement. And it wasn't months that he was in the basement. He grew tall. His muscles toned from Huldis's exercises. Time disappeared when he was down there, but now, he saw years had moved on. It didn't leave him behind, it drug him forward with it. Forgotten by all but time, which refused to let him rest. He worked and worked and grew and aged.

This isn't the boy who went into the basement. And it wasn't months that he was in the basement. He grew tall. His muscles toned from Huldis's exercises. Time disappeared when he was down there, but now, he saw years had moved on. It didn't leave him behind, it drug him forward with it. Forgotten by all but time who didn't let him rest. He worked and worked and grew and aged.

"Who are you?" he asked, not recognizing the boy staring back at him. "Elijah," he answered.

Huldis remained silent.

"Dad called you Nicky," the boy in the mirror said. "But Nicky died. Dead in the alley, and now there's only Elijah."

Was there a hint of the boy, the frail little boy who let his family die in the alley? Did Nicky come out of the basement? Did he ever go into it? No, Nicky never left the alley. He died with his mommy and daddy. Elijah came out of the alley, birthed in the blood of his father and the smashed gaze of his mother.

From then on, Nicky was gone. Elijah was the one in the mirror now.

A tear welled up in Elijah's eye for the passing of his family. The boy, Nicky, was the final casualty.

# TEN

The Study was bigger than the big room in the New York Library. More than the volume of books, it was the height of the ceiling that stunned Elijah. He got dizzy looking up and staggered backward into the room. There was a painting on the ceiling of a naked woman trying to touch the finger of an old woman with long white hair wearing a red robe. They were sitting in clouds and surrounded by children and those green-eyed pooka creatures who looked hungrily at the younger woman.

Bookshelves stretched from floor to ceiling and covered the walls. Elijah thought the number of books to be countless as they were orderly shelved with some stacked to fill the shelf space completely. There were plush couches spotting the giant room with finely crafted wooden tables on both sides of the couch.

The old woman in the wheelchair sat at a large table. She stared through a magnifying glass held by a jointed copper pipe arm. Elijah thought it amazing, but the old woman paid it no mind as she examined an ancient book. He waited at the door for an invitation, clasping his hands at his stomach and rocking quietly.

She looked up and smiled.

"Mr. Elijah Adams. A pleasure to finally meet you," she said.

Elijah smiled and lowered his head in a bow, like he'd seen in the movies. She looked like a queen and so he acted accordingly. No one else was in the Study yet.

"You may speak to me."

Elijah shook his head, grimacing, sorry to disappoint her. He knew Ms. Fiona said never to talk to this lady, her mother, and he didn't want to upset Ms. Fiona.

The old lady knocked on the wooden table with three sharp raps. He snapped to her attention.

"I. Make. The. Rules," she said slowly. "My daughter is brilliant. When God formed my little Fiona, she poured in intelligence and left no space for kindness or compassion. She seeks to protect me. I needn't protection."

Elijah nodded quickly to calm the old woman, who was wheeling towards him now. As she spoke, as she approached, her presence filled the Study darkening the room as if a cloud passed over the sun. This darkness congealed in Elijah's guts, becoming a boiling fear. The closer she came, the more intense her oppressive tension grew until she was directly at his toes. He wanted to step away from her, but his body wouldn't comply.

Elijah stood before her, drowning in her presence. A power swelled within her until she saw he felt it. He felt the electric thrumming coming from her, the surging of an unseen force. Then the shade passed. She released him and said, "You will address me as Madam Geeze, or simply Madam if you wish. There is no other Madam Geeze. And you will speak when spoken to or when you have something to say."

Elijah nodded quickly.

"I heard you like Frankenstein." She wheeled away, taking her oppressive presence with her. "Why is that?"

"I understand it," Elijah answered in his slow tone. "The Monster was alone."

Madam shook her head. "No. He was not. He had Victor, his maker."

"They fought," Elijah answered. "They were not friends."

Madam huffed a laugh that turned to a cough. After she recovered, she swallowed hard and said, "Relationships are never so simple. Maker and Monster were defined by their conflict with each other. The Maker cannot ignore the Monster anymore than the Monster can live without the Maker."

Elijah looked to the ceiling and saw the old lady in the painting wasn't reaching for the young lady. She was pointing. The pookas were seeing where the old lady pointed as if taking direction. Their snarls could have been to attack, but Elijah didn't think they appeared scary, only fierce. As was the old lady in the painting.

They were not being sent to attack the young lady, but perhaps, being instructed to teach her ferocity. Were the pooka teachers? Were they guardians? Student and teacher. Mother and daughter.

But not mother and son. His mother wasn't here to protect him. She died.

"We don't always get to choose our path," Madam said. She patted his arm. "And some people never get to walk the path meant for them." She joined him in looking at the painting. "The world is hard. But we need each other. No one can survive alone. In this painting, the old woman isn't just the teacher, she's the world. The pooka aren't just the protectors, they are the fangs of the world devouring the weak. The young woman is inheriting the world and all its problems. It is a cycle worthy of a grand painting."

"But we hate?" Elijah turned from the painting. "The Maker hated the Monster," he twisted his fingers, trying to find the right words. They uncoiled in his mind with some effort, but Madam was patient. "We kill what we hate."

Madam nodded. "Some do." She laced her fingers into his. Elijah felt her dry papery skin and would have recoiled if not for her cold touch being the only touch from an adult he's had since his dad held him in the alley. "Not'all. They're scared. Monsters get scared. Makers get scared. And sometimes you cannae tell which's which."

In this moment, Elijah could have turned back. He could have returned to being Nicky, the kind, innocent boy. Life would have been different for so many people if Elijah would have smiled at Madam Geeze and said what he wanted to say, "I want to go home." Back to New York, to the Millers and the police to tell them what happened, and get justice for his parents and Mr. Lions. To start life again and perhaps be a professor, or a teacher, or maybe even study here with Madam Geeze. She was kind and wonderful and could be the Maker to his Monster.

But before the conversation could open that path for him, Fiona entered the Study. She stomped to her mother without looking at Elijah. Worry creased her brow, her hair frizzed in panic. Warm clothes wrapped around her with a thick covering of snow coated her shoulders.

"Mother, we have a problem," Fiona grabbed the back of the

wheelchair and pushed her out of the Study. "Elijah, Anna will be here shortly. Please eat without us."

Elijah nodded and avoided eye contact with Ms. Fiona. Did she hear him talking to Madam? He hoped not. He should have listened. No talking to Madam. Now she's going to take him back to the alley. She said she would, and Ms. Fiona wasn't one to make idle threats.

Elijah approached the table where Madam Geeze had been reading. A dark spiral, etched into the aged page, caught his eye. It looked like the spiral on the stone Anna received for Christmas, but this one had doors between the lines—like a maze. His heart raced as he traced the lines with his eyes. What was it?

Then Huldis's voice echoed in his mind, clear and certain. *That is the Lazarus Spiral. That's how you can get your family back. But you'll need Astrid's help.*

Elijah froze, staring at the spiral. Get his family back? Huldis had never lied to him before. The promise of his mom, his dad—it surged through him like a tidal wave of hope. No Fiona, no alleyway, no blood. Just life before. Just Nicky.

"What is the Lazarus Spiral?" Elijah asked.

Before Huldis could answer, Anna walked in and waved.

*Wave back so she doesn't get suspicious. We'll need her to get the blocks back. Astrid has the keys to the Spiral. Help her and get your life back.*

Elijah waved.

# ELEVEN

Mid-day meal came and went. Dinner came and went. There was no sign of Fiona and Madam Geeze.

Elijah asked Anna where they went, but she was too pre-occupied with Zelia trying on new clothes to pay any mind to her mother. The two children sat in the Study for most of the day. Elijah reading. Anna playing. After dinner, one servant came for Anna and motioned for her to follow him. None of the servants ever spoke.

He took Anna and Elijah to a white room with large windows and three enormous beds. There were servants in here as well, but they were dressed in all white. Fiona was pacing at the bedside while Madam Geeze was being helped by numerous servants that Elijah assumed were doctors. She was bleeding and hissed through horrible pain.

"Anna, Nana has been hurt. She needs your attention while I attend to another matter." Fiona gave Elijah a doubtful look, then strode toward the door. As she passed him, she said, "Come."

Anna went to her grandmother, and Elijah followed Fiona. The servants closed the door and locked it when he left. Fiona moved quickly. Elijah struggled to keep up. Her long legs and wide stride kept Elijah at near a run to keep pace.

"I need another set of hands," she said and walked faster.

"I can help," Elijah said. This was his moment to show Fiona he could help in the house. He wasn't a thing to be in the way or just another mouth to feed. He could help like he used to help his family and the neighbors.

"You've helped enough," Fiona snapped back. "You and that damn puzzle."

"Huldis?" Elijah wondered aloud.

Fiona scoffed. "Huldis," she mocked. "Who else? That thing has been nothing but trouble."

"Why did you help?" Elijah asked the question Huldis had pondered while they were alone in the basement. "You came to help."

"Anna heard the call and came for you. We were in the city for a shopping trip, and she heard the puzzle call out. Her insistence was undeniable."

Elijah wasn't surprised. Fiona wasn't the kind of person to help someone. At least he didn't think she was. But Anna seemed like she'd help anyone who needed it.

They walked out of the house and into the garden. Fiona led the way to the hedge maze. When Elijah saw it, he staggered back. The snow capped greenery was well manicured and would have been pleasant if not for the stories Anna had told about Zelia encountering monsters within it. But Zelia was a doll, and that was, possibly, years ago. It could have been made up? A kid's fantasy.

"Keep up," Fiona said as she walked into the hedge maze.

She was wearing a red jacket that was a stark contrast to the snowy surroundings. Since they came outside, the snow had intensified now, making it hard to see far ahead. The red jacket stood out, but Fiona didn't wait for him. She charged into the maze. Elijah ran after her.

While Fiona easily stepped over the snow, Elijah had to wade through it. Drifts in the maze came up to his thighs, and the snow kept coming down. His suit was warm, but now it was soaked through, his pants clinging to his legs like icy clamps. Cold came up from below him while it fell from the sky, pressing down on him. A frozen vice squeezing the heat from him. At least the snow smelled nice. It was winter, the flavor of a candy cane, but now it was choking him. The snow pressing into his lungs as it fell into his mouth and pushed on him through his soaking wet suit.

Fiona moved, unphased by the cold. Snow built on her jacket and then melted away. Elijah thought it must have been waterproof or something because it didn't look like the snow was drenching her like it was him.

Now the downfall was so dense, Fiona's red jacket was fading away. She was moving too fast.

"Wait." Elijah said, but with the roaring wind and the crunching snow, she didn't hear. Or didn't want to hear. "Wait! Ms. Fiona!"

Two quick turns and Fiona was gone. The snow was falling harder now. "Ms. Fiona!" He called, but the wind threw his voice away from the maze. Snow built on his shoulders as he stood and looked for any sign of where to go. He saw Fiona's footprints, but soon those were covered in fresh snow. Even his own steps to backtrack and escape the maze were gone. "Ms. Fiona!" He called again but there was no answer.

Unsure what to do, he thought of Huldis and asked with his thoughts, *What do I do?*

The puzzle didn't answer. Driving wind filled the world around him. Fluttering snow gathered in Elijah's ears and eyelashes. He brushed it away. More came. The world was blurred and muffled.

As he cleared his ears, a snarl came on the wind, followed by a thick, hungry growl. Elijah perked up like a rat smelling a cat. The growl came again. Snow muffled the sound. The wind throwing the sound in all directions. Snow crunched behind him. Elijah spun to see what was creeping up on him. Nothing was there. More crunching, quick steps rushing towards him came from his left. Nothing was there.

"Ms. Fiona?" Elijah asked weakly.

In the fog of snow, green flaming eyes came out from behind the hedge maze turn in front of Elijah. The Pooka snarled and growled in a low rumble the boy could feel in the ground. Snow coated the top of the black creature, steaming away moments later. It stood quivering with potential energy, ready to pounce as it bared its teeth, three rows of teeth, much more than a dog should have. It wasn't a dog. It was a pooka. Whatever that was.

Terror filled Elijah. Between the cold and the wait for this creature to attack, he couldn't breathe. But then a quick breath came, breaking through the fear with recognition. "Jasper?" He thought this pooka looked exactly like the one Anna told him was named Jasper when he first arrived at the house.

The pooka leaned back, relaxing as the growling quieted, then stopped. It sat and faced Elijah, eyes still flaming green but now more contemplative, less ready to kill.

"Jasper?" Elijah said again and motioned for the pooka to come to him like a dog. It didn't, and for a moment Elijah thought he saw the pooka roll its eyes. "Not a dog," Elijah chided himself.

Jasper looked to his right, behind the hedge wall from which he came and then walked that way, disappearing behind the snow-covered greenery.

Elijah held himself and shivered as Jasper stuck his head around the hedgerow.

"I follow you?" Elijah asked. And again, the pooka seemed annoyed at the question. Not wanting to be a bother, Elijah walked towards the pooka. As soon as he did, Jasper disappeared behind the hedge.

When Elijah reached the place Jasper stood, the pooka had moved to the next turn and walked off when Elijah saw him. The boy ran to catch up. No matter how fast he ran, Elijah was never much of an athlete. Jasper was always at the next turn. There were no paw prints between turns, only faded footprints. Fiona's footprints.

Another few turns, and Elijah came to an opening in the hedge maze where Fiona stood over a blob of black goop. Spindly spider legs stuck out of the blob at odd angles, with too many joints. A cluster of eyes was at the smallest part of the blob. The entire body was steaming, and no snow settled on the mass.

"Dead?" Elijah pointed to the thing, unsure if it was an animal, a pile of trash, or what. The unreality of the thing didn't scare Elijah because he wasn't sure what he was seeing. But Fiona's glare at the thing, the black sludge on her hands, told Elijah whatever the blob was, Fiona either put it here or did something to it.

The butcher near their apartment. His hands would look like this sometimes, but they'd be dark red instead of black. Was she butchering this thing?

"Do you know what that is?" Fiona asked. Her voice was sharp as usual, but it was a genuine question.

Elijah shook his head, then checked the opening to see where Jasper was. The pooka was not there.

"Huldis mentioned nothing like this?"

*Tell her no.* Huldis spoke into Elijah's mind and the boy shook his head quickly. Fiona's mouth twisted, chewing on an idea, staring at Elijah for the answer. He looked away, unable to stare into her dissecting eyes.

"No. I don't know anything about this," Elijah said.

"There were three of these trying to get into the house." Fiona hunkered down by the fleshy blob and pointed at it. "They're Guardians of the Tower. They don't belong here. Someone showed them how to get here."

Elijah listened and then stared at the steaming mass, considering Fiona's implications. She was saying someone, or something, brought these things to their house. She was implying it was him.

"Anna trusts you," Fiona stood. "Did you know about this?"

Elijah shook his head quickly. "Honest. No. I wouldn't hurt Anna."

Fiona nodded but froze when she heard Huldis add, *That's the right answer.*

Of course, it was the right answer.

It was the truth.

Elijah did not know what this thing was or how it got here. Huldis didn't tell him about this. Being a smart kid, Elijah was connecting the *tower* to maps and images he'd recently seen in the book in the study as well as the stone Anna received for Christmas, what Madam Geeze called her *birthright*.

Fiona glared at Elijah. Both of them stood staring at each other as the snow built around them. Fiona was considering something, while Elijah simply wanted her to believe him. If he protested too much, he'd look guilty, but he was innocent. He didn't want to go back to the basement.

He broke from her accusing eyes and searched again for Jasper, but didn't want to ask where he was because Fiona said to never talk to the pooka.

"Let's get this over with," Fiona barked and went to another mass that was buried in the snow. She reached into the powder and pulled a rope up and tugged it. The snow fell away, revealing a wooden sled with two shovels on it. She threw a shovel at Elijah. He didn't catch it in time, and the wooden handle cracked against his collarbone. Fiona didn't notice or didn't care. "Get that thing on the sled."

She went to the blob and put her shovel under it. Elijah copied her. The shovel handle bent against the weight of the blob, and with enough shouting from Fiona, they both lifted the thing onto the sled.

"Pull it." Fiona picked up the rope for the sled and tossed it into the snow for Elijah. He retrieved it and pulled the sled, but it didn't move.

"Heavy," he panted.

"So are lies," Fiona snapped back. "I trust you'll find your motivation to pull it with the cold. You know the way back. Take it to the incinerator. The help will take it from there." She left, going back into the hedge maze and disappearing quickly in the snow.

Elijah didn't respond. This was his punishment for a crime he didn't do. And instead of arguing, he'd do it. Then he'd talk with Ms. Fiona, show her he wouldn't do anything that threatened her or Anna or Madam Geeze.

The cold was biting. He wasn't dressed for the cold—no heavy coat, no real protection from the biting wind. His shoes were soaked and now icing over. Shouldering the rope, he pulled again, and the sled was starting to move—but his feet slipped and he fell.

Now covered completely in snow, he climbed back to his feet and pulled again.

Fiona wasn't going to help. No one was going to help. No one cared about him here except Anna. Maybe Madam Geeze would have helped, but she was in her sick bed now, Anna was by her side. There was no one else in the world now to help him. Everyone else was in the alley. They'd be there forever. Never here for him.

He pulled again, grunting, his lungs clenching, burning, his face turning red as he put every bit of strength into moving the sled. The rope bit into his palms, but they were too numb to feel it. Too cold for the blood to flow freely through his fists. He kept pulling. Once it started, he could keep it going. He just. Needed. To. Move. It.

Straining. Slipping. Falling.

Again, soaked with snow, he got up. But the weight of the snow, the weight of losing to the sled, failing Fiona, failing his family, threw him down into the snow. He was a frail boy, and that frailty, vengeful and angry, shoved his face into the snow, rubbing his face in the bitter frost of failure.

Elijah screamed into the snow. He didn't know about pressure valves, but if he did, he would have recognized his valve snapped. The strain of death and isolation had built up in him for too long without any release. He made a fist with his right hand and imagined the knife, the bloody knife that killed his dad, in that hand. He stabbed the ground imagining it was that guy from the restaurant, the guy with short red hair, the guy covered in dust, his dad's killer, the guy who shoved his mom into that dumpster, Fiona for throwing him into the basement, Anna for not getting him out sooner. But the last face he saw was his own, and that is the one he stabbed the hardest, the fastest, because it was the face of a boy too weak and frail to do anything but scream and cry and let everyone do whatever they wanted to him.

"I hate you!" Elijah snarled. "I hate you!" And as he stabbed his fist into the icy earth, killing every face there, smashing them into a blood pulp that sprayed over the snow, blooming into a gory garden, slashes of blood flung around him. The meat of his hand had split open, raw and hamburger against the frozen ground.

He screamed again, pouring the rest of his hate into the night, into the indifferent stars and moon that didn't care about a boy dying in an alley or a garden or a basement. They just watch as horrible things happen, blinking and staring without tears or expressions or sighs or gasps. Just watching, bored and unblinking.

Then he knew what to do. He would just lay down and freeze to death. It would be easy. He didn't have to do anything. He could kill the cause of all his problems without doing a thing. And the stars would just watch. A boring death to bore the watchers.

He laid face down in the snow and let it build up around him as he cried ice. When the snow blotted out the moon and all he could see was the deep blues of a frozen tomb around him, he closed his eyes to sleep and let the end come.

A rough whack hit his head. "Ouch!" Elijah sprung up away from the hit. As the snow fell away from him, he saw Jasper sitting before him with the flaming green eyes burrowing into his soul with disappointment. The snow had stopped, but the pooka was darker than the nighttime purples that came with a snowy day.

Elijah stared into those eyes and shouted, "Leave me alone!"

But the pooka didn't move. It only glared at Elijah with the deep emotions that only a dog could share with a human, and these emotions were anger, disappointment, and sadness. Elijah could feel all three from Jasper and had to remind himself the creature before him was a pooka, not a dog. Not man's best friend but a creature from somewhere else. But the stare pushed through any defenses Elijah had against the creature. It was sad. It was…he was empathetic.

Jasper pawed the ground, once, very hard. It was a command. No translation needed. *Get up!*

"Why?" Elijah said. His life was over. Why get up and keep going? Mom and dad were dead. Fiona hated him. Why go back? Why get up?

While the pooka sat statuesque, Elijah sat panting and numb from the cold. Jasper didn't move, not even a shiver in the cold, as it looked expectantly at the boy.

Elijah shook his head. "Just go." He waved the pooka away.

But Jasper didn't go. His glare intensified. What could a pooka feel? It looked like a dog stretched and strained to be a cross between fox and wolf. Its eyes were swirling green flames that left a trail as it moved, yet within those eyes Elijah felt Jasper telling him, *I'm not leaving.*

The pooka was still until Elijah whispered, "You and me?" Maybe he wasn't alone? Anna was there. She cared as much as she could. But why did Jasper help him? The pooka led him here. Fiona wouldn't have cared if he disappeared into the maze earlier and no one came out here to find him. So why did Jasper care? But he did. Elijah could feel it.

And maybe that was a start. Anna and a pooka. Maybe that could be the start of a new family?

Jasper stomped again. *Get up!* He trotted over to the sled, which was again buried in snow save for the blob which still steamed. Jasper nosed into the snow and pulled up the rope and tugged it. The sled moved easily over the snow.

Elijah stood. "You pull it?" He asked.

Jasper again rolled his eyes and nodded for Elijah to join him at the rope. The boy did and together they pulled the blob easily. Jasper could have pulled it alone however, he let Elijah struggle a bit, but not too much, to pull the creature.

The work burned away Elijah's tears. Replacing it with the pride you get from doing the impossible. He couldn't pull this thing. Now he could. And he knew Jasper was helping, but they were doing it together. Elijah wasn't alone.

Together, they pulled the creature through the hedge maze, Jasper leading the way. When they left the maze, Jasper vanished, and Elijah was alone, pulling the sled. It moved easier than before and, although exhausted, he was able to take it to the incinerator behind the house.

When he went to the main house's front door, through clouds of Elijah's panting, steaming breath, he saw Jasper watching. The pooka sat in the second story window, its green eyes looking from the boy to the moon.

Elijah followed Jasper's gaze as the moon broke free from a cloud casting silver light throughout the night.

The snow, the sky, the entire world glowed in the moonlight. There was more than darkness out here. Yes, the darkness was thick, it was still there, but a heavy snow brought light and colors to the night he'd never seen in New York. Here the snow wasn't jagged clumps of charcoal gray pushed aside on the streets, it was soft, white, gleaming. It wasn't something to grumble about and cause problems but a thing to see, to enjoy, to feel.

The beauty of the world, this world of nature and snow and open spaces, hit Elijah, making him choke on a breath. Beautiful things were lurking behind the clouds, obscured, waiting until the right moment to reveal themselves.

Yes, there were beautiful things in this new home. The books. The snow. Jasper. Anna. Things to begin a new life with if he could find his way.

# TWELVE

Madam Geeze was still in what Elijah now knew as the infirmary. She was sleeping as she had been for the past few weeks. Fiona never left her bedside. Anna stayed sometimes, splitting her time between her grandmother and her studies.

This left Elijah alone in the house with no one looking for him. Not that anyone ever did.

He missed Anna. She stopped by once in a while but was always distracted. They studied together, but Anna couldn't focus. They ended up walking around the mansion, exploring the other hallways. Most only had empty rooms draped in drop clothes and coated in dust. While they walked, Anna told Elijah about her time in the basement.

She told him of her early memories of the basement, but that she was too young to remember much. He asked her what it was like for her, but she couldn't remember. When she asked him the same, he answered the same, but the darkness of that basement, the isolation, the time out of time, wasn't forgotten—it was fresh in his memory.

There were many rooms in the house that Elijah had not explored and dared not enter without Anna. Huldis whispered into his ear to search for the blocks, and he did, but never went to the one place he was confident the blocks were kept, Fiona's room. Huldis urged him to go, to dismiss the consequences, but Elijah knew what his mom would have said about that. She would have told him to be patient, to listen to the adults, and they'd help him.

But he also knew not all adults were helpers. The men from the diner weren't helping anyone. Fiona wasn't helping him. Only Huldis helped, and he wasn't even a person.

"What is wrong with Madam Geeze?" Elijah asked Huldis. His words came easier now after so much practice.

Huldis answered, *She was bitten.*

"By the thing in the maze?"

*Yes. She shouldn't have fought with it. Old lady should have known her limits,* Huldis said.

"Will she be okay?"

Huldis didn't answer.

Elijah walked about the study running his fingers over the leather spines smoothed by age. They were mostly brown, some redder, some blacker, but mostly brown. The shelves were dark wood and recently polished by the servants. He could smell the oil lingering in the air. On the desk, the book Madam Geeze was looking at on Christmas was still open to the page she was reading. Elijah went to it.

"Can I help her with something in one of these books?"

*Focus on what's important. Help Astrid.*

He slid a small note paper into the book to keep the page Madam Geeze was reading, then turned to the beginning. The pages crackled and waved a musty smell into the air as they turned.

The first page of the book proclaimed the title in bold, crisp letters: *The Shadowed Key* by Victor DeLacroix. There were symbols drawn on the page in pencil that had withered with age, but Elijah didn't know what they meant. The next page was a print from a steel engraving where an army of women in shining armor wielding swords and hammers fought against monsters made of shadow and glass. In the following pages, Elijah read tales of other worlds and the doorways between them. He learned of creatures lingering on the edges of reality and how their eternal machinations intersect with individual people's lives in mundane ways, like the death of one's parents. How those mundane events can ripple through the universe and transform the shape of stars or the fate of galaxies.

But of all the topics in this book, he focused on the idea that one could reshape reality with the proper tools.

*I told you Astrid could help bring your parents back,* Huldis said.

Elijah kept reading. The Lazarus Spiral wasn't a tool for bringing people back to life; it was more like a loom, weaving together what has been, what is, and what could be. "At the center of the spiral, you can intersect with the threads of reality and re-string them." Elijah read the words, but not all of them made sense.

Outside the massive study windows, the sun was setting. Long shadows formed around him. He turned on the desk light to keep reading, but the rest of the study was devoured in the murky retreat of sunlight. Glowing green eyes watched Elijah from the hall. Their owners snarled and chuffed. He looked for Jasper, but none of the pooka were familiar. And they did not look at him with kind eyes, but rather with suspicion and disdain.

*Pay them no mind. If they were to do something, they would have done it by now,* Huldis said.

Elijah watched the eyes and the glowing trail left behind as the pooka moved in the dark. More of the creatures came. None entered the study, they simply paced in the hallway as if waiting for Elijah to come to the edge of the desk lamp light.

"Why are they mad?"

*Their matriarch is dying. They're scared.*

"Of what?"

*Of you.*

Elijah laughed at the impossibility of that statement. Those pooka creatures were large dogs with fangs and glowing eyes, their bodies made of shadow and darker stuff. How could they possibly find *him* scary?

He tried to return to reading but had a hard time concentrating with the snarls and growls from the dark. However, he kept reading until he fell asleep, which became his normal life. Every day he read the many tomes of the study, gathering an education about earth and beyond.

This was life for a year.

When Anna came to visit, Zelia started to be left behind on their walks. Christmas had come again, but there was no celebration. He made Anna a gift this year, having realized that he didn't give her anything last year. She had also made him something and on Christmas morning; they met where the tree should have been and exchanged gifts.

No one else joined them. There were no other gifts. Fiona had been absent from their lives. Anna told Elijah her mother was working to heal Madam Geeze, to find answers about what happened that night. There were always monsters in the hedge maze but never a Guardian of the Tower, they never left their station. Whenever Anna talked about these creatures, as she was trying to explore how this beast could have found its way to her grandmother, she'd pry with questions like, "Did Huldis make you do something you didn't understand?"

Anna didn't blame him for Madam Geeze's condition. She thought he was a pawn. But Elijah could think of nothing he did, nothing Huldis said, that could have done this.

Without any one directing the Christmas celebration, it went unnoticed by all but Anna and Elijah and even them, only for each other.

She opened his gift, wrapped in newspaper. As she saw it, her face lit up with the first genuine smile he'd seen from her since last Christmas.

"Thank you," she paused, "Nicky." She smiled her disobedient smile. And he didn't correct her. There was no point. Anna did what she wanted; that had always been the case, and he believed, always will be. She lifted the painting from the paper. It was the view out of Elijah's room; the barn, the hills, the forest. He'd worked on it for weeks and thought it was his best yet, but he knew painting wasn't his talent. The ability to capture the world with a brush was his mom's skill, not his. He'd rather read and learn than create.

"This is so good," Anna said. "You're so talented."

Elijah shook his head. "Nah, I just didn't know what else to do for you."

But Anna wasn't just being nice. She treasured the painting, holding it how she used to hold Zelia. In her eyes, those deep blue eyes that could sink Elijah's thoughts, tears built. One fell free, and he looked away, unsure what to say.

"I don't think mine is this nice," she said and handed him a box wrapped in silver paper.

He opened it quickly and smiled. It was another journal.

"I didn't know what to get you. We haven't talked much about anything other than Nana. Sorry, I'm not a good friend," Anna said.

"Wait here." He ran to his room and returned. The red leather journal from last Christmas was in his hands. He opened it and flipped through the pages, showing each filled with notes from his readings, thoughts of the day, doodles in the margins. "I've been writing in it all year. I've never had anything like this," Elijah said, then shrugged. "This is the best present I've ever gotten. Now, I can remember what I was thinking. I won't forget."

Elijah held out the filled journal for Anna to take. She did.

"Did you write about the basement?" She asked. The words caught in her throat, almost afraid to ask.

He smiled and shrugged. "Some."

"I tried to come every day."

"I know. And I loved your visits. They were the literal light of my night." Elijah chuckled.

"But you were down there for so long," Anna said and looked away from him. She pressed the painting into her chest, a shield from the anger, the blame she expected from him.

"It wasn't that long." Elijah waved away the comment, catching himself doing Fiona's dismissive flick. He wiped his hand on his leg, trying to get the habit he picked up from that bitter woman out of him.

"Four years is a long time." Anna whispered.

Elijah didn't answer that. He went into the basement before he had a grip on years and dates, and so when he emerged, that it was 1922 meant little to him. He knew the Great War was over, but what did that matter? He knew Anna had grown older, and so had he, but four years? That was almost half his life, growing in the dark.

He hadn't celebrated his birthday this year, but if he was down there for four years, then he's ten now. When was his birthday? His mom knew. Who else knew?

"That's the past," Elijah said and turned away. "Thank you for the journal."

Four years echoed in his mind.

He's ten now. Half his life has been in this house. Most of that time thrown away under the house. The rest has been spent in the study, reading about a world beyond these walls.

Victor Frankenstein spent most of his life learning. And he created a monster. What would Elijah make? Not paintings. Nothing beautiful. That wasn't in him. He's been grown in blood and dirt and ice. That doesn't make flowers. What does it make?

"I am going to go read," Elijah said. "Merry Christmas Anna."

"I'm sorry." Anna cried. "I wanted to take you out, but I couldn't. She wouldn't let me. She didn't trust the puzzle."

What could Anna really have done? Fiona was all powerful. She would have killed Elijah given the chance, given a reason.

"I know." Elijah went to the study and began reading. He put his new journal beside the book, inked his quill, and wrote on the empty parchment page: Four Years.

The words, in black, screamed at him from the page. Who the hell keeps a kid in the dark for four years? And for what? For punishment? Punishing him for not dying with his parents?

Elijah jumped from the chair and threw his journal across the study. A pooka outside yelped and ran into the deeper shadows of the house. Elijah growled and threw the ink well across the room. It shattered and splattered on the wall, but he didn't care. Let Fiona be mad. What would she do? Lock him away? Kill him? She'd already taken half of his life. Why not take all of it? He ripped books from their shelves, throwing them, screaming and snarling as he did until he stopped, realizing he was hurting the things that had been there for him. Books. Learning.

Understanding sank in that he was taking his anger out on innocent things, innocent books that did nothing more than teach him. He looked to the ceiling, seeing the old lady with the pooka in the painting, and apologized to her.

"I'm sorry. I know you're teaching me, but can't I learn easier? Can't I get easier lessons? Do they have to be so hard?"

But she didn't answer. The painting only stared at the young woman, reaching for her, looking expectantly like the worst was yet to come.

Elijah cleaned the study and returned to his books, to his lessons with a penitent mind.

Anna didn't come back after that. He didn't see her again until the Spring Equinox in March when Madam Geeze summoned him, ending this time of learning.

# THIRTEEN

"Mother wants to speak with you." Fiona slammed her hand on the desk to wake Elijah.

He startled up, and out of a pool of drool he left on the desk. Grateful thoughts flooded his mind when he saw the slobber didn't touch the pages of the books he'd been reading.

Elijah nodded with a wide yawn and hopped to his feet. The two walked through the well lit hallways. Fiona must have turned on the lights, save for the one hallway where it was always dark. All shadows in the house were chased away.

Madam Geeze was laying in the same bed in the infirmary. Her robe was white with a lacey veil covering her eyes. Anna laid beside her, holding the old woman's frail hand and crying.

"Elijah," Madam Geeze said. Her voice was weak and raspy. "You have not come until called."

He nodded.

The servants scurried around, preparing the room for a transformation. They brought in white linens and opened the curtains to show a clear, starry night through large windows. The lights in the room's corners were dimmed, creating a path of shadow from the side door to the side of Madam's bed.

"I did not want to bother you," Elijah answered with a glance at Fiona. His language had smoothed into a graceful delivery that brought a smile to Madam Geeze's frail face.

Madam laughed, but it coiled into a heaving cough. "You have lost so much." She waved for him to come to her bedside. Fiona gently pushed him forward. "You are not one of us, but you will learn." Madam appraised him, smiled and said, "I can see you have learned. You have learned so much in so short a time."

"Mother—" Fiona started.

Madam struggled to lift her hand. "I have spoken. Fiona, my daughter, you will teach him." Fiona recoiled as if hit with a physical blow to the stomach. "As he will teach you the lessons I could not."

"But, Anna?" Fiona asked.

"She must go home. Little Anna has learned all she can here. My sisters will teach her lessons she cannot learn here. Fiona, you are brilliant. You will change the world. Anna will love the world no matter what. She has the heart for it and now we must find your heart." Madam pointed to Elijah. "He is your passage to life." Madam took Elijah's hand and put it in Fiona's. Fiona dropped it as soon as the old woman let go.

"I will make you proud, Nana," Anna said through tears.

"You already have." Madam kissed Anna's forehead.

Fiona, seeing the visitors at the door, put her hand up, asking the pooka to wait in the darkness. "Mother. I beg you to reconsider. How?" She looked at Elijah, then at Anna. "I, Anna, is my light."

"As you were hers, but now both of you need to seek new shores. There are more lights among the sea, and they need you. Go to them." Madam nodded and looked at the pooka poised at the shadowy doorway. "It is time."

Anna climbed off the bed and held Elijah's hand. "I love you, Nana." Then she pulled Elijah's hand, leading him out of the room. Servants stood by the door.

"Elijah," Madam called.

He turned back to her.

"The Maker and the Monster." She chuckled weakly. "My boy, there was never a monster, only a lost soul." She smiled and nodded solemnly at him.

Elijah nodded back, but he didn't agree. Frankenstein made his creation as a monster. Never was it the thing of beauty the doctor imagined, and only when it was seen in light was the full horror of the thing understood. When the Maker sees the Monster, truly sees their creation, there is no other response than revulsion—and death.

Anna and Elijah closed the door behind them.

***

"Why?" Fiona gasped as the pooka entered the room. "Why are you doing this?"

"It is time my daughter. I love you," Madam said as the pooka came to her bedside and climbed onto the white sheets with her. "It is time. You did all you could. The Guardian's poison has set too deep, ate away too much. I can linger and suffer, or I can rest. It is time for me to rest."

"But, I, I can't do this. I can't be—you." Fiona pleaded.

Madam Geeze smiled. It faulted as pain wracked over her, but not from the bite. From her failure to prepare her daughter for a world without her. She sucked in a deep breath for her final words.

"I never wanted you to be me, my dear Fiona. I always wanted you to be you. Brilliant. Beautiful. Diligent. Greatness is within you. But it is clouded by your anger. I thought you'd let the anger go, eventually, after all those years. You have not. So, now I try another path. You shall unlock your greatness by the piece of your soul you've ignored in life, kindness. Find it and you will find your fate. Now go." The last words strained in a breathless push, expending all she had to tell her daughter what she thought she couldn't die without saying.

Fiona's eyes filled with tears of loss and confusion, then left the room.

The servants closed the doors behind her as the largest pooka, the one Elijah knew as Jasper, sat on her chest.

Madam Geeze smiled at him and breathlessly whispered something in another language.

Jasper howled. The other pooka joined in. Their howl began as a sad wail but faded into a soft, ethereal breath, blowing Madam Geeze's soul to the next life.

# FOURTEEN

Anna walked Elijah to her doll's room and sat at the desk. Elijah sat on the floor.

"I'm sorry for your loss," Elijah said. He heard Mr. Lions say that to his dad. It felt appropriate now.
Anna nodded as she quietly cried.

"Nana is going to be with the pooka now," Anna said. "She will be happy there."

"Is it like heaven?" Elijah knew of heaven and hell from the few times his mom took him to church. They never found one his mom liked. She said there's more to God than suffering, but that was all any of the preachers ever talked about. After all these years, Elijah thought his mom was wrong.

Anna shook her head. "No. Heaven is like paradise. The pooka come from somewhere else and Nana will spend some time there helping them, then she'll go to heaven."

Not understanding, Elijah just nodded and picked up Zelia, Anna's doll, and gave it to her.

"You are a good friend," Anna said and gave him a hug. He hugged her back gently.

A thunderous snap came from up the hallway. Elijah heard the scream in his mind, so loud it crumbled him to the ground.

Anna screamed, "What!?"

But Elijah couldn't talk. Splinters sprayed through his brain, gripping the walls of his skull and dragging down, shredding the bone. He held his temples and rocked on the floor, drooling, all systems shutting down from the pain lancing from his mind through his body.

When the screaming stopped, Elijah staggered to his feet, stumbled to his room as Anna followed, asking what was happening, but he knew.

In his room, Fiona held two halves of the puzzle board in a white knuckled grip. Blood bloomed through the knee of her house dress as she panted ravenously. When Elijah fell into the wall, stumbling with jelly legs, her eyes fixed on his.

"You brought this on us!" Fiona screamed. Her eyes were wild, her hair frayed from days of being unkept. She held up the board for him to see. "You did this! You brought them! You killed her!"

"Mother!" Anna pushed past Elijah.

"Don't defend him, Anna! He and this thing brought Nana's death to us. Didn't you!?" Fiona threw the board down. It clattered on the floor in a hollow rattle. "You called the Guardians!"

Elijah shook his head. "No! I didn't!" Reason would not work, but he tried. "Why would I do that? I knew nothing of them when it happened. How would I know what to do?"

Anna nodded feverishly, trying to convince her mother to see sense.

"I've learned a lot in the past year, Ms. Fiona. I still couldn't do what you think I did, even with everything I've learned."

Fiona didn't have the smiling face or laughter of the men who killed his parents, but she was going to kill him. Reason had no place in her fury, in her grief.

He knew it. She was going to kill him, and no one would stop her. No one would care.

"Anna, go pack," Fiona shouted to her daughter. "You will go to Nana's sisters, and I'll take care of this boy!" The last word was spit out like rotten flesh. Anna didn't move. "Go!"

Anna still didn't move.

She shook as her body told her to run and stay at the same time. Anna tried to form an argument, her mischievous disobedience struggling to emerge yet unable to break through her own grief. Her mother glared at her. Fiona's presence infecting the room with her intense judgmental fury. Under the weight of her mother's anger, Anna broke and ran away. "You! Get in the basement!"

"Ms. Fiona—" he started, but she slapped the air around her, sending a shockwave through his face. Elijah stumbled back, falling from the force of her strike…not that she hit him, but the force she projected knocked him down.

"Basement or alley!" She screamed.

Alley. The word dominated Elijah's thoughts. Be done with me if you're done with me. At this point he'd welcome being gutted where his family died, be done with all this. Die a quick and familiar death.

But maybe in the basement he could convince her of his innocence. After her grief cooled, after she felt the loss, maybe then she'd see reason. He could continue his studies into the Lazarus Spiral, discover how to save his family without Huldis, who was no doubt dead. The board was broken and with it, any hope of helping Astrid, who would have helped him. But this library, this study, Fiona herself, had answers. If he was dead in the alley, it was over. At least in the basement, there was a chance of continuing.

Elijah scurried to the puzzle board pieces and picked them up. He grabbed Huldis's remains, his knife, the whetstone, his journals, Frankenstein, and then ran to the basement door. Fiona was going to kill him if he didn't do what she said.

She stomped behind him as a loud howl came from the infirmary and Elijah knew Madam Geeze had passed on. Fiona didn't miss a step though and kicked him down the stairs into the dark of the basement. He tumbled down, thudding into the dirt, cracking elbows and knees and hips on the concrete under the dirt. She slammed the heavy door and shot the bolt with a final click.

Elijah heard her bark to the servants, "No one opens this door until I say." Then she stomped off, and Elijah lay in the dark, holding everything he owned.

# FIFTEEN

Food and water were provided, but no light. Light came when the door opened and left when the door closed. His eyes grew accustomed quickly to darkness and the vague shapes of his former quarters became clear after only a little while.

The darkness welcomed him back with eager acceptance. His dark vision returned. The light was no longer for him, and he pressed himself deeper into the basement's cavernous depths. Eventually he hid from the door opening to avoid the harsh pain of day light.

Elijah didn't try to keep time. He didn't care. Anna was gone. What was left?

Sleep came and went. His bed was as he left it when he lived in the basement before. Remembering Huldis's exercises, he kept his body strong. Remembering the books, he kept his mind sharp. In the journals Anna gave him, he wrote notes about the books. Without any ink, he used his knife to prick his fingers and scrawl his thoughts.

Elijah tried to fix Huldis, to no avail. He'd walk around the basement, talking to himself in his mind about what he learned over the past year and a half. Processing, connecting ideas he couldn't connect while he was reading. The dark was a canvas for him to put out everything he knew, everything he experienced and see where there were lines, cross sections invisible in the light.

Ideas emerged from the dark. Passages he read now made sense in new ways. Old ideas, ancient ideas, collided with modern science. They twisted and coiled into the fusion of science and magic. And that's where Elijah's mind dwelled for countless meals, countless sleeps.

He lost track of when he was sleeping and when he was awake. Meals were missed. The door didn't open for long stretches. But he exercised, remembered the books, and talked to himself in his mind, scribbling bloody journal entries only when his fingers had healed enough from the last time he'd pricked them with the knife.

Ghosts emerged from the dark. At first, they re-enacted memories. Dinner with his mom. When his dad came home. Murder in the alley. He watched the scenes, detached like a play and when they were over, they'd restart on a loop. Time was a loop.

Sometimes Anna came to have tea, but the door never opened. She walked out of the darkness just like his parents did, like all the actors in these scenes did. And when done, they faded into the void. No one walked away into the dark, they simply dissolved.

This was how the monsters in his nightmares, the ones he had as a little kid, the ones Nicky had, came and went. They'd walk out of the night and disappear. He'd wake up screaming and his mom would dance with him to chase away the monsters but now, he couldn't dance. There was no music. The silence of the basement had no tune, no beat, nothing to shake his hips to. Here, he couldn't chase away the monsters.

Soon the ghosts were not just memories. They would talk to him about the book upstairs. Ask him questions about other worlds, as if quizzing him on what he learned. His mother would ask questions about the Spiral. Anna would pour imagined tea into imagined cups while reviewing the Tower of Ascension's floor plan. They were aggressive, demanding answers, demanding he know more.

Sometimes they'd teach him. They'd tell him things he swore he didn't read in the books. Secret things that only the darkness knew because darkness was everywhere. It saw everything. And so it knew things like malevolent entities and tools that would help him find the Spiral.

When he'd reject their ideas, their more extreme and violent ideas like calling the Guardians to kill Fiona, to kill Anna, the darkness would scream at him. Remind him of what happened when frail boys couldn't help their family. Show him his dad being stabbed to death. Show him his mom's shattered face, removing the blur from her disfigured face where there was no more skull.

Once, after his mom demanded he stop being so weak and leave this place, he asked his mom if she was real. Would his real mom have said those things? He couldn't remember her now. Not the real her. The her from the dark was all he could remember now. This version of his mom, a shambling decayed thing, half her face smashed, laughed at his question, cackling, echoing, derisive laughter, and vanished.

It was during one of these long conversations when footsteps coming downstairs interrupted the discussion.

Were they real?

Was it Anna? Had she finally come for him? Was it Christmas again? Could another Christmas miracle be happening? He didn't have a gift for her. Maybe there was something in the dark he could give her—something hidden away. But she was a person of light. She wouldn't want anything from the dark. There was nothing here for her.

The door opened, startling Elijah, forcing him back from the light in a mad scurry across the dirt floor.

"Elijah," Fiona called. She stayed on the stairs. The brightness from the door made her silver hair and black gown glow like a halo. He'd forgotten her voice. It sounded softer than he remembered. Older.

Elijah came to the edge of darkness, shielding his eyes from her light. A cloud of dirt drifted from where he was to the stairs. Fiona waved it away. From this distance, he could smell outside on her. It was warm and flowery. She smelled like sunshine and that turned Elijah's stomach.

"Did you know Huldis's plan?" She asked.

Elijah's words wouldn't form in his throat. All the talking he's done, so much talking, has all been in his mind. But to answer Fiona, he shook his head slowly, knowing no answer would change his condition. The second floor was not for him. Life beyond the dark was no longer for him.

Fiona threw a canvas bag on the dirt floor. It hit with an empty puff.

"I do not believe you."

She waited for him to scurry over and scoop up the bag, but he did not. He kept to the darkness, finding it now much more comforting than the light. "You and your kind only take. You were not happy with your conditions and so you tried to take what you could." She flicked her hand dismissively at the canvas bag. "And see where it took you. Cast out. Your only friend broken, deceased. You alone, in the dark, and with nothing."

But that wasn't true. He had the knife and whetstone. He had the journals and book Anna gave him. These few things were enough to keep his mind busy, to hone his focus as he honed his knife.

"Mother thought you could open the way to the realm of the Pooka. She thought you could learn our ways and be aligned to our purpose, but I knew better. I know your kind. She never left the house, but I saw how your kind gathers in the gutter, tearing scraps from anyone who has them, whether they're offered or not." Fiona turned to go upstairs. "I will return you to your alley tomorrow. Take everything you brought with you out of this house. Leave none of your rot behind." The basement door closed, cool darkness returned, and the lock clicked.

Elijah went to the canvas bag and picked it up.

*No more distractions.* Huldis whispered in his mind.

Elijah startled and looked for another, having forgotten the voice of his puzzle. How long had it been? How many meals? He didn't know and didn't waste thoughts on it now that Huldis was back.

"Where have you been?" Elijah said aloud, his voice coming now that he was alone.

*I couldn't speak. She had to think me dead.*

"And now?"

*She has stopped listening for me. Hubris taught her of victory when I knew the path to triumph was patience. Complete the word and let us consult Astrid.*

Elijah knew he didn't need to see the puzzle pieces to find the right letters. He pieced Huldis back together, feeling the fit of the two sides of the board to ensure they aligned. When they did, he didn't wait and plucked a letter from the bag.

He was kneeling at the foot of the stairs, the puzzle on the steps, when he placed the first letter, D, in its place. The next letter followed quickly, O, then another O. Heavy footsteps rushed towards the basement door upstairs.

"Stop!" Fiona shouted upstairs. She was panting. Running to the door to stop him, to distract him. "Stop! How are you—"

The last block clicked in place, and Huldis spoke, *Say all the words and help Astrid. Finally, help Astrid after all these centuries.*

"Open the Door," Elijah said as the basement door flew open and blasted his eyes with the bright daylight above. The sun hurt, but he didn't flinch. Fiona was a silhouette against the glow, but Elijah could smell the terrified sweat rushing over her flesh. He looked up to her, to where her eyes should have been, and smiled before the world flickered out of existence like a burned movie reel.

He had left the Geeze House and found himself in a dim room. The air was thick with an acrid stench that made his eyes water. Bubbling liquids of sickly greens and venomous purples simmered in an array of twisted bottles and tubes. The fireplace flickered in faint smoldering embers, no longer warm but in the last throes of death.

Floorboards squeaked under heavy feet as someone was moving

around the shelves. A soft scraping sound drew Elijah's attention to someone hunched over a broom, sweeping the floor. Dust swirled up around the woman's knobby knees.

Sensing his presence, she stopped mid-sweep. Slowly, her face turned towards him—weathered and wrinkled like old leather, with eyes that gleamed unnaturally brightness in the gloom. Those eyes widened with curious surprise, fixing on him with an intensity that made his skin prickle.

"Astrid?" Elijah asked.

She straightened with every joint in her body, audibly popping, echoing in the silence. The broom clattered to the floor as she nodded and smiled. Elijah had done what he promised, but her smile, her presence, turned his stomach. Something was wrong. He thought he was saving someone and instead; he sealed his destiny.

# SIXTEEN

Astrid was a fairy tale witch through and through. Her clothes were tattered, her flesh was pale, flabby, and soggy in a strange mix of fish guts and sacks of brined pickles. A noise came from her nose like a whistling gasp that silently came in, but exhaled in a high-pitched siren. One eye was twisted to the side while the other, cataract white, bore into Elijah.

"Huldis?" Astrid asked. Her words cracked. Elijah recognized the sound of years of silence breaking away from an unused voice.

"He led me here," Elijah said. The words were as cracked as hers.

Astrid stood taller. Her back popped with a loud snap that sent her staggering to hold a chair. Elijah went to help her, but she waved him off.

"Old body," she said, laughing. "How did you find Huldis? He come to you?"

"No. My dad gave him to me. He got the puzzle from a castle in Germany." Elijah remembered the conversation from the Son Rise Diner all those lifetimes ago. His dad telling his mom, it was from a castle—no a shop beside the castle. The shopkeeper said it would help Nicky.

*Beware calling for help because you don't know if they're here to help you or help themselves.*

"Puzzle?" Astrid shook her head. "Rune board." She waddled to a bookshelf.

The room was like a twisted version of Fiona's study—but filthy, chaotic, with dust-covered shelves crammed full of books, scrolls, and stone tablets. Stacks of ancient papers spilled onto the floor, mingling with jars of foul liquids and dead things preserved in cloudy vials. It reeked of decay and neglect.

But Astrid moved with purpose, her crooked fingers plucking books from the shelves without hesitation, as though the chaos was perfectly ordered in her mind.

"Rune board," she said again and pulled a book from her shelf. "You came alone?"

Elijah nodded. He wondered what Anna would say about this place. The thick crust growing over everything, or the rancid odor pouring from bubbling vials, or the constant thrum of energy flowing from Astrid.

Unlike Anna's house, this place was not filled with light. There was a sickly green glow outside the one window, and it only showed the edges of Astrid's room. The house was one large room, filled and trashed from centuries of neglect.

"I'm here to help you," Elijah said as he noticed one jar with a snakeskin floating in amber fluid.

"Is that so?" Astrid pulled another book from her shelf. "That's a funny thing about help—"

"You don't know if they're here to help you or help themselves," Elijah finished, a chill creeping down his spine. Who was Astrid helping?

The witch pointed a stumpy finger at him. The tip was missing. She laughed a wheezing cackle.

"I'm here to help you. Then, Huldis said, you might be able to help me. I need the Lazarus Spiral."

She stopped laughing. The ambient bubbling took over the room for a long moment. "Why would you seek such a thing?"

"My parents. I want to help them. Huldis said we can do that with the Spiral."

"Aye," Astrid nodded slowly and pulled another book after some intense thought furrowed her brow. "The Spiral can do many things. But none of those things are done here. A journey is required." She placed another book on her table. It tilted on the dead rat that was already occupying that space. Astrid picked up the rat and offered it to Elijah. He politely waved away the offering.

"Where do we need to go?" Elijah looked out the one window and saw the sky filled with green gas and a shattered blue planet. The sky was dark, but not like night. It was darker than any night he'd ever seen, and the stars were infinite, unblinking, as if watching to see what he did next. Far below, were crashing black waves and a sea that extended to the horizon. Elijah imagined the house on a high stone spire. Isolated. Unable for anyone to reach other than through Huldis. Did Astrid build this? Was it her home or prison?

The latter. Without doubt, it was the latter.

"Well, the Tower of Ascension, of course," Astrid answered with a flourish. She placed the broom against a wall, then gathered the books she pulled from the shelves into a small satchel. "But first, we need to go back from whence you came."

"How?" Elijah didn't see any way out of this room other than the small window. No doors.

Astrid laughed her throaty chuckle. "You opened the door. We can go back anytime if the door is still open, but time works differently here. Let us make haste to avoid surprises." She shouldered the satchel and stood beside Elijah. He cringed as her hand rested on his shoulder, feeling the small bones of her fingers through the loose, fleshy fat of her hand.

Astrid groaned, "Huldis, open the door."

And Elijah was back in the dark of the basement. The door upstairs was open. Blinding, burning light flooding into the basement around Fiona. She gasped, raising her hand as if pushing back what she saw in those dark depths.

No time had passed at all since he left. The door was still swinging open behind Fiona. It hit the wall with a rattling clatter.

*Welcome back,* Huldis said, his voice curling through Elijah's mind like smoke.

Astrid's throaty laugh came from the dark behind Elijah. Fiona gasped, shook her head and ran from the basement, leaving the door open, the way out of the basement unguarded.

"We have a long road ahead and that lady is going to block it. Best to address that problem before it becomes a crisis," Astrid said. A phlegmy laughter erupted from the old lady as she waddled into the darkness.

Huldis cheered. *Good to have you back, Astrid.*

She picked up the puzzle, the bag of letters, and walked upstairs in her hunched wobble.

Elijah followed.

# SEVENTEEN

Elijah pressed through the painful light of the stairs. Emerging from his silent darkness into a bright chaos.

The servants were fleeing the house. Many had nothing with them. They just walked quickly, almost at a run but too proper to run. As with everything in the Geeze house, they were orderly, going to the door and closing it quietly behind them.

Silent to the last.

Elijah thought that must have been how Fiona preferred them, silent. No voice. No protest. Just do as they were told. Why didn't they ever talk? No voice, no noise, just going about the house without a sound. Perhaps the ones who did speak were thrown into the basement and then cast out?

Astrid didn't wait for Elijah. She moved slowly through the kitchen and into the foyer.

But Elijah couldn't see in the light anymore. His eyes were attuned to the dark. That didn't happen last time. He must have been down there even longer. Longer than four years? In the kitchen, he noticed how big his hands were, how his arms and legs stretched, and his head almost reached the doorframe of the basement.

His clothes stretched awkwardly over his frame—the shirt that once fit him now stopped short of his wrists, the slacks hovering above his ankles. He was taller, thinner from the meager diet and constant exercise in the basement. But it wasn't just his body that had changed. Years had passed. How many? He couldn't know. But everything about him felt stretched, like he had outgrown more than just his clothes—he had outgrown the boy who went down into the basement.

How much of his life was in that darkness? Anna never came. Fiona never came. Only the visitors in his mind and all they had were scenes of torment, harsh lessons, derision. Once there was hope that he could convince Fiona with reason, that he could prove he was a good boy. Now anger had hollowed that hope away and there was no use in being a good boy. He wasn't even a boy anymore.

In the foyer, the servants were still fleeing as Elijah felt his way through the light to the stairs. His gut knew where Astrid was going. The study.

But why?

The stairs climbed beneath him, the light above searing in its intensity. The Christmas tree was long gone, the space where it once lived still empty, awaiting another happy moment to fill it—yet that kind of moment would never come again in this house.

A pleading whimper pulled Elijah into the dark, where he could see glowing green eyes staring at him. Their soft expression was strange on Jasper's face. But the message was clear: *don't go.*

"I can't stop now." Elijah answered.

The pooka chuffed and stomped his front paw. *Yes, you can. Stay here.*

Jasper laid down, putting his face between his paws, which stretched before him, touching the edge of the light. Smoke curled off the pooka's paw where the light sliced across it and it whined, reaching for Elijah through the burning pain.

Elijah stood over Jasper to shade his paw, to stop the burning. He said, "I'm sorry Jasper. I have to fix this. I'm on the wrong path. I should be with my parents. Astrid's going to help me do that." Elijah pushed Jasper's paw out of the light and left the pooka to go to the study. Jasper again whined but retreated into the darkness, letting his boy make his mistakes.

Elijah whispered back to Jasper, "sorry, the Monster has to confront the Maker."

In the study, the windows were open and midday sun poured through them, making Astrid hiss and flinch in their brightness. Elijah's eyes remembered the light now, still pained, but able to see more clearly.

For as long as Elijah had been in darkness, Astrid had been longer. Huldis said centuries. Seeing her gray skin, her bagged eyes, Elijah thought centuries was a conservative estimate.

"You best finish your work before the dark comes. Before the pooka return," Fiona said. She faced Astrid with the defiance that Elijah expected, the same defiance Anna wore with her mother.

The words were laced with venomous hate. She stood at the desk where Elijah used to sit reading about the Lazarus Spiral. How long ago? He didn't know. She threw him away and forgot him like the rich always forget the poor. They forget the poor are humans, just like the men in the diner forgot his parents were people; the coloreds were people, everyone just wants to live and grow their life but no. They can't because the rich want the poor to stay poor and the racists want everyone else to go somewhere else.

"We'll be done long before then. Where's the book?" Astrid snarled.

"How did you do it?" Fiona asked Elijah. "Huldis was broken. Did you want it to live so much you willed it back to life?"

*I'm more durable than wood.* Huldis answered in their minds. *You were foolish to believe the physical manifestation would have any impact on my spiritual binding.*

Fiona nodded, seeing her hubris. "And you?" She motioned to Elijah. "Are you caught in the tsunami or are you the earthquake?"

This didn't make sense to Elijah, but he answered, "You kept me in the basement. Why?"

"You don't get this!" Fiona said as she motioned to everything. "This isn't for your kind!" Her lip curled in disgust, as if the very thought of him—of someone like him—daring to touch the knowledge within these walls was an insult. "What would you do with any of it? Burn it for warmth? Sell it for pennies to feed your childish whims? You lack the heritage, the intellect, to grasp the truths in this place!"

Elijah stood his ground. "Why do you hate me so much?" His voice was steady, but inside, the years of abandonment, the darkness, the isolation—they all burned to the surface. "Anna didn't hate me. But you did. The moment you saw me." He took a step closer, his eyes meeting hers with the cold certainty of someone who had been through hell. "Your mother was right—there isn't a shred of kindness in you."

"You!" Fiona shouted. "Your kind took everything from me! Everything! And you won't do it again." She pulled a gun from the desk drawer. Her hand rattled as she pointed it at Elijah. He closed his eyes and breathed easy. The thunderous crack deafened Elijah. And he waited to feel metal rip through him. Was this what his dad felt from the knife?

But it never did.

Astrid waved her hand, and the bullet fell to the ground, hitting an invisible wall.

"What is this?" Astrid asked and smirked. "Throwing metal? Where is your craft?" She looked around. "All this and you use a metal bead as your attack?" Flicking her hand, the gun was thrown from Fiona's grip. "Shame. Your dogs kept you lame. No gifts." Another flick threw Fiona against the bookshelves, grinding her back against the wood as Astrid lifted her to the third shelves and slammed her to the floor with quick flicks.

Fiona grunted as she pressed to get up from the floor, but something heavy, invisible and impossibly heavy, kept her pinned down.

"The book?" Astrid asked and pushed her hand down harder. Fiona flattened on the floor.

Elijah read about magic while in this study, but he'd never thought it was real. There were times he suspected Fiona used magic on him, but he was never sure.

He was seeing it now.

The air thrummed with energy with a metallic tang flavor filling the room. Anna never mentioned magic. Never talked about much outside of tea and life, but Elijah thought Fiona was holding back. Her presence held power. Fiona vibrated with energy, but it was nothing compared to Astrid's thrumming, quaking power pulsating off the ancient woman.

Fiona pressed against the floor to lift herself up, screaming with focus, but she couldn't get up. Instead, the wooden floor creaked, then splintered under the pressure.

"The book!" Astrid screamed.

Fiona collapsed, her body heaving with the effort. But her hand still moved, twisting the air as if pulling on invisible threads. With a sudden yank, Astrid was wrenched from her feet, crashing to the floor as if the ground itself had been ripped from beneath her.

Elijah could have stepped in front of her, could have tried to stop her, but he didn't. He watched her leave in curious wonder where she'd go. The kitchen, the infirmary, the basement are the only places he'd been in this house, but he knew there were countless other rooms.

Would she leave like the servants?

He didn't think so. She was buying time. Sunset was coming, and the dark brought the pooka.

Elijah glanced to the ceiling, seeing the painting of the old woman, the pooka ready to pounce, and knew this was her plan.

Astrid recovered from the fall slowly. Her many years took their toll, as they do on all the elderly. Fiona was still young enough to recover quickly, but ancient bodies like Astrid, like Madam Geeze, did not bounce back so spry.

"Find her," Astrid said to Elijah as she went to the bookshelves.

"Bring her back here. I, we, need that book—if we're going to the Spiral."

Elijah lingered in the study's doorway, his heart pounding. The house was filled with light—too much light after so long in the dark. But the hallway across from Anna's room remained cloaked in shadow, and there, at its edge, stood Jasper.

Other pooka gathered behind him, their glowing green eyes tracking Elijah's every move.

Jasper's soft growl echoed in the silence. It was a warning. A plea. But Elijah couldn't stop. He had to keep going—he had to find the truth, even if it meant facing the darkness once more.

He listened, heard nothing, and remembered what he left in the basement. If Fiona found him, he'd need his knife. Who knows what weapons she had throughout the house and if she attacked, he'd need something to defend himself.

And so he returned to the basement to get the knife that killed his dad.

# EIGHTEEN

There wasn't much difference between a house full of silent servants and one that stood empty. Elijah's steps echoed through the stillness as he made his way to the basement. He moved quickly, the absence of life around him making the grand home feel like a tomb.

At the basement door, he stopped. Dust drifted in the shaft of light pressing down the stairs into the dark below. His hand trembled on the knob.

He found a heavy sack of rice nearby and propped it against the door. No more locks. He tugged on the door to make sure it wouldn't drift shut, to ensure he wouldn't get trapped down there again—not this time. He couldn't afford that.

It would be quick. Run down, grab the knife from the table, run back up. Nothing else. No encounters. No distractions.

As Elijah descended the wooden stairs, the boards groaned under his weight. Footprints scattered in the dirt at the base—his, maybe Astrid's. He ignored them and pressed forward, his focus narrowing. The table was where it had always been, but its shine had dulled, coated now in years of dust. The knife lay there, untouched and gleaming—its edge still sharp from hours of honing with the whetstone. His whetstone, and Frankenstein—both lay beyond the edge of the light, buried in the shadows.

Elijah stepped around the table, into the dark. His fingers brushed over the letters on the book's cover, whispering the title to himself… Frankenstein, the Modern Prometheus.

Anna.

He wished she were here.

"Are you happy now?" Fiona's voice floated out from the deeper darkness. "You've done what I did to you."

Her voice was distant, coated in regret, yet still cold, still confident. Always confident. Elijah froze, uncertain if she was real or if his mind was playing tricks on him. He promised himself there would be no encounters down here. He grabbed the knife, feeling its weight in his hand, and turned toward the stairs.

"Elijah." Fiona's voice softened, almost gentle.

He shook his head, gripping the knife tighter. "Are you real?"

"Yes."

He stepped off the stair, keeping his knife ready, but something in her tone made him hesitate. "No. I didn't want you to be here. This is my place."

Fiona chuckled lightly, like the soft chime of silver bells. "Your place? Boy, you were simply the latest occupant." She stepped closer, the sharp edges of her face catching the faint light. Her cheeks glistened with tears, but her eyes remained steady, keen even in the gloom. "Fitting that I'd end where I started."

Elijah's vision adjusted faster than before. The surrounding blackness lifted to shades of gray, and he could see her now—standing by the table, watching him. Her eyes were hollow, but still piercing.

He moved closer, knowing the knife was useless at this distance. It was a weapon to be used up close, where you could feel your victim's life wash over you as it fled their body.

"And I suppose it's fitting that you'd be the one to do this," Fiona said, her voice calm, almost resigned. "We can't escape our fate. Maybe we run from it for a while, but it always catches up."

Elijah stopped. "Go upstairs," he demanded. "Give Astrid the book so I can save my parents. Then I'll leave. You'll never see me again."

Fiona shook her head, her laugh hollow and bitter. "Your parents are dead. You can't bring them back."

"Huldis said the Lazarus Spiral—"

"Oh, I'm sure he did," Fiona cut him off with a smile that twisted into something cruel. "I'm sure he told you all sorts of things. And that's why the poor stay poor. You're so easily led by promises—promises that never work the way you think they will." Her voice dripped with venom. "The poor are stupid. It's easier that way."

"What do *you* know?" Elijah shouted, his grip tightening on the knife. He wasn't stupid. His mom wasn't stupid. His dad was a hero. They weren't stupid.

Fiona's expression shifted, her voice losing its edge for a moment. "My parents were just as stupid. They trusted the union, and we starved. When my dad crossed the picket line to make money for a meal, they killed him. Came for my mother and me that night. Got her. Carla found me before the mob could."

Elijah's knife lowered, confusion flickering across his face. "Who's Carla?"

"Mother. Madam Geeze. Her name was Carla."

"She wasn't your mother?" Elijah's voice softened. She wasn't lying. He could see it in her eyes.

"No. Just like I didn't give birth to Anna. We find children. We raise them in the Geeze family. All of us are orphans."

Elijah stepped back. His knife fell to his side. Who was this woman? He had thought she was born into wealth, entitled from the start. He had never known hunger, never wondered where his next meal would come from. But she had. And now he was here to destroy everything? Was that how she saw it?

"If the Maker had cared for the Monster, taught him how to speak, showed him love instead of disgust—what could have been different?" Elijah wondered aloud, thinking of Frankenstein. Humans couldn't bear to show kindness to things that reminded them of death, of poverty, or who they once were.

"How long was I in the basement?" Elijah's voice wavered. He braced for the answer.

Fiona didn't hesitate. "Six years." The words were cold, factual. "The first two were to ensure Huldis was destroyed. The next four to make sure you wouldn't try to reconnect with Anna. I wanted you to hate us."

Elijah didn't hate Anna. He hated Fiona. Six years. Who had he been talking to during that time? Imaginary people? Was Huldis working in his mind without exposing he was still alive?

Six years.

He was in this basement for two-thirds of his life.

What good can grow discarded in the dark?

Reading his expression, Fiona scoffed hard and pushed off the table. She said, "Yes, six years. And before that, just less than four years. Ten years. Count yourself lucky it was only ten. Some of us did much more."

Ignoring her comment, Elijah asked what he wanted. While he grew up in the darkness, he was human and rarely heard what others said. He simply waited for his turn to talk.

"Did Anna ask about me?"

Fiona sighed, her composure cracking for a moment. "Every time." She looked away. "But she'd never come down here to find you. I told her you'd gone back to your life, such as it was. That you hated her. You hated us."

"Why?" Elijah's legs buckled. He fell to his knees, the weight of the question—of all the years—crushing him. He hit the floor hard, but the pain was nothing compared to the emptiness inside. "Why did you do this?"

"Because people like us are poison to people like them. Carla, Anna—we're a rot in their hearts. No good comes from us." Fiona's voice grew distant, her words measured. "So, I kept you from her. Anna isn't from my womb, but she's my daughter. I've raised her to be everything I'm not. And you will not ruin that."

The knife pulsed in Elijah's hand, throbbing with every heartbeat. It wanted to stab Fiona like it stabbed his dad, angry and hate filled for doing the horrible things she did, just like it stabbed his dad for doing horrible things. Things like helping others. Like eating dinner.

Like protecting his family. It wanted to drink her hot blood, chew her guts, leave her in a pool of blood for Anna to crawl into — and the thought burst there, the image of Anna screaming for someone to help and no one coming until she couldn't scream anymore. It turned his guts.

He never wanted that for her. Never wanted her heart broken, her soul corrupted by something so much darker than this basement.

"Go upstairs!" Elijah screamed, his voice cracking with tears. "Go! Now!" He slashed the air toward the stairs. "Don't make Anna find you down here!"

Ficna hesitated, but something in Elijah's voice—some deep, terrible restraint—compelled her to obey. She walked around the table and made her way to the stairs.

"I won't die down here," she said quietly. At the bottom step, she turned, looking into the dark one last time. Her lips moved silently, mouthing the word *goodbye*. Then she ascended with the same stately composure she had always worn.

Elijah lingered in the dark, his tears hot against his cheeks. A ghostly image of his father flickered from the shadows.

*Nicky.*

Elijah turned to the voice. "You're not my dad. You can't call me that!"

*I know you're confused, champ.* The voice was soft, familiar. He hadn't heard his dad in so long, he couldn't be sure this was what he sounded like. *But your heart knows what's right. Just listen to it.*

"Go away!" Elijah shouted, bolting up the stairs.

But the ghost was gone by the time Elijah slammed the door shut, locking the basement—and its ghosts—behind him forever.

# NINETEEN

Astrid was still in the study when Elijah and Fiona arrived. The two walked in without a word, one at the point of a knife and the other at the point of no return.

Elijah knew this was it. His destiny was locked in many decisions ago, but now he was on a train taking him deeper into wherever the future went without windows or a map or even a known destination. Each step forward wasn't a choice, it was autopilot.

"No luck?" Fiona said to Astrid in her defiant, dismissive tone.

"Not yet," Astrid said. "Be a dear and help an old lady."

But neither woman moved. Having been through the study many times, Elijah volunteered, "Which book?"

"The map to the Spiral," Astrid answered, and eyed Elijah with curious hope. Fiona looked at Elijah and he wasn't sure if it was a wordless command to stay silent or a question of whether he knew what Astrid was looking for.

"Why do you need that…book?" Elijah paused on the last word, wondering if it really was a book Astrid was searching for. Besides, why would she need a map if Huldis said she could help? How could she help if she didn't even know where to go?

"It shows the starting point to find the Spiral," Fiona said. "Astrid does not know where to begin. How could she help you? She's just a lost old lady."

The old woman wobbled to Fiona and slapped her sharp across the face. A jagged nail ripped a gash in Fiona's high cheekbone, but the younger woman did not flinch. She stood as if stone against Astrid's aggression. Elijah stepped around Fiona and kept his knife high.

"Why would you need a map?" Elijah asked. "Huldis said—"

"Huldis said what you needed to hear, boy," Astrid spat at Elijah. She went to the broken board, held it up, "He's a Fylgjur, his loyalty is unwavering. I made him that way and if he needs to lie to babies, he will!"

She swatted at Elijah. An invisible force slammed into him, throwing him out of the study. He slid across the floor; the knife tumbling out of his hand, and stopped by the hallway to Anna's room.

From the study, he heard Astrid and Fiona arguing, but what did he care? He knew neither wanted to help him. Left to Fiona, he'd be thrown away in the alley with nowhere to go, no one to help him. Left to Astrid, he'd be thrown to the pooka as she ran away. He was on his own and perhaps he always would have been after his parents died.

The sun was setting outside. Darkness was coming and with it, the pooka. Fiona was screaming in pain from the Study now. Astrid had moved to torture to extract the information she needed. Elijah left the screaming behind when he went into Zelia's, Anna's doll's, room. This was the first place Anna brought him. A place where maybe things could have gone differently for him if he stayed in this room. If Anna stayed and the two of them had tea here instead of in the basement. He went to the bookshelves and looked at the spines, reading each and remembering the stories Anna read to her favorite doll.

Outside the large window, the last sliver of sunlight was waning. Anna's room was as magnificent as he remembered it. Nothing had changed. The white flower dresses still hung in the closet, but now they were longer. Yellow flowers adorned everything except the black stone orb sitting on top of her wardrobe dresser. It was held by a stand that showed the map she was given by her grandmother on Christmas morning all those years ago. Elijah couldn't believe that delightful happiness, was *years* ago.

After his own studies, the discussions with ghosts in the basement, he recognized landmarks on the stone.

He took down the stone. The map wasn't a book. It was a carving, chiseled to last forever. It was warm in his hands, warmer than the stone should have been.

Anna was the only one who cared about him. Maybe Madam Geeze did, but a few talks were not enough to know. The racists didn't care. The rich didn't care. The powerful, even though he saved her— freed her, the powerful didn't care. And because no one cared, now he had what they all wanted. A map to change the world, however he wanted it to be changed. And Elijah knew just what he wanted to change.

Everything.

What was the point of bringing his parents back into this horrible world?

He took the stone out of Anna's room and stopped at the

shadowed hallway where the pooka lived. Their flaming green eyes watched him, snarling and growling. They inched closer to the study as the shadows extended from their hall.

"I'm not going to hurt you, but I am leaving." He held up the map. "Tell Anna I said I'm sorry for taking her map." Elijah picked up his knife from the hallway and one of the pooka followed him in the sliver of shadow through the hall. He looked twice at the pooka, who was watching him calmly. It was Jasper.

"Are you coming with me?"

It nodded.

*Where are you going?* Huldis asked Elijah in his mind.

"To change things," Elijah said and waved for the pooka to follow him. It trotted up to him as the sun fell under the horizon and the pooka flooded out from the hallway. They raced around Elijah, paying him no mind, and rushed into the study. Fiona's screams of pain paused as Astrid's began.

Elijah stopped at the front door and looked up to the second floor, to the study. Screams kept coming from both women. Yelps echoed from the pooka.

*Astrid needs your help. She's going to die,* Huldis said.

The rich fought the powerful. Each wanting more without caring about anyone else. Let them kill each other. What does it matter to him? He didn't matter to *them*.

"If she dies, what happens to you?"

*I die too. Her binding magics will unfurl, and I'll be spun into the Spiral.*

"Will she kill Fiona?"

*Yes, that horrible woman will die before Astrid. Death is already coming for her.*

"Then I'll wait." Elijah sat on the throne by the fountain where Fiona watched Anna open her gifts.

There were brown, rotted pine needles on the floor where the tree was all those years ago. How much had the world changed while he was away? Did anyone ever look for his family? Was New York still a giant city? What happened in Harlem with all those artists? He thought about these things as he sat and waited for the noises in the study to cease.

*Help her!*

Elijah wondered if the servants would come back. If they would cast him out or just resume business as usual without Fiona.

Would Anna come back?

He hoped not. She liked Nicky, and Nicky never left the basement. Now only Elijah remained. Perhaps he'd go to the basement to find Nicky. Maybe the boy was still down there, ready to step back into the world with enough quiet, enough time, enough darkness.

Huldis kept pleading, and that told Elijah Astrid wasn't dead yet. The yelping stopped. A gust of frozen wind whooshed through the house. That brought Elijah to his feet, and he rushed to the study. Jasper followed him and whined as he saw piles of dead pooka littering the floor. They looked like smoking pools of shadow and smelled like winter snow before it fell. Astrid was gone. Huldis's pieces were still on the desk where she left him.

*She fled.*

Elijah didn't answer.

He knelt to Jasper and stroked his head. "I'm sorry for your loss," Elijah said.

Jasper whined and nuzzled him. Elijah hugged the creature and pet its flank. Under some of the pooka, Fiona's hand stuck out as if reaching to grab something but dying before she could grasp it. Jasper went to it, nuzzled it, but the hand did not move.

He howled at the loss. Other pooka joined in, the howl raising to the ceiling and fading to the ethereal breath that Elijah knew would carry Fiona's soul to the realm of the pooka.

*You can open the door again. Save Astrid.*

When the howling stopped. Elijah knelt to Jasper and said, "Let's get cleaned up." The two went to the stables.

A frozen winter night gripped the Geeze estate with frost and ice crystals growing over the grass. The stars were out. They blinked and flickered as if processing all that had happened this night, these past years. Elijah, filthy from years without washing, went to the stables and cranked the hose to wash himself. The water was an icy knife scraping away the old Elijah, the one who was born from a nice kid, and leaving behind the Elijah who let Fiona die. Someone his parents didn't know. They would have helped. They were helpers. And they died for it.

No, Elijah was their son. He never came out of the basement. Nicky died the first time. Elijah the second.

"Ely." Elijah said. "I'm Ely."

Jasper nodded, understanding, and released a howl into the night. The howl he let out when Madam Geeze died and Fiona died. This marked the passing, the final ecdysis, the final skin shed. The frail boy shed. The student shed. Now only Ely remained.

Huldis kept asking for help, but Ely, as that is how he thought of himself now, never answered him again. The board pieces and the bag of blocks were put in the shed and locked away.

***

Days later, the servants returned. Wordlessly restarting their duties and serving Ely now as master of the house.

He expected nothing from them. Ignored them mostly as he went about his studies. Words were not required in the Geeze house and thus never used save between Ely and Jasper.

All the windows were covered. Jasper roamed freely in the house, but Ely rarely left the study. He read. He slept. He learned.

The darkness never bothered him as he'd simply turn on a light when needed, but always kept it low to not bother the pooka.

Every night he'd go to the basement to sleep. Jasper would join him. Ely would pet the pooka as it laid on the floor and the two would let the darkness take them. Every night, Ely hoped when he awoke, he'd find the lost boy in the darkness. Nicky would wander out from some corner and he'd find his way back into the light. But Nicky never came out of the dark.

Loved ones never came to visit him again. Not his parents. Not Anna.

# TWENTY

Six years later, in the summer of 1934, Elijah had read every book in the library. Some multiple times. He understood the world as an academic and had ventured out to see the changes brought by science.

There were many new wonders.

He brought many of them home to explore and learn from. Radio components were strewn through the study over books. Light bulbs and batteries lined the shelves beside books and relics he'd found in antique shops across the world. Of all these items, his favorite, for it held a place of honor in the study for any who entered to see, was a phonograph. It played almost constantly, only stopping when Ely went to sleep. The music that rang from the large brass horn: jazz.

He never sang along, nor danced, only listened and remembered the streets of New York. The music mixed with the fighting. The poetry intertwined with the police whistles. Fighting and playing. Death and creation.

Yesterday, he had acquired the final components he needed for his long journey. Today he listened to his latest jazz record, reclining in the study and calculating all he needed for his trip. He held Anna's stone; the warmth coursed through his arms.

He was going to the Lazarus Spiral to set things right, but prior to doing that, he had one last piece of unfinished business.

"Are you joining me?" Ely asked Jasper. He pet the pooka behind the ears how it liked, and the creature licked his face to confirm. "I had this made for you so we can travel until we get where we're going."

The pooka walked into a thick wood and steel box that kept all the light out. Ely closed the door to the box and looked at the other pooka gathering in the study's shadows. Over the past years, more appeared from the shadows and while Ely never asked where they came from, he knew this was their home. "I will see you all soon. Keep the house in order until I return."

Ely left the study and summoned the servants. "Please take Jasper's travel case to the car. Summon Mr. Jones and," he took a deep breath, "please notify Ms. Anna Geeze of my departure."

Ely handed a note to the servant. The nameless man took it without a word as the servants did all things and went about their assigned tasks.

The car was pulled around and loaded for Ely. He wore a deep black suit with a silk black shirt underneath it. His hair was finely coifed, and a red silk pocket square peeked from his jacket. At twenty-two, Ely had grown into a pale, yet fit man. Not tall but lanky, thin from exercise and never growing an appetite beyond the essentials to survive. Yet none would look at his face and mistake him for a kind man. Deep pits surrounded his eyes with sharp-angled bones straining his skin where softer cheeks and chin should be.

People avoided him in the city and in his travels. Left him alone, which was exactly what he wanted.

The driver opened his door; he climbed in, and Ely's journey continued.

His first stop was back to where it began. As Fiona said, it is fitting to end where you began, and this chapter was over. From here, he would never be back, or at least that was his plan, but plans rarely go according to plan.

They drove to the alleyway where Fiona and Anna found him. He pulled on black leather gloves and exited the car into the winter night. His breath fogged around him like a dragon ready to set the world on fire.

The alleyway's darkness swallowed him. Son Rise Diner was now *Nelly's*. Elijah knew that was Mr. Lions' daughter, Nelly Lions, who reclaimed her father's business after his murder. She had fallen on hard times and received a gift from an unknown benefactor to keep her business open until tonight. The benefactor was no mystery to Ely, as it was him. He wanted to ensure Nelly was here for his business with Mr. Jones tonight.

"Has Mr. Jones arrived?" Ely asked.

The driver nodded.

"Summon Ms. Lions."

The servant nodded and went into the restaurant.

In the alleyway, two large men, both in the common attire of his servants, stood beside four hooded men on their knees. Ely nodded to the servants, and they unmasked the four middle-aged white men. Their rough lives shone on their faces through deep lines of poor choices and furrowed brows of regret.

"Mr. Steven Jones. Stevie, as you were known," Ely said. "Recognize this?"

Ely pulled his knife from his jacket. The knife that drank his dad's blood all those years ago. The knife a little boy took from this very alley almost twenty years ago. The man on his knees recognized the knife because it was his before it was Nicky's.

"Recognize where you are?" Ely motioned to the alleyway.

Steven Jones said nothing. He sunk, knowing this day had finally arrived. Relief fell over the man's face, which pissed Ely off. He kept things short so the relief couldn't be enjoyed for long. "Peter Adams. Bethany Adams. Nicky Adams." The backdoor to the restaurant opened and Nelly came out. She was short and plump and shocked at the scene behind her place. Ely met her stunned gaze and said, "Mr. Moses Lions. You murdered them."

"We didn't kill the boy!" Jones shouted. Denying this charge as if the murder of a child was too heavy for his conscious yet the murder of race traitors and a colored man meant nothing.

Ely ripped Jones' head back and exposed his throat. Leaning close to the kneeling man's face, he whispered, "Yes, you did." Recognition contorted Jones' face as he saw the boy in the man before him, but the shock was quickly replaced by another look, that of surprise. The surprise of a man who can't believe what just happened, that someone cut their throat, someone took their life without giving a shit about that person's family, friends, the impact of one death on the world, let alone four. Ely threw Jones into the alley's pavement without the relief he hoped for, only the emptiness of a checkbox checked.

Nelly screamed.

He held the knife handle out to her and pointed to two of the men. "They killed your father. Stomped him to death right where they are kneeling."

Nelly stopped screaming. The fear drained from her. Hate poured into that empty place, the place that had been waiting to meet the bastards that took her daddy, but she shook her head. Ely saw a memory pass over her face, chasing away the hate, leaving behind a resolute certainty. "Jesus calls us to forgive. Even the worst of us."

She wasn't a monster. Her maker was kind, gentle, caring.

Ely nodded and motioned to the servant behind her. In his most genteel voice—the voice of the wealthy and elite—he said, "Please accept my apologies for your loss. Your father was a good man." Ely almost smiled as his mouth watered, the hunger for something beyond sustenance stirring in him for the first time since his last visit. "He made excellent pancakes." Ely looked away from her. "We will clean this up, and you'll never see us again."

"Forgiveness can be in your heart too." Nelly reached for Ely. "You can let them go. I'm sure these boys didn't see nothing here tonight. Did you, boys?"

"No, ma'am!" one answered. He'd pissed himself when Ely held out the knife to Nelly. The stain was spreading, and streams trickled down his leg as the smell drifted into the alleyway. It was thick and heavy, like the smell of blood in such a small place. He must have drunk heavily at the bar where Ely's men found him tonight to make such a pool at his knees. The other men's shoulders caved down as if relieved of a heavy burden.

"Please. Sir. Forgive them for your soul's sake," Nelly pleaded. "Through Jesus, forgiveness can be in your heart. I know my daddy's recipe for those pancakes. Come in. I'll make you a batch. Jesus will help you forgive these boys. He can be in your heart."

"No, he can't." Ely slashed the pisser's throat and kicked his knees out so the man would lie face down in piss and blood. "My heart's already full." The next throat was slit. The final man started screaming for help. "Please, go back to your business, Ms. Lions. My servants will ensure you are compensated for your inconvenience tonight."

"I'm not pleading for them, sir. I'm pleading for *you*." She reached for his arm, and when her hand touched him, she recoiled. The heat of hate, of the inevitability of tonight's actions, boiled from him like a fever. Nelly crossed herself and covered her mouth, as if to shield against catching his infection.

"Shut him up!" Ely shouted to one of the large servants. The man grabbed the screamer's face and jaw, smashing them closed with a sickening crunch as crumbling teeth spit through shut lips. "Thank you for your care, Ms. Lions. But to go where I'm going, I need to close all the doors of my life. Their blood is my key to lock the past away."

Nelly noticed two servants collecting the blood of the other men into glass jars. "Are you going to Hell?" she asked, trembling at the answer.

Ely shook his head. "No. I'm going deeper."

That was the last she could bear and went inside, closing her restaurant for the night.

Ely went to the last man, stood in front of him, and waved the knife for the man to see. The final man was weeping with seizing sobs.

"Please," he mumbled through the gravel remains of his teeth. "Please. I have a family. I've been a sinner, but I can do better. I can change." He whined and kept his eyes away from the knife, away from the monster before him.

The servants poured the other men's blood into the alley, making the shape of a spiral. Ely watched them finish and touched the edge of the spiral with his knife.

"No one changes for the better." Ely sighed, then tapped the edge of the spiral. "Open the door."

A crimson spark ignited on the edge of the spiral and raced around the lines to the center. Fire leapt up from the center, burning all the lines in the spiral and making the whole form glow with a demonic crimson light. "Stab this in the center, and you can leave," Ely said. He dropped the knife at the man's knees.

"I won't say nothing," the man cried. "I, I, I don't even know who you are."

Ely held out his hands, gesturing that the man must recognize him—must know the face of the boy who died in this alleyway. And if not that face, then the face of the teen who rotted in the basement for so many years. And still, if not that face, then the face of this man before him—the face of death that has come for him and so many others. "I'm Ely. You and your friends killed Nicky. The Geeze family killed Elijah. Now, there's only Ely." He motioned to the knife. "Let's finish this."

The man with broken teeth looked at the servants surrounding him. They didn't move. He asked, "I just put this in the center and go home?"

"Sure," Ely shrugged. "Let's be quick before I change my mind."

The man scrambled to his feet and hurried to the center of the spiral. He looked back at Ely to make sure the deal was still the deal, and Ely flicked his hand in the dismissive motion he had picked up from Fiona. Realizing this, he shivered in disgust but knew: you can't choose who shapes you, only what you do with that shaping.

The remaining man—he thought himself the lucky one—bent over and stabbed the center of the spiral. The spiral inhaled sharply, then exhaled molten light that dissolved the last man before he could scream, before he could admonish Ely for going back on his word, before he could do anything but wish he had been a better person so he could see his son again.

His wish went unheard.

As the spiral's mouth yawned open, the servants brought all of Ely's belongings. Without a word to or from them, Ely pushed the bags in, then Jasper's container, finally jumping through the portal himself.

It closed a moment later, and the servants began scrubbing the alleyway, disposing of the bodies, and returning this place of death to the empty, dark void it always was.

# TWENTY-ONE

Anna received a letter when she returned home from the cliffs. She loved to walk among the rocks while the tide was out. It was time for her to reflect on The Emergency as the locals called it, or World War II as the rest of the world knew it. Now, the cliffs were empty as many fishermen joined the British forces, leaving Anna with the waves, the wind, and her thoughts.

The note was handed to her by a servant, a man wearing the standard dress of the Geeze family. He said nothing, as was the custom. She took the note, paper worn and weathered from a long trip, opened it quickly to confirm this was the note she'd been waiting for.

*Dear Ms. Geeze,*

*We have located the man you set us to search for. He has established a homestead in West Virginia, United States of America. As instructed, we have maintained distance and avoided contact. Please advise as to next actions.*

*Sincerely,*

*Mr. Calvin Huber*

Anna refolded the letter and nodded to the servant, dismissing him from her. She wondered where Nicky had been since his last correspondence in 1934. When he left New York, he did not specify where he was going, but apologized for taking the map her Nana had given her. She knew that was where he went, but wished it were not so. The Lazarus Spiral was not a place for good people or kind hearts.

After the treatment Mother gave him, could he have anything but malice in him? Anna knew he was thrown away as soon as she left. Mother said so, but after Mother died, she thought she'd find Nicky. She looked. But the search never found anyone. Her old house, the Geeze estate in upstate New York, would never let her enter. Was it the pooka keeping her out? Or did Ely hate her so deeply that he barred her from her own home?

She never did until now.

In her own study, she opened a map of the United States and found West Virginia. The Atlantic waters were full of U-boats if the movie reels were to be believed, but Anna knew better than to trust faceless voices in dark rooms.

She went to her shaded hallway, the home of the pooka in her home. Their green eyes glowed and trailed sickly flame as they prowled in the dark.

"I am returning to the New World. At high tide, would you kindly negotiate a safe voyage for my ship with your sea-bound brethren?"

One pooka came forward in the shadow, nodded and walked back into the darkness.

It had been years since her last trip home. Mother had already passed, and Nana's sisters were in their final years. Now, Anna was alone save the pooka, and she hoped after a visit with Nicky, she'd be alone no more.

Anna didn't know of Astrid, nor Nicky's second basement exile. She hadn't known the darkness that festered within the kind boy she met before monsters infected the world. Some of those monsters were actual creatures from other worlds, but most were people who forgot they were people. Monstrous creatures were just animals, but people, they had agendas beyond survival and manipulations unknown to the animal kingdom. People were the worst kind of monsters, monsters that hungered with a belly that never filled.

"Ready my car," Anna called to one of her servants. "I'm going home."

# INVENTORY ITEM 32

Inventory Item: 32

Components:

Broken wooden puzzle board

Wooden alphabet letters

Collection: Public

This came to me in pieces, literally. When I showed up for the trade, the trader had a canvas sack filled with wooden parts. He dumped out the contents and it was something I wasn't expecting. A wooden board broken in half with recessed areas where letters could be placed like a puzzle. The wooden letters spilled out too, and I asked if he had all the letters. He said he did.

There was a little energy coming from the object, and I think that's because it was broken. My gut told me this would be a good trade, even though it wasn't all that powerful.

I asked about the backstory, as I always do, and the trader, I never got his name, said it came from a mansion in Ireland that was owned by some rich lady. For the next twenty minutes, I asked a flurry of questions to find out who *some rich lady* was, but he clearly didn't know. He claimed the bag came from an estate sale, but it sounded stolen to me. In this business, we don't ask how each of us got the object, only where it came from and only that when we actually care about the history of an object—like I do.

The letter board looks ancient. It is finely crafted, but the edges of the wooden letters are worn by ages of use, or perhaps a single person using it constantly for countless years. There are also singe marks, as if the board and some letters survived a fire.

I searched for mansions who had a fire in the region of Ireland the trader claimed this came from and couldn't find anything. While I'm going to sink a lot of time into figuring this one out, I am curious about what this thing was before it was broken, burnt, and worn out over the years.

Well, I'm keeping it in the public collection and will trade it for something more useful when the chance arrives. For now, I'll just throw it on the shelf and wait for it to cycle out of my collection.

# 41

# ONE

"There are worlds beyond this one. You must have suspected as much. Few, however, understand that these worlds are held together by threads—threads that stretch from the Lands Beyond all the way to your Core Worlds," the man—or whatever it considered itself, spoke with the casual tone of an old friend, like someone sharing a lesson learned long ago in university.

But Charles Bracker was no friend of this thing. The tone, though always inviting, always kind, didn't fool him. As an experienced toy collector, Bracker knew this wasn't a friendly conversation—it was a game. And he was already struggling to keep up.

Alone in his house in the woods, Bracker was a cautious man in all things. He had enough food and water for the road, the only road to his house, to be closed for two months. That happened sometimes up here when the snow hit hard, but it was fall, and while there was no snow, a heavy rain like they had the other day could wash out the road. Visitors were rare, and that was just how the old man liked it.

The only visitors were other old men, other haunted toy collectors like him, but tonight's visitor wasn't one of them. It wasn't even a man.

It was a thing—a thing from one of those toys.

Bracker had been collecting haunted toys for over forty years without incident. None of the demons, ghosts, or monsters within the toys ever escaped, until tonight.

And tonight was no accident.

He activated the toy genie lamp driven by a question. The question took to seed weeks ago when Neil screwed him over with a bogus trade. But after Neil's death, the question burned in Bracker's mind; it demanded attention in every waking moment.

When he slept, it whispered in the background of his dreams and was seen in everything from the swirls in his coffee to the clouds in the sky.

Why did Neil want this toy so badly that he'd betray their long history in the trade to get it?

"You seem distracted?" The creature asked.

Bracker shook away the idea. "Just listening."

But the thoughts of Neil's betrayal kept gnawing at Bracker. It was that betrayal that led to Bracker calling Neil for the man's final trade. Charles Bracker sentenced Neil Lessman, a colleague—a fellow trader, to death.

Bracker didn't kill him. The horrid Death Doll did. Once the doll saw Neil, he was a dead man unless he gave up his toy collection, like Bracker did. But Neil would never do that. He was too wrapped up in this nightmarish world to let it go.

"Well then, let's continue. It is through these threads that I can grant your wishes. Three wishes, to be exact. Often your kind begin small and if you adhere to the rules, you may wish for almost anything."

The creature settled into the recliner across from Bracker in the dimly lit living room. They sat in silence. No crackling flames in the fireplace. Not a single clock ticked. Even the faint hum of electricity flowing into light bulbs was missing. Only the muted cries of nature outside broke the quiet. Insects chirping and pleading for a mate to come and break their loneliness, to be with them as the night grew darker and the brewing storm gathered.

They sat as if sharing whiskey—though only Bracker held a glass—and cigars, which he puffed at steadily. The genie, or at least that's how Bracker thought of it, didn't smoke cigars, but a thick black cloud continuously drifted from its form.

Tendrils of dark smog curled up from the genie, coiling like snakes in the air before dissipating. The sharp scent of burnt cinnamon cut through the rich haze of cigar smoke, leaving Bracker uneasy, though he kept his gaze fixed ahead, as if nothing was out of place.

Unlike the tales from Disney, this genie was not the answer to Bracker's wishes, and the old man never wanted a friend like this.

The creature's skin was deep onyx. Under its flesh were thick muscles, as if it spent all those years trapped in the toy genie lamp exercising. Silk black pants fit loose against strong legs, then ballooned by his ankles.

But the most striking mark of its inhumanity was the boney ridge that jutted from its forehead. The forehead bulged like the tectonic plates of this creature's skull had collided and thrust from that collision sharp horns at its hair line. Behind the row of horns, the creature's hair was black, slick, and relaxed.

Everything about this creature was far too relaxed, far too comfortable for Bracker. The thing's casual confidence and *just folks'* manner kept the old man on high alert.

"Well, what wish would you like to start with?" The creature asked.

"Let's not start yet. Perhaps first, we can discuss the rules? I don't want to gaff," Bracker said. He chuckled and sipped his whiskey to return the conversation to his control. The genie's golden plastic lamp was in his lap.

Without realizing it, Bracker had already made a major gaff tonight. By simply touching the lamp and summoning the creature within, he had begun the first of many mistakes tonight. But the question needed to be answered. It could wait no longer.

Unlike Neil, the old trader didn't listen to the backstory, the oh so ever important backstory. Neil treasured the story over all things but the toy itself. Bracker wasn't much for history, preferring completed transactions to storytelling.

Tonight, that would be his doom.

"Oh yes, certainly," the creature leaned forward, its eyes gleaming. "To begin, you must understand the resonance of your request. To manipulate the threads of reality, I must..." It paused, searching for the right words, and then, with disappointment, continued, " I must align with the tune where your wish emerges, riding along the strings of existence. The song must flow, naturally bending toward your desire. I cannot simply cut in—the melody of the universe must continue uninterrupted."

That didn't make sense. This wasn't a music class; it was a wish. Wasn't it just words spoken to create an outcome? Genies grant wishes. What else is there to it? But maybe that's why Neil wanted this thing so badly? He knew something that made this make sense. If Bracker didn't give Neil the Death Doll, he could have asked, but now...

Taking a stab at understanding, Bracker asked, "So, is that like a time constraint? I cannot ask for something that would redo, undo, or alter a past event? Because that would be like cutting in?"

The creature pointed at him with a boney finger, then it smiled, revealing long fangs erupting from charcoal gray gums. "I knew you were a smart one. Brilliant. Most do not understand so quickly."

This wasn't news to Bracker. He knew he was smart. Smarter than most, and that knowledge had been his downfall on more than one occasion. However, tonight he thought he had this creature well in hand. Wishes could only change what was going to happen, not what *had* happened. That was easy enough.

But this wasn't what he wanted to know. What did Neil wish for? That had to be why he wanted this toy. Neil didn't do anything other than collect haunted things. There was no online presence for him outside the subreddit. And rumors said Neil had dozens of haunted toys where other collectors had five at most. What could such a man wish for?

"Has anyone ever tried to break the rules?" Bracker asked. He tried to push away the heaping praise, knowing the creature was attempting to worm into his good graces. Bracker knew this game was one of winners and losers. Losing meant death, if he was lucky, fates far worse, if not. The board was set. The pieces moving. The outcome was in flux, as man and monster attacked and defended. But the game continued, and flattery was only one move.

The creature relaxed into the recliner, nodding with plastered sorrow. "Yes, many. Many have thought themselves above the rules. Wisdom, it appears, is for the select few." It motioned between itself and Bracker as if to invite agreement. Bracker said nothing. He only sipped his whiskey and considered where to move his pieces next.

What question would navigate the game board? How could he put the creature off its strategy? What did it want?

But over all that, there was only one question Bracker really wanted to ask: Why? Why did Neil screw him over? And the answer had to justify giving Neil the Death Doll.

Neil chose death.

Bracker didn't kill him. Neil could have done what the doll said and lived. His death was not Bracker's fault.

Then a proper question came, one that would move the game along and to his advantage.

# TWO

"What are common first wishes?" Bracker planned the followup question. His mind spun potential answers and next questions, then answers to those. It was verbal chess and, like any master, he needed to focus to keep track of all the potential moves between him and his opponent.

"Wishes from wise fellows like you or fools?"

While Bracker wanted to steer the conversation towards Neil, the djinn was intent on flattery, so a red herring was in order. "Fools," Bracker smirked and chuckled. With its attempts at flattery, the genie would have expected Bracker to ask about the wise.

But if the genie was thrown off, it didn't show. "Ah, yes. The brilliance of fools to entertain, to teach, and warn." The creature leaned forward. A wave of smoke flowed toward Bracker from the motion. It reeked of burnt cinnamon, filling his throat, choking him. "Often fools want money. They equate income to wealth and wealth to power and power to happiness. Yet they learn quickly that the chain breaks before it begins. They assume their poverty, actual or imagined, is due to not having the right chance. They do not understand the fundamental flaw is not their lack of fortune but their lack of foresight, their lack of self-discipline, and their unwillingness to sacrifice," the genie shook its head and clicked its tongue, *tsk tsk tsk.*

"Like a lottery winner?" Bracker chimed in. "They get the windfall and are miserable until they lose it all." What would Bracker wish for? Not that this is what he wants. He wants answers about Neil, but what would he wish for if he could?

The genie smiled, letting its lips peel away from neat fangs. "And there is why you are no fool. You learn from others."

But Bracker chided himself, knowing he *was* being the fool. The genie was directing the game, not him, and even this move was played off by his opponent. Control must be sought through other means, and that began with rethinking this creature. It was not a genie, not a fun faerie tale creature. It was a djinn, a villainous monster. A thing deserving fear and cautious handling.

He downed the last drops of whiskey in his glass and held it up for examination. The djinn nodded, confirming the glass was empty. Or that Bracker did well to finish it, but then Bracker inserted his redirection. "Would you like another?"

"I have not had one yet," the djinn smiled.

The comment was designed to plant the seeds of hubris into the creature. To make the djinn believe the whiskey was doing its work and that would lead to confidence, which could be turned against the creature.

The toy collector shrugged and apologized for the confusion, then offered a drink to his guest. The djinn held up a polite hand and declined the offer.

"This is indeed a prize whiskey," Bracker went to the bar. It was in the living room to the right of the djinn. An old oak bar with brass railings and heavy wooden stools lined the wall. Behind it, a large glass cabinet held whiskeys from all over the world.

He pulled out the one he'd been drinking and placed it on the bar for the djinn to examine. The creature rose from the recliner and saddled up to the bar to inspect the deep amber liquid within the rectangular bottle. No label or marking on the bottle signified its importance, but both creature and man knew this to be a sign of true greatness as the greatest never needed to identify their greatness.

"Fellows Bourbon." Bracker poured himself another shot. It was a heavy pour, more for show than for anything he actually planned to drink. He re-corked the bottle and placed it back on the shelf. "A close friend gave this to me many years ago. I only drink it on special occasions."

"Like a night where your wishes come true," the djinn eagerly interjected.

"Like such a night," Bracker nodded, cheered and sipped from his glass. "Now, this one." He pulled another bottle from the shelf. This one was labeled with a white sticker that simply read #313. "Batch 313 from the One Legged Racer still. They don't make it anymore. 313 was the last batch and to my knowledge, this is the last bottle." It was full. Blood red wax sealed the cork. A tab stuck out of the seal that had been pulled but not completely opened.

Bracker almost opened it the night he learned Neil had died. The night the doll killed him. He gave Bracker this bottle, not as part of a trade but as a thank you for connecting Neil with another collector. Yes, the doll killed Neil. If Neil would have listened to her, obeyed her, he'd still be alive. Bracker didn't kill him. And remembering that fact made the old man's hands tremble. His next move in this game was muddled, then drowned in Neil's memory.

"Is that your wish?" The djinn appeared puzzled in the turn of conversation. "To have another bottle?" He chuckled at the simplicity of the ask.

"No," Bracker said. There were no friends in the haunted toy trade. And so Bracker got his head back in the game, returning to a move he started earlier. "But what would someone like me wish for? I still don't understand what people wish for. Is that why people seek you out? For wishes?"

There isn't much Bracker needed in life. He loved his isolation and had no interest in the mortal world, but perhaps wishes were not constrained to this world? The idea itched in his mind.

The djinn smiled, wagging a finger as if catching Bracker mid-maneuver. "I see what's happening here. You have a specific wish in mind, but you're wondering if someone's already beaten you to it."

"Do you get a lot of repeat wishes?" Bracker asked, cautiously.

"Most people ask for the same things. Sure, they phrase it differently, but it's always money, power, sex—the standard stuff. Although..." The djinn's eyes gleamed. "I did have one person ask for their dog back. I delivered that one, no strings attached. Didn't even charge a wish."

Bracker set his glass down, startled. "You can do that? Choose what counts and what doesn't?"

The djinn nodded, as if offering a secret. "How about this: your first wish, if it's small, won't count. Use it as a warmup—if you make it right now."

Bracker wanted to resist, but the greed within him was too great. Rumors said Neil always knew if a toy was really haunted or not. Everyone said he'd just look at them and know.

How did he do that?

If Bracker could have done that, the trade that killed Neil wouldn't have happened. Bracker would have seen the Matchbox car was just that, nothing more. And the trade would have fallen through. Bracker would never have called Neil to push the Death Doll on him.

And so Bracker asked for what Neil had. "I wish I could see the haunted toys like Neil Lessman could. He could see if they were really haunted or not. I want that." And with that, he'd never have a bad trade again.

"Done. That will require new eyes." The djinn nodded a sharp, single nod. "And Neil didn't see the power. He felt it like a magnetic pull or sometimes like a heat. But you'll see it because that's what you think you want, and your wanting, your willing it to be, is how this works."

Bracker's eyes dried out. He rubbed them, desperate for moisture, feeling his eyelids scrape like sandpaper, but only steam hissed from the corners. The sockets around his eyes quivered, rippling as scorching heat pressed against his eyeballs. The pressure, as if the djinn were thrusting a molten poker into his face, drove him to his knees, the whiskey glass slipping from his hand and shattering on the floor.

Shards of glass sliced into his palms as he collapsed, but the pain in his hands was nothing compared to the searing agony in his head. He screamed, hoping to release the pressure building behind his eyes, but it only intensified. Blood smeared his face as he clawed at his eyes, but even that steamed away. Bracker threw his head back, and with a sickening pop, his eyes burst—like overripe zits, exploding in a spray of blood and steam.

As the pair vanished and he pulled his fingers from where his old eyes once were, he could still see. But now everything had a dull sheen to it, like over polished glass. He stood.

The djinn was no longer a solid figure, now appearing as pure smoke. It hadn't shed its human-like façade; instead, with Bracker's new sight, he could see the true face of his opponent. Strangely, it was less monstrous than its attempt to appear human, and that brought Bracker an unexpected sense of ease. Now, at least, he knew the real face of what he was up against.

In the mirror behind his bar, Bracker examined his new eyes. Where there was once white was now pink, with splotches of red dripped throughout. Golden irises glimmered and sparkled, reflecting in the beautiful fractals of the mirror. He assumed his eyes burst, but they were still there, just stripped of their original blue coloring.

Silver strings wreathed him, lashing out, writhing and rippling in the air. He reached to touch them. "It's like cilia."

"It is," the djinn agreed. "And all living things have it. Well," it chuckled humorlessly, "almost all living things."

Bracker looked at the genie lamp and saw the cilia like strings radiating from it, but they didn't wiggle, they simply stood straight as if reaching for anything close to them. All the strings pointed at him and glowed bright silver. Some strands entwined with his, locked together and tightening, coiling into each other for a stronger grip.

"You didn't say it would hurt." Bracker bent forward, examining his eyes closer. Inside the gold irises were strands of light, like fiber optic cables surging with messages from sensors.

"All magic requires sacrifice," the djinn sighed as if to say, *that's the breaks.*

The game was now deeply in favor of the djinn. And Bracker was losing ground as his new eyes took in the world around him. His goal for the night, drifting away as the taste for what could be surged within.

That was the free, small wish. What could be done with a powerful wish? What did Neil wish for? Could he have wished away the Death Doll? If so, then why didn't he? Why didn't he save himself? He chose death…

Bracker's mind swam in possibilities, which was exactly where the djinn wanted him.

# THREE

"Such a powerful wish, and for free." The djinn shook his head, chiding itself for such generosity.

Bracker ran his hand through the silver strings floating around him. While he couldn't feel them with his fingers, their energy sizzled against his flesh. Perhaps just knowing it was there was enough to bring his nerves to life. The strings flowed between his fingers in the mirror behind the bar as if seaweed reacting to a current.

"And now, what would you like for your first official wish?"

The game came back to Bracker, the realization that he'd lost control. And so, he repositioned himself, going for a more direct approach than a circuitous one. "Why did Neil want you so badly? That is not a wish, only a question."

And it was the question that had been burning in Bracker. The question that led him to activate the lamp, to touch it, to unleash the creature within—to invoke resolution, as it was known. Yet the answer was worth the trouble, because there was more going on here than Bracker knew. Why else would Neil burn him on a trade for this lamp? There must be more here than he understood.

"I wouldn't treat such a request as a wish. It is only a question of curiosity." The djinn stood from the bar stool and went to the lamp. "Neil never summoned me. I had no interaction with him."

As an experienced liar, Bracker knew false statements when he heard them. The djinn's smokey cluster where a face should be didn't match the words or perhaps it was something in its coal eyes, but there was more than what was being shared. This only incited Bracker more. This was the first lie he felt from the djinn. The game was turning to Bracker's favor.

The djinn knew something, or Neil knew something. In hindsight, Bracker should have asked Neil before giving him to the Death Doll. If Bracker knew why, would that have changed things?

"Did you know Neil stole you from me?" Bracker took another glass from the shelf, this time pouring himself a taste of whiskey from a spherical bottle. The cork on top was shaped like a golden racing horse sprinting along, the jockey riding forward and eager to win.

The djinn looked appalled at the news of the theft. "No. I was unaware. Within the lamp, I am not privy to the machinations of you collectors."

Bracker saw his chance and rolled into the next question, resetting his focus on understanding what the djinn's true value was. "What do you do in that thing all day? Seems like a cramped space for one such as you?"

"Oh, it isn't as cramped as you might think. I'm a trans-dimensional being and the lamp is the gateway. When I enter it, I leave this physical world for another." The djinn circled his hand in the air as if to say *you know how it is* and moved to Bracker's bookshelves. Above the books were a collection of old BluRay disks and above those, music CDs. "I have my distractions within there, as you do here."

"So, are you a prisoner of the lamp?"

"Absolutely not. The lamp is the doorway, but I am free to roam the other dimension. When the lamp is rubbed, I am summoned, but as soon as I go back, I am free."

Perhaps Neil's interest in the lamp was about this other place? Bracker considered the possibility of interdimensional travel, whether the secrets of crossing worlds was known by Neil, and if this lamp was only a doorway to the man?

Many of his fellow collectors had long suspected that Neil's interest in the toys went beyond mere fascination. In private messages—never out in the open—whispers circulated. Neil was more like the infamous Ely Adams than anyone wanted to admit. Ely, the trader everyone knew to avoid. Too many collectors had gone to him for deals, only to disappear without a trace. By the end, Neil had become just as much of a boogeyman as Ely.

Some believed that Ely was mixed up in something far darker than the haunted objects themselves. Now, it seemed Neil might have been too.

"Certainly, Neil engaged you in some manner?" Bracker asked. He took a sip of whiskey and went back to his recliner. The game was more stable there and perhaps a return to the chair would help him set things back in his favor.

"I did hear him talking." The djinn tapped his chin as if trying to remember. "Yes, he was talking about, well, dark things." Quickly, the mood changed from a game to a forbidden topic. The djinn shifted, came back to its chair and, like Bracker, sought to regain the game of old. "Now, about that wish."

A mistake! The djinn said moments ago that it couldn't hear outside the lamp, but now it said it could? Bracker had him on the ropes and avoided the redirection.

"No. Tell me more. What darker things?" Bracker knew Neil's reputation for dealing in taboo, for the rumors of doing things others wouldn't to get the most haunted of haunted toys. The dead man was driven to be the best, and that drive ultimately led him to his death.

Once Bracker heard Neil went to Iceland for a toy and upon collecting it, took it directly to trade with a collector in Egypt. But the Egypt trade wasn't for a toy, it was for a book. Another story was how Neil researched making haunted toys by killing children and stuffing their souls into the toys. Bracker always dismissed this because if Neil could do that, why would he be in the trade? But why were any of them in the trade?

Like many others, Bracker did it for the oddity of it. He also collected CDs and vinyl albums. There wasn't anything driving him other than the awe of his peers for his strange items. Neil was different. He was obsessed. And it wasn't just the toy he wanted, it was always the story. When it came to trade this lamp, Bracker knew little about the story. Neil was frustrated but not deterred by that. Did Neil discover something about the lamp? Did he get the story? Is that how he survived the lamp?

"I do not wish to speak ill of former owners." The djinn gave a cordial grin and steepled its fingers.

"Neil's dead. Killed by one of his toys," Bracker said.

This news, and by the djinn's expression Bracker was certain this was news, shocked the creature. Its hands fell, lapsing its focus for a moment as a dumbfounded expression slithered over its face. The djinn sat taller and leaned forward. "Are you sure?"

"Told by a reliable source." Bracker thought of the girl online who told him Neil was dead. She had the Death Doll and disposed of Neil's collection at the Patticon River, which is where his contact recovered this lamp. The contact, a local police officer, refused to go at night and instead went in the morning. He reported finding the lamp beside a dripping wet ten-pound weight on the muddy shore of the river. "He's dead."

The djinn sat back in the chair. It silently processed this information. Why did the djinn act like Neil's death was impossible? There was something it knew—that would deny the possibility of Neil's death. Did he wish for immortality? Could Bracker wish for that? To live forever? To cross worlds?

Bracker refocused, seeing the djinn on its heels and wanting to keep it there. "The Death Doll got him."

At this, the djinn sprang to its feet, the recliner chair toppling behind it from the force. "Viola is here? Vilhelmina the Reckoning? Acolyte to Lady Chelus, Fiend of Dokkalfar and Valkyrie of the Realm?" Each name pierced through the djinn's calm, another nail driven into its confidence. Its form rippled, shaken by the mere mention of such a being.

Then it appended the name that Bracker recognized, the name that brought his soul low, just as the others must have done to the djinn: "Ely Adam's Death Doll?"

Bracker nodded, assuming it was the same, but never caught the doll's name. He only did what she said. No questions, no deals, no debate, just execution. She demanded he get rid of his collection, and so he did. There weren't many items of genuine interest remaining, but it was the idea—the idea of getting rid of all the things he'd been collecting for years, all the deals, and the crappy trades he suffered. And poof, she made him give it all away. And in the end, it was only a few toys, but the thought of making Neil give it all away, a punishment for that damn trade, was what Neil deserved. Just not death.

Why didn't he give up the collection? "What dark thing was Neil into?" The answer to that question could unravel every question Bracker needed answered.

"The Lazarus Spiral," the djinn moaned in horror. It paced, biting at its clawed fingertips. It stopped, realization sinking into its face, black smoke billowing intensely from its body. "That's why she killed him. He was seeking the Spiral. And, and he found it…or at least a doorway…" The djinn looked at his lamp and shook his head, denying the thought.

The Lazarus Spiral? In all his years collecting, Bracker couldn't remember ever hearing that. "Lazarus? Like the guy in the Bible?"

"No, not Lazarus of Bethany, Lazarus Alexandros. Lazarus of Alexandria. He was a mathematician." The djinn stopped in front of Bracker. "He discovered the Lazarus Spiral theoretically and then actually found it, the real place."

A hard quiver darted through Bracker's stomach. The game had changed. The djinn was in free fall, its game was over, and it was just trying to get out of here before the Death Doll came back. But Bracker did what she said. He got rid of his collection. Sure, the police officer gathered a few items from Patticon River for Bracker and the collection was restarting, but she wouldn't come back for just a few things…would she?

"She's here for those who can access the Spiral…" The djinn quickly glanced at his lamp again, very fast, but not fast enough to prevent Bracker from noticing. "We have to leave." The djinn rushed to its lamp, stopping short of touching it as Bracker interrupted.

"Wait, what is the Lazarus Spiral?" Bracker asked.

The djinn could be bullshitting him, but sweat was beading on the creature's head and it moved so quickly around his room that it must have had a compulsion to burn off nervous energy.

The djinn sighed and put up a hand. "Before I begin, I have to be clear. Rule two, you cannot wish for something that is directly impossible. It has to be able to possibly happen without breaking the threads of reality."

"So, if I wish to be rich, which I am not," Bracker emphasized the last words, "then it could work because I could get a lottery ticket tomorrow and be rich."

The djinn nodded. "I mention this now because when people wish for power, they are asking for a laughable fraction of what is possible with the Lazarus Spiral. If you ask to go to this place, I cannot send you directly there. It would be impossible for you to go there from this world. You'd need a door."

Bracker suppressed a smile. Understanding dawned as to why the djinn's eyes kept darting to the lamp. The lamp was a door. It could be a doorway to this place, whatever it was. If Neil was looking for this place, the trade now made sense. Yet, if Neil would have told Bracker, if he would have negotiated…things could have been different. Not that Bracker did anything wrong, but Neil had always made good trades and if not for this last one, he would have not been the first person Bracker thought of when the Death Doll said she needed to be passed to another. This trade was full of assholes. Bracker never thought Neil was one until he was.

Taking a deep breath, the djinn sat down, its heels bouncing on the floor, and began. "Remember, I talked earlier about the threads that hold the worlds together?"

Bracker nodded.

"The Lazarus Spiral," the djinn breathed, its voice dropping into a reverent hush. "It is where the threads that hold the worlds—all worlds—converge."

Bracker blinked, his mind catching on the word "all." All worlds? His chest tightened, an involuntary reaction to the sudden, dizzying scope. All worlds. Did that mean…?

The djinn didn't seem to notice Bracker's struggle to keep up. "It is where you can… reconstruct… everything," the djinn whispered, drawing out the words as if savoring their taste. "With just a thought."

Bracker's mouth felt dry. Everything? The vastness of the implication pressed on him, like a weight he couldn't fully grasp.

"And it isn't like magic. It doesn't require careful wording or focus, or sacrifice. The Spiral understands your intent and delivers it, whether you understood your true intent or not."

For a moment, silence hung between them. The room felt suffocatingly still, as if even the shadows were listening. Bracker didn't move, afraid the next breath he took might shatter the fragile web of secrets the djinn was spinning. He searched for an analogy. Struggling to organize his thoughts with the flood of possibilities gushing in, he settled on asking, "It's a wishing well?"

The djinn rolled its eyes as a nervous laugh slipped out. "It isn't *a* wishing well, you don't ask, it is a *willing* well. There are no rules here. Nothing is impossible. Nothing is off limits. You simply *will* whatever you want into existence. And it is."

Earlier in the night, the power of the djinn was intoxicating for Bracker. Now, discovering there was a power beyond anything he could ever imagine, Bracker's agenda for the night moved beyond survival, beyond the djinn's wishes. He never had been one hungry for power, but he was an opportunist. And he clearly heard opportunity knocking to give him everything he ever wanted.

The game was over.

# FOUR

The djinn began its tale of the Lazarus Spiral.

"Before time's clock was wound, before the stars lit the void, two worlds were created," it began, its voice a low rumble. "The birth of one brought forth the other, and between them… the threads were woven."

Bracker's pulse quickened as he leaned forward, drawn in by the weight of each word.

"But the First Builder knew those threads alone would not hold. They were fragile, strained by the forces of creation." The djinn paused, letting the tension build. "So, the Builder crafted something stronger—a support beam to bridge the worlds."

The djinn's voice deepened, as if recounting a secret long buried. "To do this, the Builder twisted the threads, binding them tighter and tighter, until their tension became power. And at the heart of that power, the Spiral was born."

Bracker's breath caught, the room itself seeming to close in around him.

"The Spiral," the djinn continued, "was sealed with a stone—a lock placed at the center, where the threads pulled against one another. This lock is what holds the worlds together. Without it, they would collapse, folding into chaos."

The djinn's eyes gleamed as it spoke, its smoky form shifting restlessly. "But with it… the Spiral remains, a nexus of all worlds, all realities, humming with energy. The energy that you can now see."

Bracker struggled to absorb the enormity of what he was hearing. This wasn't just a story. The Spiral was real—the point where every world and possibility converged.

"Wait, *First Builder*? You mean, you talking about God?"

The word didn't register with the djinn. It shrugged and continued. "The First Builder built all and all that has come since." That explanation fit Bracker's expectation of God and so he waved to continue.

The djinn did. "As time began, and the worlds went to war, a third world was constructed to provide the two worlds with a neutral place in which to deal with their differences. The stone lock was the center of this third world and to seal the threads, protecting the nexus point between the two worlds, the Builder designed a tower on top of a mountain which was only accessible through a hidden trail in the mountain range."

"Wait!" Bracker interrupted. "I have questions."

The djinn huffed at the interruption, then circled its hand to invite Bracker to be out with it.

"One support beam?" He asked.

The djinn nodded, but it wasn't as certain as Bracker expected. It was the answer of someone who assumed, or didn't care, but the old man let it go and asked his next question.

"Why have it accessible at all? I mean, if it was so important, why not lock it away from the world…worlds?"

This time, the djinn shrugged, but Bracker didn't buy it. The creature knew more than it let on. Still, pressing now would do him no favors. Playing along—letting the djinn think him gullible— would take Bracker much further in this game. So, he didn't push, just yet.

"Sorry, just a curious sort." Bracker waved for the djinn to continue, and it did.

"The tower, known by my people as the Tower of Ascension, is guarded by fierce creatures on the upper levels, where intruders are often caught, imprisoned, and devoured." The djinn delighted in this a little too much. "But deep in the tower, under the mountain, is the stone holding everything together."

"The Lazarus Spiral?"

"Yes, Lazarus Alexandros believed there was too little tethering the heavens to the earth. Legend has it, a voice whispered in his ear, guiding him to this realization." Again the djinn shrugged like it didn't know who would possibly whisper such a thing, then continued. "Regardless, he was a mathematician by trade and thus he devised an equation—a proof, in his mind—that a nexus point must exist, holding the worlds together. To him, the worlds were simply heaven and earth. He didn't grasp the true complexity of what he sought. Still, he pursued his theory relentlessly. After discovering a passage into my realm, he found the Tower of Ascension, braved its dangers, and eventually descended into the Lazarus Spiral."

"What did he wish for?" Bracker leaned forward in his chair. For a man who worked for everything he ever had, the idea of wishing seemed abstract. There were no wishes to replace doing the work. Never in his life did he utter the words *I wish I had* until tonight.

Wishing was for the weak willed. And that made the possibilities he could wish for too vague. He needed models beyond the obvious.

"To go home," the djinn answered and gestured to Bracker as if to ask, *what did you expect?*

But that weighed heavily on Bracker, sinking him into his chair with a deep, audible sigh.

Why would Lazarus settle for home?

At the center of all worlds, with the power to reshape reality at his will, why would Lazarus only wish to go home? The mathematician could have uncovered the universe's deepest secrets. He could have become a god, lived forever—yet all he wanted was to go home?

The simplicity of it unsettled Bracker. Merely hearing this story stirred a wonder in him. The djinn might grant some of these wishes, yes, but there would be consequences—Bracker had no doubt of that. Magic requires sacrifice.

The Lazarus Spiral, though, that was where one could make a wish without paying the price. A wish with no consequence. Bracker pushed aside his questions, for now, leaning forward as he asked, "Then what happened?"

"Lazarus recorded his journey, but the text was lost for centuries. It was found in an expedition to Iceland by Victor DeLacroix, who published his findings in his iconic work *The Shadowed Key*. Many generations of sorcerers have studied the text, but Lazarus left out some key pieces of information on finding the tower."

"But *you* could take someone there who asked? Someone who wished for it?" Bracker jumped at the question that had been building since the story began.

The djinn was terrified of the Spiral, or maybe his mind was still on the Death Doll, who he called Viola. Regardless, Bracker felt certain the djinn knew the path to this Tower of Ascension.

"No," the djinn shook its head. "Rule 2. I can only do things that are possible and to access the World Between Worlds would be impossible from here."

"But not through your lamp?" Bracker countered, a smile tugging at his lips. He knew the game the djinn was playing. The lamp was a passage to another world—and through it, other worlds could be accessed. This was the sort of evasion he'd expected, a half-truth to avoid the power balance tipping in Bracker's favor. When it came to truly powerful wishes, there was always a catch—always some reason they couldn't be fulfilled. But not this time. The djinn slipped too much, too many details not meant to be shared, given in the djinn's distress over Viola.

He leaned forward. "Wishes are in the details, right? If I wished to go to the Lazarus Spiral through your lamp, that would work."

The djinn sucked a deep hiss through its teeth. It shook its head, then shrugged as it thought through the request. "It would have to be two wishes. The first would be to go into the lamp and then, once in the lamp, to go to the Lazarus Spiral."

"Is that what Neil wished for?"

The djinn froze, which was all the answer Bracker needed. Whatever dark things Neil was into, he went to the Spiral. What did Neil wish for at the Spiral? Was he really dead? Maybe the girl who said she had the Death Doll was wrong? Yet here was the lamp. Found exactly where she said she disposed part of his collection.

"What will happen to me? If I wish to go into your lamp?" Bracker pointed to the lamp. "You said magic requires sacrifice. What will happen? I just want to know."

"As I came out in smoke, you will go in as smoke," the djinn said. "The lamp is a little small to climb in as you are." It grinned and chuckled a humorous laugh. Bracker agreed it was funny to think of climbing into something so small. "It won't hurt. Once you're in there, I'll join you for the second leg of the trip."

This is what Neil wanted. He hadn't stolen the lamp just to hoard it—he'd used it to achieve some darker, twisted agenda. He'd screwed Bracker over, sure, but Neil wasn't dead. He couldn't be. Somehow, he'd outmaneuvered the Death Doll, and that girl online had gotten it wrong. Neil didn't need his collection anymore; he'd moved on to something far more powerful.

Bracker's mind raced. How did Neil know? How had he uncovered the lamp's true potential? Bracker bit his lip, cursing himself for not paying more attention to the stories. If only he'd listened, maybe he'd have understood. Lesson learned—next trade, he'd get the full story.

But what Bracker hadn't yet realized, what he couldn't quite see, was that there would be no next trade. He wouldn't be trading haunted toys again. Not ever.

Still unaware of his fate, the toy collector nodded and downed the last of his whiskey, savoring its warmth as if it were the final thing tethering him to his old life. He turned to the shelf and reached for the bottle of Batch 313—his special bourbon, reserved for only the most significant moments. Going to the center of all worlds, and having anything, *everything*, would certainly qualify. He pulled the tab, ripping off the wax seal with a satisfying snap. The cork popped, and Bracker poured himself a full glass, the rich amber liquid swirling in the dim light.

"See you soon, you slippery bastard," Bracker muttered, raising his glass to Neil. That Neil wasn't dead, not really, took the weight off of Bracker's soul. There were no friends in this business, but perhaps Neil was close? The doll didn't get him. Bracker didn't seal his friend's fate. But what is Neil up to? Time to find out.

He took a slow sip. The drink was sweet at first, a familiar warmth that turned smokey as it slid down his throat. By the time it hit his stomach, it burned. It wasn't the best, but it was the rarest, and that made all the difference.

Smiling, he nodded to the djinn, who watched from the corner, silent but knowing. "Let's do this," Bracker said, the eagerness in his voice betraying his confidence. He lifted his glass, savoring the moment before he spoke the words that would change everything.

"I wish to go into your lamp."

"So, it shall be." The djinn nodded, and black smoke billowed around the creature.

Instantly, pain erupted through Bracker's body like a thousand razor blades slicing into his spine, each cut followed by the violent fizzling of pop rocks exploding in raw, exposed tissue. Every cell inside him seemed to crackle and burn, popping uncontrollably.

His muscles convulsed, skin tingling, then erupting in flames as if every nerve ending was being seared alive. His body jerked as if it were tearing itself apart from the inside, every fiber of him dissolving into agony.

Eyes wild with terror, he turned to the djinn, desperation and betrayal etched into his contorted face. Why? Why did this hurt so much? His mind screamed for answers even as his body rebelled against him.

The djinn, unfazed, met Bracker's panicked gaze with eerie calm. Its smoky form flickered, but it provided the answer without delay, its voice smooth, almost mocking.

"Why do you humans always think I'm honest?" The djinn smiled, all humor gone, replaced by the satisfaction of victory.

"You said it wouldn't hurt!" Bracker snarled through the pain. He fell to his knees and coughed out the red mist that was filling his insides.

"I also said I'd join you. Guess you can't believe everything." Black smoke drifted away from the chair where the djinn had been sitting and towards the lamp. It stopped and reformed its body from the smoke as the red mist foaming from Bracker's body was sucked into the lamp.

"Wait—what did Neil wish for?" Bracker's voice cracked. The words barely made it past the smoke filling his lungs, desperate to grasp the one thing that might save him from this nightmare. He had to know. Had Neil escaped the same fate? What had he done to survive?

"Neil didn't make your mistake. He never called for me to come out of the lamp." The djinn smiled.

"The Spiral? He wanted the Spiral?" Bracker pleaded.

"Everyone wants the Spiral. I tell them about it, and they can't resist wishing for more. The path they ask for… is never one they survive."

Bracker saw the djinn never stopped playing the game. Where the toy collector was constantly distracted, the djinn never lost his strategy.

"Why? Why'd you do this?" Bracker asked his last question.

And the djinn answered, "For fun."

It laughed and leaned closer to watch Bracker's realization that there was no reason to kill him beyond a whim. No rational explanation for tempting him with the Spiral other than to get the old man to ask to die.

This was never a game. It was a prolonged execution scripted to make Bracker feel in control, to make the realization that he was never in control even more horrible. He was dead the moment he rubbed the lamp.

Seeing his failure, Bracker screamed until his throat filled with his evaporated insides and then he just coughed, gagging on himself. His flesh imploded and curled up into his chest as he kept hacking out the mist. Then, with one last heavy choke, his skin popped and all the blood mist in the air flowed into the lamp's small spout.

The last thing he heard was a heavy knock on his front door. A visitor had come—but who?

Bracker never found out.

# INVENTORY NOTE 41

Inventory Item: 41

Components:

Plastic Genie Lamp

Collection: Private


I thought this was the last toy. The power radiating off this thing makes my teeth numb, but Dodslav has not come yet. Perhaps it takes time to travel from wherever he is to the dollhouse's spiral. After Bracker discovers the car is a fake, I'll be done in the haunted toy trade. Word spreads quickly in this small community and now is when my reputation will either carry me through a bad faith deal or ostracize me forever. Then how will I complete my collection? How will I trade for Drew?

But I couldn't give Bracker anything from my collection. I need every ounce of spiritual energy to draw Dodslav.

This toy is rumored to grant wishes. It is my ultimate weapon against Dodslav should things come to that. For years now I've gathered toys to trade for Drew, but the past private collection toys are my weapons, my armor, my gateways, to take my brother back. I never trusted Dodslav, a creature that fed on my brother's weaknesses. I always knew things would come down to this.

With this lamp, I can wish for immunity from resolution and freely use these toys as an all-out assault against that demon.

When I do, Drew will come home, and we'll leave this place for the farm in Italy I bought a few years ago. I've kept this world of haunted toys away from there, mostly. Arcane studies don't count. Besides, I know Dodslav won't leave me be if I take my brother back. Those weapons in Italy are more like home defense than tools of war. Regardless, Drew and I will escape and be done with all this.

As much as I hate the idea, I must go to Sister Wendy one last time. She's the only one who knows how to kill creatures like Dodslav and I don't plan to leave his world without his head. Thirty years of work won't end with me constantly looking over my shoulder. According to her journal, the little black book that has been with me since the start of all this says, demons are immortal in our world. But, there's a note at the end of her journal that suggests demons like Dodslav can be killed here. She doesn't specify how? I assume it has to do with her faith. Could there be more to it? Something I could do?

Before I engage the genie, activating a toy on purpose, something I've never done since Drew was taken, I need to see if one or two more toys will summon Dodslav. I need to give him the chance to make good on our deal, but I'm so tired. Burning Bracker like this is just another dark deed added to my ledger dripping with sin. When will the Ferryman come to claim his due?

According to Bracker, this lamp contains a djinn. Real genies are monstrous tormentors, not friendly blue buddies. Every wish has a twist and so I have been thinking carefully about what I'd ask. I'm certain the ability to grant wishes is some kind of dark magic. In which case, wishes will require some kind of price to be paid by the one benefiting from the act. I'm no sorcerer, but my arcane studies have taught me not to mess with magic unless I'm desperate.

And I am. So desperate to be done. To wash my hands at all this, but could my hands ever be clean? If Bracker tries to trade that car I gave him with the wrong person, they might kill him. That's not to think about the people who were literally killed to make the toys I have amassed in my basement. When is enough? Is Dodslav just watching and laughing as I keep doing more and more to get more and more, never having enough until there's nothing left inside me? When is enough?

I guess I'll find out.

God, I hope the next toy is the last. Please, let it be enough. Please let it be the end to all this.


*NOTE: This was one of the toys Viola made me throw in the river. It is drowned, like her, in the Patticon River. - Lucy

# EPILOGUE

The djinn drifted through his black smoke to the front door. It was white and solid, without a way to see the visitor. Regardless of who it was, the djinn knew anyone would be easy work with his charms. Besides, perhaps he could get another meal out tonight? Another serving of mist for his pleasure.

It opened the door and prepared to greet the visitor, but the visitor didn't wait. He was an old man, in his early seventies, and pushed through the djinn without question. The man was solid for an old guy, with eyes that were set in his purpose.

"Fotham? Also known as The Wish Breaker?" The old man went to the plastic genie lamp and picked it up. He was wearing leather gloves but seemed unbothered by the danger of resolution.

"I am," the djinn, Fotham, answered. "Do you seek me for wishes?" The creature did not think this was the case. Without a moment of surprise or even wonder, the old man knew of Fotham's kind and, the djinn thought, this wasn't the first Dokkalfar the man had encountered.

"No. Keep that shit to yourself." The old man's voice was cold, dismissive, and disinterested. He moved through the cabin. Sharp eyes examined the house for any sign of distress, anything that would raise an eyebrow if investigators began looking for the guy who lived in this cabin. There was no rush in his movements, just the steady precision of a trained professional. "I'm Lee. The Artist sent me to gather you." Fotham recoiled from the name, *The Artist.*

Being this far in the woods, Lee assumed the cabin's owner didn't get many visitors and probably wouldn't have anyone coming to check on him. But Lee's training kicked in, and it was standard Sector-7 protocol to ensure a victim's last location appeared properly disturbed for the persona and profile of the person. This guy Bracker was a neat freak and everything throughout the cabin was in its place, save for a bottle of whiskey on the bar. He must have been drinking prior to the djinn's trickery. That likely made the outcome easier for Fotham.

"The Artist?" Fotham's voice wavered. Even the djinn, trapped in a plastic genie lamp to serve its sentence, an unfair and cruel sentence by the Valkyries for corrupting humanity centuries ago, knew to fear The Artist. His name was whispered among the Valkyries, among the worst of humanity, but this man—his emissary, said it without fear, without care. "He, he has sent for me?"

Lee nodded as he placed the whiskey bottle back in the cabinet. His leather gloves left no prints. The glass was washed, dried, and placed in the cabinet where the others were kept. "He's asked me to take you to the hive."

"You are his emissary?"

Lee snarled at that. "No. Just another caught in his wake."

For thirty long years, The Artist had pulled Lee's strings, reducing him to a puppet in a world of shadows and monsters. But for

Bobby—for his son—it was worth every ounce of pain. Bobby was safe, far from all of this. He'd grown into a good man, someone untouched by the horrors that consumed Lee's life. And that was all Lee needed. His servitude would end soon, he knew that, and with it, he'd take the curse that had poisoned him for so long. It would die with him. And the God damn phone that started it all, the Artist's haunted phone his son brought home on the worst day of their lives, would never be found. Bobby would be free.

"Get in the car."

＊＊＊

From the woods, curious eyes watched, undetected by Lee due to the observer's own Sector-7 training.

Bobby, like his father, knew how to be invisible. And while his father was the best at what they did in Sector-7, he was aging and always had a blind spot for his son. As the black sedan drove away from the cabin, Bobby followed on his silent electric motorcycle. After so many years of secrets, tonight Bobby wanted to see what was eating at his father. The last secret unshared between the two.

They drove late into the night with Bobby having to stop for a quick charge. Being prepared for such a situation, the tracker Bobby placed in his dad's car was beeping steadily. After the charge for the bike and a coffee for him, Bobby was back on the road and heading towards Annapolis, Maryland.

Lee had stopped in an industrial district outside of Baltimore. There were neighborhoods of brick warehouses for miles around and not a single person to be seen except the occasional night watch guard who flicked their flashlight around. These warehouses might have been new when his dad was a little kid, but now this looked like the land time forgot. Empty warehouses, empty shipping containers, empty roads and overgrown lots. Humans didn't come here unless they had to. No one was shipping anything from here.

Bobby left his bike near a rusted out shipping container. He covered the bike with a large tarp he found in a container.

His dad's car was parked outside an old warehouse on the outskirts of the complex. The windows were broken on the first and second floor, but the ones on the third and fourth floors were only cracked, being too high to reach for the kids throwing rocks. Some bricks were crumbling from the dead vines bursting through the grout, clawing their way up the walls. In the moonlight, the windows glistened like spider webs with all their cracks. The air carried a burnt decay that was common in these industrial complexes, but Bobby caught the scent of something else: cinnamon. He followed the smell into the warehouse and through the forest of steel poles holding up the second floor, and stopped where the smell was most intense, a steel door to the basement.

There wasn't a doorknob, just a hole where Bobby looped his fingers and pulled the door open. Most of the door was rusted and Bobby waited for the thing to crumble, or the hinges to squeal, but it held and was surprisingly silent. As it opened, the stench of cinnamon singed Bobby's eyes. He tried to blink away the tears but couldn't keep up. Bobby tucked his nose and mouth into the crook of his elbow and pressed forward downstairs.

The steps were steel, as rusted as the door, and just as silent. He moved down, pulling his service revolver to be ready for whatever he found down here. Staying in the shadows, he stopped midway down, which was far enough to see his father's nightmare clearly.

Bobby blinked hard to make sure he was seeing what was there. He remembered the creature in the construction yard, the one that broke into their house when he was a kid. He remembered the thing's boney forehead, its shimmering black skin, the claws and fangs jutting from its hands and lips. Here was that thing again. Now not just in his teenage nightmares, now there were hundreds in the flesh.

Lee pulled the demon from the cabin into a swarm. They all billowed black smoke as if the floor was an incinerator, filling the room with shadow. Every one of them had the bulging foreheads, some had horns, all had the deep onyx black skin. They gathered and hissed as the newcomer joined their cluster. Bobby tried to count how many could be down there, but he couldn't. Only assumptions could be made, perhaps a hundred, maybe two hundred, he wasn't sure.

But now he knew his father's secret. He knew what had been eating at his old man ever since they found that damn phone, the phone that called hell.

Many of the creatures wore green tunics. Nujen, the creature at the construction site all those years ago, dressed just like them. His dad and he talked about the phone and Nujen often, but never around others and never in a manner that led Bobby to believe his father was still involved in this madness. Here was all the proof Bobby needed. All the certainty that his father never left that night, never stopped calling hell and talking to the devil.

Concrete walls and iron pillars held up the basement ceiling. The warehouse was empty other than the throng of bodies now smoking and milling about the large opening. A makeshift stage was at the back of the basement. Lee stepped up onto it and raised his arms to quiet the demons.

"All, the Artist has collected you for a purpose. He is ready to complete his masterpiece, but needs your help before he can," Lee said. The demons murmured to each other, wondering aloud how they could help the Artist. Bobby had never heard of this person, but clearly everyone else here had.

The Artist must be the general or commanding officer for this legion of creatures as they all revered his name, and the one who brought his messages to them.

"Emissary, what must we do?" Someone shouted from the mass of smoke filling the basement now.

Lee's voice lacked any fire as he recited the words. "Go forth and retrieve the Dollhouse. You will know it by the Artist's touch—it's unmistakable." What should have been a rallying cry landed flat, drained of all passion. Lee wasn't leading an army, wasn't inspiring the troops. He was simply repeating instructions, going through the motions as if the task had no more meaning than the words themselves.

But those listening knew better. The words didn't need Lee's conviction—they carried the weight of the Artist's command. For the faithful, that was enough to stir the flame inside. The black smoke responded, thickening, as it drifted toward the stairs. It moved with purpose, silent and sure, and Bobby felt his breath catch in his throat. They were coming for him now.

He quietly ran upstairs, moving fast but trying not to make a sound. The warehouse was a maze of empty rooms, no cover, just rows of bare walls and floors too hollow to keep his footsteps hidden. His pulse was in his throat now. He spotted a rusted backdoor and didn't hesitate, shoving it open with a rough screech that made him cringe. They had to hear that. He needed cover, now!

Outside, his eyes locked on salvation: a dumpster, old and beat to hell, with crumbling holes in the metal, but the black lid still clung there like a lolling tongue. Bobby sprinted to it, heart pounding in his chest, and dove inside, pulling the lid down over his head.

In the suffocating dark, he held his breath. The smell hit him like a punch to the sternum—rotting food, sour rainwater, rusted metal—but it didn't matter. He pressed his back against the dumpster's damp walls, pulling his knees close, and tried to steady his shaking hands. This was better than being seen.

Billows of black smoke poured from the door, slipping through cracks in the grout and blasting out crumbling bricks. The demons spilled into the night, hunting for their prey, moving like shadows on the wind.

Bobby peered through a rusted hole in the dumpster, watching as streams of black cloud vanished into the dark, swallowed by the city's night sky. Inside the dumpster, the air didn't reek of trash but of damp, steaming moisture clinging to the cool evening. There was death in that air, outside and within. Something had died in here—maybe more than one thing—but in the total darkness, Bobby hoped nothing was still alive enough to bite.

He waited, listening. Nothing moved. Even the demons outside made no sound as their smoke faded into the night, carried on the wind, leaving only silence and the promise of their return.

Knowing someone could have lingered, Bobby settled with the dead roaches and decayed corpse of a rat in the dumpster until the first golden ray of sunrise sliced into the murky rot. Following protocol for breaking cover in a possibly hostile situation, Bobby cautiously climbed from the dumpster.

No one was around.

Bobby rushed to where he'd hidden his bike—but it was gone. Others might have thought they'd gotten mixed up in a warehouse complex this sprawling, but not Bobby. He knew exactly where he'd left it. Someone had found it. Someone knew he was here.

And that someone was watching him right now.

Instinctively, Bobby pulled his shirt up to cover his face—standard protocol when things went sideways like this. He took a quick breath, orienting himself toward the entrance of the warehouse gates.

The sun was coming up over the shipping containers as Bobby sprinted to the exit. He watched for long shadows, seeing none. He kept running.

Whoever found his bike waited for him to return for it. They saw him. And now they were following him.

A guard now stood in the booth at the gate. The gate was down and would block a car, but for someone running, it was no problem to dodge around it and escape. Bobby put his revolver in his pocket and took out his taser.

Behind him, someone shouted, "Intruder!"

The guard in the booth turned, spotting Bobby rushing the gate on foot. He stepped out, firearm raised, barking commands for Bobby to stop, to get down on the ground. Bobby didn't. The guard fired, but Bobby had already shifted into a zigzag run, making him a hard target. Besides, Bobby trusted his Sector-7 body armor to absorb a hit without slowing him down.

Another shot rang out, then another. Bobby was within arm's reach now. He slammed a taser into the guard, dropping him to the ground with a quick jolt. More shots cracked the air from behind. More shouts to stop. Bobby ignored them, vaulting over the gate's red-and-white bar. He sprinted along the chain-link fence that lined the warehouse lot.

He glanced back to see if the guards were giving chase. They were, but there was someone standing above it all, watching from a top a large pile of shipping containers. It was his dad. Bobby knew now who found the bike, but worse, his dad knew he knew.

Now would be when many people would get distracted with questions and worry. Questions about what their father thought? About what their father was doing? About what would happen next. But Bobby didn't let his thoughts wander from the objective: escape. He had time to think about everything later. For now, he needed to find a place to lie low and spotted such a place ahead.

Once this warehouse complex were houses. Some developer tore down the houses to make way for *progress* and a higher paying customer. But it appears some houses were not destroyed and instead, became corpses infested with vagrants. The first house had a few people sleeping on the stairs and the front door was open.

Bobby knew a crack house when he saw one. Dead lawn, dead eyed people spotting it, worn down exterior but surprisingly clean. From the looks of the people outside, no one inside would even notice him.

The guards had come out of the gate now and were following him but from afar. They wouldn't be able to see him slip into the house.

Bobby hurried through the open door and quickly stepped over the bodies scattered over the floor. People clustered, frail and emaciated, in the dark recesses, away from the light outside. None of them noticed him. He ran upstairs.

His heavy foot falls stirred the shadowy figures below. They rose, some of them able to gain their feet, some simply lifting their hands to him.

Were they zombies? It wouldn't be the first outbreak of a zombie-like virus Bobby had seen, but they seemed different. Not hungry for flesh, but for something else.

On the second floor, a set of double doors were thrown open, and a man dressed like a mega-church preacher, three-piece suit, bleached white from head to toe, stepped out. He spotted Bobby immediately and appraised the situation.

"Blessed be my kingdom," the preacher said and reached into his pockets. "Sleep all for my blessing."

The zombies collapsed to the floor. Not a sound made, not a motion seen.

The preacher motioned for Bobby to come to him. "Welcome to the Sleep House. I assume you are fleeing a pursuer?"

Bobby stopped on the stairs, looking down to see the guards' shadows in the yard. They were coming in.

The preacher whispered, "Come." He motioned to his office, which Bobby could now see through the door. "Come for tea. Be saved and tell me of the world beyond this place."

Bobby knew the man was dangerous. It was obvious there was something horrible happening here, but what choice did he have? Face the guards who shot first and asked questions later or have tea with this preacher?

"I'm a federal agent," Bobby lied.

"Then you wouldn't be running," the man said and waved him to join him. "Men like you are not here by choice. Come. Tell me your tale and I shall tell you mine. I am no threat to you."

Bobby believed the man and hurried into his office. The preacher pulled whatever was in his pocket and threw it down into the shadows in the foyer. Frantic motion, crawling, screaming, wailing, cries of deep sorrow and howls of pure ecstasy erupted from the house. The commotion scared the guards who had never heard a drug induced feeding frenzy like this before and they moved on to the next, much quieter, corpse of a house.

The preacher came in and closed the doors. He motioned to the chair in front of his desk as he went behind the desk and sat. Bobby didn't expect a drug dealer's office to be so organized. He expected it to be fancier.

Baby blue paint chips hung from walls. Black fuzz and brown water stain blotches bloomed under the curled paint chips. Both chairs squeaked as the men sat. On the dark wooden desk, piles of papers were stacked in neat columns. There were four columns, and a paperweight of an hourglass on each. The sands were at different moments of time for all four, which made Bobby wonder about their purpose, which was clearly not simply as a paperweight. Decorating the shelves surrounding the office were nautical tools which Bobby thought were functional based on their pristine condition. On one wall a plastic gold star necklace hung from a hook. It was out of place in its ordinariness, yet clearly held a place of honor in the room from the prominent display.

"Well then," the preacher said. "I am Mr. Dream. God of this realm. You have entered my world seeking succor and I grant it. But who are you?"

Bobby weighed his answer, looked the man in the face, and let his intuition take his words where they would go. "I'm Robert. And I'm looking for a dollhouse wanted by someone called The Artist."

Mr. Dream smiled and opened a drawer in his desk. Cool air filled the room as the drug dealer produced two paper cartons of water, then closed the drawer, taking the cool air with it. "Box of water? No plastic here. Must protect our home." Mr. Dream smiled. Seeing Bobby's hesitation, he added, "It's just water." Then opened one and drank from it.

Bobby took his and laughed at the thick black letters on the white box, *Box of Water*. Obvious but effective labeling. He opened the water, sniffed it, sipped it, then, deciding it was simply water, took a long drag.

"The dollhouse. I knew the owner, but he died," Mr. Dream said after a long sip. He nodded at the memory. "I have a pretty good idea who has it now." There was a pad of yellow paper on his desk with the stationary header reading *Hang in there*. A small cat hung off the g in hang. "I'll write the address here."

He chuckled at another memory, pausing for a moment to reflect, then continued on. "I gave someone this address once, and it took them down a very dark road." Mr. Dream tore the paper from the pad and held it up. "If I give this to you, that path will be laid before you and once you tread it, to veer from it is near impossible."

Bobby held out his hand to take the paper. "I have a feeling I've been on this path since I was a kid."

Mr. Dream nodded and did not stop Bobby from taking the paper.

"You can leave through the backyard. No one will see you because no one wants to see what emanates from here." Mr. Dream motioned to a rack of clothes in the corner of the room. It held old, ragged jackets and shirts with solid stains that crunched when Bobby touched them. "Wear our garb and eyes will find anything other than you in their gaze."

After a moment, he added, "If you encounter Wendy. I am almost certain she has the dollhouse now; tell her I'm still watching over her."

Bobby changed into the soiled clothes and cringed as they scratched over his skin. Every inch was cruddy from too many things to decipher. Best not to think about it and escape. "Thank you," Bobby said.

Mr. Dream nodded. "I help where I can. Although, my help is not always found to be helpful in the long run." He tried to smile but couldn't. "Good luck Robert. Never come back here."

Bobby left shortly after, seeing the guards checking houses further down the street. Knowing his father saw him, Bobby checked twice for Lee. Not seeing him, Bobby took to the backyard and out into the empty fields beyond the warehouse lot.

***

It was true, no one saw a junkie wandering out from its hole. And when you look like a junkie, smell like a junkie, and stumble forward like a junkie, civilized people block you from their mind. They don't want you to exist in their happy little world and so they can't see you.

Unfortunately for Bobby, Sector-7 taught Lee to see everyone all the time.

He followed Bobby through the field, through the town, and stopped only when Bobby arrived at the steak house, DiCoros.

Both men, father and son, looked at the restaurant, unsure why they were there.

But Bobby re-read his note from Mr. Dream saying the words out loud: *Ask for Nightshade.*

Lee heard and filed it away.

Bobby went through the revolving door.

# AUTHOR'S NOTE

In Stephen King's THE WASTELANDS, one character, Susanna Dean, has a quote that I think is very applicable to this book:

*It is hard to begin.*

And so it was with this book. I knew the story of the Dollhouse before I finished *Life Changing Yard Sale*. In fact, I wrote early permutations of story 1 and 42 before the first book ever came out. But the origins of Ely Adams, Dodslav, and Vilhelmina (our sweet Viola) were mysteries to me until this book. I knew their ambitions, all but Viola's—she was meant to be one and done, but by the end of 42 Revisited, I knew she wasn't going anywhere, anytime soon.

And on that note, it sounds like Bracker's helper found a clue that might cause trouble for Ms. Lucy in the next book. How would a ten-pound weight end up on the muddy shore of the Patticon River? I suppose we'll see (read Passages for a clue).

But Ely and Dodslav were very interesting characters to explore further. I didn't know how deep Ely Adams' connections to other stories ran, but his history with the Geeze family will certainly come back to us. I recognized the struggle Nicky, then Elijah, now Ely has with the world. As I started my professional career, I often found myself at odds with who I was (self-taught technologist without formal training) and where I was from (small town with no family experience in white-collar business). There were many slights (both actual and perceived) that could have turned toxic if I didn't let them go. Ely is an examination of someone who can't move on, who has the chance to let go, but cannot and thus moves forward into a very dark future.

Dodslav, on the other hand, is the artist. He's not poisoned by the world, only by his ambition. I love he recognizes he is not of the noble world yet must operate within it, and does so masterfully. I love that he's a myth, a boogie man that is disregarded until those who have flocked to him stop and actually look at him. Something tells me Dodslav might be one of my favorite characters to come out of my imagination.

And while beginning is hard, middles are equally challenging. This book marks the midpoint (I think) of the Lazarus Spiral series. We end with a legion of demons seeking the Dollhouse (find out who has it in PASSAGES: Lazarus Spiral Book 2). Dodslav has built, through his Emissary, an army within our world. Neil, the only person who we know of, ready to fight demons, is dead. But we now know the nature of the Lazarus Spiral and why some seek it. It is a wishing well where you can wish for anything without consequence. Who wouldn't want to seek that?

The next book, tentatively called RETURN POLICY, will pick back up with Lucy, Nadia, and Trudy. The villainous plans of Ely Adams and Dodslav will come to light and perhaps we'll even discover what happened to Item 13…the Worry Person. The Lazarus Spiral has coiled around all these people and more (Sister Wendy, Mr. Dream, Lee, Bobby, and others) leading all of them towards their destiny.

I do not think they will all arrive at the Tower of Ascension, nor will some see the Spiral firsthand. The world of haunted toys is deadly, claiming many victims. But for those who make it, what wish will reshape the world, all worlds?

The Lazarus Spiral deepens.


Tim Kulp

Baltimore, MD

2024

# REVIEW PLEASE

Dear Reader,

Thank you for embarking on the journey through ORIGINS: Lazarus Spiral Book III. Your support in my own creative journey means the world to me. I hope you found yourself as engrossed in the twists and turns of this tale as I was in writing it.

Your feedback is invaluable. Reviews not only help me grow as a writer but also guide other readers to discover stories they might enjoy. If you have a moment, I would be immensely grateful if you could leave a review sharing your thoughts and experiences with ORIGINS. Whether it's a few lines or a detailed reflection, every review makes a difference.

You can leave your review wherever you discovered this book. Your insights and feedback are crucial in helping me continue to write and improve.

Thank you for being a part of this adventure, and I look forward to bringing you more stories from the dark and mysterious corners of my imagination.

Until next time,

Tim

# CONTINUE IN THE SPIRAL

Continue into the Lazarus Spiral with Life Changing Yard Sale and Passages by T. Kulp. The tales in ORIGINS are just the beginning (pun intended). Watch as the people swirling around the toy collector, Neil, bring out the worst in everyone.

Begin your journey with Life Changing Yard Sale:

Available now.

https://timkulp.com/books/life-changing-yard-sale

Discover more books from T. Kulp at

https://timkulp.com/books

# NEWSLETTER SIGNUP

Thank you for reading ORIGINS. I hope you enjoyed the story and will checkout my other books.

I'd love to keep sharing my writing journey with you. If you're interested, I have a newsletter where I share updates about my work, snippets of upcoming stories, and other creative musings.

Sign up for my newsletter at

https://timkulp.com/newsletter-signup

When you sign up, you get another Lazarus Spiral story called Early Birds Pay Double.

Thanks again for your support and see you in the next story!

Tim

# OTHER BOOKS BY T. KULP

BLOTS

[dis]connection

Library of Lessons & Lies

Shadows, Stains, & Secrets

Life Changing Yard Sale

Passages

Early Birds Pay Double

16

Excess Baggage

www.ingramcontent.com/pod-product-compliance
Lightning Source LLC
Chambersburg PA
CBHW031641200726
48289CB00004BA/1134